One ROGUE at a TIME

JADE LEE

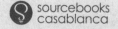

sourcebooks
casablanca

Published by Sourcebooks Casablanca, an imprint of Sourcebooks,
Inc.
P.O. Box 4410, Naperville, Illinois 60567-4410
(630) 961-3900
Fax: (630) 961-2168
www.sourcebooks.com

Printed and bound in Canada.
MBP 10 9 8 7 6 5 4 3 2 1

One

BRAMWELL WESLEY HALLOWSBY MISSED THE GREAT love of his life because he was listening to the tale of his first kill. She was right in front of the inn in a blue dress and a bonnet with a matching ribbon. But his attention was on the inside as Dicky spoke of his Brave Deed. Not Bram's assassinations of vicious men and once of a woman spy, but his very first kill at the age of twelve.

It had been a rabid bear, according to Dicky, escaped from the local fair and still wearing a bright red and green ruffle around its neck. Horribly, this only made it more terrifying to the onlookers as the young Bram stepped forward to defend a child.

"A child?" gasped Dicky's wife, Clarissa. "Boy or girl?"

"Both!" cried Dicky, gesturing with his cheroot. "Twins with kittens. One in each hand and completely defenseless!"

That part was new. Last time it had been piglets. Bram looked out the inn window, idly scanning the street. Though Dicky had easily a dozen men who'd vowed to kill him, none of them would bestir themselves this far north of London. They were in Hull now, nearly to Scotland. If it hadn't been for Clarissa's tetchy stomach, they would be there, and he could get paid. That's all he wanted. To get them to Scotland so he could get paid.

He narrowed his eyes. There was a thick brute of a man coming toward them, but then the man stopped to talk to the woman in blue. The man bowed only slightly, then spent his time ogling the woman's impressive bodice. Bram labeled him the local lecher and let his attention wander back to Dicky.

"And there he stood, one tiny boy against a rabid bear," continued Dicky as he patted the small treasure chest on his lap. The heavy thing must have flattened even Dicky's massive thighs, but the man would not give up his gold even to sit in an inn with his sick wife.

"Terrifying!" gasped Clarissa. She always gasped whenever she spoke. "Did it attack? Did it hurt you? Are there scars?"

Bram barely stopped himself from rubbing his forearm. He knew the shape and the texture of the scars there from memory. The origin of the bizarre tale that had become his legend.

"Horribly disfigured, my dear," Dicky said, clearly gleeful at the thought. "You shan't see it, of course. He keeps it well covered."

"Oh my!" Clarissa's eyes grew sultry. Then she pressed her sapphire necklace to her lips at such an angle that her husband wouldn't see her lick it. But Bram saw—as she had intended—and he idly wondered if he would take advantage of what was offered tonight. It wouldn't be the first time he had used his own mystique to open a woman's bedroom door. And Clarissa was stunningly beautiful, as was her husband. Of course, they were both rotten to the core.

As the bastard son of a duke, Bram had to make his own way through the world. Thanks to the connections of an elite education, he'd been able to hang on the outskirts of the moneyed *ton*, but it had cost him. Humiliation was the smallest price he'd had to pay as he played bodyguard and general strong arm for the peerage. He'd also had to split his mind into two pieces. One half hoped for goodness and beauty in the world. He couldn't shut it up no matter how he tried. The other half saw with clear, bitter eyes what went on and hated the world for the disappointment.

Meanwhile, Dicky continued the tale. "People were running about screaming, you understand. Everywhere was chaos as grown men dropped to their knees in terror. But not Bram. At the tender age of ten, he stood up for those poor children."

"Ten? I thought you said he was twelve."

Both husband and wife looked to Bram, and he knew they would stay like that until he answered. "Eleven," he said, choosing to split the difference.

"Eleven then. But you'd just had the birthday, right?" Dicky asked.

"Right." Wrong, but who was he to argue? Dicky was paying him to be mythic.

Something jerked in the window, and he glanced quickly back. It was the woman in blue as she'd twitched away from a grinning man. Oh. Likely she'd been pinched as she'd passed the thick-jowled man.

"The beast gave out a tremendous roar!" Dicky

bellowed as he leaped to his feet, one arm holding his gold, the other waving about while his wife squealed in mock terror.

"Uh, Dicky, you really shouldn't be so loud…" began Bram, but he needn't have bothered.

The door to their private room burst open as the innkeeper rushed in. "My lords! My lady! What is amiss?"

Dicky let his arm drop, not even embarrassed. "I was being a bear, sir."

The innkeeper was understandably flustered, and though Bram enjoyed a flustered innkeeper as much as the next man, he hardly thought it fair. But rather than point out Dicky's error—a sin for any paid servant—he redirected the man. "Have you got the posset yet? For my lady's stomach?"

"Oh, sir, not yet. But I've sent my son to find her—the woman I told you about—and not return until such time—"

"Oh, but I am so wretched!" gasped Clarissa as she pressed a limp hand to her brow, her sapphire earbobs waving wildly on their gold chains.

"A hot towel, milady? Perhaps a blanket?" Not much of the peerage traveled through here, and he was making the most of these two.

"I won't put you to the bother," she said, her voice fading.

"But milady, if it would ease your suffering—"

"Tut tut," Dicky interrupted, oblivious to his wife's need to be cosseted. "She said no. Get on with you. I was in the middle of my story." Bram sighed. "Bring her hot stew."

"I couldn't eat a thing," Clarissa protested.

"You will," he said, keeping his voice stern. She liked it when he was bold. Yes, her legs shifted restlessly, and she shot him another coy glance that made him vaguely nauseous.

The innkeeper's head bobbled yes as he rushed out the door in search of stew. Meanwhile, Dicky was annoyed that the attention had shifted off him. "Pay attention," he ordered. "I was about to get to the good part."

Pay attention to his own tale of derring-do? "Please, I adore this part," he lied as he looked back out the window.

He saw a mob of boys—four of them—barely into their first beards. They were calling raucous comments aimed at the woman in blue. Really, why was she walking alone—moving from one house to the next to the next—seemingly unprotected by a husband, father, or brother? Didn't she know better than to tempt the locals to harangue her?

"The bear attacked!" Dicky cried dramatically. He roared again, and Clarissa squealed. "Bram pulled out his father's dueling pistol and shot it right in the muzzle! Bang!"

"Bang," Clarissa echoed as she rubbed her thumb over and across the smallest sapphire in her necklace.

"And that, my dear, is the tale of how my dear Bram became the man he is today. And he will protect us, you see." Dicky returned to his seat and curled his arm around the treasure chest. "If he could protect tiny children—"

"And their kittens! Don't forget the kittens!"

"And their kittens from a rabid bear, then…"

"Then we are safe with him." Clarissa's gaze returned to him, her gaze growing more languid. "I feel so safe."

Dicky frowned, his face turning red. On any other man, it would be a hideously florid look, but it only seemed to enhance Dicky's easy charm. "That's why I hired him, Clary. To make you feel safe."

"You did a good job," his wife said, her eyes not leaving Bram.

Bram pushed to his feet, needing to stretch his long legs. "You do know that story has grown over the years."

"Tut tut," Dicky said. "We all know it's true. Or most of it."

Or none of it. When had his life become so absurd that he contemplated cuckolding a man—his employer— simply because he was bored? He despised himself, and by extension, he despised Dicky and Clarissa.

"There's no danger, Dicky. No one will chase you up here. They will ruin your reputation in town, destroy your financials simply because no one will do business with you, and certainly, you will never be invited to a *ton* party again. But there won't be a soul who offers you bodily harm."

"Course not!" cried Dicky as he patted his treasure again. "That's because you're here. That's because I had the foresight to befriend you as a child. I knew then that you would protect me. I knew then that you were a man who could save me from those blackguards…"

Bram stopped listening and headed for the door. Dicky noticed about the time he stepped into the hallway.

"Where are you going?"

"To have a look about. Just in case." It was a lie, but it was one that would satisfy Dicky, which would make sure he got paid when this was all done.

So he left the room, choosing to wander through the inn. He made it through the kitchen and out the back, to the garden behind with two lazy hounds dozing in the sun. And once outside, he took a deep breath of the summer air and a greedy look at the green land around him.

That was the life he wanted: stretched out in the sun like those hounds, with his eyes drooping shut, while a pup or three gamboled nearby. He saw no puppies, but he imagined them, and they made him smile.

Then he saw her. The woman in blue again, this time without anyone pinching or ogling her. The sight was striking enough, but then she paused under a tree, pulling off her bonnet to raise her face to what breeze could be had. Fine blond hair blew back from her cheeks, and her perfect bow of a mouth curved in delight. Beautiful. A country miss complete with a basket on her arm. Her lush, unspoiled beauty was the kind that could only grow in the wilds. In London, she would be painted and sullen, her body trussed into dresses that maximized assets and minimized flaws. But this woman had a simple gown, and while he watched, those puppies he'd imagined suddenly appeared. Four of them, barking and leaping from somewhere he couldn't see.

She smiled when she saw them, and then—to his shock—she laughed, so musical a sound that he was riveted. Bells could not have sounded so pure.

He was awed. It was his idealistic mind, he knew. The one that believed in unsullied beauty. She knelt down then, oblivious to the dirt that would coat her skirt, as she tickled the puppies, her laughter chiming in the air.

He found himself moving toward her without choosing to do so. He had no idea what to say to an innocent miss. He'd never known a woman who could be so sweet. And yet—

"Miss Bluebell! Miss Bluebell!"

A boy barely out of short pants came tearing around the corner. She looked up, her expression surprised as she held out her arms. He careened into them, so fast was he churning his short, stubby legs.

She said something too low for Bram to hear, especially as the boy kept talking right over her despite being short of breath. Rude brat.

"Da says…you come. Right away!"

At that moment, one of the puppies attacked the angel. It was nothing more than a growl and bite as it grabbed hold of her dress and shook. With a sharp word for the dog, she picked it up and took her time disentangling it from her skirt, but then the thing started licking her on the face.

He saw the wet tongue tasting her chin and neck. He heard her laugh, this time deeper—throatier—and he felt himself harden as he hadn't in years. Her cheeks were flushed, her hair now flying free as the dog laved her. His mouth was dry as he watched, and he abruptly thought of so many things, all dark and carnal.

"Miss Bluebell!" the child cried, and Bram wanted to spank the idiot child for drawing the woman's attention. *Don't look at him. Look at me!* The thought was bizarre in his mind, but it was no less loud.

The woman finally managed to pull the puppy away from her face. She must have said something because the boy nodded vigorously and pointed at the inn. At first Bram thought the child was directing her to look at him, but he soon realized the truth. Neither boy nor woman had seen him, and the disappointment of that was yet another shock. What was wrong with him?

Another puppy grabbed hold of her skirt, and he nearly growled himself to make the thing back away. For all he knew, he did make the sound because a second later the woman looked straight at him. She arched her brows, her rose-colored mouth molding into a perfect oval of surprise. He held her gaze, transfixed by the aquamarine clarity of her eyes, especially with the sun full on her face. And then she blushed.

Sweet heaven, his knees nearly buckled. The shock of that destroyed the illusion and allowed the bitter half of him to take control. He'd gone weak simply from looking at a woman, and he knew what a disaster that was. Hell, he had the scars to remind him if he should ever forget.

And while he allowed the anger to put strength in his leg, the woman rose to her feet, shaking out her skirts before grabbing her basket as the boy babbled on.

"There's a lady and gents at the inn. Right fancy, every one. They need your tea, Miss Bluebell. Right away! Right now, Da says. Right—"

"Now. Yes, thank you, Timothy." Her voice was more cultured than most, but the roots of this provincial village were heavy in her long vowels.

She started heading his way, and he noted the square set of her shoulders and the jut of her chin. She was proud then, and if the narrowing of her eyes meant anything, it was that she was studying him for a weakness. "I think she's dying!" the boy said in a loud undertone. "She presses 'er fingers to 'er mouth and she sweats to stink! That's what Da says. Wot if she dies right in our parlor? What if—"

"She's increasing," Bram said. He hadn't meant to speak. He had intended to simply watch and learn, which was his usual way of dealing with strange women. But the moment they neared, he found himself speaking simply to silence the prattling child. "It's morning sickness, but Clarissa was tired of the drive."

The miss cocked her head as he spoke, listening closely to his words. The idealistic part of him admired the color of her eyes and her honest face, but the bitter part of him knew that only liars needed to pay such close attention to their surroundings.

"So she needs something to settle 'er stomach?" the miss asked.

She needed a good spanking. She and Dicky both, for conning seven peers of the realm into giving them thousands of pounds for a make-believe sapphire mine. But that wasn't his job. Preventing this witch from poisoning the two idiots was.

He moved deliberately slow, easing his way in front of her. He was a big man, a good head taller, and he used his height to full advantage as he glared down at her.

"They don't need what you're selling." No one did. Because it was all lies.

"So you know wot a lady in 'er early months needs?"

"Please, sir," the boy piped up. "My da will whip me for sure if she don't come."

The woman dropped a calming hand on the boy's shoulder. "You won't be whipped, Timothy. Go inside."

"But—"

"Go." Bram was startled to realize he'd said the word. Worse, it came out more as a growl than intelligible speech. But it was enough to terrify the boy into bolting.

The woman shook her head. "There was no need to frighten 'im."

He'd meant to frighten her, but obviously, she was of the fearless sort. "Clarissa just needs some attention, not any magic potions."

"Magic potions!" she cried, obviously offended. "I make good Christian tisanes, sir. Nothing 'eathen about plants tended with care and picked at just the right time to ease a lady's delicate stomach." She narrowed her eyes. "I 'ave a wonder of a posset for a man with a sore 'ead too, but I'm afraid I've nothing for stupidity."

Oh, well, if she declared it Christian in her broad, flat accent, then far be it from him to interfere. He folded his arms across his chest. "Clarissa just needs some attention—"

"And I'll be giving 'er that, sir, if you would stand aside. Unless you'd prefer to let 'er aim her illness at your thick 'ead."

That, of course, was exactly why he was outside. Damn it. Not only was she a manipulative woman, but she was clever too. He had no problems with simply barring her way, illogical as it was, but he knew time was ticking away. The first thing young Timothy would do was run tell his da what was happening out here. And a minute after that, Bram'd have the anxious innkeeper on his heels, begging and bowing enough to give him a headache.

"Show me what's in your basket," Bram ordered while he tried to think of some better way to rid the area of this woman.

She drew back. "You have no cause to—"

"I've every cause to protect those two. It's my job. And you'll not interfere with that."

"Then it's your job to see the lady gets tended."

"Not by you."

"Then who?" She gestured to the few hovels that made up the town. "There's no doctor for fifty miles. And no surgeon for thirty. When people get ill, they tend to it themselves, or they call me for a tisane. If 'tis naught but a woman's complaint, then let a woman tend 'er."

He glared at her, knowing she was right. But he couldn't just give in. It wasn't pride—though he was man enough to admit that played a part—it was his whole mystique. He had to appear wholly intimidating, or his entire life would fall apart. The only jobs he had were from peers who had need of someone impressive to protect them. If that mystique fell away, so would his employment. So he braced his feet and glowered. "I'll see what you carry in that basket, or I won't let you in."

"I'll save you the trouble. I've a knife in there. As big as an ax, and I'll use it to murder you for no reason at all."

His lips twitched. He didn't want to be amused,

but she was so queenly in her outrage. Even in her dirt-stained dress with that broad northern accent that dulled the mind. With all that, she still carried herself as a queen, and he was impressed. Though not in the least bit cowed.

Sadly, he was out of time.

He heard the heavy footfalls and knew Dicky was tromping out of the inn. He heard the man's quick gasp of surprise. Stupid man would never look beneath the surface of a beautiful woman. He'd just see the flawless skin, the sweet curves of lush breasts and full hips, and he would be lost. That the man had swindled the *ton* for so long was a miracle.

"Bram, my man," Dicky said as his footsteps slowed to the tempo of a swagger. "Is this lovely creature the lady bringing possets?"

The woman shifted immediately into a demure curtsy that completely fooled Dicky. "I am, sir. Me name's Maybelle Ballenger, but everyone calls me Bluebell on account of my eyes."

"Bluebell!" Dicky exclaimed. "Charming. Absolutely charming. Lord Linsel at your service." He stepped forward and executed a courtly bow. If nothing else, Dicky knew how to impress an ignorant woman. Maybe even a clever woman too, since Miss Ballenger colored and ducked her eyes. Bram wanted to curse her for the act, but every woman colored and ducked her eyes when the ever-gorgeous Lord Linsel turned his charm in her direction. "And this rude gentleman," Dicky added with a wink, "is Mr. Hallowsby."

"Your basket, Miss Ballenger," Bram cut in, his voice cold. "Just let me see what's inside."

"Is that what the fuss is about?" Dicky said with a hearty laugh. Which is when Bram realized the man wasn't carrying his chest of gold. That was a surprise. "I hardly think this charming young miss means me harm. And besides, you're more than a match for one little slip of girl, don't you think?"

He slid his gaze to Dicky, wishing he could strangle the man. Especially when the lady continued to keep her gaze down and her expression demure. Gone was the bold-as-brass woman who'd been facing him down not one minute before. In her place stood a simpering child, which was exactly what would appeal to Dicky. He'd married Clarissa, after all, hadn't he?

"I just want to see what's inside," he said, keeping his voice cold. "You tasked me with your safety—"

"Yes, yes, of course." Then Dicky shifted his gaze back to Miss Ballenger. Or rather, to her ample bosom. "I must apologize deeply, but I am in somewhat of a pickle. Quite dangerous, actually. Would you mind terribly helping me out? Just a peek at your basket, please."

"Well, milord, since you ask so sweetly." Then she held out her basket and tugged off the cloth cover.

Bram glanced inside, cataloging the items in an instant. She did indeed have a knife in there. A small one meant for cutting fruit. It was very sharp as it gleamed in the sunlight, but the handle was old and worn. He didn't regard it as a threat. He was just noting that she had an old tool she kept sharp. Also inside were a variety of bottles, packed securely amid sachets and carrots.

Nothing damning at all, except the lies she sold in those bottles. And the overall lie of her body and smile.

"There now," soothed Dicky. "Nothing at all to fear. And will anything in there help my dear wife?"

"Oh my, yes, milord," she said with an artful smile. "But…oh." Her face fell as she glanced to Bram. "Forgive me, but is your wife in a delicate condition?"

Dicky laughed with good humor. "Clary is always in a delicate…"

"With child, Dicky," Bram interrupted.

Dicky puffed up, preening as if it had been a miracle to get his wife pregnant. "Why yes, indeed."

"Oh dear," the woman said sadly. "When a woman increases, she's quite delicate. I've only the one posset that will do." She touched a small bag. "It's strong, but made for the frail."

"Well, then you have one."

"Oh no, sir, I couldn't. It's for my aunt. She's been faring poorly, and I saved it just for 'er."

"Well, that's too bad," Bram interrupted as he grabbed Dicky's elbow and tried to steer him around. "She's got nothing—"

"Wait, wait," said Dicky, shaking off Bram's arm. "She's got the one, and Clary will be impossible if we don't give her something. You know how she is."

The lady shook her head and abruptly brightened. "Well, perhaps some of my other draughts will do. If I could meet the lady? See what she—"

Good God, she was worming herself deeper. Bram had to keep her from coming inside. He could think of a dozen reasons, but the most important was the way Dicky was looking at her. If the idiot got it in his head to seduce the witch, they'd never leave this miserable village, and he'd never get paid.

"Dicky, no," Bram said, though he knew two seconds after voicing the words that he'd taken the wrong tone with the man. Dicky was well aware of his consequence, especially in front of a pretty woman. He would never countenance a negation from a hireling. And sure enough, the man glowered down at him despite the fact that Bram was a good foot taller.

"Now, see here, you work for me. And I declare this beautiful creature will tend Clary. Do I make myself clear?"

Bram clenched his jaw, forcing himself to keep quiet. Meanwhile, Dicky held out his arm for Miss Bluebell Ballenger. "Come inside, my dear. Let us see what you have to offer."

Bram was left to trail in their wake. Damn it. They were never getting to Scotland. He was never getting paid. And he blamed it entirely on the witch.

Two

HE WAS GOING TO BE A PROBLEM, THOUGHT MAYBELLE, as she played the innocent miss taking an impressive man's arm. Not the angelic looking Lord Linsel who was angling his head to see down her bodice. She gave him just enough of a view to tantalize and no more. It was the other one, the tall one with the righteous air, who would be the difficulty. She'd met men like him before. Angry, prideful gentlemen who found every excuse to be difficult just because they could.

Fortunately, she'd been dealing with just that type of mongrel all her life, so she anticipated no problem. The key was to align her goals with his, and therefore, both get what they wanted.

He wanted her gone. She wanted to sell all of her potions and be gone. Therefore, she would simply have to recruit him to her purpose, and then they would both be happy.

So she cast a winning smile over her shoulder at him. It would only irritate him further, but she took a perverse joy in the way he glowered at her. Lord, if the man would only smile, he would be devastatingly handsome. But no, he would be sour pudding, and she would laugh when she bested him.

"Is this your first child, milord?" she said, opening her eyes wide to make them appear more genuine.

"We hope. The others have not…well…Clary doesn't carry a babe well. She's delicate that way."

"'Ow awful for you. My 'eart simply bleeds."

Was that a snort she heard behind her? Ha. If he thought that ingenuous of her, he was in for an earful. She'd barely started buttering up the obviously rich Lord Linsel.

"It must 'ave been an important matter then," she continued, "to travel when she is in a delicate way."

"Oh yes," the man said gravely. "I'm an important man, you see, and there are unsavory characters who are after me. Hence the gentleman behind us."

She wondered if that were true or he just liked being important. She could certainly see why Thomas's family was in such a tizzy to see them happy. Rich travelers were windfalls for the entire village, and everyone was right now thinking of ways to bilk them.

They passed through the kitchen, where she gave everyone inside a reassuring smile. She had everything in hand. The innkeeper, Mr. Garwick, bustled forward, his face flushed and his hands knotted from the swelling in his joints. He started to speak, but she shook her head. Instead, she patted his arm before passing him a tisane as thanks for calling her. Besides, she had a half dozen that would never sell before she left.

"For your joints, Mr. Garwick," she said. "In return for some of your wife's divine stew." She turned to Lord Linsel. "Mrs. Garwick doesn't charge half as much as she should for that beef. I have tried and tried to copy her recipe, but I simply haven't the knack. Or the meat."

Out of the corner of her eye, she saw Gillian nod in agreement. The woman could now charge these nobs double, and the man wouldn't blink an eye. "Have you tried a bowl?"

Lord Linsel shook his head. "I haven't had—"

"Oh, you simply must. It's wonderful. An important man deserves an important meal, don't you think? And this is the only place for miles to get one."

The man puffed out his chest. "Well, then I suppose I will."

"Excellent. Oh dear, 'ow I run on. I'm not used to chatting with so elegant a man. Mayhaps I could see yer wife?"

"Yes, yes. Right through here."

She didn't need him to lead her. She'd been coming to this inn selling possets since she was old enough to count money. But she let the man lead her and so entered the private parlor where a beautiful woman drenched in jewels sat looking bored.

Her gown was the most stunning thing Maybelle had ever seen, and a surge of desire went through her strong enough to make her bite the inside of her cheek. One day soon she would be attired in a gown like that. Lush green like the deepest forest, plus a gold necklace sporting blue sapphires, just like the one this woman wore. She'd have a big ring on her finger too, and…oh my.

Obviously the woman had been sick. The stink clung to her gloves. Her breath was foul, and her blond ringlets were greasy too. When Maybelle was rich, she'd look pretty *and* smell good.

None of those thoughts appeared on her face as Maybelle went smoothly to the woman and gingerly sat beside her on the settee. As she went, the heel of her foot kicked something hard hidden under the couch, but she couldn't bend down to look. She'd already scanned the room and itemized the things that were clearly owned by these three. Nothing much beyond the lady's bonnet and a long umbrella. Maybelle'd give her eyeteeth to know what was hidden beneath them.

But she wasn't here to satisfy her curiosity. Her job was to sell everything she carried. "Oh my, I've never seen so beautiful a laidy before," she said in an overloud murmur as she crossed to the woman's side.

"What?" The woman's face crumpled up in horror. "Gracious, Dicky, what creature is this? I can't understand a word she's saying."

Maybelle drew up short. Of all the things she'd expected to hear, that wasn't one of them. She always spoke perfectly clear. But perhaps the woman was hard of hearing. So she smiled warmly and spoke slow and distinct.

"Good afternoon, my lady. I can see you've 'ad a 'ard time of it. Mayhaps—"

"Oh, keep her away. Her words grate on the ears. Mr. Hallowsby, tell me her garbled screech doesn't give you the headache. And me, in my delicate condition." She pressed one hand to her belly and one to her mouth.

"I completely agree," said the difficult man. "I'm sorry, Miss Bluebell, but you must leave."

What? Without earning so much as a farthing? "You understood me clear as day outside," she snapped. Then she forcibly moderated her tone. "I. 'Ave. Possets," she said, each word distinct. "To. 'Elp. Stomach." She patted her tummy.

"I'm not a half-wit," the lady snapped. "I hear the mangled thing you call language perfectly well." She raised her hands and made a shooing motion. "Go away. Just go away."

Maybelle clenched her teeth, struggling to keep calm. It was always difficult braving the village to sell her wares. She'd been pinched and insulted for the last hour. And now to be dismissed for her language? That was beyond ridiculous. She spoke perfectly clearly. Her speech was no different than the innkeeper's.

But there were more ways than one to sell a thing. She would simply do it without speaking. And charge them triple for the trouble. So she lifted off the covering of the basket and showed the woman her tisanes and possets. Then she picked out one in particular and mimed drinking it. Then she pointed at her belly.

"Good Lord, she wants to poison my baby," the woman moaned.

That was not in the least what she had said...er... gestured. She looked to the room at large for help. Mr. Hallowsby was just standing there smirking, so she looked to the woman's husband. Turning pleading eyes on him, she lifted up her best tisane. It calmed nerves and soothed aches. Truthfully, she wanted a cup of it right now, but instead she looked imploringly at Lord Linsel.

"Clary, you're going to make the beautiful girl cry."

Oh damnation, men were such idiots. The last thing this woman wanted was to hear about her beauty.

"Don't you get loud with me," the lady pouted. "You know how it upsets me." She clenched her necklace as if she feared Maybelle would steal it.

"I'm not, dearest," Lord Linsel said, moderating his tone. "But perhaps this will help your nerves."

"What can this ignorant creature have that will help me?"

Ignorant? Maybelle was better educated than anyone else for miles. She had read Shakespeare and knew her figures. She had memorized chemical formulae and even knew Latin, though Greek had been beyond her. Naturally, none of that would show outwardly. And apparently, it didn't show in her voice either.

"Are you trying to be rid of me?" Lady Linsel continued, her voice painfully shrill. "To poison me—"

"Of course not." Worse and worse. Lord Linsel was getting irritated and now looked desperately at Mr. Hallowsby. No, no, no! He had to look to his wife.

Maybelle pushed to her feet, but was suddenly blocked by Mr. Annoying.

"Let's get out of this place," the man said calmly. "It doesn't agree with Clarissa."

She'd wager her last penny that nothing agreed with Clarissa. She looked to Mr. Garwick, but the innkeeper could do nothing to help. He simply shrugged, and she knew she would have to resolve herself to mitigating the disaster instead of reaping any windfall. Thank God she was leaving the horrible village, otherwise she'd be years trying to counter the damning scorn of this woman. Did she not understand how her one little tantrum could taint a person for decades? Maybe not in London, but in these parts, everything these three said and did would be repeated for years to come.

"I'll ready the horses, my lords, my lady," Mr. Garwick said as he bustled out of the room.

Meanwhile, Maybelle grabbed another tisane. She would have to risk speaking. There was no other way to get the information across quickly. Except she couldn't catch Lord Linsel's eye. The tall man was in the way.

So she ended up tugging on the irritating man's sleeve. He looked down at her, his expression both mocking and indulgent. Bastard. But she swallowed her indignation and held up her offering.

"It will 'elp her sleep," she all but hissed.

She could see the man considering it, but she'd spoken too loudly for all that she'd tried to keep it an undertone.

"What is that noise she's making?" Lady Linsel moaned. "Oh, I cannot I abide it!"

Meanwhile, the man gave her a rueful shrug. "It was a good try. I'm sure you have the locals eating out of your hand."

Well, what was that to the point? She wasn't staying around here any longer than another hour.

He must have seen the frustration on her face. He must have read the fury in her eyes. He had to, otherwise there was no explaining the low chuckle that vibrated through the air and straight to her belly. It was a rich sound that woke parts of her that she'd never felt before. It was a mocking, horrible noise, she told herself, but to no avail. Her body responded anyway.

Humiliating!

And now she was the one who wanted to leave and damn them all. These nobles, the provincial village where she'd been harassed daily, and most especially, this man.

"Good-bye and good riddance," she all but spat. Then she grabbed her basket and...

And why were there three more men in the room? Not just men, but huge burly brutes the size of Vikings? Their shoulders were twice the size of normal men's, and their fists—the size of hams. They were dressed better than most, but not as well as the three here. And there was a clear leader. A man in a gray waistcoat shot with gold.

And they all had pistols in their big fists.

"Jeremy," Mr. Hallowsby drawled in a self-mocking tone. "Why didn't I remember you?"

The giant in gray nodded with a cordial smile. "It's because I'm so hard to see."

A joke, obviously. Nobody laughed. Not even the other two brutes. Clearly they were there for brawn not brain.

Meanwhile, Lord Linsel puffed himself up, though anyone could see he was terrified. "Now see here, good man. We were just leaving. We'll just grab our things and be out of your way. Whatever business you have in this village is none of our—"

"Awwwr, but our business is with you."

Maybelle winced at the Cockney accent. And they thought she sounded awful? What did they think of him?

"Who are these people?" Lady Linsel demanded in a shrill voice.

It was Mr. Hallowsby who answered. "This is Mr. Jeremy Dudding, bastard son of Lord Sturman." He looked at Lord Linsel. "You remember Lord Sturman? He's the man who invested over ten thousand pounds in your sapphire mine."

Lord Linsel visibly paled. "It's not my fault. I lost everything too. I believed there were sapphires."

Maybelle narrowed her eyes. She could see Mr. Hallowsby thought that a bald-faced lie. His expression flattened, and he exhaled a slow breath. But then he lifted his hands slowly in a kind of *what now?* gesture.

"What is it that you're looking for, Jeremy?"

"Mr. Dudding."

Mr. Hallowsby looked hurt by that. "I've known you all my life. We're both bastards. We played marbles together as boys. Shared the same tutor. Jeremy—"

"Mr. Dudding."

The tall man sighed and nodded. "That's hurtful, but very well. What is it that you want here?"

"I'll take his gold lockbox, if you please. See—I know he's got the profits. Just ain't sharing them."

Lord Linsel huffed out a breath. "There were no profits! I swear on my life!"

At which point both of the silent Vikings lifted their pistols and aimed. It took Lord Linsel a few breaths before he understood what he'd said. That it truly was his life at stake here. His wife had a quicker intellect, and she squeaked in alarm.

Mr. Hallowsby eased his weight sideways, slowly moving in front of the lady. Obviously, he was protecting her, and Maybelle felt a little slighted that he wouldn't stand bodily in front of her. But then again, she was already shrinking in his shadow.

"How about we let the ladies step out and talk

about this like gentlemen?" said the irritating man. Except he wasn't being irritating right now. He was acting rather heroic, though she was loath to admit it.

"Ladies?" Mr. Dudding mocked. "It's that blighter's wife who got my father involved."

"That's not true!" cried Lady Linsel. "Not a word of it! I have nothing to do with my husband's schemes."

Not the best choice of words, and her husband shot her a glare. Then Mr. Hallowsby was speaking again as he stepped further away from Maybelle, which, sadly, drew attention to Maybelle.

"What about her?" the difficult one said. "She's just a local witch-woman. She's got nothing to do with anything here."

Mr. Dudding looked her up and down, his gaze insolent, and she felt herself grow cold. Certainly, she'd defended herself against lechers before, but not one of his size, and certainly not one carrying a pistol. "She looks plenty ladyloike to me."

Mr. Hallowsby made a show of disgust. "I'm trying to handle this like gentlemen, Jeremy. You know me. I'll deal honorably with you."

"You cheated at marbles!"

"You taught me how."

The Viking glared, then slowly shook his head. "She stays," he said with a sneer. "She looks to be the lady's maid to me. And that means—"

"For God's sake," Mr. Hallowsby huffed. "Miss Bluebell, would you please tell him what you're doing here?" His gaze never left the Viking. "Just listen to her voice, Jeremy."

Well, if that didn't just take the cake. They could

understand the brute's Cockney but had to point out her accent? She had half a mind to—

"Miss Bluebell," Mr. Hallowsby said, his voice tight. "Please tell him what you're doing here."

She straightened up to her full height, which barely topped the man's shoulder. "I am no' a witch! I'm selling possets." She held up her basket so he could see.

"That looks like carrots."

"Possets, tisanes, and carrots," she corrected.

Jeremy snorted. "Awrite. She ain't no laidy's maid."

And what was that supposed to mean? "Of course I'm no laidy's maid—"

"But she stays 'ere nevertheless."

Mr. Hallowsby stepped forward. "She's got nothing to do with this."

The Viking shrugged. "I like the way she looks." His eyes narrowed. "And I don't take orders from hired bastards."

She glanced at Mr. Disagreeable and found that he wasn't insulted by the name. Or perhaps he was simply unaffected. Either way, he shifted back, such that he shielded her partially from view.

She didn't want to be grateful, but she was. Profoundly grateful.

"So you're in charge, Jere—Mr. Dudding. What do you want?"

Jeremy appeared to think this over. His eyes narrowed, and he seemed to hold his breath. At first she thought he might have some sort of digestive ailment, but in the end, he spoke up.

"He 'ire you to protect 'is lockbox?"

Mr. Hallowsby shook his head. "Just to get him to

Scotland safe and sound." He pointed up the north road. "Twenty miles. Let me get them escorted there, get paid, and then you can have him."

"Bram!" Lord Linsel squeaked. "That's not what we agreed."

"On the contrary," Mr. Hallowsby said with a slow drawl. "That is exactly what we agreed." So he turned his charming smile on the Viking. "So what of it, Jeremy? Honor among bastards? We both get what we want."

Sounded like a gypsy bargain to her. One where the thieves got everything, and the honest Lord Linsel lost it all, but she didn't dare speak. At this moment, she wished she'd just headed for London this morning without trying to gain a few extra pennies first.

"Hmmm," murmured Jeremy. She could already tell he was merely pretending to consider the offer. "I'd rather get wot I want and forget about you."

"We once were such friends, you and me."

Jeremy didn't appear to think much of that. "Where's the lockbox?"

Which is when she realized the truth. It flashed across her awareness as quick as a divine gift, and she weighed the possibilities. If she stayed silent, then maybe she could get out of this alive but with no profit. Most days that would sting, but today of all days, she needed that money. She was still undecided when the Viking took another heavy step into the room.

"Tell me," he said with a growl, "or I start shooting, beginning with him." He pointed at Mr. Hallowsby.

Well, that was hardly fair. By all rights, the man was

simply doing his job. And he'd been a fellow playmate as well. No reason to kill him first.

"There is no lockbox!" Lord Linsel squeaked.

"Awrite then," he said as he pointed his gun at Mr. Hallowsby.

The irritating man didn't seem to even blink, but he shifted away from Lady Linsel. "Why not take her jewelry?"

"What!" the lady gasped. "No!" she cried, clutching her necklace tight.

The Viking laughed, and the sound was not pleasant. "We all know that's glass an' paste."

"Is not." The lady sniffed.

Really? Maybelle thought as she peered at the gemstones. Meanwhile, the Viking huffed out a breath. "The lockbox, or I kill you, Bram." He cocked the pistol, and suddenly, Maybelle was speaking even though she hadn't planned on uttering a word.

"No!" she cried. "I know where the box is. I can give it t' you."

"What the devil are you saying?" gasped the lady.

Was the woman an idiot? Maybelle planted her hands on her hips and glared. "I. Know. Where. The box is."

"You couldn't possibly," the woman said with a sniff, thereby confirming that she could understand Maybelle just fine. And also, that there was a lockbox.

Maybelle revised her estimation of the lady's intelligence downward.

"I do," she said as she turned to the Viking. "I'll tell you if you buy all me goods."

"Wot?"

She sniffed and stomped around Mr. Hallowsby. He was giving her a bemused expression, but she turned her back on him. Sadly, that only made her spine tingle with awareness, though she focused totally on the Cockney Viking.

"They's good Christian possets 'ere. For 'eadache, for fever, for a laidy's increasing pain." She shot Lady Linsel a glare.

"Oi don't need that," said the Viking.

"And carrots. Do you need carrots?"

"I loike carrots well enough, but I don't mean to be paying for them."

She folded her arms across her chest. "Well, I'm selling them. And I won't tell you aught about the lockbox without you buying every single piece of it. Basket too." The basket was a last second inspiration, but she counted it worth a shilling at least. "There's quality goods in there. Great for whatever ails you, even if it's hunger. Especially if it's hunger."

"I don't need any old lady possets!"

"But you do need the lockbox, and I know where 'tis."

Lady Linsel leaned forward. "I tell you, she couldn't possibly know anything at all."

Lord Linsel huffed. "Because there is no lockbox!"

"One guinea for the lot."

"I don't 'ave a guinea," the man growled.

A low voice interrupted, the words laced with humor. "Course you do, Jeremy. You love flashing that gold."

The Viking looked up and glared. And after a furious gesture at his men, the pair stopped looking at her carrots and re-aimed their pistols at Mr. Hallowsby.

"What are you going to do?" Mr. Hallowsby taunted. "Even up here, there's law. The innkeeper's seen you by now. And his children. There's folks in the street too. It's a beautiful afternoon. Everybody's out. You planning on shooting everyone? Pay the woman, and then leave us be."

"Bram!" Lord Linsel cried.

"Dicky," Mr. Hallowsby responded. "You paid me to get you safe and sound to Scotland. I'm trying to do that if you'll just be quiet and let me handle things."

"Not when you're—"

"A guinea," she interrupted. She had to, or the men would start squabbling like chickens. "And another for the basket."

"Wot!"

She lifted her chin. "Keep wasting my time, and it'll be a guinea per carrot."

"I'm not paying that!"

"Then I'll be on my way, and you'll never find that lockbox. Not in a million years." It was a lie. Even these brutes likely knew how to search a room.

The Viking glared at her. Then it became a glower. He even rose up practically onto his toes to try and intimidate her. She didn't so much as blink.

Then suddenly he was huffing and puffing as he pulled out his purse. "I don't have two guineas."

He had one and several other coins.

"Your men have purses, don't they?" she challenged.

They did, but they were loath to hand over their coin. Until Jeremy kicked one. "Your sis is increasing, ain't she? Think she'd like a potion?"

The other one nodded slowly. "It's 'er birthday Tuesday."

Maybelle smiled. "There you go. Drop it in boiling water. Let her smell the steam, and then drink it. Wonderful soothing."

"Which one?"

Maybelle pointed. Behind her, Mr. Hallowsby was stifling his laughter. He covered it well. Made it more like a snort, but she knew. And she almost smiled as well because this was a strange windfall today.

And so it was done. The coins counted out clearly. They didn't have two guineas. Just the one and coins to add up to enough. She pocketed them quicker than any gypsy, and then gave them a demure curtsy.

"A pleasure, sirs." She was about to turn on her heel and leave, but they stopped her. Honestly, she didn't think they'd let her get away, but she wanted to be closer to the door. She'd like to slip away when they went looking for the box. Sadly, she didn't get more than a single step nearer.

"The lockbox?"

"Under the fainting couch. Over yon." It was the hard thing she'd kicked with her heel when she'd sat down at the very beginning. It was covered by a large blanket, but it was the only logical possibility. Unless it was a chamber pot. Or one of Timothy's toys. Or any of a thousand other things.

But then Lord Linsel exploded into sound and fury. "There is nothing under the settee. She's a mad witch! You can't possibly expect her to know anything. Who knows what she'll do to you when you bend over to look…"

Nobody paid him the least mind. And lest she think she could escape, Jeremy Viking kept her standing there while he motioned one of the other men to go look. And sure enough, right there under the couch was a heavy iron box painted gold. A huge padlock clanked as they set it down on the table.

"Look at that," said Lord Linsel, overly loud. "Oh goodness. What do think the innkeeper is about, keeping that there?"

Again, no one paid him the least heed. In fact, Mr. Dudding pointed at it and barked out an order to Lord Linsel. "Open it!"

"Well, how am I supposed to do that? I haven't got a key for it."

And they called her an ignorant provincial? Did he truly think anyone believed him?

Meanwhile, Mr. Hallowsby huffed out a breath. "Don't be stupid. Just shoot it." And then when two of the henchmen lifted their pistols, the man took two quick steps forward with his hands raised. "Not here, you idiots! There are people everywhere. Don't you think someone will come running when you shoot off those pistols? Then how would you explain things?"

"Damn it, Bram," Lord Linsel huffed. "I paid you to protect me, not help them!"

"I am protecting you, Dicky. Or would you rather they drag you off and shoot you instead?" Then he glanced back at the Viking. "Don't think it. Because then I would have to fight you. And neither of us wants that."

Mr. Dudding seemed to consider that, and Maybelle spent an interesting couple seconds looking from one man to the other. Whereas Mr. Dudding just seemed to be thinking, she saw something quiet die in Mr. Hallowsby's eyes. As if he truly was seeing the end to a friendship. Which was odd. What kind of man would count this thief a friend?

But in the end, Mr. Dudding nodded. "I'll just take the box then. And be grateful I didn't do to you what I did to your carriage. But I will…if you follow me."

To which Mr. Hallowsby groaned. "I told you, I just have to get him to Scotland. A few hours' ride. That's all."

"Guess you'll have to walk then," said the Viking as he jerked his head at his men. Then he paused long enough to tip his hat to her. "Miss."

She curtsied out of reflex, her attention split between the withdrawing Vikings and Lord Linsel as he began screaming.

"What? Wait! Damn it, Bram, do something! That's my property!"

But again, no one was listening to the man, who was turning purple in his rage. So purple, in fact, that he started to rush forward. Mr. Hallowsby was there in a second, blocking his way.

"He'll kill you, Dicky. Listen to me! If you follow him, he'll shoot you just because he can. And do you think there's a surgeon anywhere here? One that can save your life?"

Well, she could answer that. "None, sir. No doctor for fifty miles, and no surgeon for thirty."

And yet still the man struggled. Physically, he was no match for Mr. Hallowsby, who easily held him back, but he did fight and rage enough that Maybelle began to feel sorry for him.

"That was everything, Bram. Do you hear me? Everything I have is in that box."

Well, she could hear him, as well as everyone else.

"You have your life. Your wife is well and increasing. Be happy with—"

"*Everything.* How am I to live? Damn it!"

Meanwhile, Maybelle shifted to look out the inn window. She saw the Viking on a horse, his two companions, and a fourth as well. And they were leading away a pair of matched bays as well.

"Your carriage horses, I'm guessing," she said. She didn't think she could be heard over the noise of Lord Linsel's tirade—or Lady Linsel's moaning—but Mr. Hallowsby must have heard her because his head shot around.

Helping him out, Maybelle went to the curtains and drew them back so he could see the group leaving. He didn't say anything, but Lord Linsel was quite vocal with his curses.

"Shut up, Dicky," he said. "Let me think."

"Shut up? Shut up! I hired you—"

"To get you to Scotland. And I will—"

"What good is Scotland if I don't have any money once I get there?"

"You've got all your money squirreled away in Scotland. And I've got your damned gold in the boot of the carriage. Hidden in a rucksack. Or I did. Don't know if they found it."

Maybelle's eyebrows rose at that. Well, that was a bit of keen foresight. Apparently Lord Linsel thought so too, though it took him a bit longer to comprehend the information.

"I don't have any money in Scotland. That was all… Wait…what?"

"Only an idiot goes around clutching a lockbox like it was gold."

"It was gold!"

"It was paper and pounds sterling. And it's in a rucksack in…" No need to finish speaking, Lord Linsel was out the door and running to the carriage house as fast as his long legs could carry him.

Lady Linsel was on her feet as well, moving quickly after her husband, though with much more dignity. Which left Maybelle alone with Mr. Hallowsby.

"You still have to get them to Scotland," she said.

The man nodded grimly. "And without horses."

Well, then. This day was turning out to be the biggest windfall of all.

"As to that, sir, perhaps I could help."

His eyes narrowed onto hers. "You have horses? A carriage?"

She grinned. "Mayhaps. For a price."

She started laughing the moment he groaned.

Three

BRAM SAW THE MERCENARY GLEAM ENTER BLUEBELL'S eyes and knew they were in trouble. He could resist the wiles of a beautiful woman, but Dicky was hopeless in that area. And if she suggested an easy path to Scotland, the idiot would insist on taking whatever she offered. And pay whatever she wanted.

"Let's have it," he said in his coldest tone. "What are you offering and at what price?" He had to get them out of this annoying village as soon as possible.

In the distance, he could hear Dicky and Clarissa as they made it into the barn. If he knew Jeremy—and he did—then the carriage would be damaged beyond use. And sure enough, he heard Dicky's howl of rage.

"You need 'orses, yes?" she said. "To get to Scotland."

He nodded, offering no more information than that. But she was a clever girl and knew exactly the predicament he'd been mulling in his mind.

"It can't take long for the big man to shoot open that lockbox. 'E'll see that you tricked 'im and be back quick as a wink."

"What do you suggest?" he bit out.

"I know a farmer with 'orses. One's a draft, but quick enough, especially if you don't follow the main road north. Only got one, but there's another two mares as well. Both young, but serviceable. Especially over the 'ills. It won't be easy, but it'll keep the Viking off your scent."

"Viking?"

"Mr. Dudding."

Oh yes. He did have a Viking look to him. "Thank you, but no. I'm sure the innkeeper will be convinced to part with some horseflesh, especially with enough—"

"'Cept he's only got the one. An old mare sweet as can be but slower than molasses."

He bit back a curse. He didn't want her to hear it and jack up the price even more than it was. Sadly, her smirk told him she already knew they were in trouble.

"How much for three horses?"

She blew out a low whistle. "For you? Wouldn't be possible. But if I approach them—"

Dicky burst through the room door, his face flushed and his hands clenching the bag of money. "They've taken the horses and broken the axle on the carriage. Can't leave like that." Then he swallowed as he glanced out the window. "Do you think they'll come back?"

"As soon as they find out they haven't got the real money." Dicky paled, and for a moment, Bram thought the man would faint. So he spoke in a soothing tone. "Don't worry. Miss Bluebell knows of some horses to borrow—"

"How much?" Dicky interrupted as he turned to the woman. Not much of a negotiator was Dicky.

She smiled, all sweet innocence. "Mr. Heady has a

pair, and Mr. Mockler, a draft. If you want a carriage, though, we've got—"

"Just the horses. Where?" Dicky demanded.

"I can have the pair here quick as a wink. The third will take a mite longer—"

"Just the pair. We'll ride overland. Clary's grabbing what we need now. Bram, you wait until the carriage is fixed and take it up to the estate in Scotland."

Bram nodded, but he could see the canny light in his one-time friend's eyes. He knew what was coming next. "I'll do it, but you pay me now."

Dicky pulled up short, his eyes wide in mock innocence. "You'll get paid when I reach the Scottish estate." His phrasing confirmed Bram's fears.

"I'm not as stupid as you think, Dicky. I know you're not planning on going to that estate," he said.

"Course I am," he said with mock outrage.

"Dicky—"

"And besides, your job was to get us safely into Scotland. We're not in Scotland—"

"Damn it, Dicky. I'm not arguing with you. You pay me what you owe, and I'll see you safely into Scotland. But not—"

Dicky dug a hundred-pound note out of his pocket and slapped it into Miss Bluebell's waiting hand. "For the pair."

"Oh, sir, we may be far from London, but that only means what we got is precious."

"What?"

"This'll only pay for the one horse."

Dicky had no compunction about cursing in front of a woman as he pulled out another note.

"You're a smart man, Lord Linsel, you are. But you've forgotten the tack and saddles. Especially a lady and gent such as yerself—"

He slapped another hundred note into her palm. "Now be quick."

She smiled, then took two steps into the hallway. All the inn folk were gathered there listening. Damn it, if Dicky wanted a quiet escape, he was going about it the wrong damn way. Meanwhile, Miss Bluebell caught the arm of the boy, Thomas, and whispered something into his ear. He nodded, then took off at a run.

Looked like the horses were taken care of.

"Look, Dicky, we can just—"

"Take the carriage to Scotland. You'll get your pay there."

No, he wouldn't. He crossed the room just as Clarissa stumbled in under the weight of two heavy satchels—clothing presumably. He nodded once, pleased that her color seemed to have returned, and then he grabbed Dicky's arm and spoke low into the man's ear.

"I know you plan to board a boat for the Colonies. Pay me now, and I'll see that your tracks are covered. It'll be years before they start looking elsewhere for you."

It was the wrong thing to say. Clearly Dicky had thought he could escape to the New World without anyone ever thinking of him again. But one of the men he swindled had a shipping fleet. He could find Dicky if he put his mind to it. But Dicky hadn't thought that far in advance, and he gaped at Bram.

"Surely no one will find us out there."

Bram sighed. "Dicky…" he began, but was interrupted.

"No, no. Damn it, I'm sorry, but we need every copper."

"You just overpaid for two hacks and a pair of saddles," he snapped.

Dicky nodded. "Exactly."

More important, the money he'd promised Bram was a good deal more than three hundred pounds. "I'm only going to say this once. You'll regret this. Pay me what you owe, and I'll—"

"I can't!" It was a wail, and Bram knew that Dicky actually believed what he said. And given their spend-thrift ways, they probably did need every penny. And a good deal more besides.

"We were friends once, Dicky." That was a stretch, but he'd use it. "Would you do this to a friend? You gave me your word as a gentleman."

"Take the carriage. It's yours."

It wasn't worth half what he was owed. "Not good enough."

"It's all you're going to get."

Bram pulled up to his full height. He put on his most frightening glower. But Dicky wasn't a complete fool.

"You're not going to beat me. Not in front of my wife. Not in front of these people. You only hurt people who deserve it."

"You deserve it," he said.

"No, I don't. It's only money, not blood. You fight for blood."

He'd never quite phrased it that way, but Bram supposed the man had the right of it. It was only money, and Dicky wasn't worth dirtying his knuckles. Besides, he knew he'd get his pay another way.

"Last chance, Dicky."

The man wavered. Bram saw uncertainty in his eyes. Fear and regret, mixed with a true terror of his circumstance. But before he could choose the honorable path, the boy returned. "They're bringing round the horses right there."

Thomas pointed, and sure enough the boy's older brother was leading out two yearlings, prancing in their tack. Lively things, but not worth what the man had just paid, especially since the saddles looked older than his grandfather.

"Come along, Clary," Dicky said as he grabbed his wife. The two rushed out. The fact that Clarissa didn't protest told him what he'd always suspected. The woman was in on all of her husband's schemes, and the two were made for one another.

He followed the others to the door and watched them mount up and ride out. Dicky didn't even help his wife, but clambered up his mount, then waited impatiently as she struggled with her skirts.

Then they were gone, pretending to ride up the north road, but he knew they'd veer off as soon as they were able. In another day, they'd be aboard a ship and headed far away.

He released a sigh of satisfaction, finally allowing himself to relax. Another job done and well paid. He whistled as he wandered over to the carriage. Popping open the boot, he saw that his bag was there. Feeling from the outside, he knew that the wad of bills he'd taken from Dicky's treasure chest was still there.

"You're awfully chipper for a man who just got left with a broken-down carriage and no pay."

He'd been aware Miss Bluebell was following him, but had hoped that ignoring her would encourage her to be on her way. Apparently, she was of the stubborn sort. Worse, she was smart.

"You took your pay already," she said. "When you switched out the money in the lockbox. I'll wager you took double."

He had actually, but he was uncomfortable with the way she'd figured him out so easily. "I would have given back the extra had he been honest."

"And now you got double pay and a carriage. A good day's work for you, I'm guessing."

Actually, it had taken much more than a day, but she was right. He'd made sure there'd been solid profit for the trouble. "Good enough," he said as he slanted her a glance. She was standing in the doorway, the afternoon sun making her hair shimmer like gold. He especially liked the way the tendrils escaped her chignon to curl about her neck and lower to the bodice of her dress. Pretty as a picture, his mother would say. *Pretty as a viper*, he thought.

"Stop guessing, and be on your way."

She smiled, and everything about her turned even lovelier. Rosy cheeks, sweet bow of a mouth, even the subtle way her breath lifted and lowered her curves. All of it added up to a woman who meant to entice a man to ruin.

He turned away, though it was damned hard to do. Even knowing what she was.

"What you planning for that carriage? It'll take Mr. Grummer a couple days to replace the axle."

He grunted. "I suppose you have an idea of who might like to buy it."

"I do. Though what she'll be wanting with a carriage, I haven't a notion."

"How much, you think?"

"For you, too much. She don't like men."

He straightened and allowed himself to look at her, though only because he needed to read as much of her face as he could while they negotiated. "So I'm thinking you want to buy it off me for a song and then sell it to this woman, whomever she is."

"You're welcome to go about asking who might want a fine carriage." Then she looked over her shoulder and gestured someone to come forward. It was Thomas. "You know of anyone who might buy this fine carriage off Mr. Hallowsby?"

The boy's eyes widened, and he shook his head. "It's too 'igh and too fine. Nobody has the need."

Damn. She was going to swindle him again. "What about your mother?" Bram asked the boy. "Would she know of someone?" In his experience, the women knew the secrets in a village like this, not the men.

Thomas shrugged, and Bram flicked him a copper. "Go ask her."

The boy nodded and ran off.

"I'd save your blunt if I were you," Miss Bluebell commented. "You still have to pay your shot at the inn, and I know 'ow he'll charge you."

Bram shook his head. "He just saw me left high and dry—"

"Except I know the truth."

Yes, she did. Damnation. This is why he hated little villages. Every single one of them out to rook the outsider. "I'd rather pay him than you."

She offered him a sunny smile. "Suit yourself, but I'm the only one who knows who might buy that carriage off of you." Then she gestured down the road. "I live just up the road. Ask anyone. They'll show you. When you're ready to sell that carriage, you let me know."

Then she sauntered off, her skirts swaying, her face lifted to the sun. Her bonnet dangled off the back of her neck, doing nothing to keep her skin from turning brown. But he knew that sight would haunt him for the rest of his life. Sweet creamy skin, high cheekbones, and that soft smile about her rosebud lips. The sun danced in her golden hair, and her eyes crinkled against the sun, but he knew the brilliant aquamarine clarity of them. The lust was almost an afterthought. Her beauty was that absorbing.

And then she was gone. Rounding the bend out of the inn yard as she hummed to herself. And even that soft sound lingered in his thoughts as he stared after her.

"Keep looking," said a male voice beside him. The innkeeper, he realized, joining him as they looked to where Miss Bluebell had disappeared. "All the men hereabouts look, but she's got eyes for only one man."

He turned, his brows arching. "And who is that?"

"Vicar's son about eight miles that way." He jerked his head to the west. "All the girls are like mooncalves after him. He's a bookish boy, but handsome as sin. Smiles like he has a secret that he won't share unless you're nice to him."

Bram ground his back teeth. He didn't want to think about Miss Bluebell with anyone but him, illogical though that was. He didn't want her. And if this book-ish vicar's brat wanted her, then good riddance.

"Are they engaged then?" he pressed, not sure if he wanted the answer.

"Lord no. His father won't hear of it."

So the father saw what the son couldn't. "She's not so fine a woman, then."

"Bluebell? Nonsense. Known her all her life. She's grown into a right smart girl, but there's a question, you see."

Bram shifted to look more closely at the innkeeper. With girls like her, there was always a question, and the more he knew about her, the better he'd be able to negotiate on the carriage. "What question?" he pressed, but the man shook his head.

"Not right of me to share gossip. She's a fine girl. Will make someone a fine wife."

Obviously, the man needed some inducement. "Dicky gave me this carriage here, but the axle's been cut."

"I know. Miss Bluebell told me by way of Thomas. I've sent round for Mr. Grummer, but it'll take a couple days."

A couple days in this backwater hole was not what he wanted. Worse, at the end, he'd have a carriage with no horses and no place to put the thing once he got to London.

"Right. Know anyone who'd want to buy it?"

"That thing? We don't have much call for a fancy carriage around here. Can't think of a soul."

"Miss Bluebell says she knows of someone."

The man's brows arched. "Well, then I'd trust her. She'll drive a hard bargain, that one, but she always delivers. Got that from her mother. Honest folk, those two. It was the mother who made sure of it."

There was a story here. He was sure of it. "The father a bounder?"

The man harrumphed as he wandered to the carriage. "Don't know. Never met the man."

"Missing?"

"Dead. Miss Bluebell's mum comes here six months pregnant and settles down. Says her man's dead in the war, and she's got to make her own way. And she did. My wife and me, we helped out here and there, like we do with everyone, but wasn't much need with them. She tended her babe, grew her garden, and then soon enough there was little Bluebell mixing and making possets and selling them for some coppers." Then his expression shifted to a fond smile. "That little girl could sell wings to a bird, but you don't mind when you're paying her. She's always so sweet about it."

Of course she was. That was part of the job when tricking a man. Smile and promise with everything you have and make it a pleasant experience even as you're fleecing them. He knew. His mother was a master at it.

"So that's the problem then, isn't it? No husband. What about the aunt she mentioned?"

The man screwed up his lips and spit. "Never seen her. Never visits, never writes. It's been just her and her mum, leastways until recently."

"Recently?"

"Her mum died. A cough plagued her for years, and the winter was the end of her. Though it took until a few weeks ago for 'er to give in. Strong was that woman."

"So now it's just Bluebell all alone," he murmured.

The man's gaze sharpened. "Now, see here, we look after one another out here. Have to, you understand. If something 'appens to her, I'll be coming to see you."

It took a moment for Bram to realize what the man was thinking. "I'm not going to touch that girl!" he said, meaning every word. "But I do need to sell this carriage, and I drive as hard a bargain as she does."

"Well, that's a sight I'd like to see," the man said with a grin. "Some fancy nob getting the better of our Bluebell."

"I have no desire to get the better of anyone. Just want a fair deal."

"Uh-huh."

"And I'm not thinking of anything beyond that."

"Then you ain't a normal man. Everybody looks at 'er and thinks of more. She'll be by tonight. You'll see her then."

With the whole village watching? And invested in making sure Miss Bluebell got the better of the outsider? Ha! Might as well hand her the carriage for free then, because he wouldn't get more than a copper for it.

But he didn't say that aloud. Instead, he nodded and smiled as if that was exactly what he'd do. And ten minutes later, he was sauntering up the road to see where Miss Bluebell lived all alone.

Four

"I'VE FOUND A WAY, MAMA. IT'S LIKE YOU PUSHED HIM my way just 'cause I needed him."

Maybelle blinked back her tears as she ground the foul muck with her pestle. She was in their tiny kitchen, making up the last of her stock before she left for London. She spoke to her mother's portrait even though it was in the main room and couldn't be seen in here. It was a sketch done by an inexpert hand, but her mother looked so young and vibrant that it had sat on the mantel long after the paper had yellowed and the artist's signature faded to a smear. But it didn't matter. She knew every line by heart. Had even sketched it over and over as a child to practice her "lady arts," as her mother had called them.

And now that her mother was gone, this was all she had left, except her memories and the legacy the woman had sworn her to before she'd died. A legacy that was even now coming to fruition.

She heard his footsteps long before he appeared. She'd long since trained herself to catch every rustle upon their steps, because a visitor usually meant money coming in. Someone needed a posset, an extra egg from their chickens, or the butter that her mum had churned, day in and day out.

But this time the tread was heavy, the sound like the boot-falls of quality, and she barely kept herself from dancing a jig. He was her means to London, and she'd bet every coin she had that he wouldn't leave tonight before agreeing to everything she wanted. And she wanted a great deal.

His knock was equally ponderous, and she had to school her expression to surprise and a bit of disappointment.

"A moment!" she called by way of stalling. The window was open, allowing whatever breeze there was to deal with the stench of her ingredients. So she gave her mixture a last grind before crossing to the door. *Soon*, she thought. Soon she'd never ever have to make that disgusting potion again.

He stood in the doorway, framed by the late afternoon sun. As it was still summer, the light shone down on him, and she whispered a prayer of thanks to her mum for sending him to her. Before this morning, she'd had no idea how much she had yet to learn. And now she had not only a teacher, but a handsome man to boot, prettying up her little cottage.

"Why, Mr. Hallowsby! Whatever are you doing here?"

"You told me where you live."

"But I'm sure Mr. Garwick said I'd be in tonight—"

"You told me to come."

Well then. His tone was hard, and there was no mistaking the anger in his eyes. So it was like that, was it? Armed with his distemper, he was ready to negotiate for the carriage. Well and good. Since she'd already guessed that he'd come prepared to drive a hard bargain, she had her tactics well in hand.

Stepping back, she gestured for him to come in. "I was drinking my tea. Would you care for some?"

"No, thank you, miss."

She flashed him a smile, making sure her dimpled side showed. "Best tea in the land, but suit yourself."

"I've come to sell the carriage."

She heaved a sigh as she settled in her seat at the table. Then she looked disconsolately into her tea. "It's no good. I stopped by the lady in question, and she doesn't want it. She did more'n a week ago, but now…" She shook her head.

"What?"

She looked up, doing her best to appear heartbroken. "She don't want it, Mr. Hallowsby. I tried all my ways on her, but nothing worked. Can't force people hereabouts to buy what they don't need."

His eyes narrowed. "Was there ever a woman at all?"

"Well, of course there was!" she cried, pushing her air of injured innocence. "Did you think I'd lure you out here for some other reason?" She shoved up from her seat. "I'll have you know that I'm a good Christian woman. And there's souls not more'n a hundred yards that way. They'll hear me scream if you—"

He held up his hands. "I have no designs on your virtue, I assure you."

Had he shuddered as he said it? Did he truly think her ugly? Couldn't be! She had a mirror. She'd known since she was a child how pretty she was.

She folded her hands demurely in front of her, the picture of chastened purity. "I apologize. I am sorry to misjudge you so, sir. And double sorry that the lady no longer wishes the carriage." That wasn't exactly true, but it was close enough that her conscience didn't quibble with it. "But I have thought of an alternative."

He folded his arms and leaned back against the door frame. He hadn't even bothered to come fully inside her home, but stood there blocking the light. It was a position guaranteed to emphasize his height and breadth.

"Of course you do," he drawled. "Out with it, then. Let's hear what you want."

She frowned at him, startled by his stubbornness. She was doing everything she could to be charming, and he was having none of it.

"Are you sure you won't have some tea? And in a half hour I'll have stew. Goat's milk and honey with eggs and good vegetables grown by my own hand."

"I'm sure you did everything but nurse them with your own teat."

She stiffened. No one spoke to her like that. "There's no cause to be crude, sir."

"What do you want, Miss Bluebell?"

So he would have it straight out. She understood. She preferred the plain-speaking ones too. Told her exactly when they softened. So she huffed out a defeated breath and nodded.

"Very well, sir. I believe there's a market south of here. A carriage house that will buy what you've got, or know someone else who wants it."

"Which will do me no good, because the thing won't travel."

"Well, as to that, you have the pay to fix it up right

and tight, and Mr. Grummer is ready to do the work. All you want is a horse to take it there."

He was silent a moment, his eyes narrowed. She usually allowed the quiet to linger, knowing that it discomfited others more than her. But this time, she was the one who fidgeted. What was he thinking? Why did he hate her so on sight? And not for the first time this day did she lay the blame on something entirely new in her experience. Something she'd never thought of before she'd met Lady Linsel.

Her speech. Her accent. Having thought hard on it all afternoon, she realized that when compared to Lady Linsel, her tone was different. The way she spoke was different. That had to be the reason this man despised her so readily, even in the face of her beauty.

"Am I to guess that you have a horse?" he asked.

"I do. She's none too pretty to look at and none too fast. But she'll get you there well enough."

He grunted, the sound like a bull. "I'll see it first."

"Of course you will."

"But I'll not buy it. You'll have to get it back from the inn somehow."

She turned on him, her hands planted on her hips. "Now, how am I to do that, I ask you?" It was all for show. If things went exactly as she planned, she'd be down there with him, taking sweet Mina with her all the way to London.

He shrugged as if to say it was not his problem. She glared at him and decided to let him feel like he had won. "That will double the price, you know," she said in her most waspish tone. People liked it when they thought they'd gotten the better of her.

"No, it won't. Because I'm not as vain as Dicky or as hoodwinked as your neighbors. It'll be a fair price, or I won't be borrowing your horse."

"Renting," she stressed.

"Even so."

She glared at him because it made his lips twitch into an expression that stopped just shy of smug. Then she gestured behind her.

"Mina's penned out there."

He bowed to her, then turned on his heel. She got a good look at his backside, which was as fine as his front, and had an unusual moment appreciating the view. He had a way of walking that tickled her low in the belly. A slow, languid stride that drew the eye to parts she wasn't supposed to notice. But she did look, and it made her cheeks flush hot.

Then she realized he was pulling ahead of her. His height made it such that she had to scurry to keep up, even though he walked slowly. It was a tactic, she was sure. Done to make her feel small and insignificant. Sadly, it was working, especially since Lady Linsel had begun the work earlier.

They made it quickly to Mina's pen. Maybelle only had a small cottage, so there was little space for keeping animals. And now that she'd sold the goat and chickens in preparation for leaving, there was only poor Mina looking sad with a ratty tail as she cropped the grass.

"That's a sorry looking nag."

She knew he was baiting her. Knew that her own estimation put Mina in such a sad category as well. But she felt the wound nonetheless.

"She's a truer horse than you'll ever know. Mina and

I have been friends since she was a foal. She may not look so fine as your London-bred prancers, but she'll get you where you need to go, be satisfied with the grasses at her feet, and be ready to move in the morning."

"Nursed by your very own hand…" he said, his eyebrows raised as he called her bluff.

"Not nursed. She came to us a little older than that, though I played with her as a child."

"Of course you did—"

"And I feed her my right fine carrots. By hand." Then just to prove the point, she clucked her tongue, and Mina trotted over, mouth eager for the carrot she pulled out of her pocket.

"The carriage needs two horses—"

"You can switch the hitch for one."

He grimaced, and she knew she had him. He was thinking of the expense and the bother. But if he'd a mind to leave the carriage behind, he'd have given up by now. Which meant he was here for at least a few days while the thing got repaired.

"You should add a coat of paint, you know," she said as if she'd just thought of it. "It will sell better that way."

"And what would you know about selling carriages?" he grumbled.

"Not a thing," she lied. After all, selling was selling. It was all about finding out what people really wanted and giving it to them, even if it was simple compliments and attention.

Which brought her thoughts to him. What exactly did he want? Coin, obviously, but that was the only thing. With his looks, he wasn't in need of attention.

So what did he want that she could sell him? Did he want to feel important?

She turned so that she looked more fully at him, but her profile was still in his view. Her mother said her figure was her best asset, along with her smile. And so she left it on display as she spoke.

"May I ask your advice, sir?"

His brows went up in surprise and wariness entered his body. "Of course."

She flashed her dimple, but kept her expression anxious. It wasn't hard to do. She was worried. "Lady Linsel said she couldn't understand me. That I speak—"

"Clarissa makes sure to insult the prettiest woman in the room."

"Oh, sir! Surely she couldn't mean—"

"I'll think about the horse, Miss Bluebell," he interrupted as he took a step back. Clearly, he did not appreciate false modesty. "Good day." He gave her a shallow bow.

No! She couldn't lose him now. They hadn't reached a bargain yet. "But sir, please tell me! Please…" She swallowed. He'd put on his hat. "Teach me."

He frowned at her. "What?"

"I want t' speak like a proper lady."

His head tilted as he studied her. "It's not how you speak, it's what you say."

"No, sir, that's not true," she shot back. "I am always respectful, always sweet."

"All the best courtesans are."

She blinked, shocked to her core. Had he just called her a whore? An expensive one, but still a woman who spread her legs for money. And said in such a matter-of-fact way that she was shocked. As if it were a foregone conclusion of little import. It was that last that truly bothered her. Most men who insulted her looked for a reaction. He had said it as calmly as if he named a carrot or a tree. And in that moment of frozen surprise, she lost the upper hand.

"You know," he said as he touched her chin, slowly closing her mouth, "there was a time I would have been completely fooled by you, taken in like all the other peasants in your life. But I am not, Miss Bluebell." He stepped closer to her, letting his height dwarf her into insignificance. "You are a woman who gets everything she wants. A grasping tart in the most beautiful package I have ever seen."

Never had anyone complimented and insulted her in the same sentence. And so she reacted purely from the place of a wounded animal.

She punched him square in the jaw, following with another to his gut.

Except he was faster than her, stronger than her, and definitely better at fisticuffs. He caught her fists in his palms, the smack adding insult to the sting in her knuckles.

So she slammed her knee upward as hard as she could. That, he avoided quickly, though she at least had the satisfaction of seeing his eyes widen in surprise. She tried to follow it up. She wore sturdy walking boots that stung when she kicked a man. So she did that, but he used his height to his advantage.

Before she realized it, he had gripped her hands and spun her around. Her shoulders wrenched with the force of his twist, and then abruptly, she was wrapped up from behind. His corded arms bound her across the chest, and when she struggled against him, he lifted her feet off the ground.

Easy enough from that position to bang at his legs, but he had on sturdy boots as well. They were planted solidly on the ground, and all her flailing did nothing but elicit a grunt in her ear.

Then suddenly he was lifting her up. High up, her legs swinging away from him for all that she still tried to kick. Then she came down.

Feet first, banging hard into the dirt. And before she could use that as leverage, he stepped backward such that she couldn't get purchase. She was fighting with her torso, twisting and flailing as she tried to find some way to hit him, but she was pinned. And he was so damned strong.

A second later, her bum landed on the ground with a teeth-jarring thump. She twisted with her legs, but they were splayed in front of her, and her skirts were getting in the way. Only then did he stop.

It took her a moment to realize he wasn't moving. That she was sitting flat on the ground while he held her pinned from behind. And the more she scrabbled with her legs, the more dirty and tired she got, whereas he just crouched behind her seemingly without a care in the world.

She began to curse him. They weren't English words, but Romany ones she'd learned long ago. She called him a dog and worse, though she truly didn't know what "worse" was. Just garbled sounds that she made when she was so spitting mad she couldn't speak at all. And worse, tears sprang into her eyes, leaking out the corners, and no doubt making tracks in the dust she was kicking into the air.

"I can sit here all day, Miss Bluebell."

She quieted. She stilled long enough to catch her breath, and then—abruptly—she sprang into life again. She kicked and twisted for all she was worth.

Nothing. He didn't budge and she only got more tired.

In the end, she stilled. Taking a shuddering breath, she came to terms with the truth. He was stronger and a better fighter. He could do whatever he willed with her, and she was terrified—

"What do you want, Miss Bluebell?" he asked. His voice was hoarse in her ear, a low rasp that ratcheted up her fear another degree.

"Let me go!"

"Not until we have a conversation—you and I. An honest one, if you please."

"I want to be let go!"

"I'm not going to hurt you. I just want to speak without lies. Do you know how to do that?"

"Of course I do! I have never lied—"

He choked her. His top forearm slipped up her chest until it pressed against her throat. Not hard enough to hurt, but the message got through.

"I told you. No lies."

"I wasn't," she whispered, tears of frustration burning in her eyes.

"I count half truths, slight omissions, and even things you wish to be true as lies, Miss Bluebell. And those times when you pretend to be dumb? Those are the worst lies of all. So think again. Have you ever lied?"

She swallowed. Of course she had. She'd told ugly

women they were beautiful, fat men they'd lost weight. She'd flattered and cajoled. And she'd hidden her intelligence almost from the very start. Boys had taught her young that they didn't like to be bested by a girl.

"I'm a poor orphan. I've done what I needed to."

"I'm sure you have," he said conversationally. "And I don't damn you for that." She didn't believe him. There was condemnation in every word he uttered. "But Miss Bluebell, if we're to deal with one another, I need the truth. What do you want? Is it this?"

He leaned down, and she felt his teeth at her neck. It wasn't a bite, per se. More of a slow compression of his teeth, drawing the edges across her skin while her body trembled beneath him. She whimpered, truly terrified, and then he licked where he had bit. His tongue was hot and wet, and she slammed her eyes shut trying to find a way out.

Could she scream before he choked off her breath? Would anyone come in time? She tried to still her racing heart as she gathered her breath to try.

But then he stopped and drew back. "You don't want that," he said, obviously startled.

She screamed.

As loud and as long as she could, while he released her and stood back. She scrambled to her feet as soon as she could, screaming for all she was worth. And she kept going while her throat went raw, and he stood there looking bemused.

Then she had to draw breath, and in the pause as she pulled air in, she realized he wasn't fighting her. He was just standing there, confusion all over his face.

She stopped screaming.

He swallowed. "I'm sorry. I thought…I believed…" He shrugged, then gave her a deep bow. "I was mistaken."

She stood there, shaking and staring, not understanding what had happened. Her hair was in her eyes, dust coated her dress and face, and he wasn't moving to attack. He wasn't doing anything but standing there looking as innocuous as a doddering old hound.

And yet…

Her neighbor came thundering up the road. Mr. Bray was a good man with seven children and big, thick fists. She'd sold her goat and chickens to him for less than they were worth, and he was as close to a father as she'd ever had. His face was set into murderous lines as he came at them, an ax held in his fists.

The moment they saw him, Mr. Hallowsby raised his hands and stepped back. Then he stilled and waited while Mr. Bray slowed as he approached, his great chest heaving and blowing air like a great bellows.

The man looked back and forth between them. He saw her dirty dress and mussed hair, and his mouth set in grim lines.

"Wot's to-do 'ere?" he demanded.

"A misunderstanding, is all," Mr. Hallowsby said, keeping his hands raised high.

Mr. Bray looked to her. "Bluebell?"

"He didn't hurt me," she said slowly. "He just…" She swallowed. Never would she say aloud that he had licked her.

Mr. Hallowsby slowly let his hands down. "Just confused you?" he prompted. "Startled you?"

"Did 'e touch you?" Mr. Bray demanded.

"Yes. Yes! I tried to punch him, and 'e caught me—"

"I kept her fists away from me. And when she began kicking, I flipped her around." Mr. Hallowsby slowly moved his hands through the motions he'd made.

Mr. Bray straightened, though he kept the ax ready. "Why'd you punch 'im, Bluebell?"

"He called me…" She could not say courtesan. First of all, Mr. Bray probably didn't even know the word, and she would not say whore. "He said I lie."

"We're good Christian folk, sir. I've known Bluebell all 'er life, and there's no lie to 'er. I suggest you go on back to—"

"He's going to buy Mina to take that fancy carriage to London." And right there she was suddenly aware of how easily the lie came to her lips. Except, it wasn't really a lie because he was going to buy her horse. He'd have no choice with Mr. Bray looking threatening.

"I never said that," Mr. Hallowsby stated.

"There ain't others around 'ere that would serve," she said firmly.

Mr. Bray nodded. "Everbody else needs their cattle. Mina's a good horse. Worth…" He looked to her.

"Fifty pounds," she said.

Mr. Hallowsby's hands went down. "Fifty pounds! For that nag?"

"Yessir," Mr. Bray agreed. "Fifty pounds."

Maybelle felt her lips curve. She'd learned the basics of selling from Mr. Bray. And the first thing he'd taught her was that a thing was worth what someone would pay. No more and no less. And right now, Mr. Hallowsby would pay exactly fifty pounds for Mina.

She watched the understanding build in Mr. Hallowsby's body—not his face—as he came to understand the situation. His shoulders tightened, and his feet slid slightly apart as if he were about to fight. His hands even tightened into fists, but he planted those on his hips rather than lift them. She knew from experience that if Mr. Hallowsby ever chose to fight, he would move much faster than she could see coming. So that meant he would pay, though it clearly angered him.

Good.

She was angry too.

"Fine. Fifty pounds," he ground out.

"Pay it now, if you please," Mr. Bray said, all smiles, though he never lowered that ax.

"This is robbery, plain and simple."

She was about to argue, but she needn't have bothered. Mr. Bray was before her, lifting his chin. "It were a misunderstanding, yes?"

Mr. Hallowsby met the man's eyes, and the two stared at one another. Maybelle tried to comprehend what was passing between the two, but she couldn't. It was as silent as the grave. But in the end, Mr. Hallowsby's gaze dropped.

"Yes. My mistake." And so he silently pulled out his purse and counted fifty pounds.

Add that to the money she'd already gotten from her basket of possets, and she was richer than she'd ever been in her entire life. Good Lord, this was a lucky day.

"Thank you, Mr. Hallowsby. You've bought yourself a fine horse." Then she looked up at him, her expression serene. "Will you be taking her now, or shall I keep her until you're ready to leave?"

He looked at her, his expression turning grim. Then he silently pulled out another note and slapped it in her hand. "That will cover the cost of stabling her, I believe."

"Of course," she said sweetly. "That, and my lessons, that is." Normally she wouldn't push this. Normally, she'd take her fortune and run laughing into the house. But this wasn't a normal time, and he was the only one who could teach her what she needed to know.

"Lessons?" he said slowly, his eyes narrowed in fury.

"In how to talk like a lady," she said.

"Aw, Bluebell," interrupted Mr. Bray, "wot you need—"

"I need them," she said quietly. And she knew he understood, not her reasons, but that she would have them. Just as she'd had her mathematics lessons and her astronomy teaching and her plays by Shakespeare.

Then she looked to Mr. Hallowsby, trying to judge him by his manners. But his face gave nothing away. And any clue from his body was lost amid the way he straightened and squared his shoulders.

Was he angry? Would he lie to her? Had she just pushed him too far? The questions battered her mind, but she said nothing and neither did Mr. Hallowsby. They simply looked at one another, eye to eye, raised chin to clenched jaw.

And then he smiled. Slow and sweet, before he sketched a too-deep bow.

"It would be my honor indeed, Miss Bluebell, to give you a lesson."

"In talking like a lady," she stressed. She could hear the threat in the way he'd phrased it.

"Of course," he said as he put his hat on his head, nodded once to Mr. Bray, then turned on his heel.

She watched him walk away, his loose-limbed stride taking him quickly off her property. She saw his height and his confidence. She remembered the feel of his arms as they'd restrained her and the fear that had consumed her when he'd touched her neck.

Except it hadn't been complete fear, had it? If she were honest with herself, she'd been taunting him from the moment she'd laid eyes on him. She'd made sure to show him her most beautiful aspects. She'd given him her address when normally she managed all her affairs in the village. And most of all, she'd purposely pushed him when she usually let things be with a man.

She was attracted to him—truth be told. She was adult enough to know when a man interested her. But was he too much for her? Was she too bold?

"He's not your usual gent, Bluebell. Won't be led around by the nose."

"I know," she said softly. That was, after all, why he intrigued her so.

"You don't 'ave to go to London, you know. Ain't nothing there that you don't already got here."

She looked at the man who was as near to a father to her as she had ever known. She loved his craggy face and salt-and-pepper hair that stuck straight up from his head. He'd held her hand when she was sick and taught her how to ride a horse. And if she stayed here, even without her mum, he would see to it that she married a good local man and lived a life such as he had. A passel of children, a farm that grew fine some years, and not as fine others.

Not a bad life, she thought. Maybe even a good one.

"I can't," she said as much to him as to herself. "I have to go to London."

"And wot's there that ain't here?"

She swallowed and looked away. She didn't want to hurt him with the truth.

He waited a breath. Then another. Then he sighed and spit into the dirt.

"Keep yer secrets then, Bluebell. But if you ever have need, even when ye're in London, you send me a post. I'll get to you. I swear it."

She knew he would, and she impulsively threw her arms around him and kissed his weathered cheek, letting the scratch of his beard abrade her lips. "Thank you, Mr. Bray. Thank you so much."

"Ain't nothing. Now go get some o' yer stew. We'll add it to my Beth's and have a good dinner."

She nodded and did as he asked. But it wasn't until late that night when she was lying alone on her pallet in her silent house that she thought again of what he'd said. Not Mr. Hallowsby, though he'd certainly been in her thoughts all evening. No, what she thought about was the man who waited for her in London. The one who would make all her dreams come true.

What was in London that wasn't here?

"My father," she said. "I'm going to find my father."

Five

THUNK.

The knife sunk deep into the tree trunk, the sound satisfying to the base of his spine. Sadly, Bram had been throwing at a different tree, so he was less than pleased with his performance.

He was trying out a new way of throwing daggers while he waited and worried about when Jeremy would come back. But since his childhood friend hadn't shown up so far, Bram was trying to distract himself with dagger practice. Instead of standing with his knife poised before the throw, he was drawing across his body from his hip and flicking the knife at the target. When done right, he could draw the weapon and throw it in a single, quick motion. But it was less than useless if he couldn't aim properly.

Grunting his displeasure, he stomped his way to his knives, where they lay scattered about the clearing. He'd been practicing all morning but hadn't improved one bit.

He blamed it on the woman and the damned flowers that dotted the area. They didn't even have to be bluebells, though a few were. If it was a flower, he thought of her. If he was eating food, he thought of carrots and wondered if she'd grown them. If he thought about the carriage he needed to sell, he thought about her suggestion to paint the thing. She was everywhere in his thoughts, and he didn't like it.

He stomped back to his position and tried to focus. Draw, throw.

Ping.

Right tree this time. Glancing blow.

Maybe if he envisioned her on the tree, he could stab her straight through the heart.

Whoosh.

Apparently not. He'd missed by a mile. And he didn't like picturing human targets anyway, much less a beautiful woman who drove him insane.

She wouldn't be everywhere in his thoughts if he could just pin her down to one thing. Best he could come up with was that she was frustrating as hell. He'd only known her a day, but in that time he'd labeled her a beauty beyond compare, a conniving tart, a manipulative witch, and an ignorant peasant. But none of those labels fit her well.

She was a beauty, all right, but up close he had seen the flaws in her skin. She had freckles and a slight golden-brown cast, because she clearly didn't wear her bonnet enough.

She was a conniving tart to be sure, except that when he'd teased her neck with teeth and tongue, she'd gone still with shock, and then terror. A tart would know that was foreplay, not violence, but she'd reacted with a virgin's fear.

Manipulative witch was certainly true, because

she'd clearly gotten the local populace wrapped around her finger. Except she wasn't a witch at all, but a girl on her own. By all accounts, she'd grown up with no one but her mother to aid her, and together they'd not only managed but thrived. That took strength and determination. And likely, no small amount of manipulation to get what they needed to survive.

And the last was ignorant peasant. That was patently untrue for all that she sounded like a stupid northern provincial. He'd seen the books in her small home. Mathematics, agriculture, Aristophanes, Latin. She had a library in her home and yet only one bed, likely shared with her mother. That meant they'd spent their money on her education, though why they'd made that choice he hadn't a clue.

And now she wanted lady lessons. As if he had a clue how to be a lady. And yet he'd promised—one lesson—and he would deliver.

She came to him after another ten minutes of frustrated throwing. In another hour, he'd have chipped all the bark off the trees in this clearing. He smelled her the moment she appeared behind him. It was a lemony-green scent, though in his mind, it was mingled with the peppery taste of her skin. Objectively, he knew it likely came from the bloody cranesbill flowers he'd seen all over her yard, but in his mind they were her scent, and the pepper was her spice.

"Stay back," he said, his voice gruff. "Don't want me to accidentally skewer you."

"You'd never hit me, at least not on purpose. You're too good."

He was about to laugh at her statement, but then

he did it. He drew, flicked, and *thunk*—dead center of the tree he'd been missing all damned morning. He rocked back on his heels in surprise. Had he finally gotten the knack of it? He drew again and threw.

Ping.

Close, but not quite what he'd wanted. The tree trunk was narrow enough that were it a man, he'd have hit something vital. On the tree, he'd carved off more bark. Still, it was closer than he'd been all morning.

"How did you learn that?" she asked, her words suffused with awe.

He glanced back at her. Was she truly impressed, or was that a lie? He couldn't tell. She was a master at stroking a man's ego. He'd seen her do it with Dicky.

"I practiced, is how." He stomped over to retrieve his knives.

"But where'd you get the idea? I've never seen anyone throw knives like that afore. Not drawing from the side."

He didn't answer, choosing to let her think about it. Would she take the hint and go away, or persist with her questions?

"Please, sir," she pressed, and though she'd used the word *please*, there was no begging in the tone. "'Ow'd you think of it?"

"What do you think?"

She pursed her lips, and he regretted looking at her. He'd see her wet, puckered mouth in his dreams tonight.

"I dunno," she said. "That's why I asked."

Well, at least she wasn't prone to flights of fancy. That was a rarity in his experience. Most people developed elaborate tales about how he learned a thing. It helped that he encouraged them in such thinking, but with her he simply shrugged and told the truth.

"Saw a gypsy do it once. Got a spider from twelve paces away."

"And you 'ad to learn it?"

He shrugged again and studied her. He looked at her face, her body, her everything. He couldn't stop himself from seeing her pert nose in the sunshine, the way her pale blue muslin dress pressed against her body in the breeze. Her blond locks were tucked neatly in place today, and he wished they were in disarray, tumbling about her face and shoulders while he spread her out on his bed and...

He cursed under his breath and stomped back in place. He tried to concentrate again on his throw, but he knew he didn't have the ability. His mind was filled with the imagined sight of her naked beneath him, flushed and open, as he drove inside her. It was an obvious thought, though so graphic that his blood thumped inside his veins. And he couldn't draw his knife while thinking that. He just couldn't.

So he stood there, fighting his carnal nature, while the breeze took her scent to him and made his entire body ache with yearning.

"Go away, Miss Bluebell," he ground out. "I've no interest in play today."

"I'm not 'ere t' play," she said stoutly. "I want me lessons."

"Lesson. Singular. That's all I agreed to."

"That's no' true."

He whipped around, using his fiercest stare. "It is true. You'll be getting one and no more." He let some of his lascivious thoughts show on his face. "Unless you want to pay for more."

She swallowed. It was a small gesture, partially hidden by the way she lifted her chin and looked defiant. She was nervous around him, and yet so determined that he had to wonder why. What was so important that she had to speak like a lady?

"Go home, Miss Bluebell. I'm busy."

"You're sticking trees. You can teach me while you do it."

He'd meant to turn away from her and go back to throwing. But he couldn't tear his gaze from her. Not when her eyes were flashing so blue in the sunlight. Like gems on fire.

She folded her arms. "I'm not leaving 'til you do as you promised."

"Very well. Here's your lesson. Say your *h*'s. Ladies speak the letter."

"I do! I been working on that since I was a babe."

"Well, it didn't take. Repeat after me. *My husband holds my hand.*"

"Me husband holds me.'and."

He smirked. He hadn't meant to, but she was so expressive as she spoke. First with clear defiance, but then she realized exactly what she'd said. Her eyes widened, and she scowled. With a frown of concentration, she tried again.

"Me husband holds my hand."

He shook his head.

"Me husband holds my hand." Each *h* was pushed out with a huff. "Me husband holds my hand."

He still shook his head.

"I'm saying the *h*'s."

He grinned. "My husband holds my hand."

"Me—" She abruptly cut off her words, obviously understanding her error. "*My* husband holds my 'and. Damn it! Hand."

He nodded. "There you go. Lesson done."

"No, it ain't!" Then she cursed under her breath. "No, it isn't. This takes practice."

"So go practice."

"With you. You're the only one around oo speaks properly."

That was certainly true. "Then talk. I'll let you know when it's wrong."

"No. I 'ave—have t' hear you talk back."

He merely grunted in answer, then grinned when her sigh filled the clearing. He was purposely aggravating her because she'd been plaguing him all morning. And all last night. But that wasn't her fault, he supposed, so in the name of justice, he relented.

"Tell my why you want these lessons so badly."

"I want t' learn, same as you wanted to learn how to throw knives."

"Not the same. I have need at times to hurt a man from a distance. You have no need to sound any different than you do."

"And wot do you know about me needs?"

"My needs."

"What?"

"Don't say 'me needs.' *My* needs. *My* husband."

"Oh. *My* needs. *My* husband." She not only copied his words, but his inflection as well. She had the gift of a mimic, and that would help her enormously in her task. But there was more to being a lady than words. And nothing could make this sow's ear into a silk purse. Nothing. But he already knew telling her would do no good. So instead of worrying about her, he focused on his task. Sighting his target, he angled his body how he wanted. Then he drew and threw in one single movement.

Thunk.

Good throw.

Nearly perfect, in fact. And her appreciative whistle only made him more satisfied. Until he'd realized what had happened. He didn't want to draw pleasure from her admiration. It was a trap as sure as iron bars.

"Tell me about wot—what—got you traveling with Lord and Lady Linsel."

He hadn't told her to correct *wot* to *what*, but she'd heard it and done it anyway. Well done, he thought, but instead of voicing that aloud, he aimed and threw again.

A miss. Not even hitting a tree trunk but toppling into the dirt before rolling to an ignominious stop.

"What do you think brought me here?"

"Do others like it when you don't answer their questions?"

He glanced back in surprise. "They don't usually care. Most of my associates like to guess at my life. They call me a man of mystery." Or at least the silly ones did.

"Yer associates? What about yer friends?"

"Your associates. Your friends," he corrected.

"Yer…your. Your. Your friends."

He nodded and didn't answer. He thought of his best friends Benjamin and Jared, both trapped in airless rooms of an office, and yet pleased as punch with their lot. "I don't see them much."

"Who are they?"

"A solicitor and a banker."

She sighed. "Not what do they do? Who are they?"

He twisted to look at her, wondering if this was some northern way of speech that he didn't understand. "What?"

"Who are they t' you?"

"Speak slower," he ordered. He still didn't understand the question. "Ladies have all the time in the world to be heard, and they like the sound of their own voices."

"You don't have a 'igh opinion of ladies, do you?"

"You met Clarissa, didn't you?"

She nodded, her expression rueful. "But what of yer mates?" He arched a brow, and she thought over her words. "Your mates."

He nodded because she'd found the error. She was a quick study, he'd give her that. "They're my friends from school." Then, before she could probe deeper into things he never discussed, he gave her his back as he again sighted the tree.

Draw, *thunk*.

Draw, *ping*.

Draw—

"Wait!"

He stopped his motion midswing, but he'd been holding the knife loosely. It flew out of his hand—incompletely the wrong direction—as a blur of yellow hair and light blue dress rushed forward. To his horror, the knife thunked within a few yards of Bluebell as she ran forward. God, a split second difference, and he would have got her hard in the gut.

"What are you doing?" he bellowed, his heart thumping painfully in his throat.

He started forward, only to be pulled up short by the sight of her standing with hands on her hips over an enormous pig. It was probably black, but with all the mud on it and that enormous wet snout, he couldn't decide if it was a bog fairy come to life or something mundane, like a small bloated cow.

"Mr. Periwinkle, wot are you doing out here?"

He noted absently that she'd remembered her *h* but then grimaced as the creature stepped on the hilt of one of his knives. Oh, bloody hell, those were expensive.

"What is that?" he demanded.

"It's Widow Dwight's pig. He's a prizewinner, you know."

"And you call him Periwinkle?"

"Because of the bow." She gestured to a massive ribbon tied about the thing's neck, which was many colors, none of them periwinkle.

Meanwhile, the thing started to snuffle off, foraging for whatever he ate, but she grabbed at the ribbon and wrapped a firm hand around it.

"Oh no, you don't," she said. "It's back to yer pen, it is."

He stared at her. Forget that she'd risked her life running in front of his knives to catch that thing. The absurdity of her hauling on a ribbon to drag a five-hundred-pound pig to its pen was ridiculous.

"You're getting your dress dirty," he said, which was not at all what he wanted to say.

"I know," she said on a sigh. Then she looked up. "Go on. I can't hold 'im all day."

She couldn't hold him at all. The thing was already dragging her off into the woods. She dug in her heels and grunted. "Hurry up! Get the ale!"

He blinked. "I have no idea—"

"Mr. Periwinkle likes ale. Just tell 'em at the inn. They'll know what to do." She huffed out a breath as she tried to divert the pig to the right instead of the left. "I'll be moving 'im this way."

"You can't seriously—"

"Go!"

Apparently, she could. So with a bemused shake of his head, he went back to the inn. He started out at a jog, but soon broke into a run. The sound of her heavy breath as she fought with the pig-beast followed him every step of the way. Fortunately, it wasn't far to the inn, and he burst into the kitchen with a gasp.

"Big pig," he said. Then, when people stared at him in shock, he gestured to his neck. "Ribbon. Periwinkle."

The lady at the fire pushed to her feet, nodding. "We've got just wot you need." She grabbed a bucket filled with kitchen scraps, and when he reached for it, she held it back and jerked her chin at Thomas. He was already moving, and soon he'd poured a couple pints of ale over the scraps.

"What are you doing?"

"Mr. Periwinkle likes his ale, 'e does."

Well, he supposed he couldn't blame the pig. He held out his hand, but the woman held out her palm first. "Two shillings, if you please."

"What? It's not even my pig!"

She shrugged. "It ain't mine neither. Get it back from the widow."

"But I don't know—"

She waved him silent. "Miss Bluebell knows wot to do. Just trust her." Then she stood there with her hand outstretched.

He was tempted to stomp away. What did he know about pigs and widows? But the image of Bluebell being hauled willy-nilly through the woods had him cursing under his breath as he pulled out two shillings. Damned expensive for kitchen scraps meant for a pig.

He slapped the coins into her hand, and she had the gall to smile and curtsy before she handed him the bucket. "Mind you keep it back from 'im. Just rest it near 'is nose until 'e's back in th' pen. Otherwise, you'll be coming back 'ere for another bucket and another—"

"Two shillings. Yes, I understand." Though in truth, he had no idea how one let a pig smell a bucket but not bury his snout in the thing.

He grabbed the bucket and rushed back, afraid to find Bluebell missing from the clearing. He needn't have worried. He could hear her cursing from across the way.

"This way, you obstinate brute!" How many villagers in this area knew the word "obstinate?" For that matter, how many of the *ton*?

He hurried to her side and had to stifle his laugh. She was now as filthy as the pig, her hair was matted with mud, and she was being pulled straight into a tree no matter how much she dragged on the ribbon, which—he now saw—was laid on top of a heavy rope. Well, at least that part made sense, though trying to drag that thing by a rope was no more effective than by a ribbon.

"I've got the bucket."

"Took you long enough," she huffed. "Hold it out, but not too close."

He nodded and tried not to spill the thing. "What pig drinks ale?"

"All of 'em, if you let 'em."

The country was just one new thing after another. God, how he missed the black London air where all he had to deal with was footpads and faithless peers.

"Not there!" she said as she brushed the hair out of her eyes and left a mud streak across her forehead. "Lower. Not that low! He'll get it!"

But Mr. Periwinkle was more interested in something under a bush, and so it didn't matter how high or low the bucket was. The pig wanted under the foliage.

"Ow! Damn it," she cursed. "Over 'ere, Peri. We got some good mash fer ye." Her accent was getting thicker the longer she struggled with the pig. "Damn it. You take 'im. I'll hold the bucket."

He shook his head. "Not on your life. I've only got this one coat."

"Oh, for pity's sake. The widow'll wash it."

"And charge me a crown for it," he snapped. "You hold the pig—"

"I'm not strong enough."

"A giant wouldn't be strong enough," he huffed. So despite what the muck smelled like, he reached in and grabbed the remains of a turnip now soaked in ale. Then he held it out and tried to sound coaxing. "Come on, Mr. Periwinkle. You like turnips, do you?"

"Ain't no one really likes turnips," she said between breaths.

He couldn't argue with her on that. "Don't say *ain't*," he muttered as he kept holding out the turnip.

"Drop it on the ground," she instructed. "Near me feet." Then before he could say anything, she grimaced. "Near *my* feet."

"Very good," he said with a grin. Then he dropped the turnip. Sadly, Mr. Periwinkle had no interest in it.

"Splash 'im with ale."

"What?"

"So he can get the taste."

"And how am I—"

"Just grab a handful and splat 'im with it."

She was starting to tire. Her shoulders were drooping, and he would bet her hands were getting raw. So rather than argue that it was a liquid and not something he could grab, he tried to do what she wanted.

Cupping his hand as best he could, he scooped up some ale and wilted cabbage and threw it right at Mr. Periwinkle's head.

He was in luck. The thing had lifted its snout out of the dirt, and so Mr. Periwinkle got a face full of ale. Which got his full attention.

He whipped around, moving faster than Bram thought possible for a thing that size. Bluebell stumbled around as well, and she nearly kicked the bucket over. He was able to save it—getting a kick in the forearm as he did—but that didn't save them from the weight of Bluebell lurching for the bucket.

Oh, bloody hell.

Bloodydamnpissinghell.

The thing sat on him.

Getting flattened by a five-hundred-pound pig was not an experience he ever wanted to repeat. But as bad as that was, it soon got even worse.

Six

"GIT THE BUCKET! GIT THE BUCKET!"

Maybelle's hands and shoulders were screaming, but she put everything she had into hauling Mr. Periwinkle back from the bucket. She knew that the moment the pig got a belly full of ale, he'd be a drunken pig, and no one could move him until dawn when he'd wake with a sore head and worse disposition.

Entire evenings at the pub had been spent in the retelling of one Mr. Periwinkle story after another, and she did not want to add today's adventure to that list of disasters. She had too much to do yet and no strength left in her hands as the pig got the better of her.

She lost her grip and dropped to her knees. And poor Mr. Hallowsby was now flat on his bum with a hand to his chest as he gasped for air.

God no. He couldn't be dying! Getting hit by Mr. Periwinkle was no small thing, and men had been killed by less. She'd managed to maneuver the pig off him with a few well-timed shoves, but the damage had already been done. He'd been sat on, and...

Phew. He breathed, and with no grimace of pain, as far as she could see. But then he raised a hand.

He was holding a knife. The blade flashed in the sun, and she nearly swallowed her tongue. He couldn't kill Mr. Periwinkle. He couldn't! That was Widow Dwight's only means of support beyond what little she brought in doing laundry. Plus the thing had fathered half the pigs in Hull.

"No!" she bellowed, and she saw his hand stop midair.

He didn't strike. But he didn't keep the bucket away from Mr. Periwinkle. And as they froze in that tableau, the clearing was filled with the snorts of a pig guzzling ale.

Damnation.

She plopped down on her rear, belatedly realizing that she was covered from head to toe in mud and that Mr. Hallowsby wasn't much better. Baths for them both and fresh clothes before they left. Which meant she had to get that pig back to Widow Dwight's to trade for the washing. She had precious few dresses to take to London, and this was one of her better ones.

"Aw, blimey," cried Thomas from the far side of the clearing. "We told 'im not to feed 'im the grub."

Mr. Hallowsby whipped his head around and glared at the boy. "And how was I to keep that brute away from it, I ask you?"

"By running faster than a pig," Thomas shot back, disgust in every line of his body.

Maybelle pushed herself to her feet and managed to grab the empty bucket away from the pig. Tossing it to Thomas, she said, "Go fill 'er up again. He's in a better mood now, mebbe I can get 'im going."

Thomas eyed the three of them doubtfully, but he didn't argue. Meanwhile, she leaned down and grabbed hold of the rope around Mr. Periwinkle's neck. She didn't pull, though. Her gaze went to Mr. Hallowsby where he sat in the mud looking stubborn.

"I'm not paying another two shillings."

"What for?"

"The ale."

Oh, of course. Gillian would have charged him for the grub. "No bother. The widow will cover it. She does the inn's laundry."

He eyed her darkly, though in truth she didn't think the expression was meant for her. "I hate the country."

"It would appear the country is none too fond of you either," she said. "Are you hurt?"

He grunted as he pushed to his feet. "Just my pride. And my knife." Then he held up the no longer shiny metal to the sun, and even she could see the handle was broken.

"I'm sorry."

"I've killed men for less," he said darkly as he advanced on Mr. Periwinkle.

She was horrified by the thought. "Truly?"

He whipped his gaze back to her, and a moment later, he stomped over to his two other knives, where they waited sunk into a tree trunk. She thought he wouldn't answer, but in the end, he muttered something that sounded like, "Not really. But I've wanted to."

Well, as to that, there wasn't a man, woman, or child who hadn't thought of murdering Mr. Periwinkle at some time or another. In fact, she was thinking it right now as she started to drag on the rope.

"Come on, you brute. You can't be drunk yet."

She thought Mr. Hallowsby would refuse to help any longer, but once he'd secured his knives he came to her side. Setting his hand on her forearm, he spoke gruffly into her ear.

"I've got it. Your hands have got to be mash by now."

They weren't a lady's hands—that was for sure—but she'd handled worse. "What about your clothes?"

"There's no saving them now, is there?"

No, there wasn't. And maybe not her dress either. "We'll pull together."

"Don't hurt your hands."

She flashed him a smile. This close, she could see the darkness of his beard on his cheek, the rugged cast to his skin, and brown eyes the color of mink. It was unsettling, those eyes. Rich and deep, she felt like she sank into them, and her smile faltered.

So did his.

And they stood there eye to eye, while her breath caught and her belly tightened.

"I got it!" Thomas bellowed from somewhere far away. Except it wasn't far away. It was a few paces behind, and she jolted as she realized she'd been staring.

"'Old it out," she instructed.

"I know, I know," groused the boy. "Move out of the way."

It wasn't easy. It took all three of them to coax, bully, and drag Mr. Periwinkle to his pen. And during the long, agonizing process, Mr. Hallowsby was grim and sour-faced, but he didn't complain. Not even when the blasted pig lifted a leg and pissed on him.

He cursed, of course. And she worried about his

boots, but there was nothing else to do but keep hauling, while the stupid beast was off-balance on only three legs.

Then, finally, they were done, and all she could do was stare at the ruins of her favorite gown and sigh.

"Well, look at you," cried Widow Dwight from where she came out from the laundry area. Her face was slick from boiling water and her eyes red-rimmed from the lye, but she was grinning with her gap-teeth from her big heart. "Mr. Periwinkle, you been out roaming again?"

Maybelle nodded, her hair flopping into her eyes and making them sting. "He was out by the inn."

"But that's not far. You two look like you dragged him over from Yorkshire."

Mr. Hallowsby grunted from where he was leaning hard against the stone part of the pen. "It took us more than an hour. That was far enough."

"Naw," piped in Thomas. "Once my dad and Miss Bluebell dragged him from Newbald. That took four full buckets of me dad's best ale."

"That it did," the widow said with an indulgent smile.

It hadn't, but Maybelle loved how the tales expanded with age, so she didn't say anything.

"Now, 'ow come these others are covered in mud, and you're just regular dirty?" the widow asked Thomas.

"'Cause I'm faster than they are," he answered with a grin. "Bye!" And off he ran before the widow forced the child into her laundry tub for a good scrubbing with that lye soap. Maybelle knew. She'd been a mite slow once upon a time when she was younger.

Meanwhile, she gestured to her dress. "I'm afraid this one's done for. But do you have my other washing?"

"I do. And I'll only charge you half 'cause you brought Mr. Periwinkle back."

With anyone else, she'd dicker and fuss, but everyone hereabouts looked after the widow. And they didn't fuss about prices so long as the widow kept the cost low. With a nod, she fished out her purse and counted out most of her coins, giving the woman a dark eye as she did it.

"Fair counting," the woman answered. "Now go on. Get in that wash water afore the sun starts to bake you in."

Maybelle smiled, knowing exactly where her laundry would be waiting. But then she paused, all too aware of who was still leaning against the pen watching everything with his dark chocolate eyes.

"Mrs. Dwight, may I introduce you to Mr. Hallowsby?" She was very careful to speak slowly and pronounce everything just as she ought. "He's got a broken carriage at the inn and is waiting for it to be fixed and painted."

"Just fixed," he said, as he swept into a deep bow.

"That's a mistake," the widow said as she creaked into her own curtsy. "You'll get a better price with a fresh coat."

"Not with what they're charging me," he answered with a rueful smile. "I was going to do it myself, but the cost for the paint was more than anyone would pay."

The widow chortled, then gestured to Maybelle. "Let Miss Bluebell do the dickering. She'll sort it out right and tight."

"And charge me for the privilege?"

"Nothing more than I'm due," Maybelle put in, feeling the need to defend herself.

"Well, Miss Bluebell, what's reasonable in the country and reasonable in London seems to be a little different," he said. Spoken by anyone else, Maybelle might have taken offense. But he stood there covered in mud. The only *not* brown part of him was the white of his smile and the twinkle in his eye. His tone was kind with no hint of censure in it. Just a rueful charm took the sting out of his words.

Though the widow's comment hurt a bit. "I can see that you're well acquainted with Miss Bluebell's ways, then. Come on, sir. I've got some extra clothes if you like. Will trade you free o' charge for what you got on, mud 'n' all. But I ain't got a coat—"

"It's done for anyway," he said as he shrugged out of it. "Cantankerous beast chewed on the sleeve."

"It must have tasted of the ale. Mr. Periwinkle wouldn't touch cloth otherwise."

"It likely did," he said. Then he frowned in her direction. Maybelle had only moved a step or so away before stopping to watch the discussion. But at his frank regard, she flushed scarlet. Thankfully, he couldn't see underneath all the mud. "How much are they going to charge me for the bath?" he asked.

"Oh, don't you fret now, Mr. 'Allowsby," the widow said with a laugh. "There's a creek right down there. See them trees? They're shadowing it so it's cool in summer. You go on and wash there."

"Oh no." Maybelle realized too late. That meant that she had the hot tub with the lye soap. Then she perked up. "It's a mite cold," she said hopefully. "You can have the wash tub 'ere, and I'll—"

"I'll take the cold, thank you," he said, the twinkle

in his eye telling him he knew about washerwomen and their soap.

She grimaced. "Or we could take turns."

"Listen to ye," the widow scolded. "Washing in the stream like a gypsy girl. Off into my tub."

And so she had no choice. It was the proper thing to do, or at least, less improper than bathing in a stream. And yet her feet dragged as she thought about times when she had splashed about outside like a gypsy girl and regretted that she ever wanted to be a lady. But not enough to change her course.

She moved around the house. There were bathing screens set up because Widow Dwight also made money that way. A copper a bath. But no one had been expected today, so it was the washing tub with its boiling water and lye soap for her.

She stripped out of her clothes, grimacing at the mud and the tears. Even the corset was filthy. She had to wait while the water cooled off, so she helped the widow with her work, though she couldn't do much more than fish clothing out of the water and do her best not to get mud on the freshly laundered attire.

"That's a finely made man, that is," the widow said, her gaze sharp on Maybelle's face. "If I were a mite younger, I might set my cap at 'im."

"Oh?" she answered, doing her best to sound casual. She didn't think it worked, but with the widow that didn't matter. The woman knew all the village gossip and didn't share unless it was important.

"I like some hair on a man. Keeps a woman warm in winter."

Maybelle frowned at the widow, not understanding what the woman could possibly mean. Certainly she understood the male form. She'd seen workers strip out of their shirts, so she knew that some had thick pelts of hair, others not as much. But did that mean Mr. Hallowsby was hairy? And why would a woman like that? She'd never thought twice about a man's chest hair, but suddenly, she was anxious to see Mr. Hallowsby. What exactly did his torso look like?

"Water's cool enough," the woman said, a quirk to her lips that might be a smile. "In you go."

Maybelle hissed as she climbed in. It wasn't nearly as cool as she wanted, but she adjusted quickly enough. She wanted to be washed and out as soon as she could possibly manage. She had an idea of sneaking down to view Mr. Hallowsby, and she couldn't do that while being scrubbed here.

So she hurried when she might have lingered just to tease the widow into sharing some gossip. And then she climbed out and pulled on a dress that was too large for her, billowing around her body until she tied a heavy rope around her waist. Looking in the mirror, she couldn't look less like a lady with her wet hair sticking limply to her skin, her dress a dull brown tied together by a rope. But she didn't have to be a lady just yet, right? Not until London. Her heart was sad that Mr. Hallowsby would see her like this.

"Like a girl dressin' up in her mama's clothes," said the widow. "Fresh and clean—"

"And looking like a child?" She inhaled deeply, seeing her full breasts stretch the fabric. Well, at least there she wasn't a little girl.

"Not like a child," the widow chided softly. "Like a fairy girl trying on—"

"Other people's clothes," she sighed softly. "Some day I'm going to have fine things. I'll never use a rope as a belt, I'll have silk slippers for every day of the week, and people will curtsy to me just as if I were a fine lady."

"Oooee," the widow called. "And don't you have fine plans? But nothing comes of dreaming too big except heartache."

She lifted her chin and tried to look every inch an aristocrat, even in borrowed clothing. "I am a lady. You'll see. I'm—"

"That's your mum talking. Lord knows her passing was a sad day for us all, but don't be letting her dreams ruin your living."

This was an old refrain from the widow, and Maybelle was tired of hearing it. "I got my plans."

"I know ye do. Ever since you were a babe, you had plans. But girl, listen to an old woman. Plans is one thing. Pie in the sky is another. And you—"

"Thank you, Widow Dwight, for the bath. I'm going to leave now. Tell Mr. Hallowsby that I'll come by the inn later for another lesson."

"A lesson! In what?"

"In speaking like a lady."

"But you—"

"Bye!"

And then she was off, stomping toward her house as if she meant to go there. She didn't though. She had another destination in mind.

It took a while. The widow watched her for ever so long, but in the end, the old lady turned back to her washing. Good. The moment the widow went behind the tub, Maybelle cut sideways into the trees. She'd been running around this stream all her life, so she knew exactly where and how to cross it. And from there it was easy as pie to sneak through the trees to where Mr. Hallowsby should be bathing.

And there he was, lying on his back in the water, stroking gently with his hands and...

Stark naked.

She swallowed. She knew that she ought to look away, but she couldn't. She'd seen men before, but they'd all been at a distance as they worked in the field. Or sick ones that she brought possets to. He was a healthy male and...

Stand up. Stand up. Stand up.

The words were a refrain in her head as she crouched in the shadows. She couldn't see anything with him floating on his back under the trees. Only that he was there. Only that...

He straightened.

She saw his wet head pop up and then came his broad shoulders. His back was to her as he scanned the bank on the other side. So she got to see white skin, rippling muscles, and...whip scars? They were long, thin, and crisscrossed his back.

He was submerged to the lowest part of his rib cage, so she could see only the expanse of skin and broad back. She knew he was tall, but his height disguised the width of his shoulders and his lean strength.

She swallowed, willing him to stand up all the way. The widow was right. He was a fine figure of a man.

He straightened further, and she watched as his

narrow waist appeared along with the indentations before his bottom.

Next came his bum, small and tight. He was standing full upright then, and the water came to just where his thighs bunched with corded lines. Truly, there was no softness at all in the man, and her mouth went dry watching.

Then he twisted to look over his shoulder...and found her where she crouched beside a bush. She froze, thinking perhaps he couldn't distinguish her from the foliage, but his words showed her how wrong it was.

"Ladies don't hide behind bushes, Bluebell."

True right, they didn't. But she wasn't a lady yet, so she forgave herself. "I came to...I came to see if you needed anything."

"If you're going to lie, then you can leave."

She winced. She didn't want to go. She also didn't like being caught ogling a man.

"Why did you come here, Bluebell? Tell the truth this time."

Did she? Could she? Why not?

"Widow Dwight said you were a fine fig' of a man. I wanted t' see." She got it all out on a rush.

He smiled at her, the expression slow and wicked. "Slow down your words, Bluebell. Ladies speak slowly."

She stared at him, confused by his actions. He was just standing there, his back to her as he talked over his shoulder. Wouldn't most men at least crouch down into the water?

"I wanted to see if she was right," she said excruciatingly slowly.

"And is she?"

He was teasing her, challenging her to admit her interest. She knew it was a game to him, and yet she found herself responding nonetheless. "I 'aven't seen the front o' ye yet."

"Say it correctly."

"I ain't a lady yet."

"But you're practicing. Say it—"

"I haven't seen the front of you, so I can't tell."

"Do you want me to turn around?"

Yes! No! Yes!

"So far you're not any different from the men I've seen afore." Liar, liar!

"It's true, the parts are all the same. But I take issue with the idea that I'm not any different. My hair, for example—does everyone's curl so abominably wild when dry but remain completely flat when wet?"

"Lots."

"Are their shoulders so broad? Their noses so strong?"

He was pointing out all the things she had noticed, though a strong nose was not an asset in her mind. Still, he had a kind of chiseled granite to his features that she found very appealing.

"I didn't look that closely."

"Liar."

"I didn't look closely…at your nose."

He grinned. And then he dropped more deeply into the water. Gone was his tight bum, gone too were the tiny indents just below his waist. But that was as far as he sank. And then he turned around.

She gasped and pressed a hand to her mouth to silence the sound. It was too late, of course, but she tried anyway. Especially as her eyes were devouring the sight of the dark hair on his chest. Not as thick as a pelt, but it was slick with water and drew the eye from the widely spaced nipples, narrowing down to his flat stomach, and into…

The water.

She could not see more.

"Have you seen a naked man before, Bluebell?"

She nodded without willing it. "I helped the witch-woman for nearly a year until Mama found out and stopped me. But I saw ailing men of all sorts."

"Truly? For nearly a year?"

She nodded. "Mum had the cough and was sleeping whene'er she could. Hard to keep track of me then."

"So you took the excuse to play?"

She glared at him. "I worked to pay off the medicines. And I worked to learn 'ow t' make them meself."

"How to make them *myself*," he corrected.

She grimaced. It was damned hard to keep her words on track when other concerns seemed more important. But she repeated the words slowly with the *h*.

"Good. Now I'm going to stand up, Bluebell. I'm going to stand up completely and let you look your full."

She gaped at him. He couldn't truly mean it, except one look at his face told her he did. "But…" She had no other word.

"But what, Bluebell? It's not proper? That is decidedly true. In fact, a properly reared young girl would have run away squealing by now. She wouldn't still be standing bold as brass discussing things with me."

She should run. She definitely should. Even she knew she was courting disaster by talking to him like this. If the vicar found out, she would be branded a whore and worse. But she could not make her feet move. And when she spoke, it was to challenge him even more. As if she had planned her defiance.

"You said 'young girl.' I'm four and twenty. What would a lady of my years do?"

"Well, she'd be already married then and know exactly what to do with me. But she wouldn't be waiting on the opposite bank." He glided forward in the water, stepping into the sunshine where—if the angle were right—she would see so much more. But it wasn't right, and she was looking into his eyes.

He'd know if she looked lower, damn it.

And yet, she still tried to sneak a peek.

"Shall I stand up?"

"No." Not yet.

"Are you sure? Those are lessons I would be more than happy to teach you. No one expects a girl of your years—reared in the country—to be ignorant of these things."

"Yes, they do!" she snapped. The vicar had spoken oftentimes of the sins of relations outside of marriage. And if she'd missed it in church, he had come to talk to her often enough as she aged.

"A lady is expected to be a virgin, Bluebell," he said, his tone laced with humor. And temptation. "There is much that I could teach you that wouldn't change that."

She thought about it. She didn't want to, but she couldn't help wondering what it would be like to finally learn these things. She knew married girls whispered together. She knew that people found something so enjoyable that all the bellowing from the pulpit meant nothing. A little peek wouldn't hurt. A tiny peek…

"I'm standing up now, Bluebell."

But to see, she'd have to give up being a lady. Even she knew that a lady never looked at what he was going to show her. Never saw until she was safely wed.

"No!" she cried. And then she ran.

But not before he'd risen like a god before her. And she'd seen everything.

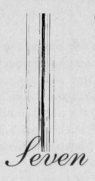

Seven

A VIRGIN. BRAM SHIFTED RESTLESSLY IN HIS BED AND dreamed of debauching a virgin.

It wasn't his usual style. In truth, he'd always equated innocence with stupidity, and that had never appealed. But one voluptuous peasant girl with golden blond hair and sweet blue eyes had him twisted up with lust like never before. So much so that he'd dreamt of her all night long when he wasn't stroking himself while fantasizing about her. It was appalling, and yet by the time dawn colored the sky, he'd come to a reluctant conclusion.

He was going to debauch her.

Not just take her virginity, but spread her thighs and do things to her that he'd only pictured in his most lustful teenage fantasies. He was going to take her every way possible, and when he was done, he'd leave her to the ruin of her life as he returned to London. Because no vicar's son would marry her after he was done with her.

That last part saddened him. He was a man who fought for those who could not fight for themselves.

Certainly he hired himself out to whatever wealthy man could afford him, but when he had the time, he worked unpaid for the unprotected. Except now he wanted to debauch one, even though she had no defense against his practiced knowledge. Damnation, he wanted her with a fever that boiled in his blood.

At this point, he almost prayed Jeremy would return just for the distraction, but the man was stubbornly absent.

So in the morning, he dressed in his new country togs. Widow Dwight had gotten a good deal on his clothes. The fine linen he'd had was worth five times what he was putting on now. But that was just as well since he had decided to paint the carriage.

He had no interest in increasing the price of the vehicle, though that was an added bonus. It was simply an excuse to stay a little longer to allow him to find a way between Miss Bluebell's thighs.

He ate his breakfast and then headed to the stable where the carriage was being repaired. Two days' work that should be nearly done by now. And as he entered, Mr. Grummer was there with a smile on his face.

"Strong as an ox is that axle now, Mr. 'Allowsby. Strong as an ox."

"Thank you. And now I'll—" He cut off his words as Miss Bluebell appeared around the other side. Her hair was tied back this morning with a soft gray ribbon that had seen better days. Her dress too, though it clung to her curves whenever she twisted or moved, tight then soft against her, in flashes that tantalized a man and made him desperate to see her without the ugly shroud. "Miss Bluebell, what brings you here this morning?"

She gestured behind her and, moving around, he saw whitewash and brushes. "I got you these."

"Really?" he drawled. "And how much will it cost me?"

"Nothing," she said. "Except to talk to me as you paint. It'll increase the price of the carriage—"

"Tenfold, so you've said."

She shook her head. "Only five or six."

He grinned. His mother was just like her, able to figure in her head with lightning speed. Although that comparison did little to endear her to him. Still, he had intended to stay, so this just made it extra easy.

"You'll need a smock to paint," he said as he glanced at her dress. Though it would be no crime to ruin it.

She shook her head. "Not me. You'll be doing the work, sir."

"Don't dirty your hands? How very ladylike of you."

She blinked, clearly unsure whether to be pleased or insulted. "I've painted afore. And dug and carpentered, and whatever else needs doing."

"That is definitely not ladylike."

"But I don't do it unless there's a need. And you, sir, are well able to pick up paint and brush."

"That I am," he said, feeling his mood improve the longer they bantered. At this rate, he'd have her in his bed by noon.

Meanwhile, Mr. Grummer clearly had other things to do. He tipped his hat, flashed a wink at Bluebell that set Bram's temper up, and then he ducked away saying something about Mr. Periwinkle's pen.

"Fix it right," he said as the man was nearing the door. "I'm not chasing that demon beast again."

"Can't rightly say you've been in Hull less'n you've chased that pig. Ain't that right, Bluebell?"

"Most definitely."

Bram snorted. "Then I have enjoyed the local custom and am ready to depart."

"After a good coat of paint, yes?" pressed Bluebell.

"Yes," he said, and his eyes went to her face, seeing that it was both eager and conniving at once. "What are you up to, Miss Bluebell?"

She blinked, too innocent. "I certainly 'ave no idea."

He arched a brow, and she thought for a moment.

"I *have* no idea."

"I don't believe you."

She sniffed. "That's as may be, but it's of no importance to me."

He chuckled, then stopped the sound with a snort of surprise. When had he last chuckled? With true good humor and an ease that made the sound so relaxed? Years, if ever. And that shocked him down to his core. Was he truly so humorless? Or so cynical?

He didn't want to answer the question, so he pulled off his coat and walked to a smock on a peg in the corner. It was meant for cleaning out stalls, but it would serve for whitewashing too. Meanwhile, she jumped up to perch on a barrel, her eyes bright as she looked at him.

"Tell me how you came to be a man who protects people for money."

"What?" He jolted, though he wasn't sure why. Of course she would ask about that.

"That's what you do, isn't it? Guard people? 'Cept you don't look or act like any guardsman."

"I'm not the militia," he said, insulted, though he wasn't sure why. He had nothing against the militia. "And say the full word. Except."

"Except," she repeated. "And there ain't—" She grimaced. "There isn't a thing wrong with being in the militia."

Of course there wasn't. It just wasn't a job for the son of a duke, even one born on the wrong side of the blanket. He squatted and looked at his carriage while trying not to think of the luscious woman a few feet away.

"That's a complicated tale," he said.

"I got all day."

"You *have* all day."

She rolled her eyes. "You *have* to start whitewashing. I *have* to *have* something to discuss."

"Very well then. I will give you my sad tale if you tell me yours. Why do you want so much to be a lady?"

"I am a lady," she repeated stiffly. "I just don't sound like one."

"Actually," he said with a soft smile, "that haughty tone was perfect for a lady."

"Really?" she said with a sudden bright smile. "I am a lady."

"Yes," he said sadly. "Just like that." He didn't like the idea of his Miss Bluebell putting on airs, but that's what she wanted, so he didn't argue. "So why do you want to sound so much like a lady?"

She was silent for a long time. Long enough for him to turn to look at her, to read that she was considering telling him the truth—the full truth—but in the end, decided on half. Or a quarter. Or whatever percentage, but it definitely wasn't one hundred percent.

"I have relations in London. I want to go talk to them."

"Relatives don't care what you talk like," he said, then immediately knew he lied. Good relatives didn't care. Most Londoners would definitely turn up their noses at someone who looked and sounded as if they'd lived all their lives in Hull.

"They might care. I'd just as soon present meself—myself—in the best possible way."

"Who are they?"

She buttoned her lip, and when he looked at her, she shook her head. "I only just learned of them from me mum before she died."

There was a wealth of emotion in those words, so he gave her something else to focus on rather than the pain. "Say it correctly."

"I have only just learned of them. My mother told me before she died."

He nodded. "Excellent. What kind of people are they? Soldiers? Merchantmen?"

"I...I'm not sure."

"Do you know where they live?"

She shook her head.

"London is a very big city."

"I'll find them."

He was sure she would, but in the meantime, there was a mystery there. "Who knows about this?" Maybe he could learn the truth from Widow Dwight.

"No one 'ereabouts." Then she grimaced. "No one in Hull."

"But they know in London?"

She shrugged.

"Delicate matter to introduce yourself as a long lost relation."

"'At's why you're helping me."

He arched a brow, and she cursed under her breath. "That's why you are helping me." Then she lifted her chin. "Your tale now. I want to hear it all."

Like she'd shared it all? Not bloody likely. But he would give her enough to chew on. "I was scrawny as a boy, and so I was picked on at school."

She frowned, but she didn't argue. Which was good, because he had no intention of letting her quiz him on his past.

"I learned pretty quick how to fight to defend myself. And then when I was pinched for money, I hit on the idea of getting paid to defend the other boys. The little ones who were like me."

"Was Lord Linsel one you defended?"

He nodded, and a fond smile curved his lips. "I charged him double on account of him being such an ass."

She nodded. "That's how you got into guarding as a boy. But as a man there surely were other ways of making a living. Did you think of anything else?"

He wanted to correct her language, but she had said everything perfect. So he pursed his lips and shrugged. "I tried my hand at other things." Mostly gambling and wenching, but neither paid his bills. "In the end, an acquaintance of mine had trouble outside of school. I helped. For pay."

"Did he deserve to be beaten?"

He arched his brow. "What do you mean?"

"Well, even I could see that you thought Lord

Linsel had done wrong, but you were getting your pay, and no thought beyond."

Not *no thought*. Just not enough thought to talk him out of the coin.

"What about this acquaintance? Did he deserve a beating?"

"*She* did not." And that was all he was going to say on the matter. So he picked up a brush and began to paint. He wasn't well versed in this. In truth, he'd never done it before. But how hard could it be? Grab the brush. Dip it in the paint. Slap the stuff on the carriage. Before long, he had settled into the rhythm and rather enjoyed it.

"You defended a woman, then."

"Yes." He answered before he could shoot her a glare. The subject was closed.

"From someone bigger and stronger than 'er. *Her*."

It wasn't a question so he didn't bother answering.

"That's like an Arthur knight."

"A what?"

"A knight of the Round Table. King Arthur—"

"I know," he interrupted.

She sniffed. "You didn't think I knew. Well, I do. I learned it young. My tutor read it to me in French to teach me the language."

"You know French?" He couldn't be more surprised.

She chewed her lower lip. "Not much. I can't remember it 'cause I don't have anyone to practice with."

"Because you don't."

She nodded and echoed him. "Because." Then she brightened. "Do you speak—"

"Not a lick. Hated anything that wasn't English.

Barely held on to enough Latin to get through school,
and the Greek might as well have been chicken scratch."

She nodded. "That's how I felt. But the French
sounded so pretty the way he spoke it. And the
stories were about saving the innocent and helping
the poor."

"I think you mean Robin Hood."

"No, I don't!" she shot back, obviously insulted.
"I know my Arthur tales. Robin Hood was someone
completely different. And I know 'is tale too. His tale."

He could tell that she did. "How did you get such
an education all the way up here?"

"Hull isn't China. We got tutors here."

"That speak French and teach girls?"

She bit her lip. "Mum insisted I get a lady's education. She said I might need it one day."

"To meet your relations in London?"

She nodded. "I'm a lady, Mr. Hallowsby. I mean to
act it in every way I can."

Her determination was never in question. What he
did wonder about was what exactly she meant to do
with her education. "So you mean to impress your
relations in London. What then? Do you ask them
for money?" No, he realized, nothing so crass as that.
"Perhaps a life there as a shopkeeper or a seamstress?"

"Do the ladies you know keep shops or sew clothing? If I had wanted to do those things, then I would
stay here."

So she did intend to go higher. "It's about the
vicar's son, isn't it?"

She jerked, and he knew he had guessed correctly,
though she tried to hide it.

"You think that London relations will make a difference to him?"

"Not to him," she said stiffly. "His father." She lifted her chin. "Me mum was married right and proper. I mean to prove it."

"Say it again."

She huffed out a breath. "My mum—mother—was married properly. In a church after the banns were read."

"Where?"

"In her home parish."

There was a story there. No woman got married right and proper and then suddenly appeared somewhere else pregnant and alone. No, that was a darker tale that no daughter would want to believe.

"It's the truth," she said, her jaw clenched tight.

"But no one here believes it?"

"Of course they believe it." She said the words, but in her eyes he read doubt. Hurt. She'd been disparaged by the people she'd known all her life. He understood that all too well. "Why not just copy the register in the church? Prove that you're legitimate. Then no tongues will wag."

She snorted. "Tongues wag no matter what. But if my London relations accepted me, well then, that would be a different story, wouldn't it? I'd be a proper lady, no questions."

Except there would be lots of questions given her circumstances. "Seems to me it'd be much easier to get a copy of the parish register."

She leaned forward, dropping her chin on her fist as she thought. "It'd help, wouldn't it, to prove to my relations who I am?"

He nodded. "Of course it would." And if there were no record in the register—as he suspected—then she would know and not be embarrassed when presented to her London folk.

"But that's all the way down in Oxfordshire," she said mournfully.

"Which is a sight closer than London. You could visit there on the way." Or stop and turn back around.

"But 'ow am I t' get there? A lady doesn't take the mail coach."

He didn't answer. And though he pretended to be focused on the paint, his mind was seething with thoughts. This had been her plan all along. To get him to take her to London in a fine carriage just like a real lady. A fine, newly whitewashed carriage.

The idea that she could have planned this from the very start stunned him, but he'd met ladies who could think deviously before. Scores of them. It was how they survived. Still, it burned in his gut that she was one of them. That she manipulated and schemed to get what she wanted.

He was silent a long time, fighting with his murderous thoughts. Just because he had been hurt by one such bitch before—nearly killed, in fact—didn't mean that Bluebell should be damned by the same stroke.

And yet his emotions didn't seem to care. While stroking white on the carriage wood, his insides turned darker and darker. By the time she noticed his silence, he was in such a fury he would frighten his own mother.

"Mr. Hallowsby?"

"Miss Bluebell?"

"Do you 'ave any ideas for me?" Then she frowned. "Do you *have* any ideas?"

"I do," he said, his fury merging evilly with his resolve. It had happened only a few times before, but each time the anger had changed the course of his life.

Just as well. He'd grown tired of his current path anyway.

"What?" she said, her face lifted in innocent query.

He looked at her, seeing her milky white complexion, the sparkling blue of her eyes, and the sweet curve of her lying lips. He saw innocence there in a mask over an evil heart. He saw so many things that had nothing to do with Bluebell but everything to do with his dark thoughts.

And so he slowly set down his brush. The white dripped, wasted into the dirt, but he didn't care. And he stalked slowly toward her.

She straightened up on her perch, her brows drawn together in confusion. "Mr. 'Allowsby?"

"Say the *h*," he corrected automatically.

"Hallowsby." But her voice shook as he towered over her.

"You want me to take you to Oxfordshire and then on to London. You want me to dress up this fine carriage and let you appear before your relations like a fine lady. You've been planning that from the moment you met me."

"Ooo, an' me a simple maid from 'Ull. Wot makes ye think I could muster all that?" She exaggerated her accent such that his back molars ground together in disgust.

"Admit it. That's what you want."

She lifted her chin. "And what if I do? You're free t' say no."

"No."

"There. Fine. Ye've said it. But I can pay—"

He grabbed her chin, pulling it—and her—toward him. Part of him thrilled at finally touching her pristine skin. Part of him watched how her eyes widened and the pupils darkened, her mouth slipping open on a gasp. Was she afraid of him? Yes. Obviously. And he tried to care. He tried to tell himself that he didn't want to punish her for crimes she hadn't committed. But she was a schemer just like the others, and so he damned her all the same.

"I will take you to London," he said, his voice low, his breath hot.

She didn't answer, and he didn't care.

"But there's only one payment I'll take."

"No," she whispered. "I'm a lady."

"Say it all you like, Miss Bluebell, but I know the truth."

She swallowed, trying to pull herself back, but she was still sitting on the barrel, so she had nowhere to run. So she stilled, but her eyes narrowed.

"Wot truth? That I want to go to London? That I want proof o' my father? Or that you're nothing but a man with ruttin—"

He kissed her. He wasn't slow, and he wasn't remotely gentle. And the fact that she was completely untutored in the way of kissing infuriated him even more. She was a lie. She deserved all the pain he could give her. She was...

She was an innocent, and he had to soften. He had

to become gentle with her, and so he did. He didn't want to, contradictory beast that he was. He liked his anger. Stoked it to a hot flame, but not against her.

So he softened. He gentled.

Where before he had simply wrenched her mouth to his, he now petted her chin. And though he had forced his tongue into her, he eased his penetration. He teased her and then pulled back.

"You are a lie," he said to her panting chest.

"You are a brute," she answered, anger vibrating out of her.

"Yes, and worse. I'm a bastard."

"You're not even ashamed."

Oh, he was. He was riddled with shame, but he wouldn't let her see it. She had to know the truth about him before she tried to play her games. "I'll take you wherever you want to go, Miss Bluebell. But *I'll be taking you* as I do it."

He felt the impact of his words on her body. She shuddered, but she also licked her lips. Part of her wanted him, brute though he was.

"I am a lady."

"Ladies spread their legs for me all the time."

"Not me."

"Then I'll not take you anywhere."

He felt her accept the truth of his words. Her body bowed, and her shoulders drooped. But when she spoke, her voice was strong with conviction.

"I don't need you to take me. I've coin eno'. The mail coach goes to Oxfordshire and London."

"You'll be prey to every bloke who sees you."

She finally jerked her chin away from the stroke of

his fingers. "'At's been true since I first started filling out a dress." And then before he could anticipate her move, before it even registered that he was in danger, she lifted her knee.

How she'd maneuvered it so perfectly, he didn't know. But one moment he was hard as a rock, still thinking of ways he could make her willing. The next there was a blinding flash of white-hot pain, and he was crumpled onto the ground.

He couldn't breathe. He couldn't think. He just knew pain. And one word:

Bravo.

Eight

BLOODY BASTARD. LECHEROUS BLACKGUARD. FAT, stupid, spurious, ignoble…

The synonyms went on in Maybelle's mind. An endless litany of invectives using her entire vocabulary, adding nonsense words when she ran out. Most of them weren't even true. He wasn't fat or stupid. But he was lecherous, as all men were. That wasn't a surprise. And yet, his kiss had surprised her. But in the end, he only saw her as a set of legs to spread for his amusement. And she had thought London men were different. She'd thought *he* was different.

Of course she was wrong. She'd known that, but she hadn't really experienced it. Not many travelers came through here. Not that she got to meet at least. And certainly not ones she could talk to or who would be willing to drag Mr. Periwinkle halfway across the county.

She relived kneeing him in the privates. The satisfaction of that moment made her smile, though she felt no joy in it. She didn't like hurting anyone. Her goals had always been manipulation for mutual

benefit. Not damage. Not pain. Not writhing in the
dirt, his lips pulled back in a grimace of agony.

She'd done that to him, and she didn't regret it.
And yet, she did. She regretted that he'd forced her
into that position. That she'd felt the need to protect
herself from his base instincts. After everything, he
was still just a venal man, and she was no closer to
confronting her father than she'd been two days ago
before Mr. Hallowsby had appeared.

Well, that was done with. The man had been a
distraction, an inspiration born of Lady Linsel's obvious hatred of her voice. Maybelle had been overcome
with the fear that her father wouldn't even listen to
her because of her accent.

But that pathway was closed, so she was back to
her original plan. Which meant the mail coach on the
morrow. But first, she had a meeting today. She was
perhaps not in the best frame of mind to meet with the
vicar or his son, but there was no help for it. She was
a practical girl, and this had to be done before she left
for London. She didn't want the vicar to think she'd
up and run off with Mr. Hallowsby.

She laughed loudly at the thought.

Then she sobered as she approached the vicar's
home. Normally, this was the last place she ever
wanted to be, but one day this might be her home,
so she needed to face her predicament square on. She
smoothed out her hair and her dress, then knocked
with quiet authority, only belatedly realizing she'd
forgotten to bring a pie.

Damn it. Charlie liked her pies.

The door was opened by the housekeeper—a

plump, rosy-cheeked woman who nevertheless looked down her nose at everyone, especially Maybelle, even while smiling sweetly.

"Hello, Mrs. Pursley," she said, dropping into a respectful curtsy. "Is the vicar in? I have need of counsel."

"Well, of course you do, Miss Bluebell. I'm sure he'd be happy to advise you."

Maybelle did her best not to react to the condescending tone. "Thank you. And is Charlie—"

"He's around here somewhere, but you won't be needing to see him. It's the vicar who will set you straight."

"Of course." Old biddy. First thing she'd do upon marrying Charlie was see that the witch was sacked.

Maybelle followed meekly inside, her eyes downcast, her demeanor excruciatingly correct. And humble. The last thing Vicar Ott liked was a proud woman. Which meant, in general, he had a distaste for most women in the county. Lord, how did he ever give rise to such a sweet-tempered son?

She was shown into the man's study. He'd been eating, as the crumbs of some sort of bread littered his desktop and the front of his shirt.

He stood when she approached, looking smug as he extended his hand. "Miss Bluebell, how are you faring? It has been my intention to visit you this last week and more. The Lord must have been whispering into my ear, but now, here you are of your own accord. Excellent. Most excellent."

If the Heavenly Father had been whispering, then why hadn't the vicar listened? This would have been so much easier if he'd come to her.

Humble, she repeated to herself. Be humble.

"I've come to speak to you frankly, Vicar Ott."

"Of course, of course. You can tell me anything."

She'd thought of at least a dozen different ways to approach this. Soften the man up with buttered rum cookies, then prove to him that she was educated in the ways of the Bible and the church. And most of all, she would show him an example of her handwriting. She had a clear, fine hand, where his was tight and crabbed. Hard to hold a quill easily in those thick sausage fingers of his. If she made him understand that she could help him with his work, then things would go much easier.

But she had been so angry with Mr. Hallowsby that she hadn't taken the time to prepare. And a lack of preparation meant disaster unless she was quick-witted. Or starkly logical.

"Vicar, it is my understanding that you object to my attachment to Charlie."

"What? What? I...of course, Charlie's mind wanders every which way. It's not for me to say where his attention lies, but I'm sorry to say that he is not attached to you, Miss Bluebell. Not at all."

"Really?" she asked, throwing doubt into her tone. In truth, Charlie was much too distractable to attach to anything but his books. It was what she most liked about the man. He was genial, kind, and prone to vague philosophical statements that made one ponder. There was nothing the least bit objectionable about the man, and best of all, he would have a tidy living in his father's place provided someone helped him manage. And that someone was going to be her.

So she lifted her chin and spoke directly. "What

Charlie thinks is between him and me. Here is what I came to tell you. I am leaving tomorrow for Oxfordshire, where I will get a copy of the register of my parents' marriage. That will finally put to rest any wagging tongues about my legitimacy."

"What? Of course, I never doubted—"

"Of course you did. And often, directly to my mother's face. But I shall prove you wrong. What's more, my father is rather elevated in London society. So not only will you gain an educated, capable daughter-in-law, but influential relations in the peerage."

"The peerage! I cannot credit—"

"It doesn't matter. I shall prove it."

The man heaved a deep breath and patted her hand. "My dear, if you need to leave for a time to…um…" His gaze dropped to her belly. "To grieve your lost mother for a period of months, then I can only—"

"I am as pure as the Virgin Mary, Vicar," she said stiffly. "I am traveling tomorrow to get proof. And then I will not have you stand in my way when I return."

"Well, naturally I would not refuse any good woman where Charlie's heart has attached."

"Excellent. Because we both know that your son will need a good woman. One who can read and write in a fair hand, who will help him with his sermons and the mundane tasks of this living. Assuming, of course, he remembers to send gifts and please Lady Claybrooks in all the ways that august personage likes to be flattered."

"I am not dead yet, my girl. This is *my* living, and I've no need for anyone to—"

"No, sir, you are not, thank God." Part of her worried that God might strike her dead for pretending to be thankful. She did not like this man, and yet she would make a bargain with him for the good life of his son. "And yet imagine how you might benefit from my possets blessed by your own hand and sprinkled with holy water."

He stiffened. "That is paganism."

"No, sir. It is only your blessing I crave. And others might pay well, if the herbs be tended and cured."

He was not a quick thinker, but in time his thoughts took him where she wanted them to go. She saw him glance at his worn vestments and battered furniture. His living was not a generous one, but it was a life that suited him and his son well. Assuming, of course, there was a woman handy who could manage the mundane tasks of life. And potentially visit the sick for him, a task she knew he loathed. And if she sold them a posset or two, then they both could benefit, instead of him constantly slinging accusations of lewd heathenism at her from his pulpit.

"I don't need help." But his words were slow, his brows furrowed in thought. It was only pride talking, but she would bet her garden that greed would win over pride.

"I'm a good Christian woman," she said, just as she and her mother had been saying since the day she was born. "And I mean to marry your son."

She stood up, not even bothering to acknowledge his ponderous frown. He would either help her or hinder her, but that would never change what she accomplished. The end would be the same.

A moment later, she heard his vague, "Go ahead. You may see Charlie."

She didn't answer, but walked out of his office and went in search of his son. She found him easily enough, sitting in the shade of his favorite tree with a book of Plato open on his lap. In this she was no help because it was written in Greek, but she could sit beside him and chat.

"Hello, Charlie," she said, and she realized belatedly that he might have been sleeping.

"Wot? Oh my… 'Ello, Bluebell. Wot you doing 'ereabouts?"

She smiled, knowing that Charlie at least would never criticize her accent. His was thicker than hers. "Were you studying?"

"Hmm? Er, I was cogitatin'," he said with good humor. "But you know I've read this so many times, I can recite it in me sleep."

"Was there a passage that you most struggled with?"

He shook his head, but readjusted his position on the grass to face her directly. "Plato, well, most of the ancient philosophers 'ad a system of question and conversation. Argument wot pushed everyone to better thinking."

"I see," she said, not seeing at all.

"But I've got no one to argue with."

Ah. Yes, his father was the closest thing to an educated man around here, and he was not one to appreciate discourse. The vicar's style was quick judgment followed by vehement damnation. But his son was more of a talk-the-matter-to-death sort.

"You can talk to me. My Greek is terrible, but I would love it if you explained it."

"Truly? It is a tad bit 'ard to follow."

She nodded. "Truly I love the sound of your voice, even if I comprehend only a tenth of what you say." That was a lie. She had a passing understanding of Plato, if not from her own tutor, then from many afternoons sitting just like this and talking with Charlie. The fact that he barely remembered she was the one who'd been wrestling with the Greek philosophers right beside him was both a pinch to her ego and a statement of the man's self-absorption.

Still, she settled in for a pleasant afternoon of intellectual discourse wherein no one would pressure her to kiss or spread her legs or any such base things. Just Greek philosophy and no worries whatsoever about how she spoke or what she said. After all, Charlie didn't really care what anyone said except that it pushed him to think deeper about his studies. And, if she simply didn't say anything, he was perfectly content to wander about his tortured thoughts on his own, even when speaking them aloud.

Simple. Peaceful. Relaxing.

And so damned boring, she struggled to keep awake.

⁂

Maybelle finally escaped Charlie to go home. She'd meant to go straight home and rest, but she'd heard from the vicar that little Sarah Grummer, the carpenter's five-year-old child, was sick with a bad fever. "A bad one," he kept intoning. "Very bad. Very sad to lose a little one."

The child wasn't dead, but she knew the vicar would wait until the girl was deceased and then go offer comfort to the grieving. It was up to her, of course, to offer what aid she could. And that meant her cool drink with the special ingredient. Medicine, yes, but she'd learned early that gathering the moss she needed was horrendous work.

Fortunately, she was so bored with Charlie that she went with alacrity. Only to begin cursing when she got to Mr. Periwinkle's trough. The creature was there, clearly distempered from a sore head.

"Serves you right for drinking two buckets of ale," she groused, then quickly got down into the muck. She'd done this enough times before, but it never made it easier. And if there wasn't enough here, then she'd have to look in worse places.

There. Mold. On the dark side of the trough. Barely enough for one drink, but hopefully, it would be enough added to what she'd made yesterday.

"Soon," she told Mr. Periwinkle, "I'll never have to do this again. Soon, I'll be dressed in fine silks and talking to earls and dukes and everything. Charlie's my 'just in case plan.'" She gagged as she began scraping. The stench was overwhelming. Muck seeped through the cloth she'd laid down, one she'd made specifically for this purpose so she wouldn't have to lie in the—

"Git off me!" she croaked as she kicked at Mr. Periwinkle. The damned beast had come snuffling at her privates. She tucked up her legs, knowing that what she did was shoving her hair deeper against the fabric. Lord, she'd stink for a week if she kept it up.

Mr. Periwinkle snorted, clearly insulted as she set her feet on his haunches and shoved for all she was worth. He moved, thank heavens. Apparently, he'd decided that she wasn't worth the attention.

She went back to her work. A few more moments. She didn't know why it worked. The witch-woman had tried the draught without the mold, and it had no effect. So it was get the thing, or let a child die of fever. She got what she needed then.

"Ewwww!"

Mr. Periwinkle pissed on her. A hard, hot stream, straight at her face. He'd missed, thank God, but she'd still gotten it full on her chest and shoulder.

"Why you..." She cut off her words, her new position showing her dark mold deep in the corner crevice of the trough. She'd have to worm her way there, but it was good mold. And mayhaps, it would keep Sarah alive.

So she ignored the stench and the pig as she squirmed her way there. The dress was ruined anyway. And a half hour later, she was able to rinse everything off in the frigid stream before tromping to her home. At least Widow Dwight had been away. If she'd had to endure a second lye soap bath in as many days, she'd not have any skin left.

She worked quickly when she got home. The fresher the mold, the better the medicine. She crushed it, mixed it with some berries and other sweeteners for taste, and then poured it in a bottle. She made it to the Grummers with barely a few hours of sunlight left.

Betty met her at the door, and her face looked worn. The exchange was done quietly, the payment not enough to cover her ruined dress. But she took what she was offered and didn't quibble. Not when there was a child at stake.

She was home at dusk, thankful it was summer and

the sun set late. "When I'm with my father," she said to her mother's portrait, "this will all seem like a bad dream. And I'll never, ever stink of pig piss again."

She didn't stop to rest. If she did, she might not get up again. So she packed what little she had left, ate the last of the food, then put on her worst gown and went to weed her garden. He found her there on her knees in the dirt. She exhaled hard when she heard his booted step on the road. There were any number of men who might walk by her small home for one reason or another. But it wasn't anyone else. It was Mr. Hallowsby, and he was coming to see her.

And while she kept her rigid back to him, she tried to decide how she felt about that. About him. She could scream, of course, if he meant to do her harm. But when she risked a glance under her arm, she saw his face was set in quiet determination, not anger. And he was calm. On him, calm looked strong and a tad bit regretful.

She shifted further, deciding to face him directly. There was no use pretending she hadn't looked. He'd been staring straight at her when she risked her peek. So she pushed to her feet and pretended her hands weren't sweating and her heart wasn't pounding in her throat.

And she waited, excruciatingly conscious of the dirt on her hands and face, not to mention her gown. She'd neglected a bonnet since it was so late in the day, and her hair was flitting everywhere about her eyes. Plus, the midges that plagued her swarmed nearby, making her swipe at them uselessly.

She was a mess, but she'd be damned if she prettied

up for him. But she wanted to. Oh, damn her, but she wanted to be beautiful for him.

"Soon," she muttered to herself. "In London." Everything would be better.

"Hello, Miss Bluebell," he said in that slow drawl that felt like honey tea on a cold day.

"Hello, Mr. Hallowsby." She might not pretty herself up, but she'd be damned if she spoke one word wrong.

"Quite a garden you have there. It'll be a sight to see come harvest."

She hoped she'd be back here by then. She would hate to see an entire summer's growing gone to waste. But then again, it wouldn't be wasted. Mr. Bray's family would take what was here and be generous in their thanks when she returned.

"You saw that yesterday," she pointed out. "Why're y' here?" Damn it. Too fast, but at least she'd used the *h*.

He opened his mouth—likely to correct her words—then stopped himself. Good. At least he felt as awkward as she did.

She waited a bit longer, her eyebrows arched and her hands clasped in front of her no matter how much the blasted midges were annoying her.

"I came to apologize," he said gruffly. "And to tell you a tale."

Her stomach knotted. She'd heard all the vicar's tales of how men were seduced by women, betrayed by women, plagued by women. No matter what the crime, it was the woman's fault. Which tale would he tell to excuse his behavior?

She found that she didn't care.

She gave him her back, squatting down to return

to her weeding. There wasn't much left to do. She'd already been at it for more than an hour.

And when he said nothing, she finally turned to look at him, a query in his expression.

He shrugged. "Normally, a person looks at me when I talk."

And wasn't that just like a man? Expecting an audience whenever he spoke. "Speak your piece, Mr. Hallowsby."

He sighed. "I'm sorry. I behaved abominably and in ways not befitting a gentleman. I've no excuse. Just my sincerest hope that I haven't hurt you in any way."

"I rather thought you were the one who got hurt," she said, relishing the memory of slamming her knee upward.

Out of the corner of her eye, she saw his expression turn rueful. "That I did. Who taught you that?"

She looked up at him. "Does it matter? I learned it. Because there have been men like you all my life."

He paled a bit at that. He didn't like being lumped in with all the lechers who had abused her trust starting from when she first sprouted breasts.

"I confused you with someone else," he said. "It wasn't right, and it wasn't honorable."

"Because I look like someone else around here?"

He swallowed, then nodded. "Not here, and she wasn't quite as pretty as you, but close. The eyes weren't as blue, the hair not so bright. And her…body wasn't as sweet."

Meaning whomever the woman was, she was flatter in the breasts and hips, whereas Maybelle could only be called generous in the curves. She sighed. "That would be the tale, then?"

He nodded, then walked around, coming to stand before her. She watched where his big booted feet went, worried for her peas, but he was careful. And he held his hat in his hand as he spoke.

"I don't make many mistakes, but when I do, I apologize." His gaze grew a little distant, and he seemed to be speaking to the air above her left shoulder. "My father taught me that. He was an honest man, which is a rarity among the peers. But he was, and he taught me to be the same."

Now, that was something she hadn't realized. His father was a peer and an honest one. Gave her hope that her father's family was equally good. But then again, if they were, she wouldn't have grown up in Hull, would she?

She thought about sending him away. She wanted to have no interest in him at all. But she did, and so she leaned back in the dirt and regarded him.

"Tell me the tale," she ordered. "Then I'll see about accepting your apology."

She could see his slight start of surprise. Women fell all over him when he apologized. It hadn't even occurred to him that she wouldn't forgive him for accosting her.

She would. She already knew that there had been a thousand ways for her to get out of that kiss, most of them before he'd approached. She'd known from the moment he started stomping toward her that he was going to put his hands on her. And she'd stayed right where she was, too mesmerized by his big body to stop it before it started.

But she wasn't going to tell him that. So she lifted her chin and waited.

"After school, I wandered around London for a couple years. I went to parties, ate their food, and…" He swallowed. "And I enjoyed what was offered."

"Drinking and whoring?"

He nodded. "Though I never had the money to pay."

"Sponging off yer friends."

He shrugged. "My mother had a friend. A woman like her who had a protector."

She held up her hand, thinking of the things he was saying. Not just his past, but his mother's past. Slowly, she pushed to her feet, then she looked at him directly.

"I've got tea inside. My own special blend. Even the vicar likes it. Will you come share a drink with me?"

His brows arched in surprise. He hadn't thought she'd be so accommodating. Neither had she, but his words were private, and so should be shared in private. Plus, he knew things about the London elite. Things she wanted to know. It only helped her cause to be nice to him if she wanted to learn what he knew.

"Come inside if you will promise not to act as anything but a perfect gentleman."

He gave her a respectful bow. "I would not break faith with you again." Then he flushed. "At least not so quickly." And when she looked hard at him, he shrugged. "What I want from you hasn't changed."

Well, that was something to set her heart to pounding. "I'm a lady, Mr Hallowsby."

He gave her a mocking bow. "Even so."

Oh. She felt her face heat, her mind twisting in on itself. Never had she felt so intrigued by a man, and having spent the afternoon with Charlie—the man she would likely marry—this felt like a betrayal. And yet she couldn't stop herself from wanting it. Mr. Hallowsby was just so damned exciting, and her life had been everything but that for so long.

She did her best not to react outwardly to his words, though her skin felt hot and her hands would not settle comfortably anywhere. She covered by leading him into her home, pausing long enough to look about her. Her neighbors would gossip, but none were about, so she led him quickly inside.

"You'll not speak of this?"

"Of having tea with a lady?"

"In her home all alone."

"No, Miss Bluebell, I will not."

"Then please," she said as she swept open her door. "Come inside."

Nine

BRAM'S GOAL WHEN COMING TO SEE MISS BLUEBELL was to apologize to her. And to explain his history with charming, manipulative blonds.

Well, that had been his outward goal. Stepping now into her tidy little home—complete with a bed some-where—he realized that his true desire hadn't changed from that moment in the barn. He meant to bed her and somehow expunge the sight of her blond curls and her sweet bow-shaped mouth from his thoughts.

Which meant his apology was only for show. Or be-cause his approach had been angry rather than seductive.

"You know," he said softly as he shut the door, "you may be a lady, but I am not a proper gentleman."

"But you can act it, can't you?" she asked as she led him deeper into the house to the kitchen.

He followed, happy to explore this small place she'd lived all her life. He saw touches of her everywhere, mostly in the plants set out to dry on every surface and rafter. It would seem her kitchen was more of a stillroom.

"You need a shed for this," he said, gesturing to some lavender that sweetened the air.

"I use Mr. Bray's shed for much of my work. He lets me have a corner of it in return for helping his wife. She's overworked with all the children. I bring the lavender here because I like the smell." Then, after stripping off her smock, she knelt to start the cooking fire.

He moved to her side because he wanted to be near her. So when she looked up in curiosity, he shrugged. "Let me make the fire. You get the water."

She nodded, then set about the small domestic chore. She worked efficiently, her skirt swishing about her ankles, and her hair curling sweetly about her temples. There was little enough light from the window, but once the fire was burning, he helped her light candles before relaxing to watch her move. Not work, just move. He hadn't realized until now how her entire body was a symphony of grace. The easy length of her fingers, the upward curve of her smile, and the seductive shift of her hips and torso as she went about her tasks.

He enjoyed himself immensely, his imagination slowly stripping away her clothing until she worked completely naked. Flushed, pert, and strong. She was a woman who had solidity, and in bed she would be an athletic partner, so unlike the frail creatures of the *ton*.

Her words interrupted his reverie. Not her voice. That was all sweet music. But her words were inconsistent with his fantasy, and it took him a moment to recover.

"What?"

"Yer mother had a protector?"

He nodded. "Still does." He watched as she absorbed that. Did she understand what he meant? His mother was a courtesan, and he, a by-blow. Did she comprehend?

"But you went to school with Lord Linsel and others. Sons of the peerage."

He nodded. "It is not uncommon. My father recognized me as his. Unapologetically."

"But you are not legitimate?"

"No." Would she treat him differently? She meant to marry a vicar's son. Would she turn him out of her house as a good Christian woman should?

She sighed. "It is a difficult way to grow. Not truly a son, not really a man." She looked in the direction of the village. "I feel like I spent my life proving I was just as good as them."

"Better."

"Wot?" She grimaced. "What?"

"You have been proving yourself better than they. Smarter, more capable, sweeter. Better." He leaned forward. "You seem an important part of this village. Did they never truly accept you?"

She didn't look at him. She was busy pulling out tea leaves, a combination from three jars in some mysterious recipe.

"I am loved by my neighbors, sought after by most who have ailments. I know all the village tales and am centered in some of them." She sighed. "But I aim for the vicar's son and the living he will have—we hope."

"So there has been a shadow."

"O' course," she snapped, her hands slapping onto the hardwood table. "Always in whispers about me mum. Always remembering I ran with the gypsies and worked with the witch-woman when Mum got sick. Was I to refuse learning when it paid for Mum's medicines?"

"Of course not."

She nodded, her eyes bright. "No. O' course not. But tell that to the pious ones."

"They won't hear it."

"They will when I meet my relations in London."

He very much doubted it. Small minds would remain small. They practically reveled in it. And in the silence, the kettle began to sing.

She pulled herself together at the sound. Her eyes might still be bright from years of suppressed fury, but her hands were steady as she poured the tea.

"Cream? Sugar?"

"None," he answered. He'd learned to like it dark and strong, and he'd rarely had money for the extra sweetness.

"Good," she said with a rueful smile. "'Cause I got no milk right now. It'd just spoil."

"Because you're leaving tomorrow?" It was a guess, but the tidiness in her house spoke of closing down for a trip.

"On the mail coach." She passed him tea in a plain cup and saucer. It was simple, but it was a good sight better than what most of the locals likely used. "And you were going to tell me of the woman. The blond like me."

Had Cara ever been like her? He couldn't imagine that woman drying lavender in her kitchen or helping a neighbor with her children. Certainly there had never been cause to drag a pig halfway across a county.

"She looked like you," he said. "And I was looking for a woman, I suppose." Then he smiled and gestured to the seat at the table. "Sit down. We cannot share tea with you fussing with the leaves."

She'd put away the jars but was now searching for

something in the cupboard. "I was looking for some biscuits and jam, but…"

"Gone?"

She pulled down a jar of berry preserves and held it to the candlelight. "Mum's favorite."

"How long ago did she pass?"

"Spring. Almost a month now."

So recent? No wonder she was still reeling. He stood up and guided her to a seat beside him. "Tell me about her."

She shook her head. "What was your blond's name?"

He winced. "Cara."

"And she was faithless?"

"She was a good deal worse than that, though I suppose that was bad enough. I nearly died because of her, and at the time I was too stupid to see her as the culprit."

She smiled. "Now, there's a tale worth hearing over Mum's jam. I'll just get us some plates."

He stopped her, then grabbed the items himself. There were only a couple cupboards, so it was quick work to find what they needed. Then a moment later he sat down beside her and took a sip of her strong tea.

"I like it," he said in surprise. Most poor households fixed it weak to conserve on the leaves, but it was not only strong, she'd done something to give it an orange tang as well.

She smiled in thanks, but didn't speak. Her eyes told him that she waited on his tale. He nodded, using the delay of drinking his tea to plan out the steps of her seduction. Because this tale would be exactly that.

"You know that I had earned money in school by

hiring to protect the younger boys. School can be brutal on the little ones, the weak ones, and the…"

"And the illegitimate ones?"

He nodded. "I grew early into my height. That helped a lot. By the time I was done at school, I'd gained a reputation for being a protector of sorts."

"And this Cara, she needed a protector?"

"Yes." And a keeper. "She came to me with bruises on her face and red-rimmed eyes. She made sure that night that I felt…" He cut off his words. "Are you not hot in that apron? There's a breeze in here, but you were working in the garden. Surely."

"She made you feel…?"

"Take off the apron, Miss Bluebell. Get comfortable. It is a long tale."

She looked at him for a long moment, then she stood and untied the cheap muslin rag. It peeled away from her body in such a way as to make him think of a ribbon on a package, discarded in favor of the much more intriguing gift underneath. She did not discard her apron, but set it neatly on a peg. And he got to watch the way her body stretched for the peg and turned—

"Miss Bluebell!" he said in pretend horror. "Are you not wearing a corset?"

She flushed and bit her lip. "I wore one in town this morning."

"But now?"

She shrugged. "I was working in the garden, and it was hot." Then she looked down. "I apologize if I offend."

He laughed in true delight, then when she looked up, startled, he gestured her back to her seat. "Shall

I tell you a secret? Men like knowing the state of a woman's underthings. Most especially if they are not wearing any."

She stared at him a moment, and her lips curled in a smile, though she hid it behind her teacup. "I think that was not a gentlemanly thing to say."

"On the contrary, ladies adore learning men's secrets."

"And you were in the middle of a tale?"

She spread some berry jam on a hard biscuit. He watched the length of her fingers and imagined where she might hold him. It was a crass thought, and he was somewhat ashamed of it, but it was there tall and proud in his imagination.

"Mr. Hallowsby? She came to you with bruises on her face and red-rimmed eyes."

"And that night I had been lonely. My friends were on holiday, you see. Not in London, as it was nearing Christmas. And my mother had a new gentleman to entertain, so I sat alone and hungry in my tiny room and thought dark, angry thoughts."

She frowned. "How dark? How angry?"

"My father had a family. A daughter and two sons. He had plenty of coal for heat and gifts under a tree at the family seat. And me? I was nothing to him."

"Nothing?" she pressed. "He educated you, he acknowledged you—"

"Yes, yes, but as a by-blow. What is that but to show me what I could not have? Let me see in my friends a life that is forever denied to me?"

She looked away, and he regretted the bitterness that still infused his words. Was he truly still angry? At a man who had been dead these last two years?

He leaned back in his chair and wiped his brow. "Do you know that my favorite thing to do at home is to take off my boots? I wander barefoot as if I were again in leading strings. Do you not enjoy that?"

Her gaze came back to his. "Barefoot?"

"On a hot summer day? Surely you have—"

"I spent most of my childhood stripping out of shoes and stockings."

He grinned, then nodded at her feet. "So take them off. Stretch your toes out of those boots. Imagine how it would feel—"

"I couldn't!" she said, shocked.

He waggled his eyebrows at her. "I promised to be a gentleman, remember? But that does not mean you have to be a lady."

"I am—"

"A lady, yes, yes. You are. But you can take off your shoes. Go into another room to do it if you like. If you are afraid of my catching sight of your pretty toes. But you are at home. Why not be at ease?"

She frowned. "Are you trying to avoid telling me your tale?"

"Not at all." Then when she looked at him skeptically, he pressed a hand to his heart. "Upon my honor, I swear, I shall tell you the whole tale." He hadn't meant to tell her the *full* tale, but now that he'd said it, he resolved to do it. "But go on. I'll be content here as you take them off. I swear I won't tell a soul."

She resisted. She had been reared too much as a lady even in this tiny little village for her to do such a scandalous thing. But he kept his expression bored as he sipped his tea, pretending that he didn't care one way or another.

He didn't think she'd do it, but the breezeless summer heat aided him, even at dusk. "It would be nice," she said. Then when he didn't comment, she flashed him a guilty smile. "I'll be just a moment."

She was gone in a flash, around the corner into where the bedroom must be. He heard the creak of the floorboards and imagined so much more.

With her gone, he could adjust his clothing. Nothing but her sweet honeypot would ease his erection, but at least he could hide it better. And when she returned, he was mopping his brow with exaggerated movements.

"Mr. Hallowsby, I had not thought how uncomfortable you must be in here. Did you wish to go outside? There might be a breeze—"

"I will stay here. But would you mind terribly if I took off my coat?" Thank God he had no waistcoat today. He hadn't wanted to risk it on another encounter with an irritated country animal.

"Please, sir. But only if you continue your tale."

"Of course," he said as he stripped to his shirtsleeves. "Much better. Thank you." Then she settled in her seat, and he tried to see if her toes appeared. In this he was disappointed. Every part of her lower body remained hidden beneath the skirt, but he could be patient.

"Where was I?"

"Alone on Christmas and bitter angry."

"It wasn't quite Christmas, but close. Then came the knock at my door."

"Cara with her bruised face and tears."

He nodded, remembering that night. He'd thought

her a beautiful porcelain doll horribly abused. "I'd spoken with her before, but I hadn't expected her to appear. She was one of my mother's associates."

"Another courtesan?"

"A talented one. But she'd chosen the wrong protector, and he'd beaten her because she was pregnant."

"My God," she whispered, her hand pressed to her mouth.

"I don't think it was true," he said gently.

"But she'd been beaten."

He nodded. "She cried in my arms. She whispered that she'd heard stories of who I was. She called me such heroic names." He felt his lips twist in a mockery of a smile. "She had read the tales of King Arthur too. Or at least knew I had."

"Did she call you Gawain and ask you to avenge her?"

He shook his head. "Lancelot. She cast herself as Guinevere, tied to another, when her heart belonged to me."

She frowned. "You knew her well?"

"Not at all," he said, "though she had a way that made even an hour in her company feel like we had been the closest of lovers since childhood."

She leaned forward, her brows drawn tight. "I cannot believe you that romantic in nature as to believe such a thing."

"I wasn't. I didn't think I was. But…" How to explain? "She said everything I wanted to believe about myself. That I was righteous when I'd suffered a grievous wrong by being born a bastard."

"Were you a fanciful man?"

Why did she not understand? "It was Cara. The

way she spoke to me, the way she clung to me, the way…" He cut off his words. The way she had stroked his cock and begged him to use it. To satisfy her yearning, just that once. Then again and again…

He cut off those thoughts, not wanting to bring that dirtiness into this place.

"Do you know," he said softly, "that in the Bible there is a tradition of washing feet? When one enters a household, the lady washes the guest's feet—"

"With her hair. She washed Jesus's feet and dried it with her hair." She tilted her head as she studied him. "Are you asking me to wash your—"

"I never thought that, Miss Bluebell. But have you ever had it done for you? Has anyone ever bathed your feet?"

She blinked at him, obviously bemused by the question. "Is this something Cara did for you?"

He shuddered in true revulsion. Though why that act would horrify him, he hadn't the foggiest idea. "My mother used to do it for her gentlemen. She said it took away the dirt and left everything clean for both her and the man." He shrugged. "She found it soothing, she said."

Miss Bluebell just looked at him, clearly not understanding.

"Let me show you," he said.

"Wot?"

He laughed at her shocked face. "Have you never put your bare feet in the stream and let it wash your cares away?"

"Of course, but—"

"Let me please, Miss Bluebell. It eases me as well."

He smiled at her, making sure he looked as innocuous as possible. "My mother taught me, and I assure you, it's a wonder for both man and woman."

"Washing feet?"

"Yes." It wasn't a lie. There was sacredness to the act. "And it's in the Bible, so you know it is holy."

"I doubt the vicar would think that."

"He would if he had a beautiful woman washing his feet."

"But I'm not—"

"Trust me."

She shook her head, but he didn't listen. He had seen the washing basin, and they had not used all the water in the kettle. So he added water to boil and pulled out the basin.

"Mr. Hallowsby, I cannot think this is proper," she said in her stiffest accent.

"It is in the Bible, Miss Bluebell. And I swear no one will know."

"No one would believe it," she said. "You, a London gentleman, washing my feet? It cannot be."

"There you are," he said, all smiles. "Come, come, where is the bold woman who dragged a pig across the county? Surely you are not so timid as to be afraid of a little soap and water."

It wasn't soap and water that she feared. The look on her face revealed a daring she knew she ought not indulge. But that was the way with virgins. Everything was a temptation because most everything was denied to them. So it was a constant game of should I or shouldn't I? He just had to make sure the most dangerous indulgences appeared the most innocent.

She leaned back in her chair and regarded him. "Are you avoiding the rest of the story?"

He looked away. "Mayhaps. A little."

"Tell me how she betrayed you."

"Miss Bluebell, how many ways can you betray a man?"

She thought about that, her even white teeth chewing on her lower lip. "She bedded other men. Not just her protector, but other men as well."

He nodded. "But I expected that. She was a courtesan under someone else's protection. I could not afford her. Exclusivity with a courtesan is expensive indeed."

It took her a moment to understand, and she colored a dusky rose as the simple businesslike nature of the rutting became clear. He was impressed. She caught on faster than most virgins would.

"But you loved her. And she went off with her violent protector."

Had he loved Cara? The kettle began to sing, and he lifted it off to pour water into the basin. There was enough cooler water in the barrel that he didn't need to run to a stream, thank God. And soon he had the basin filled at the most perfect temperature.

"Where is the soap?" he asked.

She stood and grabbed a cake from a cabinet. "It is lavender. I made it just a few weeks ago."

He brought it to his nose and inhaled deeply, but he kept his eyes on her. "Lovely," he said, making sure his gaze told her he was thinking of her.

She laughed, the sound high and tight, as if to tell him that she knew he was playing a game, but she liked it nonetheless. Then, lest he think she was completely cowed, she pressed him with the question. "Did you love her?"

"Will you let me bathe your feet?"

She hesitated, and he waited. Two heartbeats. Four. Five.

"I will if you answer all my questions."

"All!" he said in mock horror.

"Every one. As it pertains to this story of yours."

He dipped his chin. "Very well." Then he settled on the floor by her skirt. He pulled the basin forward and rolled up his shirtsleeves. She was looking at his forearms—most likely at the scars that decorated his arms—and while she was distracted, he reached forward for her—

And stopped. Her hands blocked him, holding him back until he looked up into her gaze. "I know this is indecent, my lord. I am not a fool."

"I never thought you were."

"You shall wash my feet and no more."

"Of course," he lied. There would be much more. After all, according to a ship's captain he once knew, the Chinese had a whole system of medicine done at just the feet. And though he could make no sense of the diagram he'd been given, he did understand how to make a woman moan by just touching the bottoms of her feet. "I swore to act as a gentleman."

"And then warned me that you would not."

True enough. So he looked up at her and smiled. It was his most charming look, one perfected as a boy. It held mischief and daring, but never failed to make the women laugh.

Except...she didn't. To his surprise, she let go of his

left hand to touch his face, stroking a lock of hair from his brow. "Are you always charming when you hurt?"

He blinked. "Charm is used to get one's way."

"And to hide wounds."

He shook his head, reluctantly dislodging her fingers. "To prevent them."

"Then tell me if you loved this Cara."

He swallowed. "I was young, and she was a skilled courtesan who went to extra effort to enlist my sympathies. Of course I fell in love."

"And she did not love you back, though she pretended to."

He frowned. Had he really been so naive as to expect love from Cara? He supposed loyalty at least. Even young as he'd been, he knew she was not a creature prone to love.

"She healed from the worst of her injuries in my bed. She cried as she touched me, and her kisses tasted of salt."

"Could she cry on demand?"

He laughed, though the sound wasn't even remotely light. "Most assuredly." And on those words, he escaped her lax fingers and began to lift up her skirt.

There were her feet, white and slightly clenched. She was sitting perched almost on the back of her feet with her toes pressed into the floor. As if every part of her, except her feet, were straining toward him.

He raised her skirt higher, revealing the sturdy line of her shins and the fleshy curve of her calves. Higher still, and at such an angle that he could peek...

Her thighs were pressed together, tight and afraid. And when he set her skirt just over her knees, he rested his hand on her lap to still the vibrating tension he felt there. "I am just washing your feet. It is in the—"

"In the Bible, yes, I know." She set her hands over her skirt, readjusting it so that her knees were covered, but only barely. But not before he'd seen an old scar from a deep cut. "How did she betray you?"

"She told me all about the man who had beaten her. She told me his habits and his weaknesses. She did everything but say the words aloud."

"What words?"

"Please avenge me. Please hurt this man for hurting me."

"Oh. And did you?"

He nodded, unwilling to dwell on how stupid he'd been. Always before, his protection had extended to a world he'd known, people at his school, children who had a harder time thinking of devious plots.

So he focused on lifting up her foot, gently straightening out the toes, and when she fidgeted because it apparently tickled, he made his touch stronger. Firmer. And as he set her foot into the water, she sighed in delight.

"Oh, that feels good."

He grinned and went about taking her other foot and setting it in the water. And as he knew would happen, the shift of her weight off her feet forced her to lean back in her chair. It only took a couple swishes of the washcloth before her knees relaxed too. She still held the skirt firmly in place, but there was plenty of time.

"I waited for him outside of his club. I didn't know the man. He was an older gentleman, but I'd seen the furrow in Cara's lip from his signet ring." He frowned. Knowing now what the traitorous bitch had done, perhaps that part wasn't true either.

"Were you furious?"

"I meant to speak with him. I had some innate respect for the older generation, and this man was double my age."

"Forties, then. Some might say the prime of his life."

"He was a strong man, that's for sure. And when I said I was a friend to Cara, he sneered at me."

"Was that when you grew too angry to think?"

He looked at her in surprise. "I am always controlled."

She shook her head. "A man who is always controlled has lost that control at some point. Was this the time?"

He nodded slowly, realizing now how correct she was. Certainly, he had lost his temper before, but never in such a violent fury. Never like he had then on a stranger that Cara had painted the blackest villain possible.

"Yes," he said, his voice a bare whisper. "But only after he called her vile names." Then he released a choked laugh. "I have called her much worse since then."

"But you avenged her. She'd been beaten by this man. She may be a whore, but she didn't deserve—"

"She lied. She was blackmailing him. Everything she'd told me from beginning to end was a lie."

"Oh."

"I was too stupid—too besotted—to investigate."

"I'll wager you never made that mistake again."

He looked up sharply, seeing the sympathy in her eyes, but also a kind of worldly humor. She was a virgin, for God's sake, an innocent in the ways of the world. And yet in this, she seemed to see deeper than he did. Clearer.

"I—" he began, but he had no words.

"You were a besotted young man and you got it wrong."

"How do you know that?"

She bit her lip. "I told you that I worked for a time with the witch-woman. She taught me all manner of possets, yes. But mostly, she showed me how to talk to the hurt and grieving. And one of the things she said was that the young are always stupid. That is how they become wise as they age."

He nodded, trying to think of the whole mess as simply a mishap of the young. No more significant than a tumble or a schoolboy fight.

It didn't work. He'd been a man grown, though still stupid. And whereas the wealthy and the protected could make idiotic mistakes, he was neither. But rather than say that, he applied himself to her feet. He had been stroking them in the water, cleaning off the summer dust. Now he lifted up a foot and rubbed it with the soap. And when he was done, he began to knead her foot.

She was clearly a woman who walked. Her callouses were thick, as was the strength in the tendons and muscles. That made it all the easier for him to use his full strength as he rubbed into the spaces between her bones, the hollows of arch and ankle.

He heard her breath catch as he dug his thumb into the tightest places. And he heard her sigh in delight as the knots began to release.

"Don't stop talking," she said, her words breathless.

"There isn't much more to tell. I beat the man to avenge something that wasn't true. I walked away and proudly told her what I had done and received my reward."

The thought of that night of debauchery made him nauseous. He'd spent his last coin to buy them a feast of wine and meat. She'd eaten those sure enough, but what she'd adored were the sweets he'd brought for dessert. And he had feasted on her while she licked the cream off her fingers.

"I didn't realize my mistake for three nights. And in that time, Cara had already become demanding. She told me of an earl who had hurt her more than once. And another lord who had insulted her. She was thirsty for revenge, and I was still enamored of being her knight avenger."

"Did you do it? Did you hurt them in her name?"

Bluebell's voice was still strong, though hushed. Which meant she was not seduced yet. So he applied himself to her other foot, bringing it forward into his lap, though he avoided the thickest, most insistent part of him.

"I would have, though not the earl. He was nearly eighty years old."

"Definitely too old." She might have said more, but at that moment, he pressed into the arch of her foot. Hard and sharp, as his mother had taught him, and he felt the tremor go through her body before she moaned in relief.

"I never got the chance. I was coming home one evening when the son of the first man I'd beaten found me. Him and four of his friends."

"Oh no."

"Worse, I knew him. He'd been a fair man in school, though a few years older. He'd once helped me defend a boy, and so I'd counted him a friend. But he was a younger son, so I hadn't realized the connection until too late."

"He hurt you?"

"Worse. He told me the truth. He told me that Cara was blackmailing his father. And that the blackmail wasn't even true."

She snorted. "All blackmail is true. That's the point, isn't it?"

He shrugged. "There is truth, and then there is scheme. She claimed James's father had buggered a boy so hard the child bled to death. There was no evidence but her whispers. And as the man was in the House of Lords, the scandal could have ruined him."

She gasped, and too late he realized he was speaking to a woman. Of course he had known, but somehow he'd relaxed so much as to stop guarding his tongue.

"I'm sorry," he said. "I should not—"

"I know what it means."

He blinked, startled. "But... How?"

"I visited the ill with the witch-woman and learned more than was proper. We have perversions in the country as well. Children who are not cherished, women who are savaged."

Of course they did. "I am sorry you know these things."

"Be sorry for the boy, whomever hurt him."

He nodded. He was. He was more sorry that he had beaten the man without knowing if any part of it was true.

"James's father refused to pay and may indeed have hit Cara for suggesting such a thing." He swallowed, then set to tugging on each of her sweet toes. "Cara sent me to teach him that there were consequences to not paying."

"And his son came to teach you that there were consequences for listening to Cara."

He nodded. "They whipped me." These three simple words in no way conveyed the depth of the pain he'd received. He'd nearly died from the ribbons they'd made of his back. He had wanted to die when he realized everything James had said was true. Cara had lied to him. "It was a message to her, and she…"

His voice cracked, and he felt as if he stood apart from himself, wondering how this last part was so painful. Compared to her lies and the things she stole from his flat—this was next to nothing. And yet, it burned still.

He felt Miss Bluebell's fingers on his face. The caress across his jaw and the brush of her thumb across wetness on his face. A splash from the basin, of course, but she stroked it away as if he had cried.

"What? Tell me it all."

So he looked into the clarity of her blue eyes and poured out the last of it. "I had broken ribs, you understand. And I was bleeding from the whip. I stumbled home, barely making it there before collapsing."

"Was she there?"

He nodded. "I hadn't expected her to be a nursemaid, but…" He had to take a breath. He had to focus on the darkness of her pupils surrounded by a blue more vibrant than the sky. He had to look at that before he said the last. "She left me."

She blinked, and then her eyes widened. "Just like that? She left?"

"I managed to tell her what James had said. I asked if it were true."

"And?"

"She sniffed and threw a tantrum."

"Wot?"

It was that break in her language that drew the smile from him. It made him feel as if he were speaking directly to her soul and not the facade of a lady. Somehow that made it easier to tell.

"She said that I had insulted her and stomped off. I only found out later that she'd robbed me as well."

"The blighter!"

His smile widened. He loved her accent, he realized. Every missed *h*, every rough cant. He loved it, and in thanks, he rubbed deeper into the hard places of her foot.

"She took a watch that my father had given me. And a silver candelabra my mother had given me one year."

"I hope you got them back. After you mended."

This time he grinned. "Oh yes. I got them back."

"And wot of Cara? Did you beat 'er?" She sounded positively bloodthirsty, which made him laugh. But he shook his head.

"No. By the time I discovered the full truth, it was too late for Cara. She'd tried to blackmail half the *ton*, and as one, they had banded together to oust her from their ranks. She wasn't allowed in any of the places courtesans go to meet protectors. She couldn't even buy goods from the reputable merchants. It had already begun when she'd come to me. I was her last resort."

"So she was the maker of 'er own end."

He nodded. That was certainly true. "By the time I found her again, there was little left of the woman who'd used me so cavalierly. I simply took back what was mine and left her."

"But is she still there? In London, preying on other young men?"

"No," he said, his voice softening in memory. Not in horror or even revenge. What came at the end was ugly and hard, but no more nor less than what happened to many of the women in his mother's profession. "She became a simple tart and from there a gin sot. She died later of the pox."

"I don't know whether to be grateful or sad," she murmured, echoing his thoughts.

"Do not think of it at all anymore," he said—more to himself than her.

"But you thought me like her," she said, outrage in her tone.

He looked up, seeing the crown of her blond hair, the purity of her skin, and the honesty in her expression. "I cannot explain myself," he said truthfully. "You two are nothing alike."

Except that he wanted her as fervently as the young man he'd once been had wanted Cara.

"I would never do that to anyone. I couldn't even imagine it."

He arched his brows. "Oh, surely you could. Surely you have in your darkest moments thought of blackmail."

"No—"

"You are privy to all the county's gossip. I'll bet the witch-woman knew—"

"She was a good soul!"

"Of course she was. It is not one's thoughts that determine good and evil. It is one's actions." He let her think on that for a moment, and when she was chewing her lip and nodding as if in agreement, he maneuvered her legs so that he had better access. Then he leaned forward.

"Shall I tell you a secret?"

She nodded, her eyes lighting with interest.

"I have thought of doing evil things too. Of the money I could make in blackmail."

"But you didn't do it."

"I did not."

"Why not?"

Because he remembered Cara. Because he saw where she had been leading him, and he'd sworn never to be duped again. But mostly, because it was easier to make an honest living than it was a false one. Blackmail only led to complications. It was an illusion of easy wealth, paid for daily in watchfulness and fear.

"Because it was easiest to simply wait for Dicky to betray me."

She frowned. "That's a 'orrible time. Waiting for yer friend to betray you."

He shrugged. "It pays well. And I already knew that Dicky wasn't my friend."

She shook her head. "Still horrible." She made a point of saying her *h*, and he smiled.

"It's important to know who your friends are," he corrected.

And while she was nodding, her expression relaxed and open, he set about getting his reward.

Ten

MAYBELLE KNEW HE WAS ABOUT TO TAKE LIBERTIES. She could feel it in the caress of his hands on her legs. In the way he smiled so sweetly. And, most especially, in the way he leaned into her body, moving himself closer in the guise of adjusting her foot in his lap.

It was a ruse—and an obvious one—but for the first time in her life she had trouble resisting it. Certainly there had been lots of men who had tried to take advantage. A few she had allowed. But this man with his tale of pain and betrayal, this man with his honest eyes and lying hands—this man was a contradiction who tempted her.

She wanted him to touch her. She wanted him to spread her legs and teach her what she'd missed all these years. But even more than that, she wanted to know how this man was with his lovers. After all, she'd seen him protect Dicky, even though Lord Linsel was about to betray him. She'd seen him angry enough to force a kiss from her, then soften almost immediately. And then he'd come to apologize. He was a complicated man, and she was fascinated to see all the different aspects of his personality.

But mostly, she wanted to feel him touch her. Large hands rough with callouses slowly spread her thighs. She resisted, of course, but not hard enough to stop him. And not forcefully enough to rouse her from the sensuous spell he'd cast over her.

She sighed and put her hands over his, where he pressed his thumbs deep into the topside of her knee. It felt wonderful, but she stilled him nonetheless.

"You know I cannot do this."

"I know you must keep your virginity. There is much that can be done without losing that."

She brought one of his hands to her lips, forcing herself to rouse and lean forward as she cupped his strong fingers in her palm. "You will think me a whore. Or worse, a fool."

He smiled. "I know you are neither."

"Mr. Hallowsby—"

"Call me Bram. I want to hear my name on your lips."

"Bram, you cannot have me. Not without a wedding ring."

He arched his brows, his expression boyish. "You would marry me?"

That thought pulled her straighter in her chair. She knew he was not truly offering, but the idea took root immediately. Without her willing it, reasons for and against listed themselves in her mind. He was more interesting than Charlie, that was for sure. Smarter in a worldly way, most definitely. And in the few days that she'd known him, he'd never been dull.

But he was not respectable. He was a bastard, and

the more time she spent with him, the more her own worth came into question. Not in her mind, but in everyone else's. After a lifetime of fighting for respectability, she could not give it up so easily.

"No, I wouldn't," she said gently. "You are a bastard, and I want to be respectable."

He nodded as if he had expected as much, but there was vulnerability in his eyes. As if he had hoped she could overlook such a flaw. Which was ridiculous. He wasn't truly offering, so she hadn't truly rejected him.

"Do you know…" Bram said, as he pressed his lips to the inside of her calf, "I spent years trying to be respectable? I said the right things, acted the right ways. When all my friends—legitimate children of proper parents—were cheating at cards or seducing women, I remained pure."

She heard the echo of his words in her life. She too had spent so much time acting correctly when all those she knew cheated in one way or another. "It's terribly hard."

"And lonely." He looked into her eyes. "And pointless. Those who will look ill upon you will continue to do so. No amount of correct behavior will change that."

She knew that to be true. The vicar, for certain, would not think well of her until she proved her connection to her father.

She touched his face. "So you bid me throw morality to the wind? Open my thighs, and let you do as you will?"

Sudden heat burned in his eyes, and his nostrils flared. He knew it hadn't been a true offer, but he responded as if it had been. His hands tightened, and there was extra pressure for her to spread open before him. And when he spoke, his voice was raw.

"I bid you do what pleases you, and forget the rest." Then he leaned forward and brushed his chin across the top of her knee. Once. Twice. The roughness of his stubble set her senses to tingling.

And oh how she wanted to do it. Her belly was trembling, her insides liquid. Her breasts felt heavy and her eyes languid. She spoke with slowing clarity.

"I will not bed you, Bram. Not without a ring." She said the words by rote, though her voice slowed over his name.

He closed his eyes, a tiny shiver going through his body. "Say my name like that again."

"What?"

"Bram. Say it like that again."

"Bram," she said.

"No. Soft. Throaty."

"Mr. Hallowsby." She'd meant to chastise him. She'd meant to put more distance between them. But even with his formal name on her lips, she heard the hunger in her tone. The throaty purr around the syllables of his name. And he reacted by opening his mouth and biting her knee slowly, the feel of his teeth bracing, even as he had her spreading her legs a fraction of an inch wider.

"What do you want, Maybelle? Tell me what you want."

She wanted more of that. She wanted him, but she didn't say that. She couldn't. It was too bold, and it was not what she told herself she wanted. "I want to force my father to recognize me."

He stilled, but he didn't look up at her. "With a copy of the register? In Oxfordshire?"

"Yes."

"I will take you," he said. "I will take you there and help you confront your father."

She swallowed, her body growing cold. "If I whore myself to you?"

"If you let me show you how it can feel. If you let me touch you—just my hands—and you come for me."

She didn't fully understand his words, but she gathered enough of his meaning. "That is still whoring."

"Maybe," he said, his word a bare whisper. "And I am a bastard. But I will honor my word and tell no one."

"And me? How will I feel about myself in the morning?"

He nodded slowly, his tongue licking the place where his teeth had abraded. The heat of it and the wet slide made her gasp.

"You will hate yourself and me, I suppose," he said against her flesh. "I might even hate myself for you."

She had released his hand to brace the outside of her knee. He was pressing kisses to the inside, urging her to relax. And while she focused on that, she realized belatedly that his other hand had crept up the outside of her other thigh. He was well and truly up her skirts now, and she needed to stop him soon. Very soon.

He lifted his chin. "Very well," he said softly. "I will not take you anywhere. This will be solely about pleasure."

That was not at all what she wanted, and he knew

it. "I have no need of you to take me," she said. "I board the mail coach tomorrow."

"Then who is to know what you do tonight?"

"Me."

He smiled. "Yes, you." And his left hand slid over the top of her thigh. She shuddered, a trembling that reflected the war within her. She wanted to say yes. She wanted to learn from him. He was so large, and as his fingers spread over her leg, it felt as if he touched everything.

"I will show you such things. You want to feel them. You know you do."

She did. And sweet heaven, he was doing things so slowly. She could stop him at any moment, and yet she kept thinking—in a second. Let me feel his hands on me for another moment. Another kiss.

And his hand crept higher.

She was not wearing any drawers. It was too hot for them. So when his long fingers brushed across the top of her mound, she gasped and drew up straight. But he was firmly wedged between her legs now. That only brought her more heavily against him. His fingers widened and one—

Sweet heaven!

One slipped between her folds. Wet and slick, the back of his index finger simply rolled against her. Hard and shocking. She cried out in surprise, and he stilled.

"Do this because you want to, Bluebell. Do this because you trust me not to go too far."

"Everything is too far."

"No, Bluebell. This is something you can do yourself in the privacy of your own bed. This is something ladies do for themselves all the time. I am simply showing you how."

That got her attention. This deep rub of his knuckle against her. The way it made her belly quiver and her face feel flushed.

"You lie," she whispered.

"I do not. Do you wish me to show you? To put your fingers where mine are? So you can do this yourself?"

Yes. No. She didn't know. She bit her lip and closed her eyes. This was wrong and yet… And yet…

He took her hand in his and guided it to where his were. He had straightened up between her, opening her legs so that everything was exposed. Then he pushed her skirt up to her belly. All of her was open to his view.

Her eyes flew open, and she felt her cheeks burn with embarrassment, but what she saw made her pause. His eyes were intense where he looked at her. And his mouth curved in a smile. Not a secret, guilty smile, but one of appreciation as if he looked on something beautiful.

And then his gaze caught hers. He must have understood her confusion because he explained as clearly as if she had asked.

"Look down, Bluebell," he said, his voice hoarse. "Do you see my hand there? Dark tan against your white skin… I see your tender flesh wet with dew and my fingers entwined with yours. Your curls are springy there, your petals like a ripe peach. It is beautiful, Maybelle. And I will remember this sight until the day I die."

He meant it. Every word was breathed with honest reverence, and she could not understand it. It was as though he worshiped at the place between her thighs.

She wanted to ask him to explain, but she had no breath. Not as he rocked his knuckle against her. A pulse of reaction burst through her body. A tightening. A gasp.

"Do you feel that?" he asked. Stupid question. She had all but jumped off the chair.

His other hand took hers and guided her fingers to the same spot.

"Put your thumb there."

She did as he bid. She hadn't the presence of mind to refuse him.

"Push."

He did it for her. He pressed her thumb against her, and she cried out. Hard. Hot. Her buttocks clenched and her back arched.

"Play however you like, Maybelle. Push against it. Rub a circle. Up and down. Whatever you want."

She wanted him to do it. She wanted to feel more now. She pushed again, and it was as if thunder rolled up her spine.

Then she felt his fingers spreading her open. His thumbs pushed her apart, and at his urging, her legs rolled to the outside of the hard chair. She was spread as wide as she could go, but she hardly cared as she rolled a circle over that place he'd showed her.

Oh yes. Yes, that felt good.

Then she felt his fingers push into her. She hadn't thought she could be more shocked, but she was. This was the act, done with his finger. She knew about male organs and penetration. But not this. Not that it would feel so right to have something pushing inside her.

Deeper. Harder.

She clenched around him, and he groaned.

"Sweet Bluebell," he breathed.

Then he withdrew, and she whimpered. She did not want him leaving her.

With his free hand, he pressed over hers, using his finger to thrust hers against her. Her bottom was tightening, pushing her up so that her body and their fingers bumped against where she throbbed.

And then his finger was back inside her. Not just one, she realized, but two. She felt stretched by him. Opened in a way that only a man could do.

She tightened in reaction, wanting to pull him deeper, to squeeze him harder, to…

She couldn't think.

She couldn't breathe.

It was too much, this stroke and thrust.

Flashes of sensation.

Lightning between her eyes.

Inside. He was inside her.

Yes.

Oh!

The sensations collided.

They burst together against her mind and her body as she screamed.

Such pleasure.

Such amazing sensation.

Oh yes, yes, yes, yes, yes!

Eleven

BRAM HAD ALWAYS LOVED WATCHING A WOMAN IN the throes of passion. He loved seeing if her nose wrinkled, hearing if she grunted or moaned. He liked the undulations of her body and the special way her breasts puckered. Did she shiver within her pants or thrust forward with the arch? Did her body flail wide or shrink into its pleasure?

These were the things he liked knowing, and with Bluebell it was no different. So when her eyes widened in shock and her arms flew wide, he grinned and watched with greedy eyes.

His fingers were pushed deep inside, enjoying the hard fist of her body around his fingers. Two inside her, and the others held back shallow because of her maidenhead.

Except when she orgasmed. He was so enthralled by the sight that he simply held on, his fingers pushing deeper to feel every contraction, every gasp and shudder that went through her body.

Including the rip of the membrane.

He didn't understand what had happened at first. Things were moving so explosively around him. She was wild in her completion, and his blood was pounding with her every shift and moan. But eventually, she had to quiet. Eventually, her body stopped its undulations, and she caught her breath. Eventually, he looked down at his hand and saw the blood. That was when he realized what he'd done. That he hadn't intended to rip her hymen wasn't relevant. He'd meant it when he said he wouldn't take her virginity. And he hadn't. Not really. Except...

Jesus.

Her maidenhead was ripped. By his fingers.

He looked at her face. Her eyes were closed, her body still giving tiny pulses that made her belly flutter. Her head was lying against the high back of the chair, and a languid smile played about her lips.

She was utterly beautiful.

And she was no longer a virgin.

With shaking hands, he pulled out of her. The basin was right there, so it was the easiest thing to do to wash his hands and then wash her. There wasn't much blood anyway.

She hummed, deep in her throat, when he stroked her thighs with the cloth. She let out a murmur of delight when he pressed a kiss to the inside of her thigh. And she whispered a word of thanks when he pulled her skirt down to cover her modestly, though he mourned the lost view.

"No thanks are necessary, Miss Bluebell. That was my pleasure," he said, and he meant every word.

She swallowed, then seemed to reluctantly gather herself together. She straightened up slightly on the chair and pulled her knees together. He did not interfere. Indeed, he picked up the basin and dumped the water out the back rather than let her see the tiniest tinge of pink. There wasn't any. There had been too little blood. But he was excruciatingly aware of it.

"Is it always like that?"

He shook his head. "That was like a first meal, and a good one, I hope."

She grinned. "Very good."

"But experiences are as varied as the dinners you have eaten."

She arched her brows, looking young and mischievous. "There is not much variety in the food I eat."

"Then mayhaps your every encounter will be as wonderful as this."

She nodded, but her gaze went to him. To his falls, most specifically, as he set the basin neatly away. He had not been looking directly at her. He wanted her to feel unpressured and hold on to her languor as long as possible. But he was too aware of her, even from the corner of his eye, and so he saw the direction of her gaze.

"Will you show me now?"

"Uh…what?" He turned directly to her, afraid to guess what she wanted.

"You said that what I just did…that ladies do that all the time in the dark of their bedrooms."

"Yes, that's true."

"So if this is what women do, will you show me what men do?"

He gaped at her. There was no other word for the way he stared, dumbfounded.

"We are sharing, yes?" she pressed. "As friends?"

Friends? Sharing?

She straightened fully. "We are showing each other things. It is not whoring—"

"Of course not!"

"Then…" Her eyes took on a pleading aspect, though her voice remained casual. "Share with me."

"You want to see…me?"

"Doing what men do."

Good God, she was serious. And he wanted to do it. He wanted it most desperately. "It is…" How to phrase the thrusting and grunting, not to mention the messy release—"It's not necessarily an attractive thing."

"Did you find what I did attractive?"

"Most definitely."

"Then why do you think a man is different?"

Wasn't she a country-bred girl? Didn't she understand the basics? "The man strains and moves."

"I did as well. At least, I think I did."

"And—"

She pushed to her feet, coming to stand directly before him with her chin lifted and her arms dropped onto her hips. "I showed you everything, did I not?"

Well, there was a great deal more possible, but he supposed from her perspective she had.

"So show me!" It was as much an order as a plea.

And without even realizing it, his hands went to the buttons on his clothes. When she realized what he was doing, her smile was absolutely brilliant. Both relief and gratitude shone on her face, but mostly, he saw an excited curiosity. And as he let his pants drop and set about opening his falls, she raised her hands off her hips, only to hold them nervously in front of her.

"Will you sit down?" she gestured awkwardly. "In the chair?"

The one she had just vacated? It seemed fitting. Especially as she would likely settle on the stool he had used. It did, after all, afford the best view.

He moved awkwardly, neither fully out of, nor in, his clothing. And when he sat down, she did as he expected, resting on the stool at his knees. She appeared like a student before a master, her expression eager. It was unsettling.

"Bluebell…" he said, but she shook her head.

"Do I help? What should I do?"

All at once, he was seized by the unreality of the situation. Imagine a woman asking to see this? Even at the height of his adolescent imagination, he had never guessed at this. So why not enjoy it?

He leaned back in his chair and extended his legs to either side of her while he freed himself. And there he was, tall and proud, directly before her eyes, which were as huge as saucers.

"Are you sure you want to learn?" he challenged. His voice was casual, but inside, his blood pounded with hungry excitement.

"Oh yes," she said as she shifted on the stool. Apparently, she wished to see him from all angles. "You are not exactly straight."

He nodded. A small hitch to the left. "Most men are not ruler straight."

"But there is more, yes? The sac?"

So her country education was not completely lacking. "Do you wish to see everything?"

"I thought I'd made that clear already."

Of course she had. So with a shrug, he divested himself of all the coverings from the waist down. The chair felt cold on his bare bum, but stranger was the way she impatiently unbuttoned the lower fastenings of his shirt, enough to drape it open but not fully wide. Like a stage curtain to frame the main show.

It was a truly uncomfortable thought.

He looked at her red lips, still dark from excitement. "Will you kiss me?" he asked.

She hesitated. She had cast this in her mind as a sharing of information. Kissing would make it too intimate. But it was something he wanted desperately.

"It is what men imagine before we begin."

"Kissing?"

"And more."

She shook her head. "There will not be more."

As if what they had already done wasn't intimate enough. "I know," he said, keeping his voice level. "But a kiss would be welcome."

She nodded, straightening as gracefully as any queen from her throne. Then she stretched forward over his organ, leaning in such that he could smell her scent—spiced with arousal—and see the bob of her breasts and the wet of her lips.

"Just a kiss?" she asked.

"A slow one. With your mouth open."

So they connected, lip to lip, a teasing press at first where the heat of her breath coiled with his. Then he angled his mouth one way, and she the other. Her tongue was tentative, extended into him on a shy quest. It was novel, this exploration she did, and he let her find her way around teeth and tongue.

But all too soon, his hunger took over. Where he had meant to play with her lightly, his need surged forward to make him dominate. She was leaning over him, but he boldly thrust his tongue into her mouth. In and out. Dominance and submission.

He made a passionate play of a single kiss, and when she finally broke away, her breath short and her eyes wide, he knew he had pushed her too far. The kiss had been frankly sexual, and she was overwhelmed.

So he made no move to follow her as she drew back toward the stool, though every muscle in his body clenched with the need to grab her and hold her to him.

"No more," she rasped.

He looked down to where his penis was wet and flushed, jerking toward her with muscles he could not completely control. "Do you still wish to see?"

She swallowed, and he thought for a moment she would run. But Bluebell was a bold woman, and so after a moment, she nodded.

"You may help me at any time," he instructed, "but I will show you for now."

She nodded.

He took himself in hand. He wrapped his fingers around himself, and he did a single slow stroke from tip to base. He surged into his hand, unable to stop himself, but his eyes were on her as she wet her lips and angled to see. Just how bold was this country miss?

"Do you see the moisture at the tip?"

She nodded.

"Many women like the taste. Would you like to try?"

"They…?"

He nodded.

He watched her bite her lower lip, even white teeth pressing into red flesh. He focused on that, using it to control the roaring in his blood. But then she nodded.

Bold miss indeed.

He kept himself excruciatingly still as she extended her index finger toward him. She had to do it on her own, so he said nothing. Just waited.

Then the feel of the pad of her finger across the very top had his buttocks pushing himself toward her. He could not stop it, and the brief pressure against her finger was like the press of heaven.

Then she drew back, her finger moist, the liquid pearlescent in the light. And she popped it in her mouth and sucked.

He nearly came just from the sight of that alone. He imagined himself in her mouth with her tongue swirling over his tip. With the taste of him inside her, filling her.

"Salty," she said.

"Yes."

He forced himself to let go of his grip. He opened his hand and let his organ bob free between them. "You cannot fully understand unless you do it."

"Hold it?"

"As I was. Stroke from the tip to the base."

She looked at him, her expression showing uncertainty. But then she did it. She reached out and wrapped him in a tentative hold. Her hand was cool compared to the heat of his cock, but it quickly warmed. And as she adjusted her fingers to his girth, he shuddered from the glorious feel.

"Harder," he rasped, and she complied.

White fingers, dark red head of his cock, and the pressure of her small hand around him. God, it was a wonder he didn't explode right there.

He let his head fall back, his breath ragged. She didn't move, but he saw her eyes dart to his face.

"Good?" she asked.

"Yes."

Then he pushed into her hand. She didn't resist, but went upward with him. So he wrapped his hand around hers, showing her where to squeeze, how to stroke, what to do.

It was the most exquisite torture he'd ever had. Holding himself back while he instructed her. He tried to keep things dispassionate. He tried to think of anything but the wonder of her hand on him.

Then she began to knead him. Not hard, more like the rolling squeeze of a woman who had milked many a cow. It was an unflattering thought, but oh how it felt!

His hips jerked in reaction. He let go of her hand to grip the edges of the chair. And he thrust into her hand.

Over and over, while she watched and smiled.

It was her smile that got him. She was delighted to do this for him. She was happy.

To do this.

For him.

"Ahhhh!"

He exploded. His mind went white, his hips bucked uncontrolled, and he released everything like a shot from a gun.

Everything.

Pulse after pulse.

Yes. God yes.

It was some moments before he had control of himself enough to open his eyes. When he finally did, he saw her grinning. She hadn't let go of him. She was still holding his shrinking cock while his come wet her hand. He didn't want to look to see where else it had gone. It was enough to see it there on her and him.

"Thank you," she whispered.

Thank him? The best orgasm of his life, and she was thanking him.

"Was it what you wanted?" he asked.

"Yes." She looked at him as if waiting for a sign. He had no idea what she meant, but then she glanced back at her hand. "I should let go now?"

God no. He was already starting to swell again. How could he not, with her looking so happily intrigued? But honesty forced him to nod.

"That is the essence of it," he finally managed. "There is endless variety, of course, between a man and a woman. But that is the main part."

She released him slowly, uncoiling one finger after another. Then she straightened, refilling the basin quickly, and returning with water and cloth. He had meant to put himself away by then, but languor was making his thoughts and his movements slow.

And then she was there with a gentle stroke on an organ all too willing to come to life again. She cleaned him, and he had to grasp her wrist or demonstrate again.

"Too soon?" she asked.

He shook his head. "Too hungry for more."

Her smile was wicked. "I understand."

She…what?

"You…um…" How to ask? "You wish to do that again?"

She laughed, the sound light and free. "Of course. Now I understand why women rush to the altar. It is not completely about money or even love. It is to enjoy that, yes?"

He cleared his throat. "Most women do not have such pleasure in their bed. That is why they do it alone. In secret."

She nodded as if that made sense. "Then I will have to be careful when selecting my husband."

How practical of her. He admired that, even as a surge of fierce jealousy burned through his gut. He was still sprawled in her chair, his cock ready to thrust inside her, and she was speaking of the husband she would one day wed. It was enough to make him straighten his attire, cover himself with his shirt, and put steel into his legs as he began to work his falls back up.

She moved away to give him room. As he had done, she dumped the water outside the kitchen and set aside the cloth. She restored everything to rights, but damn it, nothing was right. She'd just come for the first time. He'd just released in her hand. He wanted her to look at him sweetly. At least pretend to a warmth for him.

And he did not want it to seem—mere moments after it all—as if nothing had happened. As if she were not changed somehow by her new knowledge.

"Bluebell?" he asked. Damn it, he didn't even know her Christian name.

She turned to look at him, her skirts swishing about her ankles. She was naked beneath those skirts. *He* had been beneath those skirts. And yet, when she looked at him, there was nothing of that intimacy in her face. She was calm and relaxed. And the curve to her lips could just as easily have been because of her sunny disposition.

"I will take you to Oxfordshire," he said. "Do not ride the mail coach."

She lifted her chin. "I will not pay you."

"Of course not. It is simply a shared ride. Between friends." They were not friends. In his mind, they were so much more, but it was all she would accept, and so he used it.

"It is not proper. I need to appear a lady."

Right. "Then hire me. For the price that you would have paid for the mail coach."

"That is a pittance."

"Nevertheless, pay me that, and you will be hiring me as your guard and driver." He hated his next words, but he pushed them out anyway. "I will be your paid servant, nothing more."

She frowned, and her gaze drifted to the chair they'd used. It was her first break that told him she was not completely unaffected by what they'd done. Until she spoke.

"We cannot…share again. It's not proper. Certainly not with a servant."

He couldn't argue that, much though he wanted to. "I will come first thing in the morning."

She frowned and looked out her window. "Everyone will know."

"We'll leave early. I'll take the horse now. Come to the inn yard in the morning, and you can hire me. There is nothing improper in a day's drive."

She swallowed. "There is a great deal improper in appearing to do one thing and acting another. And people will still think the worst if I ride away with you."

Again, he could not argue. Instead he closed the distance between them. She didn't shy away, for which he was grateful. And so he took his time, touching her cheek, stroking the curve of her chin, and drawing her face up to look him squarely in the eye.

"I have lived in the demi-monde all my life. The nobles, the upper crust, even the wealthy cits—I have known many of them. There is not a one who does not focus on propriety's appearance. Actions mean little so long as the appearance is pure."

"But that is dishonest."

"Yes."

She searched his face, reading the truth in his expression—or so he hoped. Perhaps all she saw was his lust. And it was that base emotion that directed his actions now. It insisted that he stay a little longer in her company, however he could manage it.

Meanwhile, she bit her lower lip in thought. White teeth, red flesh. He would never tire of that sight. "You are living proof that people do not act as purely as they pretend," she said.

He winced. He did not like her bringing up his illegitimacy, but he could not deny it.

"Come with me, Miss Bluebell. I will see that your reputation is not harmed."

She nodded slowly, reluctantly. And then she looked at his mouth. He felt her gaze there like a brand, his flesh hot and pulsing beneath her regard.

"One last kiss?" he asked.

"Yes," she whispered.

So he took it. And he lingered over it. He burned it in his memory and hers—he hoped. Then he stepped away, feeling as if he were ripping himself away from some essential mooring. It made no sense.

She was a woman, no more, no less. He'd had many, and though this encounter was seared on his mind as intensely special, it meant nothing to his life. So he put on his hat and left.

She meant nothing.

Except, perhaps, another more exciting interlude.

He would have to handle her carefully. He would have to plan his approach. But that was something he was quite willing to do.

Bram was still thinking of ways to seduce Bluebell when he rode Mina into the barn. The horse was indeed an ugly but sweet-tempered creature, but she would serve them well. It was quiet in the barn as it was full dark, and everyone was eating or in bed. He'd be there soon enough, but he needed to settle Mina and make one last check on the carriage. The whitewashing was well done, he thought, and the carpentry—

"But why must we wait out here?" came a plaintive voice from inside the carriage.

Bram froze, his thoughts turning dark. It couldn't be. He'd sent Dicky and Clarissa to Scotland, by God. But then he wrenched open the carriage door, and there they were, looking somewhat worse for wear.

Clarissa's dress was travel-stained, her hair was askew, and her skin looked wan. Though in the lamplight, her fake sapphires still shone bright, probably because she spent so much time clutching the damned things.

Dicky still looked every inch the aristocrat, though his eyes had that desperate, haunted look that came from spending too much time in close quarters with his wife.

"What the devil are you doing here?" Bram demanded.

"Oh, hullo there," said Dicky. "Do come in and join us for a moment, won't you?" He gestured elegantly to the inside of the carriage as if he were inviting Bram to dine.

"I thought you were off to America," he snapped.

"Scotland," corrected Dicky.

"Foul things, boats," Clarissa huffed. "The waves were abominable. I couldn't possibly go to America on one of those."

"Did you try?" Bram asked.

Dicky rolled his eyes. "Of course we tried. Barely an hour, and we had to turn back."

"The waves," Clarissa gasped. "My favorite gown." Then she pressed her handkerchief to her lips.

Right. She did have a kind of stench around her.

"We need your help, my man," said Dicky with strained good cheer. "A bath for the lady, a place to bed down, and a new plan, if you please."

"I do not please. You refused to pay me, if you recall."

"You took what you wanted. Don't think I didn't notice."

True enough. "But that does not oblige me to allow you into my carriage or to feed and bathe you."

Clarissa gasped and pressed the linen to her eye, presumably to wipe away a tear. "Oh, dearest Bram, you cannot leave me in such a pitiable state. Surely, you cannot." Then she pursed her bow red lips. Far from enticing him, he felt distinctly nauseous at the sight.

"Look, my man," said Dicky, drawing himself up to his full height. "There's people after us. Surely you cannot leave us to die at their hands."

"Oh!" gasped Clarissa. "Oh no. Oh no, no, no—"

"Stop it!" he snapped. "Let me think."

Both immediately quieted. They straightened in their seats, and Clarissa even smoothed the folds of her stained gown as if they were awaiting tea service. And they waited.

"I did not say I would help you."

"Oh!" Clarissa began again, so rather than hear that, he held up his hand.

"No more of that."

"I'm trying to stop crying," she gasped, "but this has been so hard." Jesus, three days away from her gasping had not been long enough.

He cursed under his breath. "Jeremy will come back the minute he finds out there isn't any coin in the lockbox." In truth, he was surprised the man hadn't appeared already. "He'll come asking me where you are."

"And you'll tell him Scotland," said Dicky in a reasonable tone. "Which is why we didn't go there."

"I won't need to tell him anything if he finds you here."

Clarissa reached forward, her long fingers still elegant, despite the discoloration on her gloves. "You must not let that happen. What will we do?"

Bram frowned. He needed to send them far away. Someplace they could never return to plague him again. "Finland," he finally said.

"What?" said Dicky.

"Where?" gasped Clarissa.

"The North Sea is very calm travel," he lied. In truth he had no idea how calm it was. But it was the first place he thought of that would be far away from him.

"But isn't it cold there?" asked Dicky.

"The North Sea? I couldn't possibly."

"Damn it, you have to get on a boat somewhere. Jeremy will find you anywhere in England."

Dicky stiffened. "Mind your tongue, Bram. She's a lady, and a gentleman must maintain some standards."

Standards? From this pair? "Good thing I'm not a gentleman," he growled. "What about Ireland?" They could still come back from there, but it was better than nothing.

"Goodness no," Dicky said with a shudder. "Someone might mistake me for an Irishman."

Which was actually the point, but Bram knew better than to quibble. "Wales?"

Clarissa's gasp held true horror. "Among the Welsh?"

He sighed. "Italy then. You like Italians. Get a boat from Dover. Jeremy will be looking for you up here. If you travel south to Dover, the crossing isn't so bad. Then across the continent to Italy."

Clarissa's eyes brightened. "I do like Italians. The men are so very swarthy."

"Excellent—"

"But how are we to get to Dover?"

"Like I said. On the mail coach."

Both beautiful people shuddered in a very beautiful way. Tiny little tremors that displayed total disdain. Bloody hell.

"We'll take my carriage," said Dicky.

"My carriage," interrupted Bram.

"Well, not exactly."

"Yes, exactly. I did not just pay to have it fixed and whitewashed for you, Dicky. This is my carriage—"

Clarissa rubbed a long finger across the squabs toward him. "You did a fine job, Bram. No one will know it as the same equipage we came north in. It's perfect cover."

It wasn't anything of the sort. "It's not yours," he stressed between gritted teeth. "It's mine."

Which is when the waterworks began. He knew it was for show. Or maybe not, because Clarissa was not a pretty woman when she cried. She made choked gasps, and her face became blotchy. If there was one thing that Clarissa maintained, it was her beauty. Which meant these tears were real.

"Bloody hell, man," Dicky said, clear desperation in his tone. "You cannot abandon me now. Not when—"

"Two hundred pounds," Bram ground out, cursing himself under his breath.

"What?"

"Two hundred bloody pounds, and you take yourself off now." He felt bad about the horse. That sweet-tempered creature did not deserve these two. "And you leave the horse for me in Dover. I'll find her there." After all, the thing was so ugly that he'd be able to find it easily.

Clarissa's tears ended on a hiccuping snort. "You'll drive us to Dover?"

"No, I won't."

"But—"

"Jeremy will look for me in order to find you. If I'm driving you across England, he's sure to find you."

Even Clarissa saw the logic in that. So she whispered a tragic, "Very well."

Seeing that his wife had already decided, Dicky sighed dramatically. "It hurts me, how you've forgotten our friendship."

"It hurt me too when you ran off without paying me." He held out his hand.

With a sullen curse, Dicky reached for a small pot pressed near his leg. Pulling off the lid, he carefully extricated two hundred pounds.

"What is that?" Bram asked.

"It's your money," the man responded with a dramatic sniff.

"No, no. The…small chamber pot."

"Well, I couldn't keep carrying it around in a rucksack, could I?"

Clarissa brightened. "Everyone has pots, you know. I thought that would blend in."

Because everyone carried around a lidded piece of pottery wherever they went. Bram didn't argue. Instead, he pulled the money out of Dicky's hand before the man could find a way to palm some of the notes.

"It's a sad thing," Dicky drawled to his wife, "when education does not overcome breeding. Bad blood will always out." By which he meant to insult Bram's bastard blood. Too bad Bram was long since inured to such jabs.

"Oh yes," Clarissa agreed. Then she smiled winningly at Bram. "Do fetch us some stew, please, before you hitch up the carriage. I think I can manage some food now that we're away from the water."

Dicky clapped his hands. "Excellent notion, my dear. Most excellent."

Then together, man and wife gave him calm, condescending smiles appropriate to the king's drawing room. Bram almost slammed the door in their faces. Almost. But if he didn't help them, then they'd be plaguing him for the rest of the night.

So he did as he was bid. He got them stew and bread. He hitched up Mina and helped them out of the inn yard. Dicky put up a token objection that he would have to drive, but he probably needed the respite from his wife. So with Dicky driving, Bram was finally, happily, able to wave them good-bye and good riddance.

But what the hell was he going to do for Bluebell in the morning?

Twelve

DID SHE LOOK DIFFERENT? MAYBELLE PEERED INTO THE mirror, but could detect nothing unusual in her reflection. Perhaps she appeared a little flushed, but that was to be expected. She was about to leave on the trip that would end up with her being recognized as the granddaughter of an earl.

And yet, that paled in comparison to the changes from the afternoon before. What she had done with Mr. Hallowsby! What she had discovered! A whole world of surprises regarding her own body. She had not thought she could feel that way. So hot, so uncomfortable. Like a thunderstorm under the skin. And yet the lightning flashes, the boom inside her belly, the explosion, and the aftermath had changed her whole world.

It was like suddenly discovering she could fly!

She'd tried to recreate the sensations last night in her bed. She'd wanted to, but it had felt awkward and a little embarrassing. She did not want to do it without Mr. Hallowsby, even when she'd lain there reliving every glorious touch and stroke. She needed him, and so she'd settled in to a restless night's sleep without him.

She wanted to do it again. Many, many times more. But that could not happen. Not with him. She was going to be a respectable lady and marry Charlie, a virtuous curate, or maybe even someone more exalted! She wondered if Charlie knew how to do the things Mr. Hallowsby had taught her. She couldn't even envision him stroking himself, much less her. And that would be a sad disappointment in their marriage bed.

Perhaps she ought to look for someone else. But it wasn't as if she could walk around and ask prospective husbands if they knew how to give her that quickening in bed. She wasn't really supposed to know about it at all.

Which left her circling in her thoughts, right back to Mr. Hallowsby. He wasn't a potential husband, of course. He was a bastard, and as exciting as the man was, he would be a step down. She was looking to become completely respectable, not give up on it altogether. She would have to ask him if there was a way to know how a man would perform in bed. A sign…or something. Any way to find out before she said, "I do."

But that was a thought for later. Right now, it was time to get to the inn. She rushed through the last details before closing her house up for a time. Maybe as much as a month, depending on how her father received her. Then she walked as fast as she could without appearing hasty.

Her first hint that something was amiss came from the sight of Mrs. Pursley and Mrs. Bray whispering together. It was early to be about, and if they were talking in the middle of the street, then something strange had happened indeed. She needed to take only five more steps before they turned to her, speaking loud enough for her to catch most of the conversation.

"In the middle of the night, can you credit it? When all decent folks is in bed."

"What 'appened?" she asked, consciously thickening her accent so as to not give Mrs. Pursley another reason to say she put on airs.

"Why, the London gent. He up and disappeared with his fine carriage, right in the middle of the night. Rode right off like a thief! Didn't pay his shot or anything!"

Maybelle felt her blood run cold. It couldn't be possible. He couldn't have just abandoned her like that. Not after... But of course, fancy gentlemen abandoned women all the time. Isn't that what she'd been taught?

"Goodness, Bluebell, you're looking awful pale." The old biddy leaned forward maliciously. "You weren't expecting something special from that man, were you? I understand he's been teaching you lessons."

Maybelle grit her teeth, Mrs. Pursley's sly innuendo steeling her spine as nothing else could. She'd show them all as soon as she got to London and forced her father to recognize her. She'd show them all.

"Maybelle?" Mrs. Bray asked gently. She was a kind woman and Maybelle's neighbor, so her expression was filled with concern. "Would you care to walk with me?"

"Oh, thank you. I'm afraid I'm a little distracted right now. I'm going to London today, you see. On the mail coach."

"What?" gasped Mrs. Pursley. "But you can't mean to go now that he's left."

And there it was. Surely by now Maybelle wouldn't be surprised by these mean-spirited people. Mrs. Pursley must have overheard Maybelle's conversation with the vicar. She thought, in her small little mind, that Maybelle was going to run off with the London gentleman. Bitch.

"Well, what has that to do with anything?" Maybelle asked. Then before she could say more, they were interrupted by a man's call behind them.

"What ho!"

All three turned to see Mr. Bray on his rickety cart, and right beside him was Mr. Hallowsby, smiling as he jumped down from his perch. "Miss Bluebell, a fine morning, isn't it?"

Relief flooded her, dropping her breath straight down into her toes. It made no sense. She knew better than to rely on a man to keep his word. But he hadn't abandoned her. He hadn't skipped away like a thief in the night. And now he was greeting her and the other ladies as if they were at an elegant tea party.

"Good morning, Mr. Hallowsby," she said, pleased that her voice didn't sound as breathless as she felt.

"I understand we're to be fellow passengers to the mail coach. Mr. Bray and his eldest daughter, Valerie, were on their way to find you, and I've begged him for the favor of a ride."

She blinked. "So you'll be joining me? On the mail coach?"

"Yes, indeed. Appears my carriage disappeared in the middle of the night."

What? "Um, you don't seem very dispirited about it."

"Oh, I'm very dispirited, as you put it. Very much indeed. But I have to get to London, and there's no other way."

"No indeed," she murmured. Then she swallowed. "And Mina?"

His expression fell, and there was an apology in his eyes.

"Oh," she whispered. Silly her—attached to a horse. She knew better, and yet...

He took her hand and squeezed. It was a too-familiar gesture, but she allowed it. She was feeling completely bereft. "No worries. I'll recover her somehow. I promise."

"How?" she breathed.

He chuckled. "It's an ugly horse, Miss Bluebell. I'll recover her. Don't you fear."

And with that, she had to be content. In fact, she was more than content. She believed him because he hadn't disappeared in the middle of the night. And then he did the best thing ever by proving Mrs. Pursley completely wrong.

"Now, I've got to go back to the inn to pay my shot. No one was about when I got up, and so I ducked on over to Mr. Bray's home. So after that, we'll be off." Then he bowed politely to all three and headed off to the inn.

Faithful man.

And Mrs. Pursley proved to be a gossiping old biddy who got everything wrong. A perfect start to the morning, in her opinion. Meanwhile, the village had already stirred itself to gossip. Deprived of Mr.

Hallowsby, it turned on her, looking for details about her family in London. She kept it vague, as she always did, but she said she hoped to return in a month with surprising news. She only prayed that what happened matched her hopes. Otherwise, she would never live down the ignominy.

And when they pressed for more details, she told them the truth that after her mum's death, she'd decided it was time she connected with them. She made no mention of their august personage because she knew the sneering that would happen. Besides, her mum had said what money they'd had from her father's family had been on the condition that no one know her true parentage. So if there was any chance of a dowry from her father, she would keep to the agreement.

Eventually Mr. Hallowsby returned from the inn, and then it was time to leave. He held out his hand to her. She'd already tossed in her small satchel that carried all her worldly goods. Pitiful really, but it was her best two dresses and underthings, plus a few other modest items, one of which was the sketch of her mother's face as it had been drawn by her father's hand.

Right. She swallowed. This was what she wanted. This was her great chance. And yet, why was it so hard to leave? She glanced around at the faces she'd known all her life, and was startled to realize that as crotchety as some people were—and the vicar had come out to join Mrs. Pursley—it was still difficult to leave. She'd never been more than ten miles away from her home. And now she was going all the way to London? It unsettled her. Truthfully, it terrified her.

But she'd already stepped forward, and Mr. Hallowsby

had taken her hand. But when he lifted it, as one would as the lady entered the carriage, only her hand and arm moved. Her feet stayed stubbornly planted.

There was an awkward silence as she stood there, trying to will herself to move. And then he frowned at her. Not in anger, more as if he were considering a strange creature met in the wild.

"There's no shame in delaying. You need not go today."

Which meant she need not go ever. "It has been delayed too long," she responded. "I'm four-and-twenty and have never met them."

He sighed. "You could write them."

Her mother had been adamant that she not write. She had to go in person if she meant to claim her parentage. Which meant she had to get in the cart.

She looked into his eyes, trying to read his thoughts. She had no idea why his impressions mattered so much. She could have looked to any of the village, people who had known her all her life. But she already knew their opinions—for good or for ill. His thoughts were unknown. And so she looked into his eyes and saw patience. Neither support nor condemnation, just understanding, as he awaited her decision.

The idea was a bit shocking. He was not trying to force her into one way of acting or another. Certainly he was not shy about getting her to act as he willed. Yesterday's seduction had been proof of that. But today he was simply neutral. Or, if not neutral, completely silent on his opinion. Which left her to make up her own mind, which is how it ought to be anyway.

"I will go," she said, more to herself than anyone else.

His lips quirked, and she saw his eyes crinkle at the edges. "I know." He raised her hand to his lips. "You are a brave woman."

No one had ever called her that. Bold, certainly. Brassy and wild, definitely. But not brave, and not with such admiration.

How warm that made her. How her heart was beating now, and not in fear. She grinned at him, then flashed all the villagers an excited wave before climbing into the cart. She was Cinderella on the way to the ball. She was Red Riding Hood on the way to her grandmother's house and a grand adventure. She was the heroine of every great tale she had never heard.

With that bold thought, she settled back on the hard wood and grinned from ear to ear. A moment later, Mr. Hallowsby settled between her and Valerie. Then Mr. Bray in the driver's seat clucked at the horses, and they were off.

In this way, they left her village.

She named the homes that they passed, counted the farms, until they passed outside of her knowledge. Then she just looked around, her eyes tiring from the strain of trying to see everything at once.

Except there was nothing new in what she saw. It was the road. It was northern England. Perhaps she didn't have a memory associated with the trees or the bend in the road, but it still looked the same. So she smiled at her companions and listened as Mr. Bray began to whistle. That was pleasant. For a time.

Five minutes.

Ten minutes.

Fifteen.

Lord, this was tedious.

She looked to Mr. Hallowsby.

"Everything good, then?" he asked gently.

She nodded. "Perfectly."

"Excellent." And then he began to chat with them. Within another mile, they were all laughing, shy Valerie included. And in another hour, they had made it to the coaching inn.

She was an excellent companion, Bram realized with a quiet kind of shock. As they rode together at the top of the mail coach, she tried to get him to talk. First she pestered him with questions about all he had seen and done. He told her nothing. His life—or his lies—were not to be shared right now. So she chose to pepper him with questions about London.

That passed the time for an hour or more, but then he got her to talking. It wasn't too hard. She had a keen eye and a canny understanding of people, so her tales of village life were both comic and touching. He knew she'd seen the bad side of a life spent with the same hundred or so souls. The narrow-mindedness of a provincial life had always sent him running. It wasn't just the desire to fleece an outsider for every penny. Inevitably, someone discovered he was a bastard, and the whole village banded together in moral outrage against him.

So there were hints of how she and her mother had been mistreated. Some incident with boys calling her names when she was a young girl until she learned from the gypsies how to fight back with her fists and her knees.

When he didn't decry her association with those people, she opened up even more. And soon they were laughing at the myriad tales of her village. The good and the ill, all told with a kind of fondness that did not blind her to its faults.

In short, he found her heart was kind, even as she was keenly aware of the problems in her world. That made her entirely unique in his experience. Awareness without bitterness? How odd. And stranger, she was not trying to wheedle something from him. He'd already paid her passage to Oxfordshire, even sat atop the damned mail coach to protect her as they travelled. So there was nothing more for her to gain from him except a pleasant day in the sunshine as they rode lengthwise across England.

He knew that in time he would question her. It was in his nature to doubt, but for the moment, he simply enjoyed it.

In fact, the shock was that he had never had a better time in his life.

❧

They arrived in Oxfordshire too late to do more than find an inn. Bram hoped that the place they stopped would be crowded, forcing them into a single room, but he was out of luck. Plenty of space, good fare to eat, and beds separated by a wall and thick doors.

It was important to her to maintain some measure of propriety, and so he respected her wistful smile as she bid him good night and shut the door with him on the outside.

It would be another long night of tortured fantasies

of her, but by now he was familiar with them. And
besides, an end was in sight.

Tomorrow they would go to the church where the
vicar would take them to the registry. It would be hard
for her to realize that her mother lied. There would
be no banns read. No legitimate marriage recorded.
Despite all her insistence to the contrary, he suspected
that her mother had not been legally wed. In truth, some
unscrupulous nobles would write a false, special license
and get a friend to perform a ceremony. The girl would
believe herself wed when nothing could be further from
the truth. Given what he'd learned of Miss Bluebell's
mother, he guessed she was one such duped woman.

He grieved for the pain that would cause Maybelle.
All her illusions about herself and her mother would
be irrevocably shattered. But he consoled himself that
she would be a bastard then, just like him. And once
the shock wore off, a host of possibilities opened up.

After all, if you could never be respectable, then
why keep to respectable limits?

He would have her tomorrow night, he resolved.
He would make her his mistress, take her to London,
and then he would teach her such things! He was hard
and pleasuring himself most of the night just thinking
of that glorious future.

So first thing the next morning, they presented
themselves to the vicar. A quick explanation of the
situation from Miss Bluebell, then a shared look of
dismay between himself and the holy man, before all
three of them tromped to the rectory.

"Remember," Bram said as the vicar found the
appropriate volume. "Whatever you learn today, your

mother loved you. She cared for you, raised you, and gave you everything she could. The registry will not change your childhood, your mother, or even yourself. You are still you—"

"Oh, do shut up," Bluebell hissed. "I know you think the worst, but Mum did not lie about this."

He exhaled harshly. "Not lie. Perhaps she was fooled."

She cast a disparaging eye at him. "I wasn't born canny, you know. I learned to be smart from my mother."

He nodded, knowing when a woman would not listen. But in his mind, he thought that a canny woman was simply someone who had been tricked and swore to never be made the fool again. But all he could do was stand there braced to support Bluebell when she learned the dark truth about her mother.

"Here it is," the vicar abruptly cried. "Right here. The banns were read on the dates you said, and they were married all right and tight."

The man brought the record to Bluebell, and she eagerly traced the lines with her fingers. Meanwhile, the vicar smiled warmly at them both.

"It's pleased as punch I am to show you this, Miss Ballenger. You should have told me your real name."

"Oh," she murmured absently. "But I have gone by Bluebell my whole life."

"Well, you're not in the country anymore. Down here, we like to acknowledge the granddaughter of an earl."

What?

Bram looked down, his eyes widening as he read and reread the words. He knew that name. He knew that family.

Bloody hell. Her father was listed as Oscar Ballenger, son of the Earl of Cavener. But that couldn't possibly be true, could it? No, no, there was only one son. A boring Ronald or Richard or something. Damn it, what did he know?

And then he had it. He had the awful truth.

There had been a second son who'd died of a fever at school. Could that have been Oscar? He didn't know, but it was possible. Which meant Bluebell's father was gone. The first son had married and pro-created as was expected but then died in a shooting accident. That left a boy of four or five, if he recalled, who was heir to a vast estate. The mother, Bluebell's aunt, was a boring woman, unprepossessing and fat. The earl kept both daughter-in-law and heir tucked away at their country seat. All very proper, though rather cursed in terms of men.

And that was the point. The countess was a kind woman with sharp eyes and a love of fashion. She had doted on her children, and with them gone, was now lost in a vague melancholy of age.

Unless another child presented herself, one that was lively and smart, who could be dressed up and give her a reason to throw balls. The daughter of her second son, a beauty that could be brought out with all the pomp deserving of a true English rose.

Bluebell. The legitimate granddaughter of an earl.

And perhaps—right here, right now—the means to a substantial dowry. If he played his cards right. If he married her and presented it as a fait accompli. If he made sure she was his before she was presented to her grandfather and accepted as one of their own.

If he seduced her in just the right way, then it could be done. And he could have everything he'd always wanted.

The temptation burned through him, and he wanted it. He wanted it almost as deeply, as sincerely, as he'd once wanted Cara. And it was that realization that set him back on his heels.

Whenever things had appeared to go his way, whenever a gift as if from the heavens had landed in his lap—it had all gone sour eventually. There were no gifts, not without strings attached. Cara had been a lie wrapped in a pretty package.

Bluebell was no deceiver, but she was equally a lie. She'd been thrown to Hull to be raised in ignorance. Which meant the earl's family wanted no part of her. And no matter the temptation to marry her now, no matter the urge to bed her and force the earl to recognize his granddaughter, it wouldn't work. Because it never worked. And he would be a fool to pursue it.

Which meant despite everything, he had to pack her back to Hull and her life there. She had her letter from the vicar. She had proof she was legitimate. She could leave now and go marry the vicar's son as she'd wanted.

So that was his plan. He would send her away and be done with pretty packages wrapped around a lie.

Thirteen

IT WAS TRUE! EVERYTHING HER MOTHER HAD TOLD her was true! She was the granddaughter of the Earl of Cavener.

She looked back at Mr. Hallowsby, saw his stunned face, and everything in her grew even brighter. He doubted her. He doubted her mother. But it was true, and now, by God, she would go to London and demand to know why she'd been thrown into the wilds of Hull never to be acknowledged.

"I must copy this page," she said.

"Well, as to that," the vicar said, "I could write it down and affix my name to it. But my dear, if someone doubts your true heritage, you will need a solicitor to come and make an official copy."

"Thank you, sir. I shall certainly do that should it come to it. But if you would write what you can, then I would be ever so grateful." She gave him her best smile, which happened to be especially bright right now.

"Certainly. A pleasure," he said with an answering grin. And off the man went carrying the record book with him.

She laughed. She couldn't help it. It was true. She'd had her doubts. Of course she had. And there was still so much that had to be answered, but—

"Tell me everything."

She glanced up at Mr. Hallowsby's gruff words. His face was tight, his jaw tense.

"I have told you—"

"Bollocks, you have not. Look, this is a dangerous game you're playing. Do you think the bloody Earl of Cavener is going to welcome you with open arms? Assuming this really is your mother's name, he sent you off to Hull for a reason, and he might not like you coming back."

"Assuming?" she sputtered. "Assuming! It bloody well is me mum!"

"Damn it, Bluebell, listen to me. It doesn't make sense. Why wouldn't you be recognized? Why haven't you gone to a finishing school and been raised as you ought?"

"Well, that's wot I want to know! I'm going t' see 'im—"

"Mind your *h*'s," he snapped. Then he rubbed a hand over his face. "Bloody hell."

"And you mind your language. I'm a lady, if you recall."

"No, I don't recall. And you're nothing of the sort." She pulled herself up to her full height and stared down her nose at him, just like she'd seen Mrs. Pursley do to her a million times. "I am indeed a lady. That's what the book says."

"No, the book says you're legitimate. That's a miracle, true enough, but it takes a great deal more to be a lady."

"Bollocks," she snapped back.

He gripped her arm, his fingers tightening painfully. She gasped and tried to wrench away, but he held her fast. "Let me think," he said between clenched teeth.

"You're 'urting me," she said, her voice low and angry.

It took him a moment to understand her words. A moment before his eyes widened and his hand abruptly released her.

"Damnation, I'm sorry, Bluebell. But you need to let me think."

"I need to go see my father," she returned. Then she grinned, happiness bubbling out his name with true joy. "Mr. Oscar Ballenger, second son of the Earl of Cavener."

"Right. At least we know why he didn't follow your mum," he said grimly.

"Wot?" Damn it, she was a lady. She needed to speak correctly. "What? What are you thinking?"

His eyes abruptly softened. He reached out to her, but she kept back. He knew something, and suddenly, his eyes were filled with pity.

"Bluebell, you must understand. Gentlemen lie to girls all the time. What was your mother? She wasn't reared gently, was she?" He didn't ask it as a question. More like an accusation.

"She was an honorable girl. Raised proper."

"But she wasn't a gentlewoman."

Bluebell shook her head. "She was a maid in a don's house." She might as well tell him it all. "My father was a student, and he came to visit his teacher often. That's where he met my mother."

"Of course. A student trick of an uneducated girl."

"She might not have had schooling, but my mother

was smart. She learned things all the time. And she taught them to me."

"What things?"

"Philosophy. She loved Aristotle and Plato the best, but she knew all sorts of things."

He nodded. "A smart girl. Pretty, most like."

"Prettier than me," she said softly.

His lips curved. "I doubt that. But then this student comes, shows an interest. Gets her pregnant."

"Not until after they was wed."

"They *were* wed," he said.

"That's what I said!"

He sighed and didn't argue. And in the silence, the father came back carrying the heavy tome. "I've copied it down for you, but miss…" He took a deep breath. Why was it that everyone was suddenly looking at her with pity? She was a lady, and yet their eyes kept saying she was a fool. "It only says the two were married. Not who you are."

She frowned. "I'm their child."

The cleric nodded, shared a glance with Mr. Hallowsby, and then handed over the piece of foolscap. "I wish you the best of luck," he said to her. "I've seen terrible things done to naive girls, miss. It's not fair, and I try to stop it, but these are randy young boys, every year more undisciplined and cruel than the last, if you get my meaning."

No, she did not. There was clearly something of importance in his words, but without clarity, all she could do was carefully place the foolscap into her satchel. Then she watched as Mr. Hallowsby acted solemn as he shook hands with the vicar.

"Thank you, Father. I'll see that it gets all sorted out."

"You are a kind gentlemen, then."

"No, sir," he answered stiffly. "Just one paid to make things clear."

The cleric had no response to that except a slow nod and another sympathetic look. She gritted her teeth, doing her best to act appropriate to her status. She nodded, smiled her thanks, and allowed Mr. Hallowsby to guide her out. But one step outside their door, and her control broke.

"What does he mean?" she demanded. "What do you know?"

He sighed. "Come along. I'll buy you an ice. It's damned hot already and not even noon."

She wanted to dig in her heels and make him talk, but she could see by the set of his face that he would speak in his own sweet time. Besides, a queasy feeling was building in the pit of her stomach, and perhaps some tea would ease it.

So she nodded and let him escort her to what she thought must be the center square or near enough to it. She could tell he'd been to Oxfordshire before, knew where to go, and even nodded politely at a few people.

"Do you know them?" she asked.

"No, but you can tell by their clothing who they are. See the men in black robes like barristers?"

"The bishops?"

"They're not bishops. They're the dons, the teachers at Oxford. One nods to them out of respect for their scholarship."

"I see," she said as she did exactly that to another of the black-robed men.

"And because they're a priggish lot who get tetchier than a slighted countess if you don't."

"Oh."

"That's what you have to know. The dons take themselves very seriously because the boys—as a rule—do not."

"They're not boys," she said, knowing he was thinking of her father. "They're grown men who have chosen—"

"They're boys younger than you with much less sense. Worse, they're often privileged enough to think they can do anything without consequence." He sighed. "And they're usually right."

He guided her around another corner even more stuffed with people. Her whole village didn't count this many, and her eyes widened. "Why is that man dressed all in blue?"

"What man? Oh, the boy with the ugly hat?"

He wasn't even close to a youth, more like a man just out of his gangly adolescence, but she didn't argue. His pants were blue, his shirt and waistcoat blue. Even his coat and hat were another shade of dark blue, all of it of fine quality.

"It was the fashion a Season or so ago. He's out of date by London standards, but Oxfordshire is often behind the times."

This was fashion? "To dress all in blue?"

"Bottle green was the color before that."

"Truly?" She didn't think she'd ever seen a bottle green shirt before, and she looked all around trying to find one.

"Stop it," he said. "You can look about once we're

seated, but you must do it slowly. Carefully. As if you'd seen it all before."

"But I've never seen anything like—"

"I know," he bit out. "That's the point. If you want to act a lady, then you mustn't be who you are." Then he paused and gave her a heavy look. "Unless you wish to give up this mad scheme, be content as you are, and enjoy a visit to Oxfordshire."

She frowned at him. "You cannot tell me that ladies do not enjoy themselves when traveling."

"Oh, they most certainly do. They just don't act like they do."

"But—"

"Good morning, sir, lady," the innkeeper interrupted.

Together they turned to the man, but it was Mr. Hallowsby who spoke. He requested a table on the square, tea, and ices. Mindful of his instruction, Maybelle tried to adopt an attitude of boredom, but there was so much to see that it was hard. It helped that she noted two fine ladies walking together down the street. They carried parasols, had ruffles on their gowns and feathers in their bonnets, and most telling of all, two maids trailed along behind them carrying hatboxes. Fine ladies, and neither one of them smiled.

So she mimicked their sour expressions—chin lifted, nose wrinkled, and lips pursed—as they were escorted to a small table on the cobblestones.

"That's it," he said as he held out the chair for her, but he didn't sound like he approved. If anything, he had become more dour with every step.

She tilted her head, watching him—and everything

else she could see—as he settled down beside her. She'd never been served before, not like this. Not at a table outdoors by a waiter or a garçon. She knew the words, of course. Her mother had told her stories of Oxfordshire since the day she was born. But to finally experience it was exciting beyond belief.

He waited in silence, letting her gaze rove over everything. Soon they had tea and ices set before them. And he gestured for her to lift her spoon and take a taste.

Cold ice and sweet lemon flavor exploded in her mouth. It was too cold—enough to make her lips tingle—but she loved every second of it.

"Coo…" she murmured.

His jaw tightened. "Say marvelous."

"Marvelous."

"And sit up straight. Your corset isn't bone, and so you need to pretend as if it is."

She frowned, but tightened her back just as he'd ordered. It was going to be hard to maintain this posture all the time.

"I suppose I'll have to buy whalebone now, won't I?"

"Deuced uncomfortable, as I understand it."

She didn't speak. He was trying to make a point, but for the life of her, she couldn't understand what. So she just arched her brow and waited. In her experience, men could never keep themselves quiet for long. Not if they had something burning in their gut.

But in this, she was sadly out. He did nothing but eat his ice, gesture for her to serve the tea, and then glower. And he kept that up while she tried to look everywhere without appearing to really look.

"Sit up," he snapped.

She sighed, but straightened her back. "You're being very disagreeable."

"Learning to be a lady is very disagreeable." He set his arm on the table, leaning forward. "Most girls are at it their entire lives, and they hate it."

"Then why do it?"

He shrugged. "As well as ask why the sun rises in the east. Because it does. Because they do. Because that is what is expected of ladies."

Her gaze cut to his. "Then I had best start learning now."

"Or perhaps, give up—"

"Leave off," she snapped. "I am a legitimate lady. Granddaughter to the Earl of—"

"Your father died in school. Likely before you were even born."

She paused. A pair of gentlemen on horseback were riding through, splattering mud everywhere and laughing as an apple vendor cursed them. She could tell by the fine cut of their clothing that they were wealthy. No one could afford that much gold stitching unless they had money to spare. And that was nothing compared to the fine horseflesh they jerked about with no consideration for the poor beasts' mouths.

She was so busy frowning at the men that it took a moment for her to realize what Mr. Hallowsby had said. But when she did, her gaze cut back to his. "What?"

"I'm sorry. The second son of the Earl of Cavener died years ago of a fever."

She swallowed. Dead. Her father was dead. "No," she murmured.

"I'm sorry, Bluebell." Then he took a breath. "You have your paper. You're legitimate. And now we know why your father never came to find you. You can go back to Hull and—"

She slammed down her spoon, her pleasure from the dessert gone. "You have cast doubt everywhere you turn. I am tired of it. Leave if you want, but tomorrow, I go to London."

He threw up his hands. "To see what relation? Your father is long gone."

"Then I will speak with the earl."

"He won't see you." He reached forward to touch her hand, but she pulled angrily back. So he huffed out a breath and crossed his arms. "Think, Bluebell. You were sent away to Hull, your mother as well. Who do you think did that? The best possibility is that it was the earl. He will not acknowledge you now. In truth, he will do everything he can to discredit you in front of everyone, because he will not admit how badly you have been treated." He took a breath. "And that is the best possibility."

"Rubbish. Utter rubbish. I am legitimate, and he will acknowledge me." She said the words. Part of her swore the words, and then she lifted her chin and stared down her nose at Mr. Hallowsby. She did everything she knew to be intimidating, and it had no effect. He was steadfast in his regard. Just as she was sure in her plan. And so they waited, trying to stare each other down.

He shook his head. "It won't work, Bluebell. And it will only give you pain."

She didn't even bother responding. He knew what she intended.

And then, surprise of surprises, he finally relented. "Tell me everything, Bluebell. Absolutely everything."

She was in no mood to recount this, but she realized it was important she practice it on someone. She would have to relay it to the earl soon enough. And if her father was dead and gone these last years? There would be no one to swear that it was true. No one to stand by her side. And that terrified her.

"I grew up in Hull," she said, speaking her words carefully.

"If the banns were read in Oxfordshire, how did your mother get from here to there?"

She swallowed. "I asked Mum that when I was little. She told me such tales of Oxford, I wanted to see it. But Mum said she'd promised to keep us in Hull until later. I didn't know what later meant until a few months ago."

He waited, his expression shifting into narrowed eyes and a tight mouth. She didn't know what that meant, but as he didn't speak, she had little choice but to continue.

"Mum got sick last year, but it grew steadily worse through the winter. Come February, we both knew…" Her throat closed down. She couldn't voice it, but then she felt his hand over hers, heavy and comforting.

"She was all you had. I'm sorry that you lost her."

"One evening, she said it was time I knew the full story. I was old enough and would have to decide what to do when she was gone."

"What exactly did she say?"

"She said that when she was young, she was a maid working in the house of a don. There was a student,

Mr. Oscar Ballenger. He was the second son of the Earl of Cavener, and he was a kind and wonderful man."

"Or a good liar."

Maybelle glared at him. "I grow tired of your insults."

"I'm not insulting you." He leaned back. "I've been one of these boys. I spent my childhood among these spoiled, lying—"

"Not my father." Her words were clipped and loud. It was the volume that had him glancing around as he tightened his hold on her hand.

"Steady and quiet. A lady never raises her voice."

"If you are so sure I am not a lady, then why do you continue 'arping at me?" Her words were tight with fury.

"Harping. With an *h*."

"Harping, haranguing, harboring hatred. Horrible Hallowsby."

His lips twitched at that. "No one can fault your vocabulary."

Was that a compliment?

"But no one will notice if you forget your *h*'s."

"But you don't believe it's true. Even after seeing the church registry with your own eyes."

He sighed. "Bluebell—"

"Miss Maybelle Ballenger," she corrected acidly.

He swallowed and dipped his head. "Very well, Miss Ballenger, tell me the rest. Your mother said she grew up here, met a student who was the second son of the Earl of Cavener. What happened next?"

"He drew a picture of her and signed it with his name. He even wrote, 'To my love, Anna' on it."

"What picture?"

She debated showing it to him. It was her most private possession and had been on their mantel from her earliest memory. But in the end, she needed to show him every scrap of proof she had. Because someday soon, she would be showing it to the earl, and she needed to see how someone cruel and cynical like Mr. Hallowsby would react.

So she reached down and carefully pulled it out of her satchel. It was in its frame, but she had no glass to cover it. Even if they could have afforded it, it would have broken in her bag.

She moved aside the tea and ices on the table, then set it carefully before him. Then she pointed without actually touching the paper. "To my love, Anna. Oscar B."

He looked at it. With her eyes, she traced the soft lines of her mother's face. Jaw lifted, cheeks rounded, and eyes without wrinkles. She was laughing in the sunshine—or so she'd always imagined—and behind her were vague strokes like wisps of clouds.

Mr. Hallowsby turned the picture to study it more closely. She would have snatched it away if he had been casual with it, but his touch was delicate, his gestures slow.

"Not a talent, that's for sure, but definite education. And he cared for her, I can see that."

"He married her."

He looked up. "I believe you. I believe that your parents were married in the church, their names recorded in the registry just as we saw. But I do not think he was the second son of the Earl of Cavener."

"But it *is* my name. Maybelle Ballenger."

He nodded. "Perhaps a cousin? That would be great enough, wouldn't it? For your vicar's son?" His voice took on a harder edge, and for a moment she wondered exactly who he meant. What vicar's—oh!

Charles.

Yes. She supposed any connection to the earl would be enough for him and his father. So she nodded. "But I need to know the truth. Mum said they were married, but the earl would not approve. So they called the banns and told no one."

"You cannot keep such a thing a secret."

"Mum said they did. From his family. His older brother appeared as they were in the church. Richard Ballenger."

"That's the earl's heir."

"Then he can prove—"

"Died in an accident ten years ago." He sighed. "Don't you see? Anyone who will corroborate your story is gone. They're all gone, Bluebell. You're just a country girl making wild claims. The earl will not allow it. It would be the scandal of the Season."

She began to hesitate, difficulties she hadn't anticipated rising before her. But she didn't care. "There were others," she pressed. "The earl and countess arrived the very next day, but they were all too late. Mum and Dad were already married."

"And how much later were you born?"

She winced. She'd already made that calculation from the date in the registry. "Nearly eight months."

His gaze was heavy on her face, but she lifted her chin. Many children were born early in a marriage. They were still legitimate.

"Then how did you end up in Hull?"

And that, of course, was the question. "Mum said
that there was an ugly row. In the end, she was sent to
Hull. She had money that came in now and then, but
she was to claim to be a widow."

"Why would your mother agree to that? If everything was legal, she must have known what people
would think."

She had. She did. "She said my father was to join
them. After the earl calmed down. After he finished
his studies and could provide for them as a don. That
had been his plan. To be a don in Oxfordshire."

She thought briefly of the men in black robes she'd
seen earlier. That could have been her father, dressed
like that, bowed to like that. If he hadn't gotten sick.

"But he never came for her," Bram said softly.

Maybelle looked back at the sketch of her mother.
She read again the dedication and the signature. They
were getting hard to read, the pencil strokes faded over
twenty-four years.

"He loved her. Enough to defy everyone. If he
is gone now, then I will speak with the earl." She
lifted her gaze to Mr. Hallowsby. "I will make him
see me."

"How?"

She picked up the picture, stroking the frame
rather than her mother's face. Then she carefully
rewrapped it in muslin and returned it to her satchel
beside the letter from the vicar. And then she looked
at Mr. Hallowsby.

"You will make him."

He shook his head. "You haven't enough money
for that." Then he grabbed her hand. She wasn't going

to allow it, but he was quick. "Do you understand why I kept harping at you? Correcting your language, your posture, your everything?"

"Because you are mean and like pointing out faults."

"Because I am kind and know that what I said was nothing compared to what others will think in society. There is a whole world outside the *ton*, and it is vastly more comfortable than inside it. I only know a small part of the etiquette forced on young girls, and you will hate every correction, every rigid attire, and every ridiculous restriction. But that is the world of the *ton*."

"I don't care—"

"Let us say all of this is true. If you force the earl to recognize you as his legitimate granddaughter, what then?"

"I will have proof. I will be accepted."

"Back in Hull, perhaps. With the vicar's son, possibly. Not among the peerage."

"I don't care."

"But then, why do it? You can return now and have those things. The paper from the registry is all you need. No one will question it. You have enough proof."

It was true. She knew it. If all she wanted was a life with Charles, then she simply had to turn around now. She could go back to Hull and be content there. Have her life there.

But then she would never know why she hadn't grown up with a father to care for her. Why her mother had every night whispered a prayer to God that her husband come find her. "You think if I pursue this, I will discover it all to be a lie. That I am a bastard after all."

He didn't have to answer. She could see it in the

cut of his jaw. "I know the life of a bastard to the *ton*.
It is not for you, Miss Bluebell. Go home. Marry your
vicar's son. Do not—"

"I will go to see the earl." She wasn't entirely sure
where that conviction came from, except that it had
been growing inside her from the very first moment
her mother had informed her in February. Or perhaps
earlier, when she first overheard her mum's prayer for
her husband to come find them.

"Bluebell—"

"And you will make sure he sees me."

Mr. Hallowsby exhaled loudly and shook his head.
"And why would I do such a thing? I exist carefully,
Miss Ballenger, tolerated by the elite because I have
a purpose. It will do me no good to antagonize so
powerful an earl."

She could see the conviction in his face. She could
see that he was not only hard but growing more and
more inured to her. So she touched him. She grabbed
his fingers and clung to him, using what whiles she
had. "Bram, please. You will be bringing him his long
lost granddaughter."

"Whom he doesn't want to see."

"You don't know that." She needed more persua-
sion. "I could pay you."

He snorted. "You haven't enough money for that."

True enough. "Then you will do it simply because
you know my mother has been wronged. And you are
a man who rights wrongs."

He laughed at that. Long and loud, his attitude
derisive. She did not look away. In fact, she crossed
her arms and matched him sneer for sneer.

"You have me all wrong, Miss Bluebell."

"Truly? Look deep inside, Bram. Recall how you sneered at the gentlemen who churned mud in their wake as they rode hell for leather through the streets. Remember that you have gained a reputation for helping wronged ladies like my mother—cheated and lied to through no fault of their own. What did you call the boys around here? Arrogant churls who believe they can do anything with no consequence?"

"You know nothing of me." His tone was hard, his face like granite.

"Then tell me that you wouldn't like to see me—a dairy maid—set up as one of their own. True or not doesn't matter. Think on how my very presence will shame every one of them because I will be more beautiful, more ladylike, and more proper than every single one."

His brows arched at that. "You are a sow's ear, Miss Bluebell. You will never be one of them."

She winced. She couldn't help it, his words hurt. But then, she had been called that and worse her whole life. "I will. You will see." Then she leaned forward. "Please, Bram, please help me."

She waited for his answer. A nod. A breath. A flicker of his eye. Anything to tell the truth of his thoughts.

And she waited.

And waited.

Fourteen

BRAM EXPERIENCED A STRANGE MOMENT OF ABSOLUTE clarity. It wasn't just that he saw the determination in the deluded woman sitting across from him. Or that he noted the grizzled man across the street buying from the apple vendor. Or the birds in the trees as they chirped their bird noises to each other. He felt the breeze on his face and knew the stench of the shit-laden mud nearby.

And he also knew that he had a choice.

She saw him as a knight avenger of old. An idiot of the Round Table instead of a bastard with fast fists existing on the fringe of society. He was well used to people seeing what they wanted in him. Dicky saw him as a protector. Cara had seen him as a sap. And both had wanted to exploit him.

Bluebell was no different than they. He was a means to her end as well, and yet something in her words called to him. Like a trumpet sound to battle. Or the offer of a sword and shield. He could almost feel the weight of the armor she put on him as she asked him to rise to a noble cause. He could expose the wrong done to her mother. He could give her peace, if not exactly happiness.

"This will not turn out as you want," he rasped, startled by how thick his throat was, how heavy the words in his mouth.

"Of course it will," she answered blithely. "As you pointed out, I already have what I need from the vicar. I am legitimate."

"Then why face the earl? He's a crotchety blighter. Never a kind word to anyone."

She smiled at him, actually smiled. As if being reviled by a powerful man meant nothing. "But I will speak with him. I will demand justice for me and my mother. I will look him in the eye and say my piece."

He shook his head. "It is a fool's errand that will only end in tears."

She dropped her chin on her fist, staring at him with an open expression. "You're growing tiresome."

"You're not sitting up straight."

"You'll do it." It wasn't a question.

"What makes you so sure?"

She smiled again. A pure and simple smile. Her bonnet had fallen back, so the sun sparkled in her blue eyes and turned her hair to gold. He saw the curving bow of her mouth and the white of her even teeth.

Did he become her knight and fight for her justice? Or did he walk away?

She was right, damn her eyes. He was going to help her. Even he wasn't entirely sure why, except that there was a flame she kindled to life inside him. A warmth or an idiocy, he wasn't sure which. But he liked the idea of doing something noble.

It should frighten him that he'd felt this same fire years ago with Cara. It should bother him that

Bluebell kindled the same thirst for justice in his heart.
It did bother him. And yet he could not stop himself.
Blond women with blue eyes and sweet smiles. They
were his downfall. Especially if they had a cause.

"I cannot do it alone," he finally said.

She arched her brows, her smile widening into a
grin. "Certainly we can—"

"But I know who will help. She can polish the
worst of your rough edges and get us access."

"How?"

He shrugged. "If I knew that, I wouldn't need Eleanor."

He pushed up from the table. "Come on. We still
need to get to London."

❧

The ride to London was the most miserable experience of her life. It wasn't that they were shoved
together on the inside of a mail coach this time. That
was hard enough, but Mr. Hallowsby quizzed her on
every inconsequential and ridiculous thing he could
possibly dream up. How did one sit in the company of
an earl? How did one use a fan when sharing tea? How
did one stand without fidgeting in skirts that itched?

And when she complained of the ridiculousness of
his questions, he merely said that Lady Eleanor would
demand far worse, so she'd best get used to it.

She wanted to tell him to go to the devil. She
wanted to look about her on the road to London and
see everything without listening to a word he said. But
she truly did want to know what to do if the gentleman sitting next to her stank of vomit. And what were
the rudiments of breeding a good hunting dog?

"I cannot see how this is important," she said for perhaps the thousandth time. "Why don't you ask me about mathematics or sheep husbandry?"

"Because not a soul will care if you know about that." Then he cast a glaring eye at the young man who sat stuffed in the coach along with them. "And what do you know about sheep?" She assumed the question was for her rather than the young man, who flushed and looked away.

"I grew up in Hull," she said tartly. "We all know about sheep."

"Of course," he said. "Don't tell anyone about that. In fact, don't claim to be from Hull at all."

"I am not going to lie to my grandfather!" she snapped.

He nodded slowly. "True. He will expect you to lie, so you should confuse him with the truth."

"But—"

"My mother was a courtesan. I was there when she counseled others in her trade. I was there as a boy, watching as she dealt with drunken protectors and their kin, who thought she was available for anything they wanted. This was what she taught." His eyes darkened. "London and the elite are very different than anything you can imagine."

"I can imagine a great deal," she groused.

"Then imagine yourself going through the steps of a quadrille."

"A what?"

He turned and gaped at her. "Good Lord, you do not know how to dance."

She threw up her hands. "There wasn't much call

for it in Hull. No matter how much I hummed, the
sheep refused to do the patterns."

His lips twitched, but it didn't soften his glare.
"You'll have to learn that immediately. One misstep,
and you shall be branded a provincial."

She sighed. She *was* a provincial, and she began
to doubt that all his education would change that.
And that thought began to chip away at her confidence. "Bram, I am tired. Please, can you not stop
for a bit?"

"And that's another thing. Gentlemen, as a rule, are
boring. You will have to feign interest even if you are
ready to drop dead on your feet."

She dropped her head back against the flat squabs.
"I will not be talking to gentlemen, Bram. I will be
speaking to my grandfather."

"Who will either rail at you or refuse the door."

"Neither of which is boring in the least."

He huffed out a breath. "I am trying to teach you."

"No," she said wearily. "You're trying to frighten
me." She looked down at her clenched fists and consciously opened them. "And it's working."

"Well, of course—" He stopped himself, narrowing
his eyes as he glared at her. She didn't respond. She
just looked back, relaxing enough to let some of her
fears show on her face. She was a girl from Hull. What
did she know about confronting an earl? One week
ago, she didn't even know anyone who'd spoken with
an earl, much less claimed an association with one.
Other than her mother, of course.

"This is a mad scheme," he said softly. But then he
touched her hand. She'd tightened it into a fist again,

and he soothed the fingers open. "But if anyone can do it, it's you."

She nodded and let the warmth of his hand seep into hers. She breathed softly once, twice. She inhaled his scent to her soul and let it stay there, supporting her. And in this way, she finally relaxed. Which is when he started quizzing her again. All the way to Grosvenor Square.

So she gave him her back and stared out the window. They were getting to the most interesting part of the drive. Houses near enough to see into each other's windows. Another mail coach so large she could barely believe it. People wearing colorful clothing right next to someone in rags. All things she had never seen before, every mile bringing something new.

"It's bad form to be pressed up against the glass like a country git."

She glared at him, willing him to soften, just this once. It didn't work, not even when she relied on her pleading expression. Big eyes, slight pout, even a strategic blink that suggested tears.

He laughed at her. "Be sure to use that on your grandfather. It might work on him, though I doubt it. Your eyes are pretty, but they're not quite big enough for that."

"Did you just call my eyes small?"

"No. I said they're not big enough for the weeping kitten look. Not without cosmetics. But then, Eleanor will teach you all about that."

Soon they were at the London coaching inn, and suddenly, Maybelle was struck dumb with terror. So many people! So much confusion! If she were here alone, she wasn't sure she could manage it. But Bram knew exactly how to go on. He commanded a hackney and escorted her to its door, handing her up when she was cowering inside like a terrified kitten. A moment later, he was inside the smelly thing with her.

"Almost done," he said, obviously trying to be soothing. Except she knew this had been the easiest part. Getting to London was not so hard. Getting to her grandfather would be the challenge. But first she had to meet his Eleanor.

The carriage maneuvered expertly through the crowded streets, avoiding vendors, children, and rubbish alike. And while her stomach rumbled at the smell of meat pies, it was soon turned by the scent of steaming offal mixed with spoiled fruit. Every scent imaginable found its way into the carriage, and she was both fascinated and appalled by it. And extremely grateful when they finally made it to a quieter neighborhood.

The vendors disappeared, the clothing on the people became fancier, and the houses grew larger even as they tucked tightly together. She even saw a tree or two, which was like a balm to her eyes. She hadn't realized how much she loved the towering greenery until it was gone.

And then they stopped moving.

She'd been gawking out the window, her eyes actually tired from all the staring. The view when they'd stopped was of a narrow house of five stories. She couldn't imagine living in something so grand! And on the front door sat a massive knocker in the shape of an eagle.

She felt the shift in the carriage as the driver set the brake and climbed down. Then the door was pulled open, and it was time. And just like before when she couldn't climb into Mr. Bray's cart, she sat there frozen. Just a tiny movement was all she'd need. Just a single push, and she could go again. But she sat there and wondered if she could even breathe.

Bram shifted beside her, but he didn't push. And for the first time this day, he was patience itself as he waited for her to decide.

"Don't say it," she hissed. "Don't say that I can still turn back."

"I don't need to. You just did."

She glared at him. "Bugger."

He chuckled, but his words were firm. "None of that now. If you must curse—and ladies do not curse—say something sweet like *cakes*!"

She blinked at him. "You want me to say 'cake' when I'm angry?"

"I want you to say nothing at all, but I've learned that's not possible. Is 'licorice' better?"

"I've never heard of that. Is it a sweet?"

His eyes widened. "Never heard of licorice. You have had a hard life, haven't you?"

She didn't know how to answer that. She was cross with him for picking at her all day. She was cross with herself for sitting frozen like a bump on a log. And now she was cross because she didn't know what a silly sweet was and had never had it.

Then the driver apparently had enough. "'Ere now. Out ye go."

Her gaze cut to the grizzled man, and she tried to smile. Damnation, her mouth was weak. It trembled as her cheeks pulled.

"Don't be sick in me carriage!" he snapped. "Come on. Out!"

"We'll be just a moment. Here," said Bram, handing over double the coin than she thought necessary. Then he maneuvered around her to step out first. "Look your fill right now," he said in a low voice. "But the moment you step out of the carriage, you lift your chin and look bored."

"I'll never understand why you think ladies aren't ever excited about anything. Everyone feels happy about something. Or excited or mad or—"

His heavy sigh interrupted her, and she buttoned her lip. She had enough experience with men to know that when they ceased prattling and just sighed, you'd pushed them too far. So she grew quiet, lifted her chin, and held out her hand.

He took it with a look of surprise and then helped her out of the carriage. But once on the walkway, her breath caught. Outside, the buildings looked four times as large, and the fierce brass eagle even more frightening. But it wasn't until after they knocked and a blank-faced butler opened the door that she became truly intimidated.

Inside was every lush and expensive thing in the world. Every decorative vase, every brass accent, and even the walls were gleaming bright with expensive beauty. Suddenly, she remembered that she'd been sweating in the heat of the carriage. That her clothing, even new, hadn't been as crisp as the butler's coat. That she'd never possessed gloves as white as his or seen a staircase that rose endlessly before her.

She swallowed, and her grip on Mr. Hallowsby's

arm tightened. He spoke to the man, his words echoing awkwardly in her brain.

"Good evening, Seelye. I wonder, is my sister about?"

Sister?

"Good evening, Mr. Hallowsby. Please wait here. I shall see if Lady Eleanor is at home to you and…?" It took a moment for Maybelle to realize he was asking for her name. She was still stuck on the fact that his sister was *Lady* Eleanor.

Fortunately, he was quick-witted. "Miss Maybelle Ballenger requests a word, if she has the time."

"Of course, sir." The butler glanced behind him at a footman in pristine livery. The man took a sharp turn on his heel and began mounting the stairs. Meanwhile, the butler held out his hands.

Maybelle had no idea what he was doing until Mr. Hallowsby began stripping off his hat and gloves.

"Oh," she gasped, then colored up to her ears. She was not a country git to be standing about gaping. So taking herself firmly in hand, she snapped her mouth shut and pulled off her bonnet and gloves. Her dress was sadly crushed, but there was nothing to do about that. She was to act like a lady, and hadn't Bram been telling her that attitude meant everything? Haughty. She had to be haughty and remember her *h*'s.

"This way, if you please," intoned the butler as he led them at a snail's pace to a parlor stuffed to the brim with old things. Porcelain, brass, silk—all in a complicated display of history that confused her. She had few names for them, except that she suspected they were true artifacts. Furniture sat on by royalty, clocks that kept accurate time on the mantels, and paintings done by masters hanging on the walls.

She stood in the middle of the parlor and wondered if she was allowed to sit. Were grand ladies even allowed to sit where royalty had once been?

Haughty, she reminded herself. And so she took herself to the settee. Her bum had nearly connected with the cushions when Mr. Hallowsby spoke. "Seelye, are the duke and duchess at home? I have not yet made my bow to them and would welcome the opportunity."

Maybelle froze, a curse word choked off in her throat. This was the residence of a duke and duchess? This… Oh, shite. Did she sit or not? She couldn't hang out here all day in a crouch.

In the end, gravity decided for her. Her knees gave out, and she landed with a soft *umph* on velvet cushions. At least she didn't break the furniture. That would have been embarrassing indeed.

"Their Graces are not at home," the butler said gravely.

"Perhaps next time, then. Thank you, Seelye."

"Mr. Hallowsby. Miss Ballenger." The man bowed slightly, then backed out of the room. But he remained at the doorway like an expertly clad sentinel able to hear everything that was said.

Meanwhile, Maybelle cast a terrified look at Mr. Hallowsby and mouthed, "Duke? Duchess?"

He nodded, his lips curved into a smirk. She knew what he was thinking. Would she run? Would she call everything quits and head back to Hull and Charlie?

Part of her desperately wanted to. What could a father—or grandfather—give her now that she didn't already have? Except answers to a lifetime of questions.

No, she wouldn't turn tail and—

"Lady Eleanor," the butler announced from the doorway.

"Bram! My goodness, you look like you've been sitting in a dust storm."

The most gorgeous woman she'd ever seen floated into the room. She didn't seem to walk. Her movements were so smooth, her expression so serene, she might have been a ghostly apparition except that she was very much alive as she held out her hands to Mr. Hallowsby.

"Very much like a storm, I'm afraid," he said as he took her hands and kissed the back of each one. "The road to London is not paved with gold, but mud, dust, and things much worse. You must forgive my dirt."

"I always have," she said with a beatific smile. "Because you always bring such tales when you come." Then she turned to Maybelle. "And are you, perhaps, part of his latest adventure?"

Maybelle rose to her feet, forcing herself to pretend to a nobility she didn't feel. Just so long as she didn't get sick on the rug, she could carry this off.

She dipped into a small curtsy. "Miss Maybelle Ballenger, my lady." Then she held out her hands as she'd seen Lady Eleanor do. "I'm so pleased to meet you."

The woman stared at her, and there was a moment when Maybelle thought a frown was forming. But no actual displeasure pinched the woman's brows. Instead, she took Maybelle's hands in hers and held them there, all the while looking at her face.

"Well, I can tell there is at least a tale here."

Mr. Hallowsby leaned back against the mantel. "It is not mine to tell."

Lady Eleanor cast him a glance. "No, you never tell. Very well…" She released Maybelle's hands. "I've called for tea. Will you not share some with me?"

It wasn't a real question, and so Maybelle didn't answer. She simply took her seat on the settee and prayed none of the dirt on her dress found its way onto the velvet. And while they waited for the tea tray to appear, Lady Eleanor smiled at Bram.

"It's beastly hot, is it not? I'd be in the country, you know. I can't abide London at this time of year, but His Grace thought it would be best if he summered there. And since the duke must take his duchess, I chose to stay here."

"Is that affection I hear in your tone?" Mr. Hallowsby asked. "For the sailor turned duke?"

Lady Eleanor opened her perfect mouth, but then shut it with a silent shrug.

"You are set on enduring," Mr. Hallowsby said in a dry tone.

"What else can I do?" she returned serenely.

Show some emotion, perhaps? Be happy or angry or sad. Something to show that she was human and not porcelain come to life? Maybelle sat and watched the woman with fascination. She could hardly believe that Lady Eleanor was a real person. Everything about her was so perfect. Her dress, her movements, even her smile was smooth and flat.

How very odd.

Meanwhile, the butler came in, walking in measured steps. Given the bustle that she'd seen in the streets of

London, Maybelle couldn't understand how these two were so slow. The tray was set down, the lady nodded formally, and then she leaned forward to pour.

"Miss Ballenger, can I offer you some tea? How do you like it?"

Maybelle took a moment to understand. Her first thought was to answer, "With hot water." But she saw sugar and cream on the tray, not to mention a lemon sliced neatly in half. What riches! "Um, a squeeze of lemon, if you please."

"My father used to like it strong too. None of that sweet nonsense, he used to say."

Yes, that was the reason, she thought, her lips tight to keep from giving in to a hysterical giggle. It wasn't that they couldn't afford sweets. Cream sometimes, but never for something as mundane as tea.

"Bram? You prefer it almost white, don't you?"

"I do like cream," he said as she poured, then passed him the cup.

Was this polite conversation? Tea? Dust? She took a sip and tried to keep her mind quiet and her senses alert. She drank. She nibbled at some cakes so light that she'd never thought anything could taste so empty. Meanwhile, brother and sister discussed who had left London, who had remained. Who had married whom and when.

"And what of Lord Linsel?"

"Gone. He left me in Hull, which is where I met Miss Ballenger."

"He left you? But—"

"He became frightened."

"And well he should be. Were you in danger?"

Mr. Hallowsby didn't answer with anything more than a shrug. His sister, however, narrowed her eyes and then turned to her.

"Miss Ballenger, you must tell me. Was he in true danger?"

"Three men appeared with pistols. A bear of a man and two ugly men standing on either side. Terrifying." She didn't need to fake her shudder.

"With pistols?" the lady cried, her eyes wide as she turned to her brother. "*Pistols?*"

"There wasn't any danger."

"There was," insisted Maybelle. She had lost patience with sitting like a bump on a log. It was time for her to add to the conversation. "But Mr. Hallowsby tricked them, and Lord and Lady Linsel were able to escape."

"My goodness. How did you trick them? Was it like that last time? Did you punch them insensate?"

Mr. Hallowsby sighed. "No, Eleanor—"

"Of course not," the lady said, tapping a finger on her teacup. "That wouldn't be a trick, would it? Now, don't tell me. Let me see if I can guess."

"Eleanor, we didn't come here to—"

"I have it. You distracted them somehow. You found someone who looked like Dicky and Clarissa, and the brutes followed them instead." She looked to Maybelle. "Was that it?"

"No, my lady."

"Hmmm. But he could have done that. He's done that before with an extremely dangerous murderer."

"Really?" Maybelle looked to Mr. Hallowsby, who was right then rolling his eyes.

"No—"

"He's just being modest. It was the talk of the *ton* for at least a week. Set up a decoy, and the murderer ran after the wrong person."

"But wasn't the decoy in danger?"

"Of course, but he was very fleet of foot. Got away. The murderer got lost on the London streets, and Bram was able to come up behind him and…" She clapped her hands, the sound reverberating in the room.

Maybelle felt her eyes widen as she stared at Mr. Hallowsby. "What did you do?"

He started to answer, but Lady Eleanor interrupted. "Bram killed him, of course. The man was vile. Evil incarnate. The constable was very impressed and gave Bram a medal."

"Really?"

"No, not really," said Mr. Hallowsby, clearly exasperated.

"Bram never talks about it," said his sister. "Bad form and all to talk about the people he protects. He's very secretive, you know."

No, she didn't know. He'd never seemed that way to her. Especially if she took the time to listen to him carefully. But Lady Eleanor was too busy talking over his exploits to even look at the way Bram was shaking his head.

"Eleanor, please, can we get back to the business at hand?"

"No, no. I'm still working out what you did to help Dicky."

"I gave them Dicky's gold, that's what, and off they went. They got what they wanted, Dicky and his wife stayed unharmed, and I managed to get paid."

Eleanor frowned at him. "Well, that's not very sporting."

Maybelle was also frowning. "And not exactly what happened at all. He only pretended to give away all Lord Linsel's money."

"Oh! Very clever. And after Dicky got away, did you pursue the brutes? Do away with them?"

Mr. Hallowsby sighed. "When did you get so bloodthirsty, Eleanor?"

"I bet you beat them most soundly for daring to threaten anyone you protected." She turned to Maybelle. "He did, didn't he? He won't say, so you'll have to."

"I don't know," Maybelle answered slowly. "I never saw the men again."

"Well, of course not. Bram took care of them."

"But—" Maybelle began.

"Eleanor," he interrupted. "Miss Ballenger is here to ask for your help."

"Is she under your care, then?" Eleanor asked. "Is she in danger?" The woman sounded excited by the idea.

"No danger," Mr. Hallowsby said firmly.

Maybelle shifted in her seat. "And it was my mother who was wronged, we think."

Lady Eleanor set her cup down, her eyes bright. "Tell me everything."

Fifteen

BRAM WATCHED ELEANOR CLOSELY AS BLUEBELL TOLD her tale. She did it with a storyteller's natural talent, adding enough detail to make it sound real, and even letting her voice catch when she spoke of her mother. He knew he was being cynical. In truth, he knew she truly mourned her mother and believed in the tale she told. But that didn't stop him from admiring her ability to bring everyone—including him—deeply into her story.

Except for the one clear problem that he couldn't stop himself from saying aloud.

"Was there a second son, Eleanor? I cannot remember clearly. A boy named Oscar?"

"Who died at school? Yes, yes, I think that was it," Eleanor answered, her brows drawn together. "I can't remember for sure. It happened when I was a child, but I recall hearing that it made the earl bitter." She turned to him. "Bram, do you not remember any of it?"

He shook his head. "I'm barely older than you, and I did not run in the same circle."

"Well, of course not. At that age, neither of us

knew anything but our nannies." She frowned. "His name might have been Oscar."

"Which is why he never came for my mother. That's why—"

Bram held up his hand. "Don't get ahead of yourself. We don't know if that's really the man."

"But it all fits," Bluebell pressed. She pushed to her feet. "I want to talk to him."

"But he died—" said Eleanor.

"Not my father. My grandfather. He's alive, yes?"

"Most definitely," his sister said. "And in town, I believe. He prefers the city."

Bluebell turned to him, her chin lifted in that imperious way of hers. "Take me to him. Please."

Bram set down his teacup with a click. "I told you. You can't just burst in on the man. He won't see you."

Eleanor, thankfully, agreed. "He's right, you know. If your story is true—"

"If!"

"Then it needs to be handled appropriately. Oh!" She turned back to him. "That's why you're here. That's why you came to me. To get the introduction right and to give her some polish beforehand."

Well, truthfully, he'd come here because she knew everything about everyone in the *ton*. He'd expected her to have some idea of what could have happened. Despite everything he'd said to Bluebell, he sincerely doubted this errand would go anywhere. Legitimate children—even daughters—just didn't grow up in Hull forgotten by everyone. And if they did, they stayed buried in Hull and didn't demand to be heard.

Meanwhile, Bluebell was looking at him. "That's not exactly it, is it?" she challenged.

He shrugged, unwilling to confess that he still doubted her quest despite the growing evidence that supported her claim. So he looked to his half sister instead. "Can you do it? She's got no money, but it wouldn't take much. A borrowed gown. An invitation to tea?"

Eleanor nodded slowly. "You saw the church register yourself?"

"Yes," they answered together. And for added emphasis, Bluebell handed over the vicar's letter.

Eleanor read it quickly, then passed it back. She'd already seen the sketch supposedly done by Oscar Ballenger. Then she looked first at Bluebell, then Bram. He waited, his belly tight. If Eleanor refused to help, then they were at a dead end. The earl was notoriously full of his own consequence. Bram was known as a bastard. He and anyone with him would never be accepted into the house.

Finally, Eleanor nodded. "I'll do it."

Bluebell released a breath. "Thank you, my lady."

But Bram shook his head. There was more. There was always more. "Why?"

"Two reasons. First, because you'll pay me a thousand pounds."

"Wot?" gasped Bluebell.

"You know we don't have that much." It was a lie. He had that much, but he had other plans for that money.

"It's a pittance if he recognizes you. You'll be outfitted and squired about at the coming Season."

Bram shook his head. "You know that won't happen."

"On the contrary. I wager my time and influence that it will happen, provided, of course, everything you've told me is true."

"It's the absolute truth," Bluebell said. "I swear it."

Unfortunately for Bluebell, Eleanor was looking at him. "Bram?"

"She believes it," he finally said.

"And you'll be looking into the rest." It wasn't a question. If Eleanor took up Bluebell's cause, she would expect him to find and eliminate any resistance to their plan. It's what his reputation said he was able to do.

"I'll do what I can," he promised.

"Excellent," she said with a succinct nod. "I won't expect anything until she's recognized."

"Then my grandfather will pay it," Bluebell said, her words soft and hesitant. As if she couldn't quite believe it would happen. Smart woman. He absolutely doubted its possibility as well. But right now, they were carried forward on Eleanor's certainty.

"One more thing," the woman said, her eyes dancing with excitement.

"We don't have anything else—" he began, but she folded her hands together and hit him with her most delighted smile.

"I want the truth, Bram. How did you really get Lord Haims to dower his bastard?"

Bram groaned. "You know the truth. I just talked to him."

"I don't believe it. The man is an ass. He'd never pay that exorbitant an amount unless you did something dire." She looked over to Bluebell. "That is the only reason I have any hope of your scheme succeeding. Bram has already done it, you see. Lord Haims had a girl by his mistress, but refused to take care of her. Wouldn't educate her or anything. Bram got him not only to send her to an excellent finishing school—at least for an illegitimate daughter—but also to dower her. The girl married a barrister, of all things. They're quite happy, and she's increasing last I heard. So you see, he's done it before."

But he didn't get the man to legitimize the child. And he certainly hadn't convinced Haims to marry the mistress. That was what he'd been hired to do, but even then he'd known it wasn't possible. He got the mistress money, and most importantly, helped the girl build as good a life as she could have.

"I just talked to him, Eleanor." And threatened to expose certain predilections for being tied up and spanked. As a rule, Bram didn't care what a man did in his leisure time. But certain high-ranking politicos did not want their peccadillos exposed. And given Bram's overblown reputation for exposing spies and murderers, Bram was the only man in England who would be believed if he claimed Lord Haims liked to be spanked.

But he'd promised not to reveal that, and so he had held off Eleanor no matter what the cost. Even as she kept pushing.

"You must have hit him," she said. "But there weren't any bruises. Did you hurt his dog?"

"What? Why would I touch—?"

"It's well known that he adores that dog more than his wife. You must have at least threatened his dog. Did you catch him alone? In a dark alley where you had already chained up his animal?"

"Of course not! I went to his house, Eleanor."

"Of course you did. The dog was already there."

"I didn't touch his dog!"

"But you wouldn't have to, would you? Just threaten it."

He let his head drop back as he glared at the ceiling. Good Lord, now he would have to make up something ridiculous just to satisfy Eleanor's lurid curiosity. But it was Bluebell who spoke next.

"Did he have gambling debts?"

Bram shrugged. Nothing out of the ordinary. "A few."

"And did you throw your knife at him?"

His head snapped up. "What?"

But it was too late. Bluebell had already taken up the tale for him, doing what everyone seemed to do. She was spinning an imaginary story that would be absorbed into the legion of ridiculous stories that already abounded.

"You know he can do that, right? Take a knife from his hip and fling it dead center, quick as a wink."

"Dead. Center." Eleanor breathed the words like she was speaking holy text.

"Oh yes. I watched him skewer any number of trees."

"Trees? Why ever would you hit trees?"

"He was defending me from a massive pig. They're quite dangerous in the country, you know. Largest pig I've ever seen. I could have been trampled to death."

Well, that was probably true. Damned thing was huge.

Meanwhile, Eleanor was hanging on every word. "But he threw his knives to frighten the pig? Brilliant!"

Bluebell was nodding, her glance flicking to his

before looking away. So she knew she was allowing Eleanor to spin another story out of whole cloth. But his half sister was more discerning than most.

"Is that what you did to Lord Haims? Threw your knife at him?"

"I only learned the skill recently and am not very good at it."

"He's marvelous," Bluebell said.

Eleanor nodded. "He tries to keep what he does a secret, but everyone knows. He'll never admit to it. Keeps his enemies guessing." She leaned forward. "Did you see him breathe fire?"

"What? No!"

"Learned it from a gypsy. When he needs to, he can incinerate them with his breath."

Bluebell didn't speak, obviously trying to accept such a preposterous statement. Meanwhile, Eleanor was looking back at him.

"So is that what you did to Lord Haims?"

"Which? Throw my knives or incinerate him with my foul breath."

Eleanor giggled in that musical way she had. It was obviously practiced. When she was little she had a laugh like a braying donkey. "Either one. Or both!"

He sighed, deciding to tell the full truth this time. "I simply know a secret about him. I said I knew a way to get it exposed if he didn't do what was right and moral by his child. And a man who was trying to lead the country ought to lead by example and take responsibility for his offspring."

"What was the secret?"

"Gambling debt, most likely," said Bluebell.

Eleanor shook her head. "Too many people would know about that. And entire fortunes have been won and lost on the green baize. Nothing could be more common."

Bluebell nodded, though she was obviously thinking hard. "Not if he bought up the markers. Imagine the scandal if he lost his fortune to a bastard."

Eleanor's eyes widened. "Of course. Of course!"

If he'd managed to collect the markers for a fortune, he'd have done it. He'd buy a small property outside of London and live in peace with a dozen dogs. And he certainly wouldn't have been traveling to Hull with Dicky and Clarissa. But logic didn't seem to have any sway here.

"Ladies, if I share, then Lord Haims will take back his support. And Jenny deserves better."

Eleanor lifted her hands. "She's married, and the dowry already paid. What could—"

Bluebell reached forward, touching Eleanor's arm. "But don't you see? Her husband is a barrister. Couldn't Lord Haims malign him? Make it so he couldn't work?"

Eleanor nodded. "Yes, yes, I suppose so. But I won't tell."

"It don't work that way," Bluebell said. "He can't tell a soul."

Which was the perfect way to silence Eleanor. Not the statement. He'd said something similar time and again, but everyone swore they wouldn't tell. They could keep a secret. Which is exactly what Eleanor would have said if only Bluebell had used correct English.

But she hadn't. And so Eleanor narrowed her eyes and released a sigh of disappointment. "So she hasn't been gently reared."

"Of course she has," Bram said. "But it was in Hull."

"Well, we can't say that. No one of any interest ever comes from Hull."

"I'm a good Christian soul!" Bluebell cried.

Eleanor waved that aside. "I thought you were speaking too clearly. I knew it wasn't natural for you."

"Of course it is," Bluebell said, proving the point by speaking slowly and clearly.

"She's been practicing," Bram began.

"Not enough."

True. "But that's why you're here. You're going to help her."

She shook her head. "I was just trying to measure how far I would have to go to train her. Apparently, she knows nothing."

"I know a lot!"

Eleanor didn't even look at Bluebell as she scolded. "Don't raise your voice. If we're to convince the earl you are the real thing, you must perform exactly as the lady you claim to be. He'll only go so far."

"I'm his grandchild."

"And if you appear no better than a Cockney rat, he'll toss you aside for fear of anyone associating him with you. If you don't make the man bend far, he might be willing to accept you."

"But I am his grandchild."

"And when," Bram interrupted, his tone cold, "have you ever been served by the truth?"

There were layers to his words that he hoped she'd understand. After all, she'd just helped spin a tale about his exploits. More than one, if he included the nonsense about Dicky's escape and the damned pig.

She had to know that everywhere—including her little village in Hull—no one cared about the truth. It was only the reputation.

She grimaced. "I will practice harder."

Eleanor nodded. "See that you do." Then she turned to him. "Very well, Bram. Leave her to me. Send word when you have done what is needed."

He blinked at her. "What is needed?"

"Yes, yes. You'll have to intimidate the earl somehow. Frighten his dog or gather whatever secrets you have on him. I think he's fond of his horses."

"What kind of man do you think I am to threaten horseflesh?"

"One who will stop at nothing to see justice done for Miss Ballenger."

He grimaced. "I am not a miracle worker."

Bluebell gave him a smile. The kind that lit up her face. And the room. And his organ. "Yes, you are," she said staunchly. "And you've already promised to help any way you can."

"I have," he said irritably. "I brought you to Eleanor."

"Exactly," the ladies cried together. It was disconcerting.

Meanwhile, Eleanor waved to Seelye, who had somehow appeared at the door. "Now leave her to me while you do what you do."

He shook his head. "I can't do anything."

"Of course not," his sister said. Then she had the audacity to wink at him. "Your secret is safe with me."

"And with me!" Bluebell said, her eyes sparkling with happiness.

And on that ridiculous note, he was shown to the door. Which was bad enough.

Indeed, he was still fuming about the silliness of his life when he stepped into his front hallway and nearly tripped over Dicky and Clarissa.

"Bloody hell."

Sixteen

"REALLY, BRAM," DICKY SAID WITH AN IRRITATED sniff. "Your manners have become deplorable. One does not swear in front of a lady."

What lady? he nearly snapped. But he feared if he lost his temper with these two, he'd never regain his equilibrium. "How did you get in here?"

"Your landlady let us in." Dicky spoke with the drawl that indicated what he'd said was obvious. "Not much of a butler, but sweet enough. The tea was good." He gestured to the full tea service set out before them.

"I've told you," Clarissa cut in, her voice tart. "In his situation, he has to make do. You can't expect proper servants from…oh. Well, you know."

From a bastard. Bloody hell. He looked back at the room toward the rear of the house where his landlady lived. He occupied a set of rooms upstairs. All was quiet enough with the woman retired for the night. But that still didn't mean he wanted these two mucking things up right here where he lived.

He glared back at the two, sitting as if this were a proper social visit. Except he'd never visit with anyone who looked so bedraggled. The two of them had obviously been caught in the rain—or gone swimming in the ocean—and then had the cloth dry on their bodies. Clarissa's hair was beyond repair, though she'd obviously attempted to tie up the knots with sad bits of ribbon. The only things still pristine about her were her sapphires. They still sparkled bright on her neck, though she'd lost an earbob. And as he watched, she fondled the stones once again.

Nervous habit, that. She ought to stop. But then Dicky would have to stop caressing the enormous belly of...

"What the devil is that?"

Clarissa clucked her tongue at his language, but Dicky just held up an enormous clock for him to see. It was a shepherdess with three fat sheep, one of whom had that enormous belly. It took less than a second for him to realize what had happened.

"Good God, did you put the money in that?"

"Shhh!" Dicky hissed. "The crockery broke. Can't trust anything made by a Scot, you know. So we thought this would be better. And Clary here had the idea to dress the part. See how her bonnet matches?" He gestured to the side table where an enormous bonnet sat. Clarissa obliged by putting it on and bat ting her eyes. Which might have worked if she didn't look like a drowned rat.

"I was a shepherdess at a masquerade once, and everyone said I was the prettiest one there," she said.

"Most definitely," agreed Dicky. Then he grinned at Bram. "That's where we got the idea, you see."

Oh no. No, no, no, no, no. He did not want to

know the plan. But Dicky just kept talking, and there was nothing Bram could do to stop him.

"We tried the boat, you see. Even got on the little one to row out to the big one, but Clary was so nervous, and her stomach was tetchy. She didn't like the little boat."

"I don't like boats at all," she sniffed.

"Yes, well, the rower was terrible, you see. And Clary was clutching at my hand, but I was holding on to the crockery. Then there was this wave—"

"At least seven feet tall!"

"Undoubtedly!"

Bollocks, thought Bram, but he still hadn't the wherewithal to stop them.

"And I dropped the crockery, you see."

"It broke. All those pieces and the coins and the notes—"

"Flying everywhere, and Clary and me trying to grab them."

"And the sailors—"

"And well, as I said, it's terrible hard to get decent folk, you know. And sailors are the worst lot."

"Terrible thieves."

"We got some of it, you see."

"But the wave came and—"

"Blasted sailor was more interested in my money than rowing the boat."

"And… And…" Apparently, Clarissa could barely pull herself together enough to voice the last of it. So Bram did it for her, though it was only a guess.

"Capsized, did you?"

"Into the ocean!" she wailed.

Dicky patted her hand. "Lost everything, you see. But what notes we could clutch as we waded to shore."

"Waded?" Bram asked.

Dicky's words were rushed, proving that it was a lie. "Swam. We swam to shore."

"I nearly drowned!" Clarissa gasped.

Not if they were close enough to shore to wade back in. Bloody hell.

"Well," continued Dicky, "nothing on Earth would induce me back into the water after that. Not with those thieves!"

Bram folded his arms. "Lost your passage money, didn't you?"

"Stolen!" gasped Clarissa.

Bram said nothing. He was simply staring at these two and wondering why in the hell they had decided he was to be their savior. There was only one thing about those two that he cared about. One small detail was all he wanted to know.

"Where is Mina?"

"Who's Mina?" asked Dicky. Clarissa was too busy pretending to cry delicately into her crumpled handkerchief.

"The horse. Where's the carriage and horse?"

"Well!" said Clarissa, then she shot an angry look at Dicky, who gently admonished him.

"You should have told us it was such an ugly horse, Bram. We would have waited while you found a more appropriate one."

"More appropriate? A high-stepper, perhaps, in Hull. Were you trying to flee without anyone noticing?"

Dicky stiffened. "Don't take that tone with me. Just

because we're relocating to a new home doesn't mean we should be subjected to that mongrel horse."

"Where is Mina?" he ground out.

"Well, she's stabled just down the road. Filthy place. Don't know why you abide it."

"Because I don't have a horse."

"Well, you do now. I'll not have that hideous creature as one of my own." He lifted his chin. "So you owe me three hundred pounds."

"Like hell I do."

"Bram!" Dicky huffed. "I must insist that you watch your tongue."

"Or what? You'll throw me out of my own home?" It was late, he was tired, and he was in no mood to deal with these two. Unfortunately, God apparently chose to plague him with beggars and fools. He rubbed his chin. "What do you want, Dicky?"

"Well, as to that, do you think everyone's forgotten about us by now?"

Bram blinked at the man. He couldn't possibly be that stupid. "It was a week ago. No, even the *ton* has a longer memory than that."

Clarissa sniffed even louder into her handkerchief.

Dicky sighed. "We knew that was possible, Clary," he said, patting his wife's shoulder. "So we've thought upon a plan. And we've already started on it."

A plan. Wonderful. He didn't know whether to be elated or terrified. "What is it?"

"We can't go on the water. That much is very clear."

"What is it, Dicky?"

"And everyone thinks we're in Scotland. Jeremy hasn't come here looking, has he?"

"No, he hasn't." And that worried Bram, but of course, he'd only just returned to London an hour ago.

"So he must be up in Scotland looking, right?"

That's what Bram hoped.

Dicky brightened. "So that's our plan!"

"What. Is. The. Plan."

He waved to the porcelain shepherd and Clarissa's mammoth bonnet. "We're going to live in Plymouth. As shepherds."

Bram waited. Surely he was missing something significant here. A joke perhaps. Something. But the two just stared at him with hope in their eyes.

"It's the perfect thing," Dicky continued. "No one would expect it of us. We don't have to go on the water. And we're still in England."

"Where people will find you."

"Nonsense. As I said, no one would expect us to be common sheepherders." He grinned at his own cleverness.

"Dicky, do you know anything about sheep?"

"Goodness, they're dumb animals. And I got excellent marks in school. I'm sure I could figure it out."

He barely passed his classes, and that was by paying underclassmen to write his papers for him. Bram tried to picture the two of them herding sheep. Clarissa in her massive bonnet, Dicky with shears in his hand, calmly ordering a ram to heave to so that he could shear it. He tried to picture it, but he simply couldn't. Just…couldn't.

"It won't work."

"Of course—"

"But I know something that will," he lied. Nothing

would work for these two, but this might serve everyone's purpose. If he could bring it off. "But only on one condition."

"Yes?"

"That once I have you established, you never, ever speak to me again."

"Well, I say!"

"Oh no!" Clarissa gasped.

"Not one word. Not one glance. Never again. Swear it."

In the end, they had no choice but to relent. And once he had their solemn word—not that it meant much—he ushered them out the door. Finding a hackney at this hour was hard. Sitting in it with those two was even harder. But in the end he found his friend Bernard, manager of the most reputable gaming hells in town. He was also the brother of the new Duchess of Bucklynde.

He held off telling them what they would do until the last moment. Until after he had paid Bernard an enormous fee for ensuring Dicky and Clarissa's place in the troupe. And it took him two more days of miserable travel—in the carriage pulled by poor Mina—in order to find the group. But after three days, it was done, and he could finally tell them about their new jobs.

"You're going to be host and hostess of a traveling menagerie."

Then he dumped them on the proprietor—who really did need a better showman as host—and never gave Clarissa's enormous bonnet and Dicky's ridiculous clock a second glance.

Seventeen

"THIS IS JUST A TEA," LADY ELEANOR WARNED Maybelle a few days later. "You needn't worry about anything except for how you speak. Make sure your words are slow and clear. And for heaven's sake, remember those *h*'s."

Maybelle nodded. Her grandparents were coming, and she was a knot of mixed emotions. She wanted to make a good impression, but she also wanted to confront them for how they'd treated her mother. Two goals, absolutely contradictory. She was nervous and excited and bewildered all at once, and she'd never felt so many conflicting desires apart from Mr. Hallowsby—who wasn't coming, the blighter.

"Make sure to sit up straight. Keep a reserved expression, though a smile or two of happiness would not be amiss."

Fortunately, Eleanor was displaying enough anxiety for both of them. The woman was pacing, which is something Maybelle had never thought to see. Eleanor kept touching her fingers as if she were counting off items on a list. And she no longer floated when she moved. It was more of an agitated swirling of wind and words. She wished the woman would just sit down.

"That gown is perfect," Eleanor said. "I knew blue would be your color, but then I suppose you were already aware, given your nickname. Don't tell anyone to call you Bluebell, though. That will put them in absolutely the wrong state of mind. You're a lady now. And ladies have proper names."

Maybelle's hands tightened in her lap. Her borrowed corset made it difficult to slouch, which was good. But breathing wasn't entirely possible either, and that made her feel overly hot, as if she might faint. Also, her hair had been pulled and styled until she thought she'd go bald. Instead, her coiffure was now a heavy presence upon her head, so that she thought she might soon topple from the weight.

"And don't really eat anything. You're not plump, which is excellent, but the food is for Lord and Lady Cavener. Sip your tea if you must, but only a little bit. Just pretend and keep smiling."

Since she could barely breathe, the last thing she wanted was to further limit the space inside her by filling her stomach.

"Don't forget to curtsy when they enter. You are being presented to them. Get to your—"

"Tell me another story about Mr. Hallowsby," she interrupted.

"What?"

"It will help pass the time. I'm trying not to be nervous," she lied. She was trying to breathe. "And listening to his tales relaxes me." Another lie. In truth, they made her intensely curious. Not even half of what they said about him was true. It couldn't be. No one killed a bear with his own fists, and certainly not at the age of six. So with every story, she wanted to decipher what part was true and what part was pure fabrication.

"Well, you've already heard about the bear when he was a child," Eleanor said. Then a miracle happened. The woman sat down! "Have I told you about the French spy?"

"The man?"

"No, no. There have been scores of those, one can hardly keep track. And mostly, he just knocks them out and drags them to the Home Office. I mean the woman."

"A female spy?" She couldn't believe it. Not that women couldn't learn secret things. Of course they could. She simply doubted a man could catch a female spy. There were any number of ways to sneak around, pretending to be a maid or a cook, for example. No one looked closely at servants, especially if one were not that lovely. And if the woman was beautiful? Well then, the men completely lost their heads.

"He only caught one. No matter what anyone says, there was only the one."

Maybelle took a deep breath, feeling her emotions settle as Eleanor began talking. The woman loved nothing so much as telling a Bram tale, which was lucky, since Maybelle adored hearing them. "Was she pretty?"

"Ravishing. She would slip into important men's bedrooms at night, seduce them, and then steal their papers. Quite evil, that woman."

"She'd just sneak in?"

"Well, she was a beauty. And if she couldn't drug them insensate, she would get them in the usual way."

"But Mr. Hallowsby caught her." She leaned forward, being careful with her words. Even in the midst of a rousing tale of spies and seduction, Eleanor would pick on her accent. "How did he do it?"

"He pursued her all over the Continent. Down into Africa even. Took years."

"But how did he know?"

"Oh, you know Bram. He deduced it from his friends. All he had to do was hear about a battle gone wrong, and he knew there was a seductress. The problem was catching her."

Well, that was patently untrue. Even she knew that. "What did she look like?"

"As to that, no one really knows except Bram. She wore wigs and the like. One day she'd be a meek Scottish maid, the next, a dark-skinned Ethiopian princess. But Bram caught her when she was playing a sultan's wife all covered in robes."

"What was a sultan's wife doing in England? Or were they on the Continent?"

"That's just it. She was right here in London and planning to assassinate the king!"

And right here was why she loved these tales so desperately. None of them made logical sense. Why would a woman dress as a sultan's wife when trying to assassinate the king? She would stand out like a sore thumb, and everyone would be watching her just to see what she did. Plus, what good would it do Napoleon to kill their mad king? It would rouse the whole of England to bloody murder and do nothing to harm their war effort. After all, the king had nothing to do with planning the battles. Even the Prince Regent left it to the military men. And yet a woman as smart as Lady Eleanor seemed to take these tales as complete truth.

"Now," continued Eleanor, "I only heard that part. I have my doubts about her dressed as a sultan's wife and the like. And though Bram has certainly disappeared for months at a time, I doubt that it truly took years."

Well, at least that proved Eleanor wasn't completely gullible. "So what part are you sure of?"

"I know he was in the bedchamber of Mrs. Wulfson when he heard the noise. Many would claim that it was Lady Baney, but I know for a fact that lady lifted up her skirts simply to have him as her lover. It had nothing to do with spying."

"But how do you know it was Mrs. Wulfson?"

"I heard it from my maid who heard it from her maid. Or something like that. What does it matter?"

It didn't. That was the glory of gossip. None of it came from a good source. It simply arrived fully formed from a friend of a friend who had a servant who said so.

"So it was a spy come to steal her husband's papers?" Maybelle prompted. "And Bram—er, Mr. Hallowsby—was in the lady's bedchamber?" This was the part that always soured Maybelle's stomach. If all the tales were true, then not only was Bram the most brilliant man in all of England, he was also the most notorious seducer. Every tale had him in at least one lady's bedroom, if not several.

"Well, yes. She is well known for taking lovers, and why else would Bram be there?"

"You said he tracked the spy all over the Continent. Perhaps he was pursuing her."

"He was. Which is why he and Mrs. Wulfson were together. Because he knew the spy was coming, but needed a reason to be in the house when she started rifling through his lordship's papers."

"But—"

"Then he caught her. He heard the noise, grabbed the venomous tart, and sent for the Home Office. Easiest thing in the world."

"Which tart? The spy or Mrs.—"

"Tut tut. The spy, of course—"

The knocker sounded, startling Maybelle enough that she bit her lip. Fortunately, she recovered quickly enough to swallow her curse. Or most of it. Eleanor shot her a warning look, then slapped a hand on her thigh when she would have risen.

"We are talking. You are a lovely lady come for a visit, and we are chatting."

"We were—"

"Do not rise until Seelye—"

The butler opened the parlor door. Behind him trailed an elderly couple dressed in the fanciest attire Maybelle had ever seen. The gentleman had a military coat on with medals—actual medals—pinned to the front. She had no idea what they meant, but it was very impressive, especially as his face seemed to be led by an enormous blond and brown mustache. At first, all she saw were the medals and the hair.

The lady appeared less conspicuous. She wore a shimmering, dove-gray gown and pearls about her throat. Her skin was powdered, and her hair so tall it seemed to tower over her. And though she smiled with her mouth, it did not reach her pale blue eyes.

Maybelle rose to her feet, moving more by instinct than conscious thought. The couple didn't seem real to her. More like a picture in a book come to life. Could these people be her grandparents? She couldn't comprehend it. They seemed so unlike herself or her mother.

"Good afternoon, Lord and Lady Cavener," Eleanor said as she dropped into a shallow curtsy.

The gentleman gave her a perfunctory nod that might have been construed as a bow. The lady did nothing but incline her head with a vague sort of expression.

Sad, Maybelle thought. She seemed sad, though there was nothing in her outward appearance that might suggest it. Meanwhile, Lord Cavener was frowning at the two of them.

"Lady Eleanor, you said we had something of importance to discuss. Of a private nature. We must come for tea, you said. So here we are. What is it?" Every sentence was spoken in crisp efficiency, punched at the end with a huff of air.

"Won't you please sit down?" Eleanor asked, though Maybelle thought her smile was strained. "Seelye, the tea tray, if you please."

"Of course, my lady," Seelye intoned. But he left slowly, every step filled with slow pomposity.

"Don't need any more tea today," his lordship said, but his wife set two long fingers on her husband's arm.

"I should like some tea," she said. "I know it makes little sense, but I do love a hot cup on a hot day."

"I've told you time and again," the man cut in. "It's because it makes you sweat. And that cools you off."

Eleanor tilted her head. "What an excellent deduction, my lord. I would never have thought of that myself."

"Course not. Don't teach gels science." Then he turned his bristly mustache to her. "And who is this? Introduce yourself, gel. Don't be mousy. I want to know your name."

Don't be mousy? No one in her life had ever treated her so rudely, and that included all those people who thought she was a bastard. Eleanor had spent days telling her to be kind, be ladylike, be serene. She'd listened closely and intended to be exactly like her august hostess. But at those words, her intentions went right out the window.

So she lifted her chin, looked directly at that bristling monstrosity on his face and spoke. "I am Miss Maybelle Ballenger, my lord. Your granddaughter."

Dead silence greeted her words. It should have been gratifying. That stunned horror was exactly what she'd wanted. Except that a moment later, it all turned to pieces.

Lord Cavener shoved up to his feet, his facial hair quivering, with an icy stare for Lady Eleanor. "What is the meaning of this ridiculousness? How dare you—"

Eleanor shot to her feet as well. "Please, please, Lord Cavener, I know this is sudden. We haven't even had tea."

"Bollocks on the tea and you! Such schemes are beneath you, Lady Eleanor. I knew your family had sunk into the mire, but I had thought you at least would maintain your breeding. I can see—"

"You will control your tongue, sir," Eleanor said.

And if tone alone could freeze a person in place, hers would have done it. Unfortunately, it could not.

Lord Cavener spun on his heel, held out his hand to his wife, and spat a frigid, "Good day," over his shoulder.

Except his wife had not moved. Maybelle hadn't noticed at first. His lordship was commanding all the attention. But when his wife did not move so much as a muscle, all eyes went to her. And she was...

She was simply gazing at Maybelle.

"Sarah!" his lordship snapped, but his wife simply tilted her head and shifted so as to see more clearly around her husband.

"Maybelle was my mother's name," she said. Her words were soft, almost inaudible. After his lordship's booming voice, her quietness seemed to surround and lift her words to everyone there.

Meanwhile, the man would not cease snorting. "Any jack-a-dandy would know that," he snapped.

His wife ignored him, her eyes glittering bright where before they'd only seemed a dull wash. "Tell me your parents' names."

Maybelle reached to the floor behind the settee. She'd set the items there for safekeeping, but now she drew them out. First the letter from the vicar.

"Anna and Oscar Ballenger. They were married in Oxfordshire, and I am their daughter."

"Ridiculous!" the earl spat, whirling back to face her. "My son would never marry a chambermaid."

"And this is the picture he drew of my mother." She pulled out the framed sketch. "You can see his signature there." She pointed and repeated his name. "Oscar B. My father."

Maybelle's eyes were on her grandmother as she picked up the sketch and lovingly stroked the signature scrawled there. "I'd forgotten that he had talent with charcoal."

"He did not!" the earl said. Then he stomped forward and snatched up the vicar's letter. He didn't even look at it as he ripped it to pieces. "There was no wedding. There was no child. You are a scheming whore."

Maybelle didn't think. She leaped to her feet, her hands clenched at her sides, and her words came faster and faster as her accent slipped in thick and hard. "I am as pure a Christian woman as there ever was. It's you oo are a lying 'ypocrite. You tossed off me mum like she were rubbish, but she was strong. She raised me alone. Educated me better than anyone. And she waited all 'er life for her 'usband. Ever day, ever night praying that he'd come find 'er. But 'e's dead, ain't he? And you never bothered to even tell us!" It was that last bit that had her words choking off. The years her mum waited for a man who was dead and gone. Years.

Meanwhile the earl's face had purpled with rage. "You insult the very air," he bellowed. Then he rounded on Eleanor, who was sitting statue still, her hands flat on her lap. "How dare you upset her ladyship like this? How dare you bring this woman—" He spat the word. "Into her presence?"

Eleanor tilted her head, her expression so smooth it didn't appear real. "Oh look," she said, pointing over his shoulder. "Seelye has brought the tea tray. Do sit down, my lord. I find everything much clearer with tea, don't you think?"

"No, I do not!" Then he snatched the framed

picture out of his wife's hands and slammed it on the table. The cheap wood frame broke into splinters, and Maybelle cried out, but she was too late. Too slow.

The bastard—her grandfather—was going to destroy the only thing she had left of her parents.

"No!" she screamed.

And then a male voice cut through the air. It was so familiar, and yet so cold as to be unrecognizable. And it froze everyone in place the way Eleanor had failed to do.

"Touch that page, my lord, and I will hurt you."

Eighteen

BRAM WAS RUNNING LATE. LADY ELEANOR'S ELEGANT home was in a vastly different neighborhood than his less-than-aristocratic bachelor rooms. Which meant he'd had to resort to a hackney, but had chosen badly. He was carried to Grosvenor Square by the slowest, oldest, most rheumy hack he'd ever seen. But it was better than walking, so he'd tapped his foot, kept patting his pocket, which held a blank piece of foolscap, and counted the seconds until he could get to the tea.

He wasn't invited. He knew that. The last person Lord and Lady Cavener would accept was a known bastard. But as he'd stewed in his rooms, he realized that there was no way he could avoid this meeting. Bluebell and her grandparents were an explosive combination. She was headstrong, and they were arrogant. He doubted that even Eleanor had the ability to keep the situation polite.

So he'd rushed over, cursing the slowest hackney in London, and then slipped in the servants' entrance. He didn't want to intrude if he wasn't needed. He'd walked into the hallway in time to hear Bluebell state as baldly as possible her identity. And he'd stayed quiet there—with Seelye balancing the tea tray beside him—as they'd listened to the horrifying scene continue until he could remain silent no longer. Lord Cavener was a big man in a temper. Which meant he could be dangerous.

Bram was already pushing into the room when he saw the man rip Bluebell's picture out of his wife's hand. He heard the crash as the frame splintered and knew that the bastard would destroy the picture. And so he'd spoken. He'd used his deadliest tone and prayed that it worked.

"Touch that page, and I will hurt you."

Everyone in the room froze—for a second. He saw the women look at him, their eyes a mixture of confusion, hope, and sparkling adoration. That last was from Bluebell, and it terrified him as much as it warmed him. What if he couldn't stop this debacle?

And sure enough, the earl ignored him. He made a show of grabbing the paper and lifting it in his fist. Fortunately, he was slow, and Bram was there at almost the same instant. He grabbed the man's wrist and dug in his thumb as hard as he could at the vulnerable place just beneath the palm.

"Put it down," Bram said, his voice crisp enough to be an order from a commanding officer. The earl had been in the military. Perhaps he'd respond—

"You bastard," the earl ground out.

Bram couldn't tell if it was a curse or a statement of recognition. Either way, he twisted his hand, forcing the earl's wrist into an untenable position. The paper slipped, and Bluebell grabbed it and began to smooth it out.

No, it wasn't Bluebell. It was the countess, her hands shaking as she tried uselessly to fix a rip with her finger.

Then the earl shoved him hard. Fortunately, Bram was used to sparring with men with three stone more muscle. The earl's weight was equal parts fat and aging bones. It was a simple thing to stay steady against such a force. And within seconds, Bram had twisted and thumb-jabbed enough to get the man to sit back down. Or collapse, depending on your perspective.

And once the earl was seated, Bram showed his lips into a semblance of a smile.

"I believe you wanted tea, did you not, Lady Eleanor?"

His sister's eyes were huge, but she was equal to the task. After a quick double-blink, she gripped the bellpull and rang. She needn't have bothered. Seelye was already there, maneuvering to set down the tray.

"Here you go, my lady," the butler said as he walked briskly into the room. Who knew the man could move that fast? Seelye spoke with extra animation. "Cook has found some delightful cucumber at market. She says they are quite crisp."

"Thank you, Seelye," Eleanor said with a bright smile. "I understand cucumber is the earl's favorite."

"Oh yes," said the countess, her voice so breathy, there seemed to be extra air in every syllable. "He does like cucumber. And two dollops of cream in his tea."

The earl grumbled deep in his throat and made to rise. "I will not—"

Bram clapped a hand down on the man's shoulder, keeping him firmly seated. "I had not meant to intrude," he said dryly. "But as the earl insists on dragging this conversation into the gutter—"

"Mr. Hallowsby, please," Eleanor interrupted. "Tea is no place for such talk."

Bram frowned. That had been entirely his point. Especially as the earl was gripping the sides of his chair hard enough to make the slender wood creak. "And so I will remain to be sure that—"

This time it was the countess who interrupted. "Teatime is really a ladies' place, don't you think? The men are simply obliged to sit and listen to us chatter."

Had he just been told to sit down and be silent? Like a boy in short coats? Apparently so. He consoled himself that the message had been for the earl as much as himself. But still...

He eased off the man's shoulder but stayed standing directly beside the chair. He wanted to be right here in case the earl didn't like being told what to do any more than he did.

Which is when the man rounded on his wife, his expression fierce. "I will not have you upset," he said. His glare encompassed Bluebell, Lady Eleanor, and most especially Bram. "I will—"

"I know, my lord," interrupted his wife as she gestured for the teacup. She took it from Eleanor with a smile before firmly setting it in her husband's hand. "Two dollops of good cream. I just know you'll love it."

The earl stared at his wife, but he didn't throw the fine porcelain cup back at her. And then a moment later, his wife set a cucumber sandwich firmly in his other hand. And there he was, sitting rigid with fury, but with a teacup in one hand and a triangular-cut cucumber sandwich in the other. Then his wife turned to address Bluebell.

"You are quite pretty." She looked at the sketch of Bluebell's mother. "The eyes are the same, I think. But the bone structure is much stronger."

"Mum said I favor my father in that."

"Yes, the Cavener nose is quite distinct."

Bluebell's eyes widened, and she pressed her hand to her nose. Personally, Bram thought it one of her best features. Not the flattened button that most women seemed to want, but a strong beacon of direction. It fit her character. She had always been quite determined in her choices.

"And the ears, I think. I remember looking at Oscar's ears when he was a boy and finding them most delicate. His hands were all his father's." She glanced at the earl, but he hadn't moved, and his fingers were hidden beneath the food. "Do you study like he did?"

Bluebell lifted her shoulders. "I try, but there's been little money." There was a bite of accusation in her tone.

"But you managed an education," cut in Eleanor gently. "Bram said you have quite an understanding of agriculture and possets."

"That's how we survived. We had a garden, of course. Everyone does, but I began mixing possets for Mum when she got the headache. They were so good, I sold them."

"Commerce!" spat the earl.

Bram's voice was excruciatingly dry as he spoke. "And how else were they to live with no money, tossed up to Hull, and denied her birthright?"

"Now, see here—" began the earl, but again

Eleanor stopped the tirade, this time with a cluck of her tongue.

"Really, Bram, I know you were taught better manners. Cease harping at him." Then she smiled brightly at Bluebell. "What of mathematics? Do I remember that correctly? You studied that and Latin too."

Of course Eleanor remembered that correctly, but Bluebell nodded sweetly. "Cyphering came easily to me, so I managed the money—"

The earl released a strangled sound, at which his wife gestured to him without even looking. "The cucumber is quite excellent, don't you think, Reuben? I vow our own cook is too heavy-handed with the dill. Go on. Take a bite."

And to Bram's shock, the earl exhaled a full and angry sound...but still took an obedient bite. In fact, while Bram watched, he took steady, precise, military-style bites until the sandwich was finished.

"But what I really enjoyed," continued Bluebell, "was the philosophy. I couldn't understand it in Greek. I tried, but it was too hard to learn on my own."

Eleanor set down her teacup with a click. "I should think so."

And the countess seemed to blink back tears. "You know, Oscar tried to teach me Greek as well. I could never make heads nor tails of it. But he loved it so."

"That's what Mum said. He would read to her in Greek because she liked the sound of it. She said he had the most beautiful voice when he read."

"Oh yes," the countess agreed. "He did." But then she frowned. "I don't understand. Why do you say there was no money?"

"Because there was none. A Christmas gift ever' year that paid our rent. But how we lived and ate…" She shook her head. "We had to find that on our own."

The lady looked down at her hand. "And still you managed to learn philosophy and mathematics. Amazing. Did your mother teach you?"

That apparently was too much for the earl. He stiffened and swallowed his last bite. "Of course not. An ignorant chit, if there ever was one."

Well, that was progress. He'd all but admitted to the relationship, if not the marriage. But Bluebell didn't hear that. Instead, she stiffened at the insult to her mother.

"Mum could read and write and taught me the same. She had other knowledge—practical bits on how to keep a house and serve tea."

The countess brightened considerably at that. "You know how to serve tea?"

"I know the steps," Bluebell hedged. "But I never did it except for my mum. And we didn't stand on formality often."

Meanwhile, Eleanor casually set another cucumber sandwich in the earl's hand. "But how did you learn the other things?"

"There was a tutor who came through ever' few weeks. Mum washed his clothes in exchange for teaching me." She smiled, flashing her dimples. "He would use me to shame the boys into studying. 'How can a little slip of a girl know so much more than you?' he'd say. It's a sad state when a—" Her voice caught, and Bram's gaze left the earl to study her expression. She was pressing her lips tightly together, and that told him all he needed to know about the rest of the sentence. But the others didn't. They didn't have cause to understand.

"Go on," the countess prompted. "A sad state when what?"

Bluebell shook her head. "It's not important."

The hell it wasn't. That's why they were here in the first place. "It's a sad state when a bastard girl of no account knows more than a boy," Bram said.

The countess's eyes widened in horror, but it was Eleanor who released a heavy sigh. "Bram, please. I've asked you not to—"

"It's what they said, isn't it, Bluebell? You weren't even allowed to use your real name, were you? How old were you when you found out your true name?"

She looked at him, and he saw misery. He saw an entire lifetime of being slighted and abused simply because her father hadn't been there to protect her. He knew. He'd experienced some of the hatred, but at least he'd known his father. He'd felt some kindness from the man. And some protection. Which was a good deal more than Bluebell had ever gotten.

"Just tell them the truth," he said softly. "It's why we're here."

So, holding his gaze, she nodded. "Everyone called me Bluebell. It was just a few months ago when I learned I had more of a name. Mum told me everything this winter. She said…" Her gaze shifted to the earl, and it turned hard and cold. "She said that she and my father were married right and proper in the church, but that the earl was a cold and angry man. He had her shipped off to Hull, quiet like. A few coins every Christmas to pay the rent, and only if she never told anyone of the connection."

She looked at the countess, her eyes bright with anger. "Mum changed us from Ballenger to Ball. I was christened Maybelle Ballenger in secret, and we lived."

"But there's always been a shadow," Bram continued for her. "Everyone in her little village thinks she's a bastard. Do you know what that's like? To live in a little place like that and never be treated as an equal? Laughter is the easiest of the problems. Without a father, people try to take advantage. There's no one to defend them, you see. A woman and a child alone with no money and no family. Do you know what happens?"

They didn't. They couldn't. But he could guess. That she'd survived and even thrived was a miracle. And a testament to Bluebell's strength.

"She needs to be recognized," he said harshly. "She needs the shadow removed."

Meanwhile, the countess was shaking her head. "But why wasn't there enough money? I sent a hundred pounds every Christmas."

The earl stiffened at that. "You!"

She set aside her teacup with a wobbly hand. "Of course me. I wasn't going to let my grandchild starve!"

"Enough to pay the year's rent, my lady," Bluebell said. "And not enough in the last few years. The landlord kept raising the price."

"Raising the price," she echoed softly, and Bram could tell it never occurred to her that prices could change. That money one year wouldn't be enough in the next. He sighed.

Bloody idiot.

Meanwhile, it appeared that Bluebell was just now realizing that everything she'd hoped was true. She was legitimate. Her grandparents had known she was alive, and her grandmother at least had taken steps to keep her that way. Bram could see warring emotions run through her expression: joy against hatred, hope against fury.

"So my father is truly gone?"

The countess looked away. She didn't cry, but the sorrow that surrounded her seemed to scream out of every pore. And he abruptly remembered that his mother had once called her a loud woman, brash and wild. There was nothing of that left now. Only an aching sadness.

"Sarah," the earl said, his voice thick. "We should go."

"No," she said, her voice getting stronger as she faced off with her husband. "Absolutely not." Then she turned to Bluebell. "We learned of the wedding too late to stop it. I won't tell you what was said when we finally got there. Suffice it to say that... well, that Oscar loved your mother and would not set her aside."

Bluebell nodded, and Bram detected a sheen of tears in her eyes. "That's what Mum said."

"But Reuben..." She shot a look at her husband. Bram couldn't interpret it fully, but it was both an apology and an accusation. "Reuben sent her away and later told Oscar..." She swallowed. "*We* told Oscar she'd died in childbirth."

Bluebell's mouth opened in shock, but it was Eleanor who said what everyone was thinking. "That's why he never contacted her again. He thought she'd died."

"Yes," the countess continued. "He got sick soon after that. A broken heart perhaps."

"Stuff and nonsense!" the earl said. And though his words were strong, his body had deflated. The shoulders that had been held rigidly taut now slumped into his chest and against the chair.

"He grew sick and…and…"

Eleanor touched the countess's arm. "He passed, and you have grieved as every mother would. He was your light, wasn't he? The one who always made you smile."

Bram had no idea how Eleanor could know that, but the countess nodded and made no attempt to hide her tears. It was a heartbreaking scene, and he had no wish to pile more grief onto the pair, but there was more to the story.

"But you paid their Christmas gift every year," Bram pushed. "You knew she was alive. That they both were alive."

The woman shook her head. "I didn't know where. I've never known where they were, but I instructed our solicitor to give the money. I couldn't think of Oscar's child like a filthy beggar. I couldn't—"

"But you set the terms, my lady, didn't you? Even if you went through the solicitor, you told Bluebell and her mother that there would be no more money if anyone found out. If she once came forward to demand an explanation."

The woman nodded miserably. "I was waiting for…" Her gaze went to her husband.

Waiting for the earl to soften or to die. Year after year, waiting, while Bluebell grew up wondering if she really was a bastard, if her mother was a whore, and she no better than she ought to be.

God, the pair disgusted him. At least he had known from the beginning. At least his father had faced his sins and provided some shelter. But these two... They had left Bluebell and her mother to rot.

He must have made a sound. A noise of disgust perhaps, because Eleanor was again chiding him.

"Bram, please. They did the best they could in a difficult situation."

"The best they could?" he mocked. "That's a piss poor best. Do you know how she's been living? Do you know what it's like in Hull?"

It was Bluebell who answered this time. Bluebell who shot him a warning with her eyes even as her words were aimed at the countess. "Mum and I were happy," she said clearly. "It wasn't easy, but I am here now." Then she looked directly at her grandparents. "I can forgive the past." Then she moderated her statement. "I can try at least. But what are you going to do to make up for what you've done to Mum?"

"Well, that's easy," inserted Eleanor. For a woman whose expression was completely serene, she seemed almost gleeful as she spoke. "They're going to acknowledge you, of course. With a little tutoring from me and the countess—and especially, if I sponsor you—you can have a Season, marry as you ought, and be a credit to your parents." Then she smiled warmly at the picture on the countess's lap. "For my part, I think she gets her strength from her mother. Imagine the courage it takes to raise a child all alone. Impressive."

But the earl sprang back to life. "Acknowledge her?

After her mother killed my boy? Consorting with her was what did—"

"I think it's an excellent idea," the countess began. "I never had a daughter to launch."

"Well, as to that," said Eleanor with a laugh, "I'm becoming quite an expert at taking raw girls and helping them shine. Between you and me, I'm sure we can work things out exactly at they ought."

Bram had gotten complacent. The earl's fury had abated somewhat, and so Bram had been caught up in Bluebell. In the shift of emotions on her face. The clench of her fingers and the shift of her foot when she tried to hide her thoughts. He'd been watching her, so he missed it when the earl suddenly shot to his feet.

"I will not acknowledge a maid's brat. I will not—"

"You don't have to," Bram cut in, his voice cold. It was time for him to play his part. He only prayed he could bring it off.

"What?" exclaimed Eleanor and Bluebell as one. Though Bluebell's came out a little more like, "Wot?"

"He doesn't need to acknowledge her, but the truth will be in all the papers by tomorrow."

"You bastard!" the man bellowed.

Eleanor tsked deep in her throat. "Bram, really. They won't believe you."

Bram tried not to wince. Though she was his half sister, their differences were never clearer. She thought nothing of implying quite baldly that he was illegitimate, and therefore, had no reputable standing no matter what he did. It was the frustration shared by all the aristocratic by-blows. Fortunately, he'd already thought of that.

"True enough. No one would believe me." He sneered the words, some of his long-standing bitterness showing through. "Which is why I went to visit Bishop Trotman." He'd been driving over half of England to get Dicky and Clarissa settled. It was practically on his way to visit the Bishop of Oxford. "That's the man who married your parents." In truth, he'd gone and been refused entrance. The bishop would have no dealings with a by-blow. "He's willing to acknowledge the marriage. After all, it's recorded in the register and was legally executed." He looked directly at the earl. "You can't rip up that, no matter how powerful you are."

It was another lie. He knew for a fact that the powerful elite could make any number of things—and people—disappear. But sometimes, he thought, with a smile to Bluebell, the truth came out.

"I have his letter here," he added, pulling the foolscap from his pocket. He showed enough to prove that he had a paper, not what was on it. Because there was nothing on it. "I'm headed to the newspaper straight from here. So you see, my lord, it matters not whether you acknowledge her. The truth will come out."

At which point Eleanor gave him a beaming smile, and she leaned toward Bluebell. "And that is his magic. I don't know how he does it. I would think he couldn't even have gotten past the front door, but there you go. Bram is ever amazing."

"Oh yes," Bluebell said, pleasure in every line. "I know."

No, they didn't. Because it was all a lie, but at least it was a lie told in service of the truth. Meanwhile, everyone turned to the earl. It was up to him. If he stayed firm, then they were all in for a rough time. They needed his word.

"No," he said. "She killed my boy."

The countess sighed. "She did nothing of the sort, Reuben. Don't you remember? His lungs were never strong." She glanced at Bluebell. "Did you learn to make possets from your mother? I believe that's how she and Oscar met. She made him a tea that eased his chest. And she certainly knew how to read. She would sit by his bed and read his books to him when he was ill. He told me that before the end. He said she read to him."

"No," ground out the earl. "Oscar would still be alive if—"

"Oh, have done!" the countess said as she pushed to her feet. "I'm acknowledging her. You may do as you like. You always do."

"Excellent!" cried Eleanor as she too leaped to her feet. "Now, we haven't much time before the Season begins."

"Much time? We have no time," the countess said. "The first ball is in four days."

"Fortunately, I have already gotten things started." Then she frowned and looked around. "I had Helaine draw up some sketches. That's Lady Redhill, you know. Now, where did I put them?"

Bluebell stood up. "We were looking at them at the breakfast table."

"Oh yes," Eleanor said as she linked arms with the countess. "Let me show you." Then she led the woman out of the room. Just took her arm and walked her away, leaving Bluebell with the two men, one of whom was staring slack-jawed at his wife's retreating form.

Bram waited, ready to stop whatever happened. If the man became violent…

But nothing like that occurred. The earl sniffed at Bluebell and glared at Bram. "You will pay for this," he growled. "Mark my words, there will come a time when I can end you completely. And I will."

"Him!" Bluebell cried. "He's got nothing to do—"

"And you will learn your place." He shoved to his feet and puffed himself to his most intimidating size. But Bluebell was never one to be intimidated.

"Oh, I have, *Grandfather*. I have learned my place very well as an acknowledged granddaughter to the Earl of Cavener."

To which the man growled, a low and feral sound, before rounding on his heel and stomping out. Bram watched him go, but there was no more threat in him. He collected his hat and coat from Seelye and stormed out of the house.

But Bram knew violent men, and the earl was not one. For all that he thundered and growled, he was defeated. His words were for show, and Bram was finally able to relax his fears for Bluebell. She would have her Season.

"You've done it," she whispered, while the sound of the front door closing reverberated in the air. "You've made him accept me."

"I haven't done anything like that," he said. Or he tried to. Instead, his words were lost as she threw himself into his arms. He caught her—barely—but once she'd pressed flush against him, he lost no time in wrapping his arms around her. In lifting her up in a hug. In looking in her shining eyes and taking what he'd missed for three long days.

Her kiss.

He kissed her well and deep, and she melted against him as if there were no other place in the world that she wanted to be. He thrust into her mouth, he played with her tongue and teeth, and he touched every part that he could reach.

And he was still doing it when Seelye's loud cough penetrated his thoughts. And even then, his hands were on her hips, his groin hot and hard. But all he could think of was Bluebell in his arms.

She broke the contact, her breath now coming in deep gasps. And then he heard the cough again.

So he set her down. Then he forced himself to step back, though it was the hardest thing he'd ever had to do.

Oh hell. He'd been kissing her in full view of the servants. He'd been ready to do a lot more and might very well have, if the butler hadn't been making a scene.

He rubbed a hand over his face.

"I can't see you anymore," he rasped.

"What?"

He winced, because she said the word correctly. And didn't that just emphasize what had happened in the last few minutes?

"You're recognized. You're the granddaughter of an earl now. You're going to have a Season."

She looked up at him, and her entire body seemed to glow with happiness. "I know. And it's all thanks to you."

"No, no," he said, forcing himself to take another step backward. "It was your right from the beginning."

He gripped the back of the nearest chair, his knuckles going white as he processed what he had done—what had to happen.

Jesus, it had worked. She was now well beyond his touch. He'd known it was possible, but hadn't chosen to dwell on it. Truthfully, he'd thought it a remote possibility that any of this would come to pass. He'd expected to be found out that he carried a blank page, not a letter from a bishop. He expected the countess to meekly go on with whatever her husband said. She had for years, so why expect a change?

He thought a thousand other things would happen except for what did.

"I'm a by-blow, Bluebell. We can't see each other." He spoke loudly so that Seelye would hear. So that when the man told Eleanor about the kiss—and he *would* tell because servants always told—then Seelye would also say that Bram had called it off. That it was done between him and Bluebell. Bloody hell, he'd have to start calling her Maybelle now.

"I know who you are," she said, lifting her chin in that defiant way of hers. "I don't care."

"It's different now. You're above my touch." He looked at his hands. He'd never kiss her again. "It's good we never went further," he lied, but he had to make sure Seelye heard everything. "It's all different now."

"I'm not different. You're not—"

"*It is!*" he bellowed. Then he moderated his tone. "You're to have a Season now. I couldn't be happier." Lies on top of lies. And to think he'd once prided himself on his honesty. "But that means we can't even be friends."

"Wot?"

This time he winced because she'd slipped. But he didn't correct her. He hadn't the right anymore. "Eleanor will explain it to you," he said. "You'll see. You'll have your choice of eligible gentlemen now. There will be blighters about you aplenty." He made a vow right then and there to keep the worst of the buggers away. He'd have to tell Eleanor to keep him abreast of her offers. He knew secrets about the *ton* that even someone as well connected as his sister couldn't possibly know.

"Mr. Hallowsby," she said stiffly. Then she took two quick steps forward. "Bram. You have been by my side from the beginning. I will not cut you off simply because I have changed."

Of course not. Because she was at heart a good Christian woman in the best possible way. He'd tried to think the worst of her, but every day, every moment, she'd steadfastly proved herself better than he thought. Better than he'd thought possible.

"You won't cut me off," he said gruffly. "I'm doing it for you."

"But—"

"We can't know each other." And the pain of those words cut so deep that he nearly cried out.

She looked at him, her expression tightening. It became resolute in a…a… He swallowed and looked away. She appeared as any aristocrat when she declared that something would be. There was no hesitation in her expression. Simply a strong, absolute clarity of purpose.

"Bluebell—" he whispered, mourning the loss of his country miss.

She walked slowly to him. He could have moved away. He did shy slightly to the left, but she just followed. So he stood his ground and smelled her sweet scent. That cranesbill flower clung to her here, even in the heart of London.

"Bram," she said softly. "I will not give you up."

"You don't have a choice."

Her mouth flattened, but her gaze had cut sideways to Seelye. He watched her eyes flicker and saw her fists tighten. When she spoke next, it was almost inaudible.

"Can you climb walls?"

"What?"

"Can you climb the side of this bloody house?"

He blinked at her. "Yes. And don't curse."

"Eleanor's put me on the southern side. I'll leave the window open."

He pulled back, appalled by what she was saying. "I cannot—"

"Or I will climb out, Mr. Hallowsby, and wander the streets until I find you."

He closed his eyes, doing his best not to envision the horrors that could happen to her wandering all alone in London. "You are the granddaugther of an earl. It's what you wanted. I will not let you throw that away." Not for him. Not for a bastard. She was so much better than him, not only in status, but because she was at heart a good person.

Why hadn't he seen that before? Why hadn't he realized what a treasure she was from the very beginning? But even if he had, would he have done anything differently? Would he have resisted her charms? Or taken steps to tie her to him irrevocably?

He touched her face, stroking the soft skin of her cheek, letting his thumb caress the full red of her lower lip. "Maybelle," he said softly. "You must know I cannot."

She arched her brow. "I will wait until midnight. And then I will go looking for you. And if you ever call me anything but Bluebell, I will punch you in the stomach."

He snorted. She was so fierce, this little nobody from Hull, who was in fact the most amazing woman he'd ever met. He had to tell her flatly that he would not see her. But while he hesitated, fighting his baser nature, the chance to answer was taken from him. At that moment, Eleanor breezed in, steel in her words for all that she sounded polite.

"Mr. Hallowsby, I hadn't realized you were still here. Goodness, but I'm afraid it's well past teatime now, and we have so much to do before the Season starts."

He stepped back, his heart wrenching inside as he did. "I was just taking my leave."

Eleanor wasn't a fool. Her gaze hopped between him and Bluebell, no doubt seeing her flushed face and mulish expression. "Forgive me for being blunt, but you know—"

"I cannot be associated with Miss Ballenger. I know."

She sighed, and for a brief moment, he saw true sorrow on her face. "You would have made an excellent duke, you know."

The knife cut deeper into his gut, twisting slowly. He knew she meant her words to be a compliment.

He knew that given a choice between a bastard and the seaman who inherited the title, she would have chosen him. Because he at least understood what was needed of the elite. He knew how to behave because he perpetually danced at the edge of society, neither part of it nor completely excluded from it.

He knew.

But her words just churned the resentment. If only his father had recognized him. If only he had been born legitimate. Not only would he have the title, but he could have Bluebell as well. He could marry as high or as a low as he chose.

He could.

If only.

Bitterness surged inside him, but he turned from it as he turned from Bluebell. "Then I bid you both good day," he said as he gave them his most respectful bow.

Then he headed for the door. Seelye was already there with Bram's hat and coat in hand. A moment later, he was outside the residence, the door shutting with a ponderous thud.

Outside.

Unworthy.

Bastard.

He'd never hated his father more.

Nineteen

MAYBELLE WAS FUMING. IN A DAY FILLED WITH EVERY feeling she'd ever thought to experience, everything now settled into one strong emotion: seething fury. She just had to decide what she was going to do about it.

"I do not understand why you insist on treating me as an ignorant girl with more hair than wit!" She used her most pompous tone and glared at her grandmother and Eleanor.

It was early evening on the day they'd forced her grandparents to recognize her. Now she was in the parlor with Eleanor and her grandmother to plan her coming Season. Or so they'd claimed. Instead, the two women had felt it necessary to instruct her—for four hours now—on appropriate behavior. She'd tolerated it for a while, but when they began to discuss gentlemen, it became clear that Mr. Hallowsby was definitely in the *not suitable* category. And that was when she lost her temper.

But far from being upset by her outburst, the women clearly took it as a sign that she was overwhelmed instead of furious.

"I know this is difficult to understand," said one.

"It is all happening so fast, I can barely credit it," said the other.

"But you must trust us to know what is best. We have been doing this far longer than you have."

"Indeed, I cannot think of two women who would steer you more clearly in the social waters than us."

"I quite agree."

"Yes, definitely."

Maybelle huffed out a breath and wished she could loosen her damned corset a little. Instead, she attempted to moderate her tone.

"You forget," she said coldly, "that I was reared under the daily shadow of being a bastard." Her grandmother flinched, and Eleanor compressed her lips, but Maybelle did not soften her tone. "I knew from the earliest age that I must act more correct, more proper, and more stifled than anyone else just to maintain our dubious place in the village."

"But a village in Hull is not London."

"No," Maybelle snapped. "I suspect it is harder to change people's minds up there."

Which is when her grandmother reached out a comforting hand. As she'd stripped off her gloves, Maybelle could see the age spots and the slight tremor. She knew the thin skin and the frail bones of age. And so she did not throw off the condescending pat.

"I know this is hard, and I'm afraid it's going to get worse before it is better. But you must listen."

Eleanor nodded emphatically, then began ticking items off her fingers. "You require dancing lessons, singing lessons, a speech tutor—"

"Oh, definitely," her grandmother said with a nod.

"The dressmaker already has your measurements, but you will have to practice in the corset. You still look awkward."

"Because it's b—" Maybelle swallowed the "bloody awkward" she was about to say and shifted it to something less scandalous. "Pinching me to the point that I cannot breathe."

"Exactly," Eleanor confirmed. "You must get used to it."

"And you must all get used to the idea that I will be friends with Mr. Hallowsby. Without him, I would not have made it to London. I would never have met you, Grandmother. And I would certainly never be trussed up in this corset and discussing singing instructors. I have a terrible voice!"

Both elegant ladies looked at her, their expressions excruciatingly sad. It seemed to be what aristocratic ladies did when upset. They tilted their heads, let their eyes droop and their shoulders settle, while they sighed heavily with great feeling. Meanwhile, Eleanor's hands had clenched into fists, and her grandmother's foot would not cease tapping.

"The man is a by-blow," her grandmother said. "He is not received."

"He was received here."

"Through the servants' entrance," Eleanor said crisply.

"But he is your brother."

"*Half* brother. Goodness, you are worse than Wendy," Eleanor snapped. "There is good *ton* and bad *ton*—"

"You have been singing his praises since I first

arrived. I have heard about his service to the crown, to any number of poor ladies, and I have experienced his kindness myself."

"And yet he is still a by-blow," her grandmother said. "He is still not an appropriate companion for a lady."

"He has been my companion since I left Hull."

Grandmother reacted to that with a gasp and a press of her handkerchief to her mouth. Eleanor simply sighed.

"I told you that we would not speak of that," she admonished.

"But it is the truth, and—"

"Maybelle!" Eleanor snapped. "There are rules, and this is one. You will cease being familiar with Mr. Hallowsby. If you do not listen, then I wash my hands of you. Is that what you want? No Season, no dowry, no entree into society."

Maybelle bit her lip, trying to comprehend the depth of their hypocrisy. "You would throw me over simply for claiming a friendship with your brother."

Eleanor remained intransigent. "I do not claim a friendship with Mr. Hallowsby."

"But—"

"We have become known to one another only recently."

There was something in her tone. Some waver in her words, important if only because until that moment, there had been no compromise in Eleanor's manner. But it was there now, and Maybelle was furious enough to boldly push for more despite the woman's obvious discomfort.

"How recently?" And when Eleanor would not

speak, Maybelle composed her expression into an icy glare. "Recall that I have been independent most of my life. As soon as I could read, I began managing our money and furthering my education, not to mention caring for my sick mother and earning what little I could by making possets."

Her grandmother shuddered. "Pray do not mention that again."

Maybelle stopped herself from rolling her eyes. She was focused on Eleanor and would not be distracted. "I am not a woman to be put off by hurt feelings or illogical assumptions. If I were, then I would have starved to death by the age of seven. So you will explain yourself logically. Why would you refuse to acknowledge your own brother?"

Eleanor sighed and nodded. "I met him when my father was ill. You recall what happened to my family?" She asked the question of the countess, but Maybelle was grateful for the details.

"Illness. Very tragic. I cried for you."

"It was scarlet fever," Eleanor explained. "It struck my grandfather first. There were so many of us gathered for Christmas. Everyone was there." She swallowed, her gaze going very distant.

"This is how the seaman came to be the duke," Maybelle said.

Eleanor nodded. "Looking back, it happened so quickly. Grandpapa. Then my uncles and cousins. My brother, Seth. Papa tried to be so strong. Mama had passed a few years back, but as the new duke, he tried…" She swallowed and looked down at the pages of dress sketches beneath her fingers. "Well, Papa tried to be strong."

The countess now patted Eleanor's hand as she began to speak. "It is the usual procedure when the men die that the solicitors look to the heirs. Every effort is made to keep one safe, but in this case, everyone had already gathered. They were at His Grace's bedside when he died. They were there—"

"To catch the illness," Maybelle said. "So it was too late for the heirs."

"Yes," Eleanor whispered. "That is when I met Bram. He and his mother came up from London. The entire county was reeling from the disease. It wasn't just us, you see. It was the servants and their families. I have never seen so many people die before. So many mourning. So much…" Her voice faltered.

Maybelle had heard of such things. Entire villages wiped out from a sickness that ran rampant. She'd heard that it began with a few victims, but fear quickly takes over. Soon there are people barricading houses, locking the healthy in with the sick. No doctor would come, no supplies delivered. No one to cook or clean. No one but the ill tending the ill, and nothing for the dead.

The countess spoke again. "It is the hope of the mistress to become the wife. With Eleanor's mother gone and her brother passed, there would be no heir. Most of the family had forgotten about the seaman, you see. Or never known he existed."

"Papa remembered," Eleanor said.

Maybelle tried to piece it together. "So with everyone dying, Bram and his mum went there to…" She shook her head. "To marry a dying duke?" That was ghoulish and not at all what she thought of Bram.

The countess nodded. "It was that, or let the title die."

Maybelle sighed, her heart breaking. "But your father wouldn't do it, would he? He would rather the title die than go to Bram."

Eleanor looked down. "He knew about Radley."

The countess shook her head. "What a terrible choice—a seaman or a by-blow. How he must have suffered."

Suffered? As if either man were less, simply for not being reared as an aristocrat. "How could he have done that to his own son? Cast him aside like that?" Maybelle couldn't fathom it. And yet to these two ladies, it seemed like the most logical choice in the world.

Eleanor's gaze was vague. "I'd never met Bram before that. Though I'd heard whispers, people in our set don't discuss by-blows. Certainly not with unmarried ladies."

"Was he terribly angry?" the countess asked. "When he did not get the title?"

"Angry?" Maybelle asked. Why not hurt? Betrayed? Bitter?

"I do not think he expected it," Eleanor answered. "It was his mother who was hopeful. And when my father passed, she left as soon as could be. Returned to London and…"

The countess clucked her tongue in disapproval. "And the life she had made for herself here."

By which Maybelle took it to mean that the woman had a different protector. "And Mr. Hallowsby?" she asked.

Eleanor looked up. "You understand that there was

no chance by this point. That my father had…" She swallowed. "My father was gone, and the title passed to Radley, though I didn't know him at the time. Bram had no reason to stay behind where everyone was ill."

"But he did," Maybelle guessed. "He stayed to help."

Eleanor nodded. "Two months. He did everything. He helped with the dead. He cooked, he cleaned, he even worked with the harvest. I have never seen a man do so much." She bit her lip, clearly fighting tears. "He would have made an excellent duke."

But he hadn't been legitimized. He hadn't received the title. He had simply helped. Because that was what Bram did.

"And yet you still won't recognize him? He has to come through the servant's entrance?" She hadn't thought a woman could be so hard-hearted.

The countess shook her head. "You don't understand."

Eleanor echoed the statement. "How can I recognize him when my own father would not? When he would rather the title go to a seaman no one knew than to his own son? How can I ignore what my father decided when so much was at stake?"

And that was the final word. Maybelle could see it in their nodding heads. In their teary eyes and the way they held each other's hands for support. They were so enmeshed in what was proper that even when they saw Bram's worth, they didn't acknowledge it. They didn't see him.

She could rail at them. She could point out the illogic of having a by-blow, only to refuse him no matter what he became. The ridiculousness of

educating that man, but not allowing him entrance to
the very world in which he'd been reared. She could
talk until she was blue in the face, but that would
make no dent in these women's perspectives. It was
too entrenched in who they were.

"I see," she finally said.

Both ladies exhaled in relief. Clearly they thought
she meant she would do as they asked. That she would
turn her back on Bram just because he was a bastard.
And she did nothing to disabuse them of that idea.

And while she smiled and pretended to go along,
she privately made her own plans.

Twenty

BRAM PACED OUTSIDE HER WINDOW. IT WAS NEARLY midnight. Her window was open, the candle burning brightly just inside. He'd watched as one light after another was extinguished—Eleanor's and the servants'. But Bluebell's still danced in the breeze.

He shouldn't be here. He shouldn't even be thinking of the easy climb up the ivy to her arms, but he needed to tell her the truth. He needed to confess his sin from a week ago when they were in Hull. He'd taken her virginity—albeit accidentally—and she needed to know that before she accepted any high society marriage proposal.

He had to tell her. Which meant he had to go up there. He had to risk it, but he consoled himself by the knowledge that once he told her what he'd done, she would throw him out. She would toss him aside as was good and proper. And then she'd go on to the life she was meant to lead as the granddaughter to an earl.

He resolutely shoved down the black wall of bitterness that rose in him at that thought. An honorable man—bastard or not—would do this. He would ensure that she tossed him aside so that she could have the life she deserved. And so with that thought held firmly in mind, he stripped off his shoes and began to climb.

He'd gone barely three feet off the ground when he felt the knife cut across his ribs. Not deep. Barely grazing the skin, though his clothing was ruined. And while he was still processing the sharp bite of pain, rough hands jerked him down hard enough that he lost his grip.

He landed on the hard stone with a thump that rattled his teeth. It was only a quick roll of his hips that saved his head from getting split open.

"What—"

"Good evenin', my old friend."

Jeremy. He'd know that bear of a bastard anywhere, if only by the looming shadow and the man's foul breath.

Bram blinked several times, pretending to be knocked stupid. It wasn't that hard. He'd been so focused on Bluebell that he had no idea why Jeremy would be here with him.

And then he was pelted with rocks. Very specific rocks. Tiny ones that smarted where they hit his chest and his arms. They only missed his face because he was shielding it behind his battered forearms.

"What are you doing?" he cried. *Ow. Ow.*

"This 'ere's my treasure from Lord Linsel," Jeremy growled. "Rocks. Rocks in a chest meant to 'old gold."

Right. He'd known back in Hull that things weren't over with his old childhood playmate. But a certain blond-haired vixen had distracted him so much that he'd clean forgot.

Jeremy had run out of rocks, so Bram was able to

lower his arms and peer at the man. He hoped his expression looked ignorant. "There were rocks in that chest? Rocks?"

The brute stepped into the moonlight, his blood-shot eyes doing more to worry Bram than the welts from the rocks. The man was drunk, and with Jeremy that meant mean.

"Where is 'e?"

"Who?" Bram pushed himself upright slowly. If he was going to get a boot in his ribs, then he wanted to be balanced. And maybe see it coming. Fortunately, Jeremy wanted to talk right now, so the two men who flanked him were lurking back in the shadows.

"Lord Linsel, ye blighter." And then he did go for the kick. Fortunately, Bram was ready.

He twisted away from the blow, grabbed hold, and jerked Jeremy forward. He was a large man, but drunk, he was off balance. Bram was able to force him sideways at a stumble while still gaining his feet. Then he had his fists raised and was eyeing the two men in the shadows.

"I don't know where Dicky is. He took my money too," he lied. "Then he ran off while I was trying to get the damned carriage fixed." He glared at Jeremy. "That same carriage you tore apart. Probably with your bare hands."

He hoped that the backward compliment would stave off the man's fury. It was a touchy thing talking to a drunk. Especially when the man was spoiling for a fight.

"I'm going to tear you apart—" Jeremy growled.

Bram cursed. Too pissed to reason with. But

perhaps he could narrow the odds. He glared at the two shadows. "I got no quarrel with you. Linsel played us all for fools, and I got—"

"Me father was right furious when I gave him that treasure box. Rocks!"

Worse and worse. He'd thought Jeremy would open the box long before London, but he hadn't. He must have proudly offered it to his father, only to see what was really in there. And Jeremy's father wasn't a forgiving man.

"Dicky did it. I thought there was gold in there, same as you."

Jeremy had regained his footing and was now clenching his massive fists as he started stomping forward. Like the steady creep of a damned behemoth.

"Where is Linsel?"

"I don't know! Scotland?"

"I went there. 'E never showed."

So that's why he'd had this week's respite. Jeremy had been up to Scotland and back.

"He sailed for the Colonies, Jeremy. Went up to Scotland and took a boat from the coast." Well, he'd tried to at least. "Jeremy, think. Why would I give you a chest full of rocks?"

"Because you 'ave it."

Bram felt his belly clench with fear. He could hold his own against Jeremy despite their difference in size. But with the two others? His odds were not looking good.

He scanned the alley. One side was blocked by Jeremy's men. The other side was choked with debris, but he could probably get away in that direction. He was tensing to do just that when he chanced to look up. One last glance at Bluebell's window, only to see a small figure in breeches climbing down the wall. And she was carrying something long and badly wrapped in cloth.

What the hell? Idiot woman!

Even as he thought the question, his mind scrambled to reevaluate. He couldn't run now. Not with her about to drop into the fray. Bloody hell, what did she think she could do to help?

"Jeremy, the blighter didn't pay me either. Took off to America, and I haven't a bloody clue where they are!"

Jeremy straightened, his eyes narrowing and his fist coming up. "You know what I think?"

Not a lot and not well. But he didn't say that aloud.

"I'm dying to know." Probably not the best choice of words, but his mind was split between Jeremy, his men, and Bluebell as she dropped silently onto the ground.

"That's just it. Dying. I think they tried to run off, but I think you caught 'em."

"I was stuck with the bloody carriage and no horse."

"You've done more with less," Jeremy said as he cracked his knuckles. Oh shit. He always did that before a fight.

"Exaggeration. Some of it outright lies. I haven't done half of what they say—"

"Half is enough." Then he took a slow, halfhearted swing. Damn it. It was a testing blow just to see how Bram reacted. The man might be drunk, but he still knew how to fight. "I want me father's money."

"I don't have it. Dicky does."

"Dicky's dead."

"What?" A shot of panic went through him. "How would you know that?" Such was his distraction—trying to watch Bluebell without actually looking at her—that he was being stupid. Jeremy hadn't a clue where Dicky was, but Bram had already spit out the question. It had been a thoughtless response, not meant to imply anything, but suddenly, Jeremy was grinning.

"I knew it. You killed him."

"Are you daft?" Bram asked.

"You just said it. You said he was dead. How did I know it? I know 'cause you said it." Jeremy advanced slowly. "'Cause you did it. For him trying to run off with yer money."

"I didn't kill Dicky! Bloody hell, we were friends."

"So were you and me," Jeremy returned logically. Of all the times to resort to logic. And this time his punch was quicker. One side, the other. Bram evaded every swing, but he was being maneuvered around. Shifted until he was in the center of the three men.

Normally he wouldn't have allowed it. He would have sprinted down the alleyway in the other direction. He was faster than any of these blighters. But not with Bluebell gripping—

What the hell was that? She'd pulled the cloth off the thing she was carrying. A bed warmer? Part of him was impressed that she'd made it down the wall while keeping that quiet. The other part was thinking that she was absolutely, completely insane.

He had to make a show of it. Now. Before Bluebell got any crazy ideas. "Don't do this, Jeremy. If I killed them, I can kill you." He pulled a knife from his hip.

He had the other still strapped to his other side, but he was saving that for a surprise, just in case. And because he only fought well with his right hand. His left was better at punching. Or grabbing. Or anything else except wielding a knife with skill.

But Jeremy wasn't listening. He bellowed, "I want me money!" and rammed forward.

Bram sidestepped, then slammed his fist into Jeremy's jaw, whipping the man's head around. He stumbled but recovered quickly. Damn, the bastard's head was like granite.

Meanwhile, Bluebell was raising the warmer, preparing to strike.

"I'll get you the money," Bram tried desperately. "Whatever you need. I'll get it. Just go."

That was enough to make the other two pause, but not Jeremy. He either knew Bram was bluffing or didn't care. Either way, he attacked again, this time with his own knife drawn.

Bram leaped backward, avoiding the flashing blade, but he couldn't go far. Not with a brick wall to his back and rubbish fouling his footing. Jeremy swung again, and Bram countered.

Quick swipes, quicker footwork. Anything to keep the man dancing as Bram drew the fray away from Bluebell. Maybe she would be smart. Maybe she would wait until Bram took care of Jeremy before revealing herself. Maybe—

Clang.

He heard the impact of the bed warmer on someone's head. So did Jeremy, and he swung around to look.

Fortunately, Bram already knew what was going

on, so he wasted no time in attacking. Jeremy was
the leader. If he could subdue him, maybe the others
would run.

First punch was to the knife hand, and Jeremy's
weapon went skittering away. Then he followed up
with blow after blow, while he held off sticking him
with the knife. Even with Bluebell on the line, he
was loath to make anyone bleed. If he could knock
Jeremy unconscious—

The brute came back at him tenfold. For such a big
man, he was quick with his fists.

Clang. Clatter.

"Eeep!"

It was the cut-off cry that set him off. No more
holding back. He rushed at Jeremy with a vengeance,
knife and fist working hard. He got a few good cuts
in, but nothing deep. All he managed to do was slow
the bastard down.

"I got 'er! I got 'er!"

Bram slammed a hard blow to Jeremy's face. He
was desperate to end this, but it wasn't enough. And
the pause as Jeremy stumbled backward gave the idiot
enough time to hear his henchman.

The bastard straightened slowly, one meaty fist
rubbing his jaw as he peered down the alley. Bram
was already looking. At least Bluebell had gotten one
of them good.

Of the two other brutes, one was on his hands and
knees, shaking his head, clearly dazed. But the other
had his arm wrapped around Bluebell's throat, another
clutching her waist.

She was struggling, but the more she fought, the

tighter the hold on her throat. Much more and she would be strangled.

"I got 'er!" the man said again, as he wrenched his arm tight.

That ended the struggle and made Bram's vision run red. "Let her go," he said softly. "That's the Earl of Cavener's granddaughter. You want him angry at you?"

"That's no granddaughter. That's the chippy from Hull," said Jeremy. "Wot you doing all the way down 'ere? And with 'im?"

He stomped forward, his eyes narrowed. Bloody hell. Jeremy was none too easy with his women. He was downright brutal with his enemies.

Bluebell didn't have the breath to speak, but she was a master at making her opinion known. Even without breath, she screwed up her face and spat straight at Jeremy. Which was the wrong thing to do.

The bastard raised his fist, ready to subdue her. Bram didn't hesitate. In truth, he didn't think about what he was doing at all. He simply drew from his hip and threw.

Thunk.

The knife sunk deep in Jeremy's back. A kidney shot. Hell.

Jeremy roared and reached behind him, whirling around. Bram didn't stop. He punched the man as hard and as quickly as he could.

Jeremy stumbled but didn't go down. He did go toward the mouth of the alley. If he'd headed for Bluebell, Bram would have killed him. But he didn't. He stumbled past the man on his knees and headed away, blood rapidly darkening his shirt and coat.

Bloody hell. That was a lot of blood.

The third man—the one holding Bluebell—watched with terrified eyes as Bram adjusted his grip on the other knife. "It's a close thing with you hiding behind her," he said menacingly. "But I'm good with my knife. Or you can let her go, take your other man, and run."

"Naw. Naw, I won't—"

Bluebell twisted. Apparently, he'd loosened his hold enough that she could jerk her elbow back hard. She got him under the rib cage, and Bram heard the man's breath explode out of him while she slithered down, right out of his hold.

Clear target. Open chest as he—

Bram held back throwing his knife. The man turned and ran. The one on his knees was a split second behind him.

Gone. They were gone.

And then she was in his arms.

"Are you all right?" she was asking. "Did he hurt you? Bram, talk to me." She grabbed his face, turning him to stare at her and not down the alleyway. "Where are you hurt?"

"My jaw," he muttered. "Right where you're pressing."

"Oh!" She jerked her hand back, but he had already wrapped his arms around her. He was holding her tight, smelling her cranesbill scent, and feeling the solid—alive—weight of her against him.

"What the bloody hell were you thinking?" he said into her hair.

"That you were outnumbered," she said.

"I could have run. If you weren't here, I would have—"

"And they would have chased you. And I wouldn't have known how to follow. I was too far away. I couldn't help."

"You help by staying safe. By staying away."

"No. Never. I won't."

"Bluebell," he groaned. Then he kissed her. He pressed his lips to hers, and thrust his tongue inside. He plundered her mouth, her sweetness, her every-thing, as she wrapped herself around him, gripping his shoulders like a vise. And he loved every second of it. Every heavy weight, every gasping moan, every heaving second as they separated to breathe.

"Are you 'urt?" she said against his neck. "Tell me."

"Hurt," he corrected, emphasizing the *h*. "I'm fine."

"He hit you pretty hard."

He gestured weakly to the dented bed warmer. "So did you."

She looked down to the bed warmer that was now rubbish. "It was his head that was hard." Then she smoothed her hand over his jaw, her touch both pain-ful and infinitely sweet.

"Why were they here? What did they want?"

"They think I have Dicky's money."

She spat out a curse. "Not too smart, are they?"

He shrugged. "Jeremy has his own form of logic. He was embarrassed in front of his father and wanted someone to take it out on."

"But why you?"

"Why not me? I tricked him. And he thought..." He swallowed.

"He thought you'd killed Dicky and taken their money."

"Yes." It wasn't often that his reputation worked against him, but when it did, it was very bad.

"Bram," she said softly. "How many men have you killed?"

He closed his eyes, the sight of Jeremy's bloody coat stark in his mind. "One," he rasped. "Tonight. Jeremy."

"Jeremy? But…but he ran away."

"He'll never survive that."

"And there's never been anyone else, has there? What about the French spy?"

"I thought she was a house burglar until Mr. Wulfson came home. He's the one who sent for the Home Office."

"And the bear at the county fair?"

"When I was twelve? It was a bad-tempered dog—"

"That's dangerous!"

"It was *my* dog."

"Oh. So you didn't save any children carrying puppies?"

He shook his head. "Who told you that?"

"Everyone! Eleanor especially has a love of the tales, but her maid did too. And Seelye relayed a few. And—"

He pressed his hands to her lips. "Exaggerations. Some lies. I've never…Bluebell, I threaten. I intimidate. I've never killed." Before today. Before Jeremy threatened her.

"That's what I thought," she said softly. Then she shivered.

"You're cold," he said. "And wherever did you get these clothes?"

"They're mine from home. You don't think I worked the garden every day in a skirt."

"But why—"

"I told you. You climb the wall by midnight, or I come looking for you."

He chuckled. Of course she did. And she was a woman of her word. "I have to talk to you. I have something I must tell you."

"I do too, but not out here. Not in the rubbish and the cold." She took his hand and led him to the ivy. Then with a wink, she began to climb.

"Wait!" he said, holding her arm. "You can't mean to climb back up."

"I won't risk waking the servants. What I have to say is not for their ears. Besides, I don't know where the servant entrance is."

"It's right over there," he said, pointing. But she was right. It was likely locked and...

And she was already halfway up the wall. Bloody hell, she was a talented woman. And barefoot, he noted. She'd come down barefoot, cudgeled a brute with a bed warmer, and kissed Bram senseless.

What else could he do but climb after her?

Twenty-one

MAYBELLE'S HEART BEAT TRIPLE TIME. EVERYTHING she'd ever dreamed of had come true this day all because of one man. And tonight was when she was going to say thank you. When she was going to express her heart and see if he still saw her as a deceitful chit from the country.

She made it through the window, tumbling head-first onto the rug, feeling grateful she wasn't in a corset. Then she turned to extend a hand to him.

She didn't need to. Though he was a tall man, Bram was nimble. And strong. His arms bulged as he lifted himself higher than the window before pushing his feet through. Then he landed quick and quiet on her rug while she looked up at him in admiration.

"Are you all right?" he asked as he leaned down.

"I'm fine. And you?" She scanned his body, and now, with the candlelight on him, she saw where his clothes had been slashed. "You've been cut," she gasped.

She got to her feet quickly, being forceful as she pushed back his coat and shirt, feeling sick as she touched the wet blood on the fabric.

"Take this off. I can clean and stitch it."

"It's fine." He tried to still her hands, but she shoved him to the bed.

"Don't argue. In the middle of a fight, you don't feel pain when you're hurt. Not like you do later. Take off your shirt now."

"And what would you know of fighting?"

"I was taught by the witch-woman, remember? Besides, long before that I'd been called on to help. I have a fine hand for…" She swallowed. "For closing up flesh."

"Bluebell, there's no reason."

She turned to him, her brow arched and her expression as stern as she could make it. "If you do not let me dress that wound right now, I will scream. And then how will you explain yourself?"

Bram's lips twitched as he shrugged out of his coat. "You do know how absurd that sounds, don't you? You are the only one who will suffer."

Lord, he was moving too stiffly. It might be a deeper wound than he was implying. So she batted away his hands and made quick work of his cravat and buttons. And then she was stroking his glorious chest, searching for blood or bruises.

He grunted when she found it. Not the knife wound, as he'd been right about that. It wasn't deep enough for stitches. She'd wash it clean and set a pad there to absorb any more blood. No, what he complained of was the bruising. Jeremy was right-handed, and his blows had taken their toll on Bram's left side. Though she felt nothing broken, he would be in pain for a week at least.

"I'm glad you got him with the knife," she said, looking into his face. "He hurt you. And was going to do much worse."

She stroked his side, feeling sick all over again at the memory of him backing away as three men stepped out of the shadows. She'd been looking down and had felt a surge of terror and helplessness. What could she do from up above?

Thinking back, she realized she should have just screamed. Or thrown things down at them. But she'd wanted to defend him with her own hands. And she'd seen the bed warmer and hatched her plan.

"Next time," he said as he gripped her fingers. "You will just scream."

"Which would have simply delayed the attack until the next time they found you. This way it's done, isn't it? They won't come after you again."

She watched his lips compress and his expression flatten. She knew what he was thinking, and she was sorry the idea pained him.

"You don't know that you've killed him," she said softly.

He nodded, but didn't seem convinced. "Jeremy won't come after me again. That's a wound that takes a long time to heal. If it ever does."

She touched his face. "He was going to hurt you."

He pressed his hand to hers on his cheek. "He was going to hurt *you*."

She kissed him. The horror still lingered in his eyes, and even if it didn't, her fear for him still coiled inside her gut. She needed to assure herself that he was alive. That he was still strong and vital. And when he kissed her back with a desperation that echoed her own, she knew he'd been equally frightened for her.

"He didn't hurt me," she said into his mouth.

His hand tightened on the back of her head, and he deepened the kiss. He pushed inside her, and she dueled with him. But it was a losing game, and soon he was touching every part of her mouth, thrusting in and out while her breath caught, and her belly tightened for an entirely different reason.

One of his hands slid down her side, cupping her bottom before squeezing it. But then he broke away from her. He tore his mouth aside, his breath heaving in and out.

"Bluebell," he said. "We can't."

Oh, they could. They most definitely could. But she didn't say that aloud. Instead she nodded. "Lie back. Let me wash the cut."

"No—"

She glared at him. She knew her cheeks were flushed and her nipples tight. Lord knew she was all liquid inside when it came to him. But she made sure she appeared much stronger than she was.

"Take off your shirt, and lie back."

"It's nothing." But when she did not change her expression, he sighed. He pulled off his ruined shirt, and the candlelight cast his hard muscles into a golden relief.

"Lie down," she said, her mouth dry.

He did as she bid, the mattress creaking slightly under his weight. She wrung out a cloth in the basin, and she sat on the bed beside him as she gently wiped away the blood.

"I love you," she blurted out. Then she froze. Lord,

she hadn't meant to say that yet. She hadn't meant to confess it so baldly. But there it was. She'd said it, and so she was forced to continue. "I don't know when it started. It was a quiet thing, growing from something so tiny that I didn't even notice. Like spring, when suddenly you look around and everything's blooming, and you hadn't even realized."

She watched him swallow. His eyes were shadowed and his body completely still. He was holding everything inside, and she'd never know his thoughts. So she focused on her task as she cleaned his wound.

"It happened yesterday," she continued, purposely keeping her tone light. "I hadn't heard from you in days, and everything was awful. I missed you. I wanted to talk to you. I wanted…" Well, there were many things she wanted from him. With him. "And then today you were here, and it was spring."

She set aside the cloth, hardly daring to touch him again without knowing what he was thinking.

"That's gratitude, Bluebell," he finally rasped. "It's not love."

She twisted his nipple hard. She hadn't intended to, but she'd been looking at that brown flat disk with the tight bud. She'd been seeing the golden hair that whorled around it, and then he'd made that stupid comment. So she'd pinched him, except she'd been looking at his nipple so she pinched that.

"Ow!" he cried out, gripping her hand as his belly jerked, and his legs lifted off the bed.

"Don't tell me what is and isn't love. Do you think I haven't felt thanks before? Do you think I don't know when my heart is given to a man? I'm a woman grown and—"

He jerked her forward. A heave from his hands, and she landed flush on his chest. Then his mouth was on hers. She was greedy as she lay on top of him. She thrust her tongue into his mouth and felt him groan as the sound rumbled from his body into hers. He let his hands roam, caressing her back and bottom. And there, hot against her private parts, was his organ. Big and rock hard, even through their clothing. She rolled her pelvis against him, and once again felt that low rumble between them.

But then he held her back. His expression was tortured as he pushed her up. "I've lied to you," he said.

That startled her. She pushed up on her arms, lifting her chest, but not moving off his hips or legs. She wasn't even sure how she ended up stretched out on the bed on top of him, except that she still liked the feel of him beneath her, no matter what he said.

But she didn't want a lie between them. "When?"

He swallowed. "Do you remember that time in your kitchen? When we... When I..."

She felt her face heat. Of course she remembered that. She was hoping to do it again. "I remember." Her voice came out low and husky, and his eyes locked on her mouth.

"I told you I wouldn't take your virginity."

She nodded slowly. "You didn't."

"I—I don't know. My fingers were inside you when... God, you were so tight, and then you came around them, and there was blood. I don't know if I tore your membrane. It didn't matter then. You weren't going to have a highborn marriage. But now…" He looked up to the ceiling, and she saw misery in the press of his lips. "I should have told you then, but…"

"But you didn't think it mattered. You didn't think I was legitimate."

"Not the granddaughter of an earl. I never thought…"

She pressed a hand to his lips. "So I'm not a virgin."

He kissed her fingers, then gently drew them away. "I don't know. I…I don't think so."

"Is that the only lie?"

He nodded. "I'm sorry—"

She kissed him again, a sweet joy bubbling inside her. She wasn't a virgin anymore. She ought to be angry, but instead, she embraced it. She was deflowered. She might as well enjoy it.

She lifted off him, annoyed with the clothing that kept them apart. With quick motions, she pulled off the boy's shirt. She hadn't had time to bind her breasts, so within moments she was naked from the waist up.

"Bluebell—" he choked out.

"If I've already lost my virginity to you, then let us do it properly."

He was looking at her breasts, and when he didn't move, she took his hand and pressed it to her chest. He shifted immediately. His long fingers molded to her size, his thumb brushed across her nipple, and sensation sizzled down her spine.

"What if there is a babe?" he said, his voice thick. She didn't need to answer. His gaze went straight to hers. "You know what to do, don't you? You know the potion."

She nodded. The witch-woman had taught her. "You probably do too."

He shifted slightly, drawing her closer, feeling their skin touch and heat. "I know who to ask. But it's not always safe."

She smiled. "I don't care." He squeezed her nipple, and she arched into the sensation.

"I…" He swallowed. "I have a French letter." And when she didn't understand what that meant, he explained. "A condom. A thing that goes over my penis to prevent pregnancy."

"And the spread of disease."

"Yes."

She smiled at him. "You came prepared."

"I…hell, Bluebell, I am weak around you. A better man—an honorable man—would set you aside."

"Then it is a good thing that you are a bastard."

He laughed, but the sound didn't hold much humor. Then he drew her higher on his body, pulling her so that her breasts dangled before his lips. He captured the closest nipple, swirling his tongue around it and suckling while she moaned at the feel.

He stayed that way for a while. He feasted on her breasts while she grew restless and hungry. Her legs scissored against his. Her pelvis rolled against him. And when she managed to put her hand on his organ through his attire, he groaned against her and thrust into her hold.

Then he pulled away from her breasts, and his eyes looked tortured. "What will you tell your husband? When the time comes, what will you say to him?"

There it was. He'd all but said that he would not

marry her. That she would tie herself to some other man. She wanted to ask him why. Why didn't he want her? Why didn't he love her as her heart was overflowing with love for him? But she hadn't the breath.

"I want you," she finally whispered, then with growing strength, "I will have you." So she gripped him. She squeezed him through his clothing, rolling her fingers as he had taught her.

Once. Twice. And then suddenly the world upended. He surged forward, gripping her hips as he rolled her over. She was lying on her back, and he was above her. With quick fingers, he undid her breeches and pulled them down. Within seconds she was naked beneath him, and he was stroking her skin from breast to hip. And then between her legs.

His thumb was sliding between her folds, sending bolts of hunger up her spine. She gasped as he pushed high on her most sensitive place. Then her legs slipped open, and her body began to pulse. Tiny beats from her heart as everything in her opened to him.

He sat there stroking her, his eyes trained on her face as she pushed down against his thumb. "I will remember this until the day I die."

She gripped his thigh, angry at the clothing he still wore. "All of you, Bram. Hold nothing back."

He lifted up her knee, pushing it aside such that there was room for him. She dug her fingers into the waist of his pants, tugging uselessly at it.

"Off," she ordered.

Instead, he leaned over and kissed her knee, then the inside of her thigh. She didn't understand what he intended, but had no desire to resist. He moved higher on her thigh, biting lightly before soothing it with his tongue. Higher and higher he went, while she tried to shift beneath him.

He didn't let her move. He adjusted until he was lying between her thighs, his shoulders keeping her spread. And then he licked her.

She didn't know it could happen like that. She didn't know that it could feel so amazing to feel the wet and the stroke. The flat of his tongue, the push of his fingers inside her.

He stroked her deep while she clenched around his fingers. He licked her open, and he sucked that place. The part of her that made everything in her pull tight...

Tight...

Yes!

She burst apart.

The waves consumed her, and she reveled in them. But she wasn't going to let him stay distant. She had given him her heart, and she would not let him stay back.

While she lay there languid and he looked up at her, his eyes nearly luminous in the candlelight, she touched his face. She stroked his cheek. And then she gripped his ear.

Hard.

"Ow!"

"All of you," she repeated.

She tugged him up her body. He came slowly, kissing her belly and breasts while her muscles quivered beneath the attention. But she could tell he was still trying to hold back, so she fumbled through the unbuttoning of his clothing.

And then he was free. Then she could touch him where he was thick and hot and proud. She could stroke the wet tip and hear his hiss as he thrust into her hand.

"Condom," he gritted out, his breath hot against her neck.

"Show me," she said, and he pushed himself up and away. But lest he go too far, she still held him. She squeezed and played as she wanted.

And she grinned when he groaned and thrust again into her hand.

"Coat pocket," he rasped, but she didn't let go.

He reached over and grabbed his clothes, his breath ragged as she continued to play. Tight squeeze one moment, then a long, languid stroke. A pinch at the top and then a hard pull down. She saw the sweat on his chest, and she used her other hand to stroke the contours of his body. She stopped twice to tweak his nipples.

Then she watched with curiosity as he unfolded a piece of foolscap and pulled out a sheath.

"Teach me," she said, and he did. He guided her hands as she put it on him, and he drove into it.

It quickly warmed to his body, and then he was kissing her. Hard and deep, dominating her mouth as he pushed her onto her back. She went willingly, loving the urgency in his touch, the demand in the way he kneed her legs apart.

Then he was there, his cock pressing against her, a soft push that slid the tiniest bit in.

"Bluebell," he whispered against her. He was still fighting himself. He was still trying to hold back. And so she took his face in her hands and looked into his eyes.

One last attempt. One last opportunity for him to comprehend what she was saying.

"I love you, Bram. I am yours."

He swallowed. "Mine..." he murmured.

And then he thrust.

She gasped, feeling the thick and hard intrusion. He was inside her, and he was so big.

"Bluebell?" he asked, his tone worried.

"You are everywhere," she said, loving the sensation of having him surround her, penetrate her, and kiss her. She touched his face, seeing the fierce way he held himself still, the perspiration on his lip, the intensity in his gaze.

And she lifted her knees to grip him tight.

"Is there more?" she whispered, knowing that there was.

His hips jerked, and the uncontrolled push had her quivering in delight.

"Again," she whispered.

This time he slid backward. He drew out slowly, but before he was gone from her, he slammed back in. And the impact had her crying out in delight.

"Yes," she said. This is what she'd wanted. This is the possession she'd craved. "Again!"

He was already doing it. Already sliding back before that glorious thrust back inside.

She didn't have to ask again. His tempo grew faster, the impacts harder. She began helping with her legs. She tugged him into her and moaned as he slid back.

And this time when the quickening came, it was almost as an afterthought. Her belly tightened, her body arched, but the whole of her was already pulsing, already gripping, already taking.

His rasp was loud in her ear, and then…

He moaned.

A slow release of sound while his body shuddered inside her.

And it went on. He jerked against her. Hard and harder.

His breath caught.

And then he exhaled.

Soft. Low. A release.

He'd done it. He'd given himself to her.

She knew it on a level so deep, so holy, that she did not question it.

He was hers.

Forever.

Then he kissed her. A tiny press of his lips so tender that it brought tears to her eyes. She was languid in her pleasure, boneless and awed by what they had done. And when she would have snuggled closer, he set her aside.

"Bram?"

"Shhh."

He climbed out of her bed and tucked the covers gently about her. Then he pulled on his clothes.

"Bram," she said, sadness in his name, because she knew what was to come.

"Good night."

Then he climbed out her window and was gone.

Twenty-two

BRAM WASN'T A MAN WHO DRANK. EVEN IN HIS youngest years, he didn't overindulge, because he was always too afraid of what he might say when in his cups. He had learned some things from his mother that really couldn't be told. And as he aged, the secrets he kept close only grew more dangerous. So he didn't drink.

Except tonight he was blind, stinking drunk. So bloody pissed that he couldn't stand himself. And yet he sat on the floor of his tiny room and swilled cheap gin, while glaring at the only person in the world he could risk this kind of drunk with: his mother. She'd come to see him, barging in, when he was already three sheets to the wind, and he was struggling to gather his wits.

"Love," he muttered into the jug. "You love me, Mum. I don't need her."

"Of course not, dear."

"You love every man you take to your bed. In and out. Love him. Love her. Love this one. Love that."

"Yes, dear. Have you eaten any supper?"

"I had her, and she tasted like...like ambrosia."

"Of course she did. Who is this girl, exactly?"

"Bluebell. I call her Bluebell."

"But what's her real name, dear?"

He glared at the jug this time, wondering if he had the strength to throw it across the room. Probably. But he hadn't the will. He was too depressed.

"Bram Wesley Hallowsby," his mum said sternly. "What is her name?"

"Maybelle Ballenger," he shot back. "The bloody Earl of Cavener's granddaughter."

She sniffed in disdain. "Nonsense. He's hasn't got a daughter named Maybelle."

"The second son," he shot back. "The one that died in Oxford. Of a broken heart."

This time her sniff became a "tut!" Then she smoothed a nonexistent wrinkle in her skirt. "He died of the French disease."

Bram snorted. Trust that fat-arsed earl to let his son be known as a whoremonger rather than a man who loved his wife. Bluebell's mother. And the woman who loved Bram.

"She said she loved me."

"She's too young to know her mind, dear."

"She brought me across England, Mum. Managed it just like she said she would. First to fix the carriage, next to see the registry, and then to see her grandfather. Stuffed up prig."

His mother brought him a tepid glass of tea, forcibly replacing his empty gin jug with the weak brew. "Really? And the earl accepted her?"

Bram shook his head. "Wanted her strung up and quartered. But I forced him."

"You what?"

"I forced him. Wasn't hard. The marriage was real. The child is legal. And smart. And beautiful." And she tasted like ambrosia.

"Yes, yes. Goodness, that's quite a tale."

"It's true. All bloody true." His voice broke on the last as he tried to drain the last of the gin but swallowed his mum's tea instead. Gah. It was vile stuff. So disgusting that he almost missed his next words for all that he said them clearly enough. "I love her, Mum. I love her like I've never loved anyone."

"Yes," she said softly. "I can see that." Then with a sigh and a shift of her skirts, his mother sat directly in front of him. It was a surprise. He couldn't remember a time when she'd gotten down on the dirty floor with him. Not even when he was a child. So he stared blearily at her and wondered if he was hallucinating.

"Mum?"

"I'm going to tell you something I swore I'd never tell a soul. Not a soul. And if you repeat it, I shall find a way to make you pay."

And she could. He occasionally made empty threats. Had to sometimes. It was his only hope, and with his reputation it usually worked. But not his mum. Her threats were always real.

"I don't talk," he muttered.

"Not usually, but then you're drunk. So I doubt you'll remember whatever I say anyway."

His eyes narrowed. She was getting blurry around the edges. "Tell me," he ordered.

"I loved your father. And I'm fairly sure he loved me."

Bram stared at her. He replayed the words over and

over in his brain until they slipped in past the gin. And when they did, all he could say was, "Wha—?"

"It was the happiest day of my life when I found out I was with child. Second only to the day you were born."

Again, he stared at her, blinking now to force her to come into focus. It didn't really work.

"I don't regret any of it. The love. The sex. The scandal. None of it. And I would do it again."

"You hate my father. You said so. Repeated— often. You said it often."

"He was dead by then. I could speak ill of him without risk of hurting him."

Bram shook his head. It felt ten times too large and too heavy, and his stomach sloshed when he did it, but he kept denying her words. "You hated him. Hated that he got you pregnant. That he ruined your looks. That you had to care for a babe with no one to help. You hated it."

She sighed. "No, dear. I hated what I had to do after he let me go. I hated that he left me with so little money."

"He gave you thousands per annum."

She nodded and pressed a wet cloth to his mouth. He shook it away even though it did feel nice. Then he grabbed her wrist as much to steady himself as to hold her still. "You loved him?"

"Yes. And if you have to sneak around in private behind some doddering husband, then you should do that. You shall have the woman you want even if she's married to someone else."

"No."

"Yes."

"Mum, *no*. It'll kill her. She's a good Christian woman. Says it often enough."

"What does that matter? Do you know how many Christian men have graced my bed? Ladies too."

He didn't want to think of that. He didn't want to think of the ways he sullied Bluebell by merely thinking of that. "I've already ruined her, Mum. I can't make her live like...like..."

"Like all the other married women of the *ton*? Like all the other ladies you've bedded? Like all those unhappy wives who hate their husbands and their lives?"

"Yes," he bit out. "Yes, damn you, yes! That's not Bluebell."

"Isn't that her choice? Did you seduce her, Bram? Or did she pull you into her bed?"

Bram didn't answer, but his face must have made the truth obvious.

"She wanted this life, Bram. Didn't you say that she brought you all the way across England to make Cavener recognize her? That everything has worked out just as she intended?"

He swallowed and looked away. "She's not like that. She's pure."

"Not anymore," his mother drawled.

"I ruined her."

"Or...she chose to be ruined." She touched his face. It was so close to what Bluebell did that he nearly cried. "She wants you."

"She's not like you!" he snapped, then immediately regretted it when his mother's face closed down. Her lips compressed, and she looked away.

"Mum, I'm sorry—"

"Why must men always think in extremes? I can love even as a mistress. Especially as a mistress, because I choose my protector."

They both knew that wasn't true. She chose the man who would best keep her in gowns and jewelry. Or in food and shelter.

She folded her arms before her and frowned at him. "I loved your father. We both understood the constraints of his title and his marriage. I wanted his child anyway."

Bram blinked his eyes, and finally his mother came into focus. "Why did you come here, Mum? How did you even know I was back in London?"

She tapped his knee. "Of course I know where you are, my dear. I pay a boy to watch your rooms."

Of course she did. Her current protector was very flush in the pocket. "What do you want?"

"There's another girl in trouble. I need you to threaten the father of her child."

He groaned and dropped his head against the wall. Bloody hell, why was he sitting on the floor?

"Why?" he said to himself as much as to his mother. "Why have the babe? Why let a child be born as a by-blow? Don't you know we don't fit anywhere?"

"Of course you do. You fit on the outskirts with us." She caressed his arm. "I just never thought it would hurt you so deeply. I never thought I'd have a son who was so...so..."

"Stupid?"

"Honorable. Why would you want to be like them? Marrying for money, hated by your children, saddled with appearances that can never be wholly maintained. Why would you want that?"

Because he could have her. Because he could marry her. Because he could honestly, honorably love her.

But he didn't say that. His mother would simply laugh and tell him to love her in secret. To slip into Bluebell's bedroom when her husband was away. To pleasure her in all the improper ways she knew so well.

That is what he should do.

And by the time she left, he'd come to believe it as well.

❧

Maybelle shuffled into her bedroom. It was early by town standards—just after two a.m.—but she could barely keep her eyes open. Worse, while Eleanor had been the very definition of excitement, Maybelle found herself feeling rather flat.

She'd just attended her first ball.

She wore a gown of pale blue with gold stitching, so beautiful she couldn't have imagined it a month ago.

She'd been announced as Maybelle Ballenger. She'd been escorted by her grandparents, and everyone had been stunned. Then she'd been introduced to a thousand eligible gentlemen and danced until her feet ached and her head swam.

Eleanor and the countess were in alt. They said she'd been launched perfectly.

Even her grandfather had nodded. And he'd lost that stiff-backed, narrow-eyed glare he usually gave her. Instead, he'd looked almost fond.

Which meant she was accepted. Lauded even. And all she could think was that Bram had not been there. She'd expected that, of course. She'd known from the

moment he'd crept out of her bedroom a week ago
that she might never see him again. It didn't seem to
matter that he was in her soul. That they were forever connected, heart-to-heart. He would not break
society's rules enough to appear at a ball. Certainly
not the one that was to be her come-out. The last
thing she needed—according to Eleanor—was to be
associated with a by-blow, even though he was the
son of a duke.

So he had stayed away in body, but in her thoughts,
he'd been everywhere. Every man she met was compared
to him. This one's shoulders were not so strong. This
one's breath was not so sweet. This one had too small a
smile compared to Bram's. That one was too wide.

And none of them questioned a word she said. It
didn't matter if she claimed to be a Black Irishwoman
from the Colonies or a descendent from Turkish savages. At one point, she even said her favorite drink
was boiled turnips. Not a one of them looked at her
oddly. Not a one of them noticed that what she said
was complete rubbish.

They all just smiled and patted her hand while
looking at her décolletage. They all assumed she was
an empty-headed miss, and frankly, she was shocked
to prefer Bram's way of doubting everything she said.
Or even when he called her a liar. Because that meant
at least he was listening.

All these men heard was her grandfather's title and
the amount of her now-substantial dowry. Which had
been the biggest shock of all this night.

The four of them had been in the carriage on the
way to the ball. Her stomach had been tied into knots,

and she had been wringing her hands as she tried to wipe the sweat away. The countess and Eleanor were filled with last-second advice, but in one of the few silent pauses, her grandfather had cleared his throat.

They had all looked at him when he'd casually announced that he'd dowered her. Twenty thousand pounds. A sum that left her speechless. She was an heiress. And every single man and woman at the ball hadn't cared if she were beautiful or stupid or disease-ridden. All they cared about was twenty thousand pounds.

By the midnight supper, she'd wanted to escape. By two, she'd been on the verge of screaming. Which is when she told Eleanor she was leaving with or without her chaperone. Eleanor had agreed that staying until the end of one's come-out ball was gauche, and it was best they departed.

And now she was at last home. She couldn't wait to strip out of this whaleboned torture device of a corset. Not to mention taking down her hair. The pins had been poking her all night.

She made it to her bedroom and allowed her maid to undress her. In truth, she did little more than stand there like an overly large doll. The girl did everything. And when it became clear that Maybelle wasn't going to chatter, the girl had settled into her work in silence.

Blessed silence.

And soon she was ready for bed. Her maid bid her good night, then firmly shut the door. Maybelle climbed in, took one last look at her window, and wished for Bram. Then, knowing the futility of such a thought, she sighed and blew out the candle.

Which is when she heard the sound. Low, and coming from directly beneath her mattress.

"Is she gone, then?"

She would have screamed. She should have. Imagine the man hiding under her bed until she'd finally settled in for the night. And then calmly speaking, as if she'd been waiting all week to hear his voice.

Imagine!

But she had been, and so she simply smiled. Her entire body relaxed, her breath came out on a sigh, and she thumped the bed frame hard enough to hurt her hand.

"You scared the life out of me! Why the devil would you hide under there?"

"Well, I had to go somewhere, didn't I? Besides, I thought I'd have a good view from under here."

"And did you?"

"No." He sounded so disappointed that she laughed. "Nothing but dust and your slippers."

She quickly lit the candle, then pulled the coverlet out of the way. "Well, come on. Come out."

He was already scooting over, his head popping out a scant inch from her nose. His hair was mussed, his eyes bloodshot, and there was a new cut on his lip. And he was the most handsome man she'd ever seen. Especially when he looked at her as ardently as she stared at him.

"You were beautiful tonight," he said. "I knew Eleanor would dress you perfectly."

She gaped at him. "You were there? Where? Why didn't—"

"I waited outside. I watched from the bushes until

you got out of the carriage. I bet you danced the whole night through."

"And have the blisters to prove it." She sat back as he made it out from under the bed. He took a moment to shake the dust off while she realized he was dressed oddly.

Well, not oddly, but not in the first stare of fashion. It was strange how quickly she'd become used to the bright colors of fresh dye, the tight waistcoats with perfect seams and no wear. He was dressed in brown, and what she'd once thought was the most elegant attire back in Hull, she now realized was out of date. Worse, he had a stain on the cuff and a jagged line where a tear had been badly repaired.

In short, he was not a dandy about town. He was not even fashionable. What a difference one week made in her perceptions.

"What? Have I got a spider on me?"

She shook her head. "But you have got a fresh bruise. What happened?"

He touched his lip and shrugged. "Lord Dunman owed his mistress some money. I had to persuade him to pay up."

"Lord Dunman? The big one with one ear that's…" She tilted her head and gestured with her hand.

"Lopsided and a little oddly shaped? Yes, he's the one."

She nodded. "He asked for a third dance from me tonight."

Bram's expression suddenly sobered. "You didn't give it to him, did you? Eleanor must have told you—"

"Two dances. No more. Not until I've made my choice."

"Yes."

"She told me. And no, I didn't. And now I won't if he's having trouble paying for his mistress."

"Plus a host of other gambling debts."

"Definitely no more dances for him."

"Definitely." His expression was light, but there was a darkness in his eyes that recalled the shadow that had made her feet slow and her body drag. So to cover, she scooted over on her bed, her earlier exhaustion fading.

"Sit down. Tell me what you have been doing this last week." *I've missed you so.*

He settled beside her. "I paid off my tailor bill with the money from Dicky. I've helped my mother scare off an unwelcome admirer." He shrugged. "The usual for me. And you?"

"French lessons. Dancing lessons. Fittings. Instructions. Sit right, dress right, remember your *h*'s."

"And have you?"

She nodded. "Most of the time. They don't really care what I say, you know."

"Of course they do. They're listening to hear you say yes."

"Yes? To what?"

"Whatever they want from you."

She sobered. "My dowry."

He nodded. "Your grandfather has done right by you. He may not have wanted to at first, but twenty thousand pounds is a fortune."

"So you heard."

He chuckled, though the sound had no humor in it. "Bluebell, everybody heard. You're the most exciting morsel of the Season so far."

She nodded. She knew it was true, and she ought to be thrilled. She *was* thrilled. But… She touched his bruised lip. "Does it hurt?" *Kiss me.*

"Not really. I've had worse."

Of course he had.

He caught her hand and pressed a kiss to her fingertips. "Tell me everything, Bluebell. Tell me every detail of your come-out. What you thought, what you felt, who talked to you, who looked at you wrong." He waggled his eyebrows. "Who pinched your bum?"

"Pinched my bum! The very idea!"

"Did someone?"

She flushed. "Yes. But Lord Platner is practically a hundred years old." *Take me.*

"At least. And he pinches everyone's bum. The men too, but that's because he's so blind he can't see who he's got."

She looked at him, wondering at the red in his eyes and the stark cut to his jaw. Had he always looked so lean? At least in comparison to the fat nobles she'd been meeting. Or was this a new gauntness?

She reached behind her, adjusting the pillows against the headboard. Then she scooted backward, leaving a place for him to sit comfortably beside her. When he didn't move to follow her, she tugged on his sleeve.

"Come on. There's a lot to tell. I haven't been lazing around getting my lip split by hulking aristocrats. I've been *busy*."

He nodded slowly, then began to shift on the bed, but she stopped him, again tugging on his coat sleeve.

"Take it off, Bram. You're not going to need it right now."

There. She'd said it. She'd as much as told him that they were going to make love tonight. She saw the message hit him. She saw a look of absolute hunger flash across his features, quickly replaced by a wolfish smile.

"Are you sure? Now that you've met all those wealthy, titled gents—"

"I want to see if you measure up," she said primly.

"What?"

"Well, haven't I been dancing all night with them? Haven't I been holding their hands and twirling about? Let me see if you're just as strong, if your hands are just as big."

"Everything about me is just as big," he said on a low growl. "Bigger, even."

Yes, she knew that, but she tossed him an arch look. "Then take off your coat, and let me see."

He nodded and pulled it off, setting it carefully at the base of her bed. His cravat went too after she tugged its folds open. And then he stretched out beside her, his bare feet looking large and masculine on her soft white coverlet.

He looked at her, his expression open as he extended his arm to the side, inviting her to come close. She did quickly. She settled against his shoulder and smelled the sour London scents on his shirt, but the harsher scent of lye on his skin. He'd bathed before coming to see her. She touched his jaw. He'd shaved as well. *Touch me*.

"Well," she began, "I have been terrified all week."

"You? The woman who boldly faced down Mr. Periwinkle? I don't believe it."

"A pig is one thing—"

"A massive, cantankerous pig."

"Forgetting one of Eleanor's instructions is something else entirely."

His lips curved up in a smile. "You are quite right there. My apologies. You should be terrified."

"Exactly my point."

"And...?"

"And she has kept me so busy that I could barely think, much less worry, or be terrified. Do you know she has me studying Russian? She told someone that I'm a lost Russian princess."

"Russian? You don't look anything like a Russe."

"That's what I said, but she insisted that it was the only way."

He shook his head. "I heard that you were from the Colonies."

"That's another one. I don't understand why I can't be from Hull."

"Because..."

They spoke the rest at exactly the same instant.

"No one of interest ever comes from Hull." It was funny how they both knew exactly what Eleanor would say.

Then he smiled. "Except you, of course."

She shook her head. "She said I'm not that interesting yet. Not unless I'm a Russian princess."

"I think the Colonies are more exciting."

"I was asked a dozen times what I thought of the red savages. I haven't the foggiest idea what that means."

"What did you say?"

"That they were frightening. They are savages, after all."

"Very clever of you."

Kiss me.

"I thought so." She continued to chatter, telling him of every possible thing that had been on her mind. Every feeling, every impression, every second of the last miserable week without him. Everything except for the way she'd climbed into bed at night and longed for him. How she'd relived every caress, every kiss, and wished to do it again. To do it more.

And then, right when she thought she'd go mad from the wanting, he started laughing. It was a low chuckle, but so warm that it set her heart to fluttering. Stretching up to see his face, she noted the lines around his mouth had eased. The shadow was gone from his eyes. And that...

And that he was looking at her.

Then for the first time that night, she said what she was thinking aloud.

"Love me."

He paused just for a moment. A stretch of time that made the knots in her belly quiver and her breasts tighten. She opened her mouth. She stretched against him. And finally, wonderfully, she was rewarded.

He kissed her.

He leaned over and plundered her mouth while his free hand quickly undid the ties of her nightrail.

And then he stroked her skin, sliding over her breasts, and pinching her nipples. She reveled in it, her body more than ready.

Her hands were equally busy, pulling off his shirt, exploring the contours of his chest. And when he pressed her into the bed, she slid her hands to his broad back, then lower to his pants.

She tugged at them impatiently, and thankfully, he didn't need any more encouragement. He broke their kiss, pulling back to strip off his clothes. She was equally fast as she lifted off her nightrail.

And then they were naked on her bed, letting their eyes feast on one another. His cock was thick as it stretched toward her. Her breasts were peaked, her legs restless, as his gaze went to the juncture of her thighs.

Then he started to move toward her, but she stopped him. "Bram," she said, and had to say it again because the word was too husky to be understood. "Bram, last time you…you licked…"

"Yes?"

She smiled at him. "Can I do the same to you?"

He blinked, and then said one word. "Yes."

"Teach me how?"

"It's not hard."

"How you like it best."

He nodded and repositioned. He leaned back against the headboard and spread his legs. His cock bobbed between his thighs, and she went gingerly to kneel between his knees.

"Wait—" he rasped. Then he swallowed. "Let me see you first. I have dreamed of seeing it again."

"What?"

"Stay right there," he said.

She was on her knees before him, her legs slightly spread.

"Men love to look," he said. "Touch your breasts. Squeeze them however you like."

It took a moment, but the heat in his eyes overcame her shyness. He leaned forward, guiding her so that she straightened, her bottom thrust toward him. Then he put her hand on her breasts.

"Lift them. Squeeze them."

She did. She squeezed herself just how he did, and her mouth parted on a gasp.

"Just like that. Don't stop."

She looked at him, seeing his gaze riveted to her body. Then he reached between her legs and began to stroke her. Her legs tightened, but they didn't close. They couldn't. And still he watched her while she kneaded her own breasts, and he thrust his fingers into her and rolled his thumb over that higher spot.

She moaned. She couldn't help it. Her breath was coming in short pants now, and the feel of him pushing between her folds was both wonderful and not enough.

"Bram," she moaned.

"Come for me. Right now."

His fingers were so clever as he pushed on a place deep inside.

The explosion made her back arch, her body shuddering in ecstasy.

She would have fallen, but he caught her. Even with one hand still inside her, he somehow managed to wrap the other around her waist and draw her close. She fell forward, shuddering in pleasure as her body wrapped itself around him.

He pressed kisses to her skin. Tiny presses of his lips to her shoulder, her neck, the line of her jaw. "Beautiful," he murmured. "My Bluebell."

Yes. I am yours.

It took a while for her breath to recover. It took even longer for the strength to come back to her legs.

He held her the whole time, his grip sure, his mouth pressing those tiny kisses to her body.

But eventually, she straightened. In time she pulled back and looked at his cock. It was wet on the tip, the color a dark red in the candlelight.

"You will teach me now?" she asked.

"If you want."

She did.

And he did.

And then he flipped her onto her back, put her legs on his shoulders, and plowed into her. She came for him again.

He shuddered his release into her.

And while she lay sated on the bed, he gave her a tender kiss to her lips.

She knew what he was doing, but she had no strength to fight him. And no idea what she would say anyway.

He dressed quickly, blew out her candle, and then climbed silently out her window.

Twenty-three

"I HEARD A STORY ABOUT YOU TODAY." MAYBELLE'S words came out breathless as Bram was steadily kissing down her belly.

Another week of her Season gone. He didn't come to her every night, but most nights. And when he wasn't here, she missed him terribly. Her body ached for him at night, and by day she stored up things to say to him. Secrets, funny observations, anything she thought he might like to hear.

Tonight she had two days of events to discuss, but this was the most important.

"Mmmm?" he said as he gently spread her knees. She wanted to resist. She wanted to talk, and yet this was also so very good.

He licked her core.

So very, very good.

She gave herself up to it and to him. Her body convulsed around his tongue, then it opened to his cock. His thrusts were slow this time. Gentle penetration, slower withdrawal. But before long, she was gasping his name as he rammed into her.

And then he collapsed by her side, and she gathered him close. Desperate to keep him with her, she brought up the story again.

"You were quite heroic," she said to the whorl of hair around his nipple.

"It was good this time, wasn't it?"

She pinched him. "That's not what I meant."

"It wasn't good?" He was teasing her, so she teased him right back, stroking his cock. He was already thickening again.

"I'm talking about the story I heard. About you."

"What was it?" His body had stilled, so she knew he was listening. She could tell he was worried about what she would say.

"That someone was attacking a woman, and you saved her life. You killed the man who...well, I've heard different things. Rapist, thief, murderer—the villain is quite horrible."

"That tale has been making the rounds—"

"They say you killed Jeremy. The bastard son of Lord Sturman."

He froze. Then he took a slow, controlled breath. "Oh?"

He didn't fool her. She knew he was not easy about the one-time friend he'd apparently killed.

"The tale said Jeremy died the next night."

He shook his head. "He's got a bad fever. Infection."

"So he still lives?"

"Yes. At least, he was still alive this afternoon."

"How do you hear?"

"My mum tells me. She's friends with Lord Sturman's new mistress."

"Oh." She lifted her head, wishing the candle was lit so she could study his face. But even in the dark, she could see the way he stared up at the ceiling. And she felt the rigid way he held his whole body. "You didn't mean to kill him. Just stop him."

"I know."

She touched his face then, ruthlessly bringing it round so he looked directly at her. "There wasn't anything else you could do."

He tightened his hold on her back and pulled her tight. "Did you know he loved to play jacks? He was really good at it too. Bollocks at marbles and darts, but he always had quick hands for the jacks."

"Really?" She caressed the contours of his chest, but kept her gaze on his. "Tell me more."

"He had a laugh like a braying donkey. I used to tease him about it. He said I snorted like a pig."

"Well, you do sometimes."

"I know. Then we would fight. Throwing bad punches, grappling like monkeys. It was the best time, even if he broke my toy soldiers."

"You had toy soldiers?"

He nodded. "Every boy has soldiers. Once mine were done for, we played with his." Suddenly, he was above her, spreading her knees ruthlessly with his own.

She twined her legs around him. She was wet and sensitive from just five minutes before, but anything that kept him with her longer was fine. "Did he have other friends? Or was it just you?"

"Just me. Our mums were of the same status, you see. Similar protectors, both with young sons." He pushed his fingers into her, stroking her insides in a way that never failed to make her whole body respond.

"What else did you play?"

He paused, his fingers stilled while she caught her breath. And then he was at her again, stroking her relentlessly. "Cruel games, now that I think on it. He liked to catch stray cats."

"Cats?" She hadn't the focus to say more.

"We were both so angry, you see. We knew what we were—"

"Boys," she gasped out. "You were boys."

"Bastards with no future. And so we beat on each other. And when we grew tired of that, he would catch cats."

"And…do…what?"

He shook his head. "I never knew. But I guessed. Even then…I guessed."

His thumb was on her clit now, rubbing it with vague precision. He was watching her. Or thinking of the past. She wasn't sure, except that she didn't like it.

So she surged upward and gripped his hand. "In me," she said firmly. "Come inside me."

He stilled, and then he nodded. A moment later, he had on the French letter, and he was positioned exactly as she wanted. There was no tenderness. No subtlety. He simply thrust, and she welcomed the invasion. And the ruthless pounding. She gripped him with her arms and her legs. She held on while he rode her.

Until they both burst.

And when he collapsed against her side, she realized his face was wet. Tears or sweat, it didn't matter.

She held him against her and kissed the salty taste of him. And when she brushed close to his ear, she whispered.

"I love you."

He shuddered then. And exhaled a soft, quiet moan.

They lay together like that for an hour. He, so still, while she held him tight. But at the end, he kissed her tenderly and got out of bed. He was nearly gone when she said it. A whisper, but it was clear.

"I know a way to save his life."

He froze and turned back to her. "What?"

"If you want to help him. I know a way that gives him a chance. If he's not too far gone." She straightened on her elbow. "But he's not a good man, Bram. Do you want to save his life?"

He hesitated, then slowly eased back onto the bed. "He's not a bad man. He's an angry man."

"If you get him this medicine, will he thank you? Will he keep from attacking you?"

He nodded. "He will stay away." His voice was strong, but she wasn't so sure.

"Bram—"

"What is the potion? Do you have it?"

She pushed up. "I don't have the ingredients. I can mix it, but you need..." She tucked her hands together. "Are you sure you want to do this?"

"Yes. Tell me what you need, and I will get it."

She nodded. "I need mold, Bram."

"What?"

"Mold. In Hull I got it from Mr. Periwinkle's pigpen, but the witch-woman said it was stronger from somewhere else."

He tilted his head. "Where?"

She flinched. "The side of the shit house."

He laughed, the sound tight and bitter. And then he sobered. "You're serious, aren't you?"

"Yes."

He rubbed his jaw and looked out the window, his face almost gaunt in the moonlight. "How much?"

So she told him. How to gather it. How to mix it. She climbed out of bed and put on her breeches. "I will make the rest. You gather the mold."

He sighed. "Even on death's door, Jeremy is still making me stink."

"You don't have to do this."

"Yes, I do." Then he was gone.

⁂

Bram was exhausted, and he stank of shite. He'd crawled around London's moldiest outhouse and grabbed what he needed. More than enough, he hoped, and Bluebell was now mixing the potions for him. But he had to change his clothes and wash before he brought the mixtures to Lord Sturman. And all in the hope that it would be quick enough to save Jeremy's life.

"What is that awful smell?"

"Why Clary, I think it's Bram. Good God, man, what have you been doing?"

No. No, no, no, no, no.

Bram stopped at the base of the stairs. He'd ordered his feet to keep moving, but he couldn't stop himself from turning. From looking. And yes, there sat Dicky and Clarissa, once again in his front parlor.

Bloody hell.

"You promised," he said dully. "You said you'd never see me again."

"Well, I like that," Dicky huffed. "You can't mean that you would refuse the door to an old friend."

Clarissa sniffed into her handkerchief. "I've never been more hurt in my life."

Bram didn't answer. He couldn't. He was too busy trying to wrap his thoughts around the fact that he was never going to be rid of these two. Never. They would come back over and over until he died of the nightmare.

He stepped into the room and lit a candle. It was barely dawn, and it looked as if these two had slept in the parlor chairs. Even so, he had to blink twice to sort out how they were dressed and what they carried.

Dicky was the height of mismatched fashion. Purple waistcoat—missing a button. Orange topcoat and black hat—both creased—though Dicky was right then trying to smooth out the bend in the hat. Clarissa was in a gown bedecked with mismatched ribbons on every inch. She looked like a matted ball of scrap ribbons that a child might use as a toy. Or a cat. Or a cat would hack up. She still wore the shepherdess bonnet, but it was sadly crushed, and between the two sat...

An ornamental pig. Paper and paste, shaped into the vague outline of an overly happy pig. In truth, it reminded him starkly of Mr. Periwinkle after the creature had consumed two buckets of mash and ale.

"The money, I presume?" he said dryly, gesturing to the pig.

"There's almost none left!" gasped Clarissa. "Thousands of pounds..." She shuddered. "Gone."

He frowned at her, realizing at the last that she wasn't wearing her sapphires. "Where's your necklace?"

"A goat ate it!" she cried. "And the earbob!"

"No, darling," said her husband as he patted her hand. "I think it was the chimpanzee."

It didn't matter. She was too busy sobbing into her handkerchief.

Bram sighed. "How did you get here?"

"Well, as to that," Dicky said with another huff. "I don't know why you drove us across England when the menagerie was headed back to London."

He'd have driven to Italy if it could have gotten rid of these two faster. "Why aren't you with the menagerie now? You could be the grand master of a traveling troupe. It's something I thought you'd enjoy." And stick with.

"Well, I did—" began Dicky.

"They ate my jewels!"

"Not really, Clary. It had been paste, after all."

"Not the one! Not the smallest stone on the right!" That last word ended on a wail.

The stone she'd constantly fondled. Yes, he'd guessed that one had been real. Meanwhile, he was all too conscious of the time ticking away. "Well, now we've visited. Nice to see you again, but I must run. Good-bye."

"No!" Dicky pushed to his feet, daring to come forward, though his nose wrinkled at the smell. In truth, Bram couldn't fault him for that. He did reek. "Look at her, Bram. She's miserable. I could have done it, you know. I could have lived there with the livestock and the humiliation, but Clary is of a more refined sort. She can't do this. We need to find another solution."

Another solution. As if he hadn't been doing that already, getting them to boats all over England, setting them up with the menagerie. "You cheated Lord Sturman. He doesn't forgive that easily."

"But the money's all gone!" wailed Dicky, which set Clarissa into another round of loud tears. "Just a few weeks, and it's all gone!"

As if that would make Sturman go easier on them. Bloody hell. It wouldn't have worked, even if the man wasn't about to lose his son to infection. Which was going to happen for certain, if Bram didn't get the potions to...

No.

No, no, no, no, no, no.

But the more he denied the thought, the more it pressed into his brain. He was never going to be rid of these two if he didn't solve their problem. If he didn't somehow get them back into charity with Sturman, and then, all of the *ton*. These two were society's creatures, and Bram would never be at peace unless he restored them to where they belonged.

But the potions were his way of making good with Jeremy. They were his way of doing something positive out of this whole fiasco.

But there was Clarissa sobbing in his parlor and Dicky looking miserable as his wife wailed. And now his landlady was up, shuffling into the room with her eyes narrowed and her nose wrinkled.

"What's to do, 'ere?" she asked. "And what is that awful smell?"

And then it was decided. There was only one way to handle things such that Dicky and Clarissa got out of his life once and for all.

So he apologized to his landlady and told Dicky and Clarissa to not move until after he'd cleaned up. While he was changing his clothes—and burning what he'd been wearing—a footman delivered Bluebell's potions.

And then he did it.

He took himself, Dicky and Clarissa, and the potions to see Lord Sturman.

Twenty-four

"WHAT HAPPENED?" BLUEBELL ASKED TWO NIGHTS later. He was stretched out on her bed, idly stroking her body. Reveling in the silky texture of her skin, the spiced scent of her arousal, and the languid way she coiled against him.

He would take her a second time tonight, he realized, and he couldn't muster up the will to feel the tiniest bit guilty about that. He was too pleased with her and the knowledge that Clarissa and Dicky were out of his life for good.

"I had them tell their tale, of course. Sturman isn't really a bad man. He was mostly furious with himself for being duped by them. But they're charming when they need to be. And pitiful when they need to be as well."

"Did they look pitiful?"

"It started raining on the way there, so the damned papier-mâché pig was a sodden, sticky mess."

"Goodness. And the pound notes inside?"

"All three of them. Sturman let them keep it because he didn't want to touch 'em."

"The notes or Lord Linsel and his wife?"

"Either."

She chuckled, and he paused to watch the way her breasts bobbed with the movement. "But what happened?"

"Sturman agreed to forgive them the swindle."

"Really?"

"If Jeremy lived. If they paid him back."

"But how are they to do that?"

Bram shrugged. "Dupe some other poor sot. I have no idea."

"But Jeremy?"

Bram turned, pressing a kiss to her delectable shoulder. And then he scraped his teeth along it. He settled himself between her thighs because he couldn't stop himself.

"Bram!" she huffed. "What about Jeremy?"

He looked at her and grinned. "Getting better every day. His fever broke a few hours ago. Clarissa and Dicky are tending him hand and foot because they know if he sickens, then they're back to the menagerie."

"And necklace-eating goats!"

"Unless it was the chimp."

She giggled. "Of course…oh!"

He thrust into her, and she welcomed him as she always did. Then he began a slow, easy build, relishing every second inside her. Beside her. With her.

So long as he was with her, everything was wonderful.

"Oh Bram," she murmured. "I love you."

I love you too, he thought. *With every fiber of my body and soul. You are my heart, my life, my everything.*

But he never said a word.

And a half hour later, he crept out her window.

Twenty-five

"I RECEIVED AN OFFER OF MARRIAGE TODAY. TWO, actually."

Maybelle was still dressed when he came to her room. She'd long since adjusted to town hours and had only just returned from the ball. She'd dismissed her maid two minutes before and was now pulling off the pearl earbobs Eleanor had loaned her. He slipped in through the window, silent as usual, but she glanced behind her nonetheless, and gestured for him to remain quiet.

He'd nodded and settled onto the pillows on her bed, his pose so relaxed as to be decadent. She kept speaking as she washed off the kohl that rimmed her eyes, though she kept her voice low.

"Eleanor is relieved. She was beginning to fear I wouldn't get any decent offers."

"You've had offers before?"

She nodded. "No one suitable, according to...well, everyone." She listed off the first three gentlemen who had vied for her hand.

He nodded. "Blighters, every one."

"I didn't even hear about them until days later.

Grandfather refused them without even consulting me." She was a little bit miffed about that, but as they were spendthrifts in search of a fortune, she didn't complain.

"And today's offers?"

"Well, those are more interesting, according to Eleanor." She shook out her hair and began brushing it. "Joseph Mincey. Second son, barrister, respectable income."

"Mmph," he said in dismissal as he uncoiled from his place on the bed. "He'll never make more money than what he has now. No political savvy and indifferent ability with the law. You can do better."

"That's what Eleanor said."

He came toward her and took the brush from her hand. But as he began the steady strokes on her hair, she noticed he sported a dark bruise under his eye.

She spun around, managing to jerk her hair painfully. "What happened?" She reached up to his face though he shied away from her touch.

"I've been helping out Bow Street lately. Brilliant man there named Samuel Morrison. Cleverest man I've ever met, but he's not nearly as good with his fives as he needs."

She blinked, not understanding. He made a fist. "His fives. He specializes in catching murderers, but he needs a partner to help him."

"That's you?"

He nodded. "Pays well, and it's work I'm well suited for."

Except when he took a punch to the face. He saw her looking and lifted her hand to his lips for a kiss.

"Lucky throw. Murdering thief had a partner with a jug."

"You got hit with a jug! You could have lost an eye. Good God—"

He leaned down and silenced her horror with a kiss. And after he'd thoroughly distracted her, he drew away. "Now tell me about your other proposal."

"What?"

He smirked. He always smirked when she was so lust-dazed as to be incoherent. "The other gentleman."

She grimaced. "Oh, that. The Viscount Wickersham."

"What? He's old enough to be your father."

"He is exactly the same age as my father. Or would be, if my father had survived. But he's wealthy enough, if not a nabob, and he's a good, solid candidate according to Eleanor."

"But he's old."

"I know," she said. Then she mimicked Eleanor's tone. "It's an unfortunate age. Too old to be handsome, especially with the way he eats."

"He does have a paunch."

That was putting it mildly. Then she continued in Eleanor's voice. "But not so old as to make you a wealthy widow while you're still in your looks."

He grunted. "Trust Eleanor to see the profit in a man's death."

"She says it's an important consideration."

"Of course it is," he said, his tone impassive, his face more so. She frowned, trying to understand his mood, but he gently turned her around to continue brushing her hair.

She let him, watching his face in the mirror. She'd

learned that he was most emotional when she could read nothing. But if he didn't tell her what he was thinking—and feeling—she'd never know.

"Bram—"

"Anyone else?"

"What?"

"Any other offers?"

She shook her head.

"Don't despair. It's the early days yet."

The Season was half gone already. "Grandfather will not pay for another Season. He wants me married by Michaelmas."

There was a slight hitch in the stroke of the brush, but nothing more. Then his eyes met hers in the mirror. "Is there anyone you fancy?"

"Yes. An impossible man who brushes my hair and quizzes me on other men."

His lips quirked in a wry twist that held no humor. "Sounds horrible. Best forget him. He sounds like a bastard."

"He is. But I fancy him nonetheless."

"Bad choice," he said. "Your grandfather would never allow it."

"I am of age."

"You will be tossed from the *ton* before you've even begun."

She sighed. "I have been here for more than a month. I have danced and gone to the opera. I have had ices at Gunter's and shopped at the most exclusive modiste in all of London."

"Society is so much more than shopping and dancing."

"Is it?" She hadn't really noticed. It was all prancing about and gossip as far as she could tell. Not so different from Hull, actually, except that everyone was better dressed.

The stroke of the brush paused again. "So you miss Hull?"

"I do," she said softly. "It was…quieter there."

"Not boring?"

"Definitely boring as well. And small-minded. And petty."

"Sounds like the *ton*."

She agreed. "There are ladies aligned against me here just like at home."

"They are jealous of your beauty."

"Of my dowry, more like."

He shrugged. "Either way."

"And the men try to take liberties too. Just like at home."

His expression darkened. "Where is Eleanor when this happens?"

"Probably fending off her own improper advances. It doesn't matter. Unlike your Samuel, I am good with my fives." She held up her fist and smiled.

"Did you punch him?"

"Two of them. The others…" She flashed him a grin. "Why does no man expect a women to knee him in the privates? It would seem an obvious place to protect oneself."

He shook his head, but his low chuckle was warm. "We get distracted by your beauty and forget."

"You mean my décolletage."

He set aside the brush then. And as he set it on the

table, his nearest hand brushed her bosom, leaving fire in its wake.

"Yes. Definitely that."

She closed her eyes, feeling the way he touched her. Gentle caress. Unexpected pinch. And all of it filled with a kind of possession. She was his, he said with his touch. No other man could kiss her skin or touch her body the way he did. And as he loosened the buttons of her gown, she inhaled deeply of his scent.

"Help me undress?" she whispered.

"No," he answered. "I have wanted to do this from the first time I saw you in the blue and gold gown."

He helped her stand and set her hands on her dressing table. The candlelight fell on her face and chest. He'd loosened her gown just enough for him to slip his hand underneath the neckline and pull her breasts out, and then he began to fondle the nipples.

"Bram," she breathed, her knees going weak.

"Don't move," he whispered into her ear. "Keep your hands planted right there."

Then she heard him undress behind her. Just his trousers because he was still in his shirt, though he'd discarded his coat when he first arrived. And then she felt him slowly lift her skirts from behind.

Up, up, up went the fabric of her gown. It teased the backs of her legs, and then he flipped it onto her back.

Then he was there between her legs. His fingers and his cock. She was ready by then. Wet and hungry, but he still took his time.

He did as he wanted. First playing with her breasts, then stroking between her legs. Then he imbedded his cock inside her but didn't thrust. He held her pinioned while he returned to playing with her nipples. Just her nipples as her breasts bobbed with his motions.

She was sobbing his name by the time he began to thrust. And when she came, he was watching her face in the mirror. His expression was fierce, his thrusts even more so. He bared his teeth, and then he bit her.

It was so startling the way he clamped down on her shoulder, marking her there while he exploded below. She reveled in the pain, the sharp bite of sensation. But she also loved seeing the way he pumped and pumped into her. He was completely subjected to the demands of his body—of her body around him. It was the only time she felt like she owned him as completely as he possessed her.

But then the moment was over. He'd released. He'd collapsed against her back. And now, as his breath steadied, he straightened up only to curse.

"Bram?"

"Your shoulder," he rasped, indicating the dark red mark. "You'll have to cover that up. Bloody hell, I'm sorry. I didn't think."

She nodded, not trusting her voice. Tears burned in her eyes and clogged her throat, though she couldn't explain why. And a moment later, he flipped down her skirt, and she straightened to her full height. Then she forced a smile. "Don't worry. I know what to do."

"It's right there. Everyone will see," he said.

She reached for the iron used to curl hair and set it in the coals. The weather had turned cool enough that the maid had lit a fire, so soon the metal was just the right temperature.

"What are you doing?"

She took it out, then tilted her hair away from the bite. She hated doing this. It had nothing to do with the coming pain. She hated erasing his mark on her. But it had to be done.

Then, while he watched in confusion, she set the hot iron against her skin. He cried out, but no more than she. The skin sizzled, and now she could finally let those tears fall as she adjusted the damned thing to cover the entire bite.

"Stop it!" He jerked the iron away, his fingers on the hot metal since she held the handle. It burned him too, and he tossed it aside with a curse.

She exhaled, the pain lessening, but only slightly. She'd had burns before and knew it would take a good long time to heal. She shifted, turning her shoulder to the mirror. The skin was red and puffy, the burn clearly in the shape of the hair iron.

"Did I get it all?" she asked.

He swallowed. He was looking into her eyes in the mirror, but eventually, his gaze dropped to her shoulder.

"Yes," he finally rasped. "It looks like an iron burn."

"There. I'll just say I couldn't sleep and was experimenting with the iron. It was late, I was clumsy, and it slipped."

He nodded slowly, but his eyes were excruciatingly sad. "And now I've made you into a liar."

"What?" Her gaze jerked to his, but he'd already turned away. "No! Bram—"

Too late. He resettled his clothing, then headed for the window.

He paused there, his expression completely locked down. But in his eyes—right above the swollen

bruise on his cheek—she saw the swirl of some dark
and intense emotion. She had no label for it. She just
knew that he was thinking something that meant a
great deal to him.

But he didn't speak. A moment later, he swung
himself out and was gone. And this time, he hadn't
even kissed her tenderly before he left.

She stared at the open window for the longest time.
Then she looked in the mirror, her gaze finding the
burn mark that still smelled acrid. Odd how the pain
of that mark was nothing compared to the emptiness
in her heart.

She'd offered him her love. Over and over again,
she'd told him what she felt. But he never said the
words back. She'd told herself she didn't care. She
knew he loved her. She felt it in every look, every
touch, every breath.

But the words mattered. She hadn't thought they
did, but she saw now how important they were.
Because every time he held the words back, she knew
he was protecting himself. He was never going to
marry her, so by holding back the words, it wouldn't
hurt so much when she gave herself to another man.

She understood his choice, but more than that,
she now understood her own. She couldn't give her
body to a man who would not give his heart back to
her. She couldn't nightly love a man who held back
his feelings.

Which meant she had to end these visits. It was too
painful, and it kept her from looking at the other men
in her life. It prevented her from fully searching for
a husband because she kept hoping that Bram would

find a way. But he wasn't even looking, so she had to cut him from her body and her heart. It was the only way to ensure her future. Because if she didn't find a husband by the Season's end, she didn't know what she would do.

Go back to Hull and her garden? Impossible. She'd only survived that life before because she and her mother kept hoping and planning for this moment. For when she finally stepped into her full lineage and made a good marriage, which meant she could not let this opportunity pass.

If Bram would not choose her, then she had to find someone else who would. She was so resolved she said it aloud to her reflection. She swore off Bram completely.

And yet it took three more weeks before she had the strength to do it. And even then she took the coward's way out. She used the excuse of a house party at one of her suitor's homes. She waited until after they'd shared their passion.

He knew something was wrong. He knew because she clung to him, and she rode him like a woman possessed. And when he kissed her tenderly, she said the words as if they meant nothing to her. As if it were something she remembered at the last moment.

"I shall be leaving in the morning for the home of the Marquis de Mowles's country estate."

"Mowles? Is he that French refugee?"

"He's eminently respectable. Or at least as respectable as I am, given that Eleanor's lies have come back on us. Everyone knows I'm from Hull and not a mysterious Russian princess. Or even from the Colonies."

In truth, she'd been the one to tell. She'd gotten

sick of all the lies and had confessed to a notorious gossip. She was from Hull and had never even seen the ocean, much less crossed it.

"When will you be back?" he asked.

She swallowed. "Never." She took a deep breath. "I intend to marry him."

"But—"

"And he's notoriously afraid for his safety. Keeps a guard near the doors at night. Another patrols the grounds."

Translation: *he wouldn't be able to come to her at night.* They could never be together again unless he changed his mind. Unless he wanted her as much as she desperately wanted him.

Unless…

"He's a good choice," Bram said softly. Then he grabbed the windowsill and swung himself out of her room—and her life—forever.

Twenty-six

MARQUIS DE MOWLES WAS A DEAD BORE. BUT HE also had an avid interest in perfumery, so his hothouse garden and attached stillroom were stunning. When together, Maybelle and the marquis discussed flowers, methods for distilling their scent, and the troublesome insects that plagued him.

Which was fascinating for the first couple hours. After that, Maybelle grew restless. Sadly, her relations were here and made great efforts to enumerate the marquis's many attributes. Her grandfather stressed that the man was a genius at money. Except for his odd flower hobby, he would make a solid husband. Her grandmother extolled the French title, one of the few remaining after those mad peasants cut off everyone's heads. And Eleanor—who seemed to understand a great deal more than she let on—expressed that the marquis was often too busy to notice what went on among his guests. He would likely be a distracted husband as the years went on, and that was always to the good.

Maybelle listened with a smile and a nod, giving every pretense to complete agreement. But in her

heart, she simply screamed. Nothing so soft as a quiet
sob. Nothing so unending as the ache that came from
losing her mother. This was an unrelenting scream of
frustration. How could the man to whom she'd given
her heart calmly watch her commit herself to someone
else? How could Bram have left her like that?

She knew it was the way of the *ton*. Marry for
advantage, then take a lover. But she'd been raised
differently and could not comprehend such a life. And
so the hours ticked by with horticultural discussions by
day and an empty bed at night.

And inside, she screamed.

❧

There was to be a small gathering on the fifth night.
Whereas most of the trip had been simply the marquis
and Maybelle's companions—her grandparents and
Lady Eleanor—the evening of the fifth night was
to be a small dinner party with some of their host's
best companions. It had already been agreed that on
this auspicious occasion, the marquis would formally
present his ring to her, and she would joyously accept.

The guests had been arriving all day from London.
The trip was not that onerous, and they each arrived
with good cheer and broad smiles. So much so that
Maybelle began to think of slapping the next one
who grinned at her and punctuated it with a wink.
Instead, she listed their attributes in her mind. After
all, if she were to marry the marquis, she would need
to remember them all. The other two expatriates from
the Continent were boring. The bluestocking with a
special interest in insects was odd. And then there was

the Duke and Duchess of Bucklynde, Eleanor's relations. They were stopping here for the night before
finally returning to London.

Maybelle functioned as hostess, greeting the guests
as if she truly were the new marquess, and she prided
herself that she'd not dropped a single *h* all day. And
she shoved that persistent scream into a tiny portion of
her mind and thought no more of it.

Then, as evening shadows began to gather, Maybelle
dressed in her best gown, had her hair pulled and
pinned with ruthless domination by a German maid,
and sat down to inane conversation before what was
likely to be an indifferent meal. Odd how after a few
weeks in London, she was picky about what she consumed. As if her childhood of being grateful for every
morsel had never been.

"Maybelle? Are you feeling quite the thing?"

"What?" Maybelle turned to the collection of ladies
on the settee. It took her a moment to realize that her
grandmother was the one who'd asked her a question.
"I'm terribly sorry. I must have been woolgathering."

Meanwhile, her soon-to-be fiancé pranced over to
her, his French accent thick and irritating. "I'm afraid
ze country has not ze excitement of London, *n'est pas?*"

"Actually," she said, simply to be contrary, "I like
the quiet. It's much more soothing—"

Bang, bang! Bang!

Everyone jumped as the door knocker slammed
down with such force it echoed within the house.
Maybelle turned to the marquis with a frown. "Are
we expecting anyone else?"

"*Non.* We are not." His face was pulled into a tight

frown, which, she abruptly realized, was not that different from his usual face. The man was tall and somewhat gaunt. His skin tended to sag on his face, which pulled everything down even when he was at his most happy.

Meanwhile, everyone turned to look, but this was a large country establishment. No one could see the front entrance, though they certainly heard the commotion.

"You must let me see Miss Ballenger. Damn it, you must let us in!"

Maybelle shot to her feet. Eleanor rose a moment later. They both recognized the voice, but Maybelle was the only one to voice his name.

"Bram."

The marquis shot her a look. "You know this man?"

She nodded, her mind whirling, and her heart—damn that organ—was beating triple time. And while the marquis was telling the butler to allow him in, her belly began to quiver, her breath grew short, and everything in her yearned for him.

He was here.

He was here.

He was…

Maybelle gaped as a man appeared in the parlor door. "Charlie?"

Bram was not the man who rounded the corner. Instead of a tall man with piercing brown eyes, she saw the vicar's son looking disheveled and rather frightened as he shuffled into the room.

"Bluebell?" he answered, his gaze darting about the room as if searching for a place to land. "Are you really the daughter of an earl?"

"Yes," she snapped, impatient with him already. Where was Bram?

"She's my granddaughter," snapped the earl. "Who the bloody hell are you?"

Which is when Bram finally entered the room. He looked haggard. His eyes were drawn, his mouth was tight, and his jaw was thrust forward in anger. But his gaze locked on hers and held. No words. Just a stare that went on and on, while the rest of the room faded away.

"Explain yourselves, *maintenant!*" said the marquis.

Maybelle opened her mouth to answer. She'd gotten used to soothing the marquis's ruffled feathers in just the five days she'd been here. But no sound came out. And neither could Bram speak, though he too opened his mouth. Fortunately, Eleanor was there to step into the breach.

"My lord, please allow me to introduce Mr. Hallowsby. He's a good friend and means no harm, though I know things appear very odd right now."

"And this other one?"

Maybelle blinked, then managed to snap out a command. "Charlie. Make your bows."

The man blinked, then snapped to it. He performed an adequate greeting to everyone. "Mr. Charles Ott, my lady, m'lords. At your service."

"Pleased to meet you, sir," said Eleanor, before proceeding to introduce everyone by their full names and titles. It was quite impressive rattled off like that, and Charlie's mouth dropped further open with each name. Meanwhile, Maybelle was done waiting for Bram to speak. So she gathered herself together and turned to Charlie.

"Why are you here?"

Charlie colored and gestured to Bram. "'E says you want to marry me. I will, if you want. Are you really related to an earl?"

"Granddaughter," she snapped. "And…what?"

At that moment Bram seemed to pull himself together. With a grimace, he gripped Charlie and jerked him downward. Problem was, Charlie had a solid stance—always had—and just stood there without bending.

"That's not the way to propose to a woman," Bram snapped. "On your knee, man."

"What?"

"What?"

It was both Charlie and Maybelle speaking at once. But then Charlie figured out what was required, and he half stumbled, half dropped to the floor.

"Can I have your hand, Bluebell?"

"Maybelle," hissed Bram. "Her name is Miss Maybelle Ballenger."

"Oh, right," said Charlie.

"No," said Maybelle. Then she stepped right past Charlie to come nose to nose with Bram. "Why in heaven would you bring him 'ere?" And damn it, he'd made her drop her *h*.

"You can't marry the marquis. He's got a mistress."

To which the man in question straightened in shock. "Of course I have a mistress. I am French!"

"You see!" said Bram.

"What difference does it make?" Maybelle huffed. Good God, did he not understand? One man or another, she didn't care. They were all interchangeable if they weren't Bram.

"Difference? You'd hate that!"

"So you got Charlie for me?"

He rubbed a hand over his face. "I thought he's what you wanted. He's placid enough, speaks Greek, and you said—"

"Forget what I said. I didn't know anything then."

Bram glared at her. "And now? What do you want now?"

"Can I get off my knee?" Charlie whined. "The floor is bloody hard."

"Yes," huffed the earl. "As if my granddaughter would marry just a mister."

"He's a decent man," Bram shot over his shoulder. "He won't go hieing off after a mistress. There's no debt, no vices, and his biggest fault is that he's a dead bore." Then he drew himself up to his full height, his gaze going back to her. "And you said you want him!"

She stared at him. Did he really understand so little of her? She shook her head, stunned and appalled by this scene. And heartsick. So damned heartsick because he'd dragged a man all the way across England just to have her marry someone else.

Someone who wasn't him.

So she lifted her chin and pitched her voice to be as regal as possible. "Charlie, please do stay for dinner." She glanced at the marquis. "We can have one more to dine, can we not?"

Her fiancé-to-be raised his eyebrows in surprise, but nodded. "Just one?"

"Yes," she answered firmly. "Mr. Hallowsby was just leaving."

"It is French food then?" asked Charlie. "I do like their cream sauces."

Of course he did. Which is the exact moment when Bram seemed to break. It might have been something else. It might have been because she turned her back on him and began walking away. It might have been because two footmen had grabbed hold of his arms and were dragging him backward. It might have been a number of things, but that's not what he said.

"Cream sauces? Cream sauces!" he bellowed.

Maybelle turned to look at him. Did he really expect anything better from Charlie?

"You have a chance at the most perfect woman in the world, and you ask about cream sauces? Are you daft, man? Look at her! She's kind and beautiful. She's honest and doesn't quibble about dragging a pig through the muck for a neighbor. She's taken the *ton* by storm—a girl from Hull who educated herself. And she's smarter than you, by God. Smarter than all of us!"

"Really?" asked the bluestocking. "She hasn't seemed very intelligent."

"Not book learning, you idiot," snapped Bram. "But people. She understands people and how to make everyone happy. She sold her basket of food for a guinea, and everyone got what they wanted." He looked at her, his words babbling forth without stopping. "She's generous too. And so passionate."

That was going too far. He couldn't say that here, not in this company, but Maybelle couldn't stop him. Her throat was too clogged, her mind too chaotic. He could say all this about her and still not...

"Damn it, Bluebell, you can't marry Charlie. He's not good enough for you!"

She sighed. "I'm not going to ma—"

"And you can't marry him either!" he said, jerking his chin at the marquis. "None of them are good enough for you. And I'm the most worthless of the lot." Suddenly, he shook off the footmen, his motions quick as he escaped their hold. The men would have grabbed him, but Eleanor stopped them.

"Just let him say his piece," she said.

And, at a nod from the marquis, the footmen eased back, but only by a single step.

Which is when Bram dropped to his knees. Not one knee, but both, as he took her hand and pressed his forehead to it. "Damn it, I've tried and tried to let you go. I'm no good for you. I'm a bastard. A liar, and if not for you, a murderer."

"What?" gasped the bluestocking. "What did he say?"

Eleanor shushed her with a wave of her hand. It was left to the countess to explain.

"That's Bram Hallowsby, the spymaster. He works for the Home Office and kills Frenchmen by the legion." At which point the woman must have realized she was in a Frenchman's house. "I mean the bad Frenchmen, of course."

If the marquis had a comment, Maybelle didn't hear it. She was busy dropping to her knees before Bram, forcing him to look her in the eye. "You're a good man, Bram. I've always thought so."

"But you don't know the things I've done—"

"You saved my life against Jeremy. You force miscreant lords to face up to their responsibilities. You've helped Eleanor when everything was falling to pieces around her—"

"He did," said Eleanor.

"And you've made a good life for yourself despite your birth."

"I'm still a bastard," he said. "You could have anyone."

"They why can't I have the one man I want?"

He looked at her. He just looked and let everything he felt show on his face. She saw fear and desperation and a hope that he didn't dare believe in.

"You have to say the words, Bram. You have to tell me what you want."

"You, damn it. I've always wanted you."

She touched his face. She looked into his eyes. She needed to hear the words. She needed him to say it to her, to himself, to everyone.

It was Charlie who figured it out. "You're supposed to say you love her. Even I know that."

But Eleanor shook her head. "Love doesn't matter to our set."

Maybelle sighed. "It matters to me. Bram, I lo—"

"I love you. IloveyouIloveyouIloveyou."

At last. He'd said the words at last.

Everything in her body swayed forward. He caught her easily. He would always catch her. And then he was kissing her. Not her face, which was right there, but her hands and her fingertips. He was bowing before her, his body shuddering with the force of his words.

"IloveyouIloveyouIloveyou." Like a litany, the words kept repeating. The sound was all jammed together as if he couldn't get it out fast enough.

She stopped it with her mouth. She lifted his face and kissed his lips. And when he kept murmuring the words, she thrust her tongue between his teeth. And then he was kissing her back. His arms strengthened and went around her. His posture straightened, and he began to duel tongue to tongue with her. Before long she surrendered to him, opening her mouth as he thrust inside.

And when they finally stopped, when he finally pulled away, both of them gasping for breath, he recovered first. And this time his words had power behind them. And determination.

"I'm not worthy of you, Bluebell," he said.

"Bram—"

"But you're going to marry me anyway." Then his expression softened. "Please, Miss Maybelle Ballenger, please redeem me. Be my wife. We can live anywhere you want, even in godforsaken Hull, if you like. I'll drag your pig wherever you want, bathe in a frigid stream, and buy every damned one of your carrots. I'll do anything you want. Just be my wife. Please."

"Yes."

One word. One simple word, and it was done. Her grandfather blustered, Eleanor was teary-eyed, and oddly enough, the marquis was intensely proud.

"I'm French, after all," he said. "It is an honor to witness such amour. I will give away the bride, yes? If the grandfather will not."

Which was enough to shame the earl into a grudging acceptance. That surprised Maybelle, which forced Eleanor to explain.

"It's terrible form to have a child marry a bastard,"

she said in a low whisper. "But it's even worse to let a Frenchman be part of the ceremony. That would be too humiliating for words."

The countess agreed with a fond smile.

Maybelle squeezed Bram's hand. He hadn't let go of it since the moment she'd said yes. "I'll never understand all these rules," she said. "I can barely remember to say my *h*'s."

"Oh, that's all right," said Eleanor with a breezy wave. "The rules don't apply to Bram. They never have."

"That's not true," said Bram with a frown. "I can't—"

"Go to Almacks? Dance at Lady Bedford's ball? Have you ever tried?"

He blinked. "No. I just thought—"

Eleanor smiled at them both. "After you're married, I'll throw a ball for you." She glanced over at the duke and duchess, and they both nodded. "With that kind of launch—"

The countess clapped her hands. "Oh yes, we'll see that it happens just right! You'll be accepted everywhere."

Maybelle looked at Bram, a bubble of laughter coming out of her at his thunderstruck expression.

"You're not serious," he said lowly. "I'm a bastard."

"A duke's bastard. That's almost good *ton*," the ladies said together. "Besides, she's from Hull, you know. We knew she'd have to lower her expectations the minute that was out."

Then Eleanor patted his hand. "If I can accept a seaman as the ducal head of my family, then the *ton* can allow the Home Office spy a place in their world."

"But I'm not—"

"Tut tut. You are, if we say you are."

He blinked and then looked to Maybelle. "What do you want? London or Hull?"

She shrugged. "Does it matter?" She touched his face. "Not as long as you say *I do*."

"I do. I do love you, and I will marry you."

"Now. Right now."

She laughed at the ladies' horrified gasps. "As soon as the banns are called."

"I love you," he said.

And he kept saying it every day and every night for the rest of their lives.

Epilogue

MR. AARON PLATNER, BUTLER TO THE EARL AND Countess of Cavener, fingered his notice and thought about his options. He had no real desire to retire, but a butler had to maintain his standards. After years of keeping a quiet, orderly household, suddenly everything had gone higgledy-piggledy.

The house had daily visitors of a most improper sort. Mr. Hallowsby was a bastard, and by far the worst, but the previously unknown granddaughter was equally bad. He'd heard it clear as day when the girl had dropped her *h*'s. Plus, more than once, he'd caught the two kissing in the parlor. Kissing! As if they were already married.

One week after he'd heard of their engagement, Platner had written this letter serving notice. But the housekeeper—who had a soft heart—had convinced him to wait. He'd agreed because he had a soft heart for the housekeeper, but if things didn't improve quickly, he would take his retirement. He would not play servant to a chit from Hull.

Then today, a miracle had happened.

Certainly, they'd had great lords and ladies visit before, but two new personages were now taking tea with the earl and countess. Lord and Lady Linsel had knocked, and he'd immediately received them. He had an eye for notables, and these two were dressed impeccably. Their manners were perfect, their diction elevated, and they even condescended to smile at him once.

This was the kind of lord and lady that he had been born to serve. And so he'd brought them to the countess and earl, and soon was asked to bring tea. He had immediately, lingering in the doorway to listen. Which is when he heard the miracle news himself.

A new medicine created by that chit from Hull. A potion that saved Lord Sturman's son from certain death. As a butler, Platner prided himself on a more tolerant view of the peasants. He could admit that sometimes the ignorant knew remedies that were unavailable to the more exalted members of society. Apparently, the new granddaughter was one such person. Probably her noble blood coming out.

So he listened at the door while Lord and Lady Linsel extolled the virtues of this medicine. They showed his lordship papers that listed projections and a detailed plan on exactly how everything would go. A year or less before the first profits were realized.

And then the coup de grâce. Lord Linsel invited the earl — because he was the girl's grandfather — to invest in a factory to make the medicine. Ten pounds a share. Ten pounds! And the profit would be a hundredfold at first. A thousand within a few years.

Platner had savings, easily enough to buy into such a plan. He wouldn't normally have done such a thing, but he had heard of the miracle medicine already. He'd learned about it from the footman whose sister worked as a maid for the Sturmans, who got it from the valet that Lord Sturman had cried when his son had recovered. Cried! And for a by-blow!

Back now in the butler's closet, Platner fingered his notice. Did he quit the household? Take his retirement, and perhaps invest some of his pay in this new factory? Or did he stay to serve as the earl and countess brought even more wealth to the title?

It all depended on what they chose to do. If they invested, then he would remain. If they turned down these two, then he would leave. It would do no good to serve when he was becoming a nabob on his own.

He waited an appropriate amount of time, then eased himself out of his closet. He frowned at the two footmen who were clearly eavesdropping. It was not for them to invest. Such a business opportunity was only for valued servants who had been with the Caveners for years, and these two were new, barely three years back.

The footmen scurried to their position, holding out hat and gloves when Lord and Lady Linsel took their leave. Platner smiled warmly at the lord and lady, bowed as a butler ought, and then held the door when it was time. Five minutes later, the two left in a white carriage pulled by the ugliest horse he'd ever seen.

Which is when he took himself quietly into his lordship's library.

"Will there be anything else, my lord?" Platner intoned.

"Nothing, thank you," said the earl. "Unless…" He looked up and flashed a grin.

Excellent. "So you're investing." It wasn't a question.

"I'd be a fool not to. Did you hear how it helped Sturman's son?"

"Indeed, I did. I learned of it a week ago from a man who witnessed the recovery himself."

The earl's face brightened. "Truly?"

"Certainly." Well, a footman's sister's valet's word was near enough.

"Excellent." Then the earl leaned back in his chair. "There's time if you wish to add a few pounds of your own."

"I would, my lord. Especially since it's come from your granddaughter. An excellent woman, in my opinion. Most excellent indeed."

The earl released a low chuckle. "Well, she's grown on me, that's for certain. And there's no denying the change in her ladyship."

No, there wasn't. The countess was often seen smiling these days. Then the earl pushed out a chair, condescending enough to invite Platner to sit. Fifteen minutes later, the documents were written up and signed. Half his savings invested. Not five minutes beyond that, Platner returned to his closet and ripped up his letter of retirement.

He'd remain for a few years while pulling in enough money to hire a butler of his own. And to think, it was all because of that chit from Hull.

Amazing how things happened. He'd make sure to serve her an extra measure of cream the next time she came to visit.

Imagine. A nobody chit from Hull being the means to his fortune.

Brilliant.

About the Author

USA Today bestselling author Jade Lee has been scripting love stories since she first picked up a set of paper dolls. Ball gowns and rakish lords caught her attention early (thank you, Georgette Heyer), and her fascination with the Regency began. An author of more than forty romance novels and winner of dozens of industry awards, Jade Lee delights readers with her vibrant, saucy Regency romances that deliver unusual stories with a lot of heart. Lee lives in Champaign, Illinois.

50 Ways to Ruin a Rake

Rakes and Rogues
by Jade Lee

— ❧ —

Mellie Smithson has a plan

Mellie Smithson is trapped in the country with no suitors and no prospects on the horizon except, perhaps, the exasperating—although admittedly handsome—guest of her father. Unwilling to settle, Mellie will do anything to escape to London…

Trevor Anaedsley has a problem

Trevor Anaedsley's grandfather has cut off his funds until he gets engaged. Beset by creditors, Trevor escapes to the country—ostensibly to visit his old tutor Mr. Smithson—where he meets Smithson's lovely daughter Mellie. The obvious solution is suddenly before him—but will this fake engagement go as Trevor and Mellie plan? Or will they find that even the best laid plans often go awry?

— ❧ —

Praise for *What the Groom Wants*:

"Sensual, suspenseful, and satisfying, [Jade Lee] delivers on all levels." —Eileen Dreyer, *New York Times* bestselling author

"Lee spins an intriguing tale." —*RT Book Reviews*

"Highly entertaining…Jade Lee knows how to write an explosive scene." —*Fresh Fiction*

For more Jade Lee, visit:
www.sourcebooks.com

Daniel's True Desire

True Gentlemen
by Grace Burrowes

New York Times and *USA Today* Bestselling Author

An honorable life

Daniel Banks is a man of the cloth whose vocation is the last comfort he has left—and even his churchman's collar is beginning to feel like a noose. At the urging of his family, Daniel attempts to start his life over as vicar in the sleepy Kentish town of Haddondale, family seat to the earls of Bellefonte.

Challenged by passion

Resigned to spinsterhood, Lady Kirsten Haddonfield welcomes the new vicar to stay at her family's home while his is under renovation. Suddenly the handsome visitor has Kirsten rethinking her ideas about love and marriage, but Daniel's past may cast a shadow too long for either of them to overcome.

How to Seduce a Scot

Broadswords and Ballrooms
by Christy English

--- ❧ ---

Determined to find a husband for his unruly sister, Highlander Alexander Waters strides into prim Regency ballrooms searching for a biddable English lord. To his surprise, his presence in the ton causes quite a stir, but in the process opens his eyes to the most beautiful woman he's ever seen.

Debutante Catherine Middleton is also on the prowl for a man to marry—a man with money, specifically. But when Alexander witnesses her preference in throwing knives over having tea, he knows the prim Catherine is as wild as the Highlands themselves…and needs a Highland man who can match her.

--- ❧ ---

Praise for *Much Ado About Jack*:

"Grace Burrowes and Amanda Quick fans will enjoy the strong ladies in the latest fun read from the ascending English." —*Booklist*

For more Christy English, visit:
www.sourcebooks.com

Heir to the Duke

The Duke's Sons
by Jane Ashford

❧

Life is predictable for a duke's first son

As eldest son of the Duke of Langford, Nathaniel Gresham sees his arranged marriage to Lady Violet Devere as just another obligation to fulfill—highly suitable, if unexciting. But as Violet sets out to transform herself from dowdy wallflower to dazzling young duchess-to-be, proper Nathaniel decides to prove he's a match for his new bride's vivacity and daring.

Or so he once thought…

Oppressed by her family all her life, Lady Violet can't wait to enjoy the freedom of being a married woman. But then Violet learns her family's sordid secret, and she's faced with an impossible choice—does she tell Nathaniel and risk losing him, or does she hide it and live a lie?

❧

Praise for *Married to a Perfect Stranger:*

"Marvelous…the perfect blend of interesting, emotionally complex, and open-hearted protagonists."
—*Publishers Weekly* STARRED REVIEW

"A touching, heartwarming story [that] engages readers' emotions." —*RT Book Reviews*, 4 Stars

For more Jane Ashford, visit:
www.sourcebooks.com

How to Rescue a Rake

The Book Club Belles Society
by Jayne Fresina

— ❧ —

1. Reject his marriage proposal

Nathaniel Sherringham has returned to Hawcombe Prior a changed man. Gone is the reckless rake who went out on a limb to propose to Diana Makepiece three years ago. Now Nate's mysterious new wealth has the town's rumor mill spinning. To stir things up (and get Diana's attention), Nate boldly announces his plans to marry "any suitable girl" under the age of twenty-five.

2. Run away

Diana, now twenty-seven and still single, is acutely aware of Nate's return. When her mother suggests a trip to visit a cousin in Bath, Diana leaps at the chance to escape the heartbreak and regret she can't help but feel in Nate's presence…and avoid his irritating charade to find a bride.

But for Nate, Diana has always been the one. He might just have to follow her to Bath and once again lay his heart on the line to win her attention—and her heart.

— ❧ —

Praise for *Once Upon a Kiss:*

"Feisty dialogue and strong-willed characters
make for…a winning love story." —*Booklist*

For more Jayne Fresina, visit:
www.sourcebooks.com

The Rogue You Know

Covent Garden Cubs
by Shana Galen

She's beyond his reach...

Gideon Harrow has spent his life in London's dark underworld—and he wants out. A thief and a con, he plans one last heist to finally win his freedom. But when everything goes wrong, he finds himself at the tender mercies of one of Society's most untouchable women—Lady Susanna Derring.

...and out of her depth

Susanna has spent her life in London's glittering *ton*, under the thumb of a domineering mother—and she wants out. When a wickedly charming rogue lands at her feet, she jumps at the chance to experience life before it's too late. But as she descends into London's underworld, she finds that nothing—not even Gideon—is as it seems. As excitement turns to danger, Susanna must decide what price she's willing to pay...for the love of a reformed thief.

Praise for *Earls Just Want to Have Fun*:

"Pure Galen: a lively pace, wonderful repartee, colorful dialogue, and a marvelous cast of characters."
—*RT Book Reviews*, Top Pick, 4 1/2 Stars

For more Shana Galen, visit:
www.sourcebooks.com